What Readers Are Saying About Sally John...

The Other Way Home series:

A Journey by Chance

"My favorite author has done it again! Many household chores went undone as I sat, unable to resist the urge to keep turning the pages. The characters were unique, yet believable, and stayed with me long after I finished the novel. I loved the contrast of circumstances and events taking place between a mother's life and her daughter's. I just didn't want the story to end and am looking forward to reading the next book in the series!"
—*Deborah Piccurelli*

"I couldn't put this book down!! I am so anxious to read the next book in this series. It is such a personal story for each of the characters that you can relate and feel for each and every one of them (I even wished I could read Brady's books!!) Keep up the good work of entertaining and spreading the news of God's love."
—*Anita Carbaugh*

"After starting to read *A Journey by Chance*, I found myself not able to put the book down. Sally does such a wonderful job of making you feel as if you know the characters personally....The story line is very interesting and deals with real-life issues. I have read all of her books thus far and have never been disappointed."
—*Amber Karns*

After All These Years

"The message of sin, repentance, and forgiveness is found on nearly every page of Sally John's thoroughly readable book. A tinge of suspense only heightens the reader's interest and hesitation to put this book down until completed. John has

done a good job to develop not only the main characters, but the secondary characters as well. The characters' struggles with sin in their lives allow for the gospel to be presented throughout in a nonintrusive, very natural way."
—*Christian Library Journal*

"Another great story by Sally John, full of life and living! I love her characters and description of the lovely town the story is set in—she makes you feel like you can see the town and be friends with the characters."
—*Narelle Mollet*

Just to See You Smile

"I finished *Just to See You Smile* in practically one sitting, drawn in by characters and stories that lived with me for days afterward.

"Sally John's characters are knights with rusty armor and princesses with rumpled gowns. They are men and women like us who may be marred by wounds and choices, yet who courageously move forward to honor Christ and deepen loving relationships.

"Young women readers would do well to learn from Britte. She enjoyed singleness with contentment and fruitfulness, and then she trusted God for an expanded heart when He surprised her with new adventures in love. Alec and Anne's rediscovery of a marriage blending healthy boundaries and sacrificial commitments inspired me more than a dozen 'how to' marriage manuals."
—*Margo Balsis*

The Winding Road Home

"Sally John, one of my new favorite authors, takes characters I'd love to have as close friends and places them in a town where I would love to live, but she doesn't stop there. She

weaves the lives of these wonderful people into my heart, so that by the time I'm finished reading about them, I'm laughing with them, crying with them, and hoping they'll invite me along for the ride again."
—*Hannah Alexander,* author of *Hideaway*

"Through tears and laughter, Sally John paints a lush tale of two women's quests to find happiness, instead finding true love when they least expected it. From the first page to the final word, I could not put Ms. John's book down."
—*The Romance Reader's Connection*
(www.theromancereadersconnection.com)

"I could read a hundred more books with these characters in them. God has truly blessed Sally John with a wonderful talent."
—*Christen Ralich*

In a Heartbeat series:

In a Hearbeat

In a Heartbeat is the first book in Sally John's exciting new series. This poignant tale of infertility, one of the bigger and more painful issues facing our society today, weaves a story of triumph over tragedy in the lives of a firefighter and his wife. Filled with warmth and romance with a heroic theme, this compelling novel will touch your heart. Beautifully written, Sally has created believable characters who not only will become your friends, but will have a profound effect on your own life. Don't miss this intriguing story with a heart! Like me, you'll be waiting for the next book in Sally's In a Heartbeat series.
—*Susan Wales,* bestselling author, speaker, and producer

IN A *Heartbeat*

SALLY JOHN

HARVEST HOUSE PUBLISHERS

EUGENE, OREGON

Scripture verses are taken from The Jerusalem Bible, Copyright © 1966 by Darton, Longman & Todd, Ltd. and Coubleday & Company, Inc., all rights reserved, and from The New English Bible, copyright © Oxford University Press and Cambridge University Press 1961, 1970. All rights reserved.

Cover by Garborg Design Works, Minneapolis, Minnesota

Published in association with the literary agency of Alive Communications, Inc., 7680 Goddard Street, Ste #200, Colorado Springs, CO 80920.

IN A HEARTBEAT
Copyright © 2004 by Sally John
Published by Harvest House Publishers
Eugene, Oregon 97402
www.harvesthousepublishers.com

Library of Congress Cataloging-in-Publication Data

John, Sally D., 1951–
  In a heartbeat / Sally John.
     p. cm.—(In a heartbeat series)
  ISBN 0-7369-1169-3 (pbk.)
  1. Women teachers—Fiction. 2. Fire fighters—Fiction. 3. Married people—Fiction.
4. Childlessness—Fiction. 5. Chicago (Ill.)—Fiction. I. Title.
  PS3560.O3231 2004
  813'.54—dc22   2003016841

Printed in the United States of America.

04 05 06 07 08 09 10 11 /BC-KB/ 10 9 8 7 6 5 4

For Tim,
my hero bold

Acknowledgments

As with all my work, this book is like a pot of stew. I simply gathered ingredients from a variety of sources and mixed them together. Without everyone's contribution, this particular flavor never would have been captured. However, if you come across a spoonful of disagreeable gustatory sensation, please blame the chef.

My thanks to:

Matt Shoemaker, graphic designer with Harvest House Publishers and firefighter with the Monroe, Oregon, Fire Department. Thank you for graciously, generously sharing your expertise, insight, suggestions, and real-life experiences. You represent the spirit of heroism in countless ways, and it is an honor to have worked with you.

Kim Moore, for editing with wisdom, wit, and passion. Thank you for stretching me as a writer. Your direction, as always, has been invaluable.

Carolyn McCready and Barb Sherrill, of Harvest House, for your special touches on this one.

Everyone at Harvest House. Producing a book truly is a family affair, and I am grateful for having been adopted into yours.

Chip MacGregor, for the initial "assignment," fuel to my imagination.

Tom and Sandy Carlson, for Eldridge, Iowa.

Cindi Cox, for the example of "Rachel's" courage you displayed many years ago.

Michael Skelton, for your real-life monthly romantic expression that "Vic" never would have thought of on his own.

Rhonda Roush, Elizabeth John, and Melissa Westley for providing information, thereby saving me hours of research.

Tracy and Christopher John, for reading and critiquing. Kaiya Grace, for patiently waiting while Mama and Daddy helped Nonna.

Tim, for reading and for loving me.

Come Rescue Me

I long for the mighty hero of legends old.
That noble lord who earns the crown of gold,
That fearless knight upon his great white steed,
That slayer of dragons fresh from valiant deed.
Come rescue me, O hero bold.
Come rescue me ere the night unfold.

I wait for the mighty hero of legends old.
That gallant victor over evil stronghold,
That brave defender of woman and child,
That charging conqueror of darkness wild.
Come rescue me, O hero bold.
Come rescue me ere the night unfold.

—Sally John

This is what I shall tell my heart,
and so recover hope:
the favors of Yahweh are not all past,
his kindnesses are not exhausted;
every morning they are
renewed; great is his faithfulness.

LAMENTATIONS 3:21-23

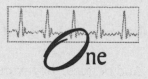

One

Rachel Koski surveyed the dimly lit ballroom and smiled to herself. What in the world was she doing there?

Hundreds of strangers milled about. The intense volume of their chatter competed with an old '70s tune blasting from enormous speakers at one end of the room. Strobe lights flashed off a rotating silver ball suspended above the dance floor, where dozens of couples gyrated as they must have 25 years ago. The scene was definitely not lifted from the pages of her own scrapbook.

She turned to her husband. "Premarital counseling never covered this."

Vic grinned and tilted his head nearer her. "Never covered what?"

"How to cope at your husband's twenty-fifth class reunion. Do you remember the subject ever coming up? It should be mandatory. I mean, I'm stumped! I don't know what to say if one more woman grabs you and says, 'Oh, Vic!'" Rachel mimicked a falsetto voice and clasped his arms. "'I had such a crush on you in high school!'" She jutted out her front teeth and fixed her eyes on the tip of her nose.

Vic burst into laughter at the beaver imitation, her stock response to ludicrous situations. She blamed the habit on many years spent in classrooms full of nine-year-olds.

"Well?" she prompted, speaking through the protruded lips and holding back her own laughter. "What should I do?"

"What you're already doing. You're laughing on the inside, doing your singsong *nah nah nah nah nah*. I win! He married me!"

She unfocused her eyes and relaxed her mouth with a giggle. "I am not."

"You should be. And besides, they were more interested in how I robbed the cradle than imaginary crushes. Hey, they're playing our song again."

"We have a song?"

"We do. Anything *mellow*." He took her hand and forged a path through the crowd to the dance floor.

Rachel slipped into his arms and followed his lead. For a guy whose wardrobe came from the big-and-tall man's shop, he moved nimbly.

He hummed in her ear for a moment. Straightening, he said, "Why don't we have a song? Maybe we should choose one."

"I already have one. That one about the hero." She closed her eyes, recalling the gist of its words. "*I long for the mighty hero of legends old? That noble lord who earns the crown of gold, that fearless knight upon his great white steed, that slayer of dragons fresh from valiant deed?*" She blinked open her eyes. "I'm looking at him."

His affectionate smile crinkled eyes that were always at half-mast. "You sang it to me on our second date."

"In your dreams! We were engaged before I had the nerve to sing that to you."

"Weren't we engaged by the second date?"

Nearly. Very nearly so. She caressed his sideburn. It was longish and a deep brown like his hair. Almost black, an espresso color.

He gazed at her, unmistakable tenderness softening his strong jaw. "So, Rache, you're not really threatened by a handful of women who think they remember me from almost thirty years ago, are you?"

"N-no."

"That was convincing."

"Well-l-l." She lowered her eyes and focused on his shoulder. He looked nice, casual in black dress slacks and a white polo shirt that showed off his arms, browned by the summer sun.

"Rache."

"Okay, I am totally *not* threatened, but how *did* you end up with me? I mean, these are good-looking women pursuing high-class careers, and I think they'd follow you anywhere."

He threw his head back and laughed in his infectious way that always drew smiles from passersby, as it did now from the surrounding couples. "Whoa! You're fishing for a compliment."

She joined in his laughter. "It sounds like it, doesn't it? No, listen. Seriously, Vic. Come on, stop howling."

At last his laughter trailed off and he grew somber. "Okay. I'm listening."

"They remind me just how grateful I am for you. I love being married to you."

He pulled her close and kissed the top of her head. "Oh, baby, every time you look at me like that with those big cinnamon eyes, you knock my socks off." His husky voice rumbled above her. "You obviously experienced a major lapse in good judgment."

"I'd say nine years is something beyond a major lapse. More like an incurable disease."

They swayed in companionable silence for a few moments.

"Rache, you knocked everyone's socks off tonight. They're all saying, *Koski's married to her? No way! The class jerk could not snag such a gorgeous woman.*"

Love had struck him blind to her imperfections, physical and otherwise. Before Vic Koski entered her life, no one had ever called her pretty or even cute, let alone gorgeous. Coming from such an earthy, realistic sort of guy, it never ceased to delight her. In her opinion, her nose dominated, her mouth was too large for her narrow face, her henna-colored hair too thick and wavy to wear in any style except short and brushed back. Those things didn't matter to Vic.

He went on. "You are extra gorgeous tonight."

She leaned back and looked up at him, batting her eye-lashes. "Stunning. Bryan says I'm *stunning*." She referred to Vic's longtime friend, the one other person she knew at the reunion.

"Okay, stunning. You are incredibly stunning in that little black number. Not only that, you're kind and charming to silly, inebriated females. And to top it all off, your legs in those stiletto heels are driving me crazy."

"There! That's what I was fishing for."

His cheeks folded along laugh lines. "Let's go home already."

"Let's." She grinned back at him. "But have you seen everyone you hoped to see?"

He shrugged. "There aren't that many. The guys I hung with aren't the type to show up at a reunion. I only showed up because you spurred me on. Coming face-to-face with my miserable past was never on my list of fun things to do."

Spurred him on? "I didn't spur. As my grandmother would say, I kvetched." Complained, peevishly and persistently.

He chuckled. "Yeah, you did some kvetching."

"Vic, honey, I'm so proud you came."

"It's been good." He drew her near again. "But let's make this our last dance. You really are driving me crazy in those shoes."

His breath on her neck flung into motion a minuscule Shirley Temple tap, tap, tapping up and down her spine. Shirley had made her first appearance the day Rachel met Vic. *Totally incurable...*

"Oh, man!" Vic stopped abruptly in the middle of the dance floor. "He *is* here! See that white-haired guy? Over there on the left."

She peered over her shoulder.

"That's Keim. I can't believe it. Come on."

She held his hand as they wove their way between couples. The older man had been a history teacher, the major influence to steer Vic off his path of self-destruction. Vic had never told him that. Their parting 25 years ago had not been amicable. Rachel didn't belong at their personal reunion.

At the edge of the dance floor, she stopped. "Vic, you go ahead. I'd be in the way."

He hesitated. "I want him to meet you."

"I know, but later, if it's appropriate. Or another time. Go." She nudged him. "I'll wait over at that table, where we sat earlier."

He nodded briskly and strode away. Even in the dim light she recognized his demeanor. What some might interpret as a lackluster expression and cold manner were, in reality, a total absorption with envisioning the venture that lay ahead. She had first seen the look while visiting the fire station, though it wasn't until later that she deciphered it. The alarm buzzed, calling him to an emergency. In the blink of an eye, she no longer existed for him. His ability to completely shut out the rest of the world was unsettling in a way.

Of course, when she became the object of his intense focus, as in a few moments ago, the quality was particularly unsettling. No wonder little Shirley still tap-danced after nine years.

Missing his supportive arm now, Rachel hobbled in the other direction, halted, stepped out of her shoes, and instantly shrank four inches. The ridiculous stilettos, which she wore perhaps twice a year because Vic liked her in them, were driving *her* crazy. She scooped the black heels from the floor, made a beeline for a chair, and sank onto it with a groan.

Propping her feet on another chair, she searched the throng for her husband. The crowd had engulfed him, drawing a curtain between her and what was sure to be the highlight of his evening. That was as it should be. The moment belonged to Vic. She felt content to sit and wait for him. Her noble lord, fearless knight, slayer of dragons, all rolled into one. Still her hero.

∽

No trumpet fanfare announced that a white knight stood outside Miss Rachel Goldberg's classroom door nine years ago. A Chicago firefighter was expected, an everyday city worker come to tell fourth graders in 30 minutes or less all about his job.

However, from the moment he walked through the door she knew he wasn't of the everyday variety. She always regretted the lack of warning. Had she known, she would have worn her spring green sweater, a much better color than the schoolmarm-ish white blouse and dark gray cardigan. She would have risen earlier and ironed a decent skirt. She would not have been left with one choice, the shortest one in her wardrobe. Of course, the knight later confessed, her outfit, most notably the skirt, intrigued him to no end. She still blushed picturing the PG-13-rated image presented to her students. Eager to demonstrate the fireman's carry, he whisked her off her feet, slinging her over his shoulder like a sack of potatoes. Through the years he maintained that his technique was so smooth, her skirt hadn't budged a fraction of an inch past decorum.

An air of assurance preceded Vic Koski into her classroom. Rachel dismissed the idea that she imagined it. Up to that point, she hadn't given firemen any particular attention. Naturally she had met a few during her lifetime, was glad somebody performed their job, and agreed with the other fourth-grade teachers that yes, they should include one in their unit on city employees. But she hadn't concocted a larger-than-life visual of them.

His height and powerful shoulders enhanced that air of assurance, but he would have commanded attention even if he had been pint-sized. The man knew who he was, knew why he walked the face of the earth. And he was, in a humble way, totally comfortable in that knowledge.

Her first inkling that she was being figuratively swept off her feet was how she stammered through her introduction of him. A six-year veteran at the volatile, racially mixed elementary school, Miss Goldberg had a reputation for being tough. It stemmed from her spunky confrontation with a knife-wielding teen illegally loitering on the grounds. The day Vic Koski walked into her room, she couldn't string two words together. Nor could she stand at the back of the room without bumping a cart and sending its load of books crashing to the floor.

His scheduled 30 minutes stretched to 60. The 60 stretched to 90 when half the students jumped at the chance to skip recess in order to try on his big helmet, enormous boots, and heavy coat yet again. Ninety stretched to a personal smile.

"Miss Goldberg?"

"Hmm?" They stood in her classroom doorway as she automatically kept tabs on the children at the nearby drinking fountain. "Jamont! Hands to yourself!"

"It is miss, then?" If his eyes hadn't been at half-mast, their brilliance would have blinded. They were a peculiar color...navy blue diamonds.

She returned his smile. "I go by 'miss' rather than 'miz' so that the children won't keep asking if I'm married or not."

He tilted his head back, laughing. "So." He propped his elbow on the doorjamb above her head. "Are you engaged to be married?"

She glanced at her watch. "Uh, do you mind just getting to the point? It's time for our math lesson."

He hesitated a long moment. "Will you have dinner with me tonight?"

She too hesitated, weighing as he must have, the consequences. How could they have known after 90 minutes?

⌒

"Rachel." Vic's good friend Bryan O'Shaugnessy sat down beside her at the vacant table, a quiet spot distanced from most of the reunion crowd. "I suggest you go rescue your husband."

She laughed. "Not a chance! My feet hurt too much." She wiggled her stockinged toes resting atop another chair. "Besides that, he's a big boy, perfectly capable of taking care of himself."

A short distance across the ballroom, a petite woman had grabbed hold of Vic a few minutes before, blocking his way back to the table. Shiny white-blonde curls cascaded about her shoulders. Although her back was to Rachel, it was evident from the tilt of her head and hips that she was flirting. Seriously flirting while Vic politely attempted to disentangle himself.

Rachel laughed again. "Look at his face. This has been going on all night, you know. These women accosting him."

Bryan poured two cups of ice water from the pitcher on the table and slid one over to her. "You're a saint to have come."

"No, just a woman standing by her man. How's your evening going?"

He gulped down his water and reached again for the pitcher. Beads of perspiration dotted his forehead. "I feel as if I've just conducted a dozen counseling sessions within the confines of a boom box." He drank more water.

Except for his curly reddish hair, Bryan could have passed for Vic's brother. He had the same rough-and-tumble appearance, was broad-shouldered, and stood a few inches over six feet. His wild younger years, those shared with Vic, were clearly etched in his face. Tonight he wore black slacks and a short-sleeved black shirt open at the neck. Without his clerical collar, Father O'Shaugnessy looked more like a cop than an Episcopal priest. Still, people were drawn to him.

"Bryan, do you ever take a day off?"

He grinned. "Rachel, do you ever take a day off from being a Christian?"

"That's different. People don't have impromptu counseling sessions with me. I guess I can hide my faith better than you can."

He laughed. "It's all in the title and the clothing."

"No way. I've seen you in sweats with total strangers unloading their problems on you. People are drawn to you. Like I've told you before, you give off Yeshua vibes." Rachel used the Hebrew term for Jesus, a habit of her Jewish grandmother. "And you should give yourself a break now and then. He did, you know."

"Thanks for worrying." He glanced again over her shoulder. "Speaking of worrying, I really do think Vic needs you now."

She turned around. A scowl had replaced the politeness in her husband's expression. His eyes were slits. Not a good sign. "Who is this woman?"

"Ellen Hamilton, née Cunningham."

Rachel swiveled back to Bryan. "And?"

"She...had his attention for a while. Senior year."

Vic had been upfront with her about his former relationships. They were a fact of his disorderly past. Nothing to be done about them except to sing the nah nah song. *He married me.*

"Okay, senior year. Is that significant, Bryan?"

He shook his head. "No, I just never liked the girl. That's why you should go over there instead of me. You can pry her loose with finesse."

"Rather than your brute strength, Father?"

"Something like that."

"Keep an eye on my shoes. They're Vic's favorite." Rachel swung her legs off the chair and padded across the rough carpet.

Intent on listening to the woman, Vic didn't notice Rachel's approach. She couldn't hear Ellen's words until she reached his side.

"I divorced him eleven years ago. And it's all your fault, Vic. If you hadn't—"

"Hi." Rachel touched Vic's left arm, the one Ellen wasn't clinging to.

"Rachel." He uttered her name with a puff of air. Relief or embarrassment?

"Aha!" Ellen cackled. "Is *this* the little woman?"

Rachel started at the woman's appearance. From the back she could have passed for twenty-five, but her deeply tanned, haggard face made her appear several years older than Vic. Her eyes were glassy, her words slurred.

Rachel recovered quickly and smiled, holding out her hand. "Yes, I'm the little woman. Rachel Koski. What's your name?"

"Ellen Cunningham Hamilton." Her breath was stronger than her handshake. "Old girlfriend."

"That's nice." According to her husband, he never had a girlfriend per se in high school. The woman was delusional and probably dangerous in her intoxicated state. Still, Rachel felt her hackles rising. What was it Bryan had said about finesse?

"Let's go, Rache." Vic shrugged his arm out of Ellen's clutch.

The woman grasped it again and thrust her face at Rachel. "I can't believe you don't have any kids. Vic Koski is one virile man—"

"That's enough!" Vic forcefully yanked his arm from her grip. It didn't end her yammering.

"What's wrong with you, Rachel *Koski?*" She spat the name.

The venomous words mesmerized Rachel. Vic's arm appeared in front of her and broke the spell. She pivoted into the shelter of his shoulder, and he hustled them away.

Ellen shouted, "Vic, don't you dare walk away from me!"

Rachel peered over her shoulder.

The woman was on their heels. "We're not finished talking—"

Abruptly Bryan stepped between them, his bulk absorbing Ellen's voice and attempts to follow.

Wordlessly Rachel and Vic hurried from the ballroom, down a long hall, and to the elevator. Vic slapped his hand against one of the closing doors as if he could manually shove it out of the way. As the doors slid open, he leaned against one and she squeezed her way into a group of noisy revelers. Inching around in the cramped space, she came face-to-face with Vic's back.

She leaned her forehead between his shoulder blades and steadied her breath.

I can't believe you don't have any kids!

Her intoxicated state notwithstanding, Ellen Hamilton had flung the conversation beyond teasing territory. Her words were not silly confessions about a bygone crush. They were mean and spiteful.

And they cut to the very core of Rachel's being.

Why on earth had Vic even talked with her?

All night long Rachel had seen the question coming at her like the pointed tip of a sword flashing in her direction. *Do you have children? Do you have children?* Each time Vic had parried for her, smiling. "Not yet. We're still newlyweds!"

The query was natural. Vic and his former classmates were 43 years old. After introducing spouses and discussing careers, the inevitable next topic was kids. She had known it would be that way. She had prepared for it and prayed she would not grow weary of asking the question in return. Prayed for an extra dose of grace as she would be obligated to view a myriad of children's and grandchildren's photos.

She and Vic had been the dynamic duo. He with his new-lywed quip, she with her thoughtful teacher-ish questions

about other people's children. She had made it through the
night with her emotions intact. And then... Undone by a
pathetic platinum blonde. Grace flew and an aching sadness
descended on her. It felt as if a sumo wrestler tromped on her
lungs.

The elevator dinged and the doors slid open. Vic slipped
his hand over hers and led her at a fast clip across the hotel
lobby. The carpet grabbed at her stockinged toes, folding
them under. She couldn't keep up.

"Vic!" Exasperated, she jerked him to a stop. "Where's the
fire?"

At last he looked at her. From his narrowed eyes, clenched
jaw, and ragged breaths, she knew she'd found the fire. Inside
of him an intense anger burned out of control, something she
had witnessed only a handful of times.

She rubbed his hand between hers. "Calm down, honey.
It's over."

"I'm sorry." Raking his fingers through his hair, he huffed
and puffed. "I'm sorry."

The man who charged into burning buildings without a
moment's hesitation was in worse shape than she was. Panic
bubbled in her chest. She needed Vic more than ever. *Dear
Lord!* The short prayer formed itself, counterattacking.

"Vic, get a grip! Take a deep breath."

He nodded, his breathing still irregular. "I'm okay." His
eyes opened wider, his jaw relaxed. He gave his shoulders a
shake. "I'm okay. Let's go home."

"Okay. But," she pointed to her shoeless feet, "will you
run back upstairs—"

"No." He stooped, gathered her in his arms like a bride,
and without another word carried her across the lobby.

Two

Rachel slid deeper into the hot bubble bath. She couldn't get warm. Late July, 77 humid degrees outdoors, not much different indoors, and she couldn't get warm.

As Vic drove them home in silence, she had listened to the thump-thump of the tires and tired to imagine them crushing the ugliness right out of those final moments at the reunion. Instead, with each passing mile between the downtown hotel and their little bungalow on the outskirts of Chicago, the ugliness mushroomed.

She couldn't remember a time in their nine years together when at least one of them hadn't either straightforwardly named the problem or annoyingly joked about the bright side until they collapsed in laughter. Tonight was different. Tonight a chasm cracked open in the middle of the car, separating the two of them.

Ellen Hamilton's vile words were nothing to tease about. They alone weren't the problem anyway. Vic had been angry before she'd spewed the words at Rachel. Was there something he hadn't told her? Why had he even spent five minutes with that woman in the first place? How could someone be so hateful as to attack a stranger in that way, at Rachel's most vulnerable spot? How had she even known they were childless?

Why would he *chat* with someone like that about their personal life?

Rachel flipped on the hot water faucet with her toes. The scent of lavender permeated the steam, relaxing her. *Lord, help him sort it out.*

Vic was outside, probably sitting on the picnic table in the backyard and gazing at the midnight sky. He would be fighting his demons in the same way he fought fires, up close and personal.

He often said, when someone asked about his work, "The only way to attack a fire is to get in its face, close enough to feel its heat and hear its hideous laugh. If you don't do that, it takes control and you lose."

Yes, he would be in attack mode right now. And later they would talk. With every fiber of her being she knew he would not leave for the firehouse early tomorrow with that chasm still gaping between them.

∽

Years ago, when Rachel and Vic first began to suspect their futures had been unalterably changed the day they met, they sat late one night in a coffee shop. He steered their conversation toward serious matters.

"There are a couple of things about firefighting, how it affects, uh, relationships…" His voice trailed off. Those navy blue diamonds twinkled, like a fine spray of sunlit water droplets showering her face.

She felt overwhelmed with childlike wonder. Shirley Temple strapped on her tap shoes. "Yes?"

He cleared his throat. "Firefighting is my life. Period. If my shift falls on Christmas, I work Christmas. If I'm off duty and a four-alarm comes in, I work my day off. When I am off, I take firefighting classes, go to firefighting meetings, talk to groups about firefighting, hang out with other firefighters. I could never give it up."

With anyone else she would have presented a dozen "what-if" scenarios, but his stern tone nixed any thought of challenging him. Did he use that tone with inexperienced firefighters? She eyed him over her cup. "I'm not sure I understand."

"I don't expect you to understand it, but I need you to *accept* it. Every woman I've dated has not accepted it. Not that I ever asked one to. Until now." He glanced away momentarily. "It's not your average, run-of-the-mill life. Just something you might want to think about. In case..." He shrugged. "You know..."

She bit back a smile and returned the shrug, too head over heels to want to grasp what such a life entailed. "Okay. You said a couple of things?"

"The other is a sort of rule that I made up for myself. For me and my, uh, hypothetical, uh, wife. We always have to be current before saying goodbye."

"Current?"

"Nothing is left unsaid. Good or bad. Absolutely no regrets between us. Every parting is almost a sacred moment."

"That seems a little impractical. Why is this a rule?"

"Because it could be the last goodbye. I might get killed on the job."

"Between heart attacks and car accidents, anyone might die on their way to the grocery store."

"True. But Rachel." He slid his hand across the table, palm up.

She set down her mug and laid her hand in his large callused one. In those early days, his touch obliterated coherent thought. Little Shirley tap-danced in double time. "Do you do that on purpose?"

"Do what?"

She inhaled deeply, her shoulders rising with the effort. "Hold my hand so I'll stop debating with you?"

Smiling, he said, "Not consciously, but I'll remember that for future reference." Then he raised her hand, turned it over, and softly kissed the palm. "Iron sharpens iron. One of your most attractive features is debating with me, exhorting me to clarify half-cocked notions. The point is..." He set her hand back down on the table and removed his from it. "The point is, I don't want to scare you away, but you have to be aware. Percentage-wise, more firefighters are killed in the line of duty than anyone else. Anyone. Even cops."

She didn't believe him. "But you mostly just sit around the fire station. Slide down the pole now and then. Extricate some victim from a smashed-up car. Go squirt a hose at some flames. Right?"

"Something like that." His mouth twitched. "Miss Goldberg, you didn't hear a word I said in your classroom that day, did you?"

"Isn't that what you said?"

He shook his head.

Later that night, for the first time, he told her he loved her.

Soon after, he invited her to visit the station. With some trepidation, she entered what felt like a foreign country. Vic's second home and the people he shared it with were an enigma to her.

Located not far from her school, the brick building struck her as aged, like most of the surrounding neighborhood. The Chicago skyline could be seen in the distance. She always imagined its yellow haze dimmed the blatant wealth those skyscrapers represented, hiding from her children that their poverty was an atrocity.

He introduced her to fellow firefighters, all wearing blue pants and T-shirts with the Chicago Fire Department insignia. Some teased him mercilessly about her presence. Vic, as mouthy as the next guy, gave it right back to them. His second home embodied the team stories her brother had often relayed to her when they were teenagers. Not athletic herself, she had never experienced such unique camaraderie.

Vic showed her the gleaming red-and-silver trucks, where his turnouts—boots, pants, and coat—waited for him, where he sat on his way to fires. He was part of an engine company, he explained, the guys who carried the hoses, the guys who "put the wet stuff on the red stuff." She saw the bunk room with its rows of beds and a sort of family room with a television, hand-me-down chairs, and couches. Vic pointed in the direction of the locker room, and then they returned to the large kitchen for coffee.

That was when the alarm buzzed. She felt as if a bolt of electricity sliced through her. There was an infinitesimal, hushed second. Between heartbeats she saw Vic's demeanor change, saw him become something she didn't yet understand. Then, before a voice on the loudspeaker finished giving directions, men moved, a blur in her vision. She watched the big trucks roll through the doors, heard their sirens scream, saw their lights flash.

Her own adrenaline pumped, and she let out a low whistle and said to no one in particular, "Whew! The boys would love this."

"Pretty impressive, huh?" One of the firemen who hadn't been called joined her.

"Very impressive. Can I follow them?"

The man studied her face as if sizing her up. "Think you can handle watching your smoke-eating boyfriend in action?"

She put her hands on her hips. "Now what kind of a girlfriend would I be if I couldn't?"

He barked a laugh. "Koski's got a live one in you!"

The fire wasn't many blocks away. Rachel parked her car at the end of a street that contained mostly empty storefronts. Smoke billowed from an open upstairs apartment window. Vic's truck was parked in the middle of the street, along with the ladder and rescue vehicles. Mesmerized, she ran to where a group of onlookers had gathered.

The scene was chaotic. Emergency workers were everywhere. Two women shrieked hysterically. Children cried. Police shouted. Firefighters carried enormous hoses. The thick scent of burning wood filled her nostrils. Ashes fell. A roaring sound grew. Glass shattered. Flames shot out another window. Waves of heat whooshed overhead.

She searched in vain for Vic. And then she realized...he was inside.

Twenty minutes or so passed. Endless hours. He emerged, his mask dangling, his face blackened with soot and streaked with sweat. He coughed. Identical to the others in his helmet, coat, and pants with double yellow stripes, he would have been unrecognizable if she hadn't noticed earlier he was the biggest one of the group.

Slayer of dragons fresh from valiant deed?

Rachel never visited another fire. She went home that day, her plans forgotten, and cried inconsolably, bewildered that God had brought such a man into her life.

That night he called, his voice hoarse, and apologized for leaving her so abruptly.

"Vic," she interrupted. "I love you."

"What?"

"I said I love you."

She understood now what he meant by *current*.

⟋

After her bath Rachel climbed into bed and snuggled against Vic, who sat with pillows stacked behind him. The fresh-scented cotton of the T-shirt he'd put on after his shower was smooth beneath her cheek. She could hear his steady heartbeat.

He wrapped an arm around her shoulders, indifferent to the affect of her still-steaming skin on the temperature of his own. But then, he tolerated heat better than most people.

The ceiling fan thrummed, circulating the nighttime summer air. Preferring the humidity to the stuffiness produced by their waning air conditioner, Vic had opened the windows. Cicadas droned incessantly.

He turned off the lamp beside the bed and kissed her hair. Faint light from a distant streetlamp shone through the parted curtains.

"Rache, about Ellen..." His voice trailed off.

"Do I need to know?"

"Yeah, you do. She attacked you. I'm trying to figure out why."

The cicadas went silent, as if holding their collective breath. Rachel felt herself go still. Vic usually didn't share details unless she asked for them. They were in his past, over and done with, covered with the blood of the Lamb. Vic was five years older and had only been a Christian for a short time before they met. Except for his stint in the Army and his work as a firefighter, there wasn't much in his past he pointed to with pride.

"Ellen was popular in high school. A rich snob. Then there was me, the cop's kid, the rebel, the troublemaker. I figured she came after me just for the shock value. Not that it mattered. I'd go along with anyone, especially a skirt who had money to burn. We hung together for a while, had some laughs. She was no Miss Goody Two-Shoes."

Rachel felt him shift slightly. "Vic, I get the picture."

"I treated her like a slut. She was engaged to some guy away at college, and I treated her like a slut."

No doubt Ellen had behaved like one. Rachel didn't point that out. Her husband would not hide behind such an excuse.

"Which was why I talked to her tonight. I apologized, asked her forgiveness. She just sort of stared at me in disbelief. She was so plastered, I didn't figure anything I could say about the Lord would begin to sink in. Then she started telling me about her miserable life. Booze and prescription drugs. A husband who didn't love her. A daughter who didn't pay her any attention. I felt, I don't know, just so mad that she'd wasted her life. Twenty-five years ago, she was the one who had everything going for herself. Money, looks, college—"

"She blamed you."

"What?"

"When I walked up, she was saying that she had divorced her husband and that it was all your fault."

"Yeah, she'd said that earlier too, which is probably what set me off. Something about if she hadn't fallen for me, her life would have been different."

"Vic, she's probably fantasized about you all these years. How did things end between you?"

"There really wasn't anything to end. My dad and Keim pretty much sat on me that last month or so of school, making sure I finished no matter how much I didn't care. She probably stopped calling. Three days after graduation I had a buzz cut and an Army platoon for bunkmates. Last I heard, she married the fiancé and moved away. I think she told me tonight that they lived a few hours from here. The Quad-Cities area maybe."

"And she's had a miserable time of it. She probably imagined life would have been different with you."

"Why in the world?" He grunted a sound of disbelief. "You women are impossible to understand."

Rachel sat up and faced him in the shadowy light. "Oh, honey, it's simple. Her parents didn't love her unconditionally. She craved attention, and even the kind you gave was better than the nothing she got at home or from the absent boyfriend. When things went sour with her husband, she fantasized about every other guy she's known. Tonight she hears you, this mature, good-looking hunk—"

"I love it when you say that." He said, grinning.

"With compassion written all over his face, apologizing to her. She's never met anyone like you in her entire life. Of course she's going to blame you for not rescuing her years ago. And she's going to hate me."

"Before apologizing, I told her all about you."

Rachel smiled. She'd overheard him doing that all evening. "Naturally."

"Naturally," he echoed.

"And you told her I was beautiful. No wonder she looked positively shocked when she saw me. You have got to start mentioning my hooked nose and big mouth. People won't believe a word you say about anything. They'll think you're dotty!"

Vic grabbed the finger she was wagging in his face and sprang forward. She squealed with laughter as he pushed her backwards. He loomed over her.

"Your mouth is perfect for kissing." He demonstrated his opinion. "Your nose is perfect. That teensy little curve..." He kissed the bridge of her nose. "Adds untold character."

She had deliberately provoked his response. Years ago, before she met his brothers, he told them she was gorgeous. She had noted their confusion the first moment they saw her. Later she pulled from Vic what he had said to them. She fussed at him and offered her realistic assessment of her looks. That time he gently tackled her in the backyard and, as he did now, set her straight about what he thought of her looks.

"Vic." She sobered. "Did you tell her we don't have children?"

"No! She didn't ask. Someone else must have told her."

Tears welled in her eyes and she didn't respond.

"Rache, if what you think is true, if she is jealous of you, then she would attack you, right?"

"But why go for the jugular? My goodness, talk about overkill."

"I'm sorry I stopped to talk to her."

"No, don't be. It was good that you did. That you faced that part of your past."

"I'm not so sure. She hurt you. Baby, I'm sorry. I'm sorry I didn't protect you from that."

"You couldn't see it coming. She was drunk. Sober, she—" A thought struck her. What would the woman do sober? Should they get an unlisted phone number?

"Sober she won't do anything. She doesn't live near Chicago. Our paths won't cross again. It's over and done with. You okay?"

She nodded. "Mm-hmm."

"I love you. And I promise, nothing more from my past will ever hurt you again."

He kissed her until the chasm closed altogether and she could no longer remember Ellen Hamilton's horrid words.

Three

No question about it, marrying a fireman had been synonymous with throwing out the calendar. Six bumpy months after the wedding, Rachel figured she could have tossed it right along with the bridal bouquet.

As a young wife, she clung stubbornly to her irrational devotion to scheduling. To *inking* as opposed to *penciling* in plans. To knowing exactly what she would be doing at a particular time seven days in advance or a month from now. God must have laughed as heartily as Vic when she finally crammed her Day-Timer pages into the paper shredder and threw the leather cover into the trash bin.

She sat now in church at the end of a pew, alone except for a couple hundred other worshipers. Vic was at the fire station. He worked one 24-hour shift, 8 A.M. to 8 A.M., followed by two shifts off. Sundays and holidays were not on the calendar, but then neither were fires and other emergencies. Nor were fires always doused and emergencies resolved by the time his shift ended. All of which explained why she had pitched her calendar.

Flexibility had been a hard lesson to learn, but a necessary one in order to keep her sanity and peace at home. She smiled, remembering how ludicrous she had been in those early months resisting his crazy schedule, wanting to inflict her sense of order on the entire Chicago Fire Department.

Little by little she accepted the topsy-turvy order of things and achieved a sense of emotional balance. She was married, but oftentimes appeared as a single person. If Vic joined her at church, great. If not, no problem. If he made it to a family outing, she welcomed his presence. If not, she was secure enough to carry on without him. Vic wouldn't be Vic if he weren't a fireman.

A movement in the aisle caught her attention. A little girl touched her arm.

"Lexi!" Rachel whispered with delight as she pulled the three-and-a-half-year-old onto her lap.

Rachel scooted the two of them down the padded pew, making space for Jessica Gray, the girl's mother. She sat, or rather collapsed was a better word. The woman appeared exhausted. Even her light brown hair, worn in a disheveled chic cut that required little attention, was flat.

"Hi, Jessie." Rachel tilted her head toward the little girl and raised her brows in question. Lexi usually attended one of the children's classes down the hall along with her older brother and sister.

In reply Jessie simply handed her daughter a book and shook her head as if to say Rachel didn't want to know.

The girl busied herself with turning pages. Rachel kissed her soft cheek. No fever. Lexi rewarded her with a precious smile, identical to her mother's on a better day. Their petite features mirrored each other, as did the teal-colored eyes.

Jessie leaned over and muttered, "Little Miss Crab. You wouldn't believe it, would you?"

Rachel saw the dark circles under her friend's eyes and crow's-feet that shouldn't be so pronounced on a thirty-five-year-old. Her wrinkled capris and sandals wouldn't cause a stir in the informal environment of their church, but they told Rachel that Jessie's morning involved more than her youngest being crabby.

"Jessie, I should have called you."

"Hey, it's the norm for a fireman's wife with three kids, right?" She blinked rapidly. "I'm a single parent half the time. I could have just stayed home."

"Or called me."

She laid her head briefly on Rachel's shoulder before turning her attention toward the front.

The two of them had met through their husbands, who were part of the same engine company. That meant if Vic was on duty, Kevin Gray was on duty. And that also meant there were three little kids and a mom who'd changed one too many diapers. The situation called for an honorary aunt. Rachel slipped easily into the role.

Like Rachel, Jessie was an elementary school teacher with a similar personality. Either one of them would, at the drop of a hat, make a beaver face or loudly sing "She'll Be Coming Around the Mountain," complete with motions and all the verses if the occasion called for it. They shared a rare lack of self-consciousness. The women would have clicked even if their husbands weren't good friends.

When the Grays' second child, Kevin Junior, was born eight years ago, Jessie quit teaching. Her plans to return to the classroom were waylaid when Lexi joined her brother and sister, Kylie, now ten. If anything, motherhood had enhanced Jessie's sparkle. Obviously something was amiss today.

Rachel settled Lexi on the pew beside her and stood to join in the singing. That morning, the day after Vic's reunion, she hadn't thought of Jessie. She had thought only of last night and of how many times she heard her husband state they did not have children.

No, that wasn't completely true. The engrossing image in her mind was of clouds gathering on the horizon. Sometime between her stocking-footed elevator ride and Vic's morning kiss, the vagueness of her uneasy feeling had been stripped away, leaving in its wake a full-fledged, all-encompassing sense of dread. It had found its way in through a wound inflicted by Ellen Hamilton, a stranger from Vic's past.

And Rachel hadn't breathed a word of it to her husband.

"All done, Lexi!" Rachel clapped and stood from her sitting position on the floor. "Good job. That was a hard puzzle. Hey, I haven't seen your new bathing suit yet. What color is it?"

"It's puhple, Aunt Wachel. I told you!"

Rachel smiled behind the little girl, who was busy dumping the puzzle pieces out for the fifth time. She loved hearing those *r*'s, even if it meant Lexi would be spending time with a speech therapist in the fall.

"Well, excuse me, Alexis Gray, but I forgot. Go put it on for me, please. I have to leave in fifteen minutes, and I *really* want to see it!"

"Okay." Without a backward glance, she raced from the kitchen.

Jessie handed Rachel a glass of iced tea, and they sat at the table. "How do you do that?"

"I've seen you do it too. It just doesn't always work with your own kids, I guess."

"It never works with my own kids. Maybe I should get back into the classroom where I have some control." She smiled. It was her first smile of the morning.

"Feeling better?"

"Yeah. Thanks for stopping by and giving me a breather. Half an hour alone in the shower works wonders. Sure you don't want a sandwich?"

"I'm sure, thanks. I was thinking earlier this morning about how I shredded my Day-Timer. Remember that?"

Jessie laughed. "Yes! You had the gang over for a barbecue at your house."

The "gang" referred to Vic's coworkers. Given the fact that day in and day out their very lives depended on each other, the firefighters were closer than family.

Jessie went on. "It was springtime, and I was way pregnant with KJ. I already knew you were pretty special to catch Vic Koski, but that day I figured special meant totally wacky. Certifiable."

"Which meant I fit right in." Rachel paused. "The point being, every time I griped about his schedule, I was griping about who he was."

Her friend grew somber. "I know, but I married a *teacher* fifteen years ago, not a fireman. And I know I agreed to his career change, but I did not factor in three kids, softball and bowling leagues, his coaching every sport his son plays, and a summer construction job!"

"It'll pass, Jessie. The second job is temporary and the kids will grow up. Tell me what's really wrong."

Jessie stood abruptly and carried her glass to the sink. She looked out the window, her back to Rachel. "We left Kevin at the ball field last night. He said he'd be right home. He didn't show up until midnight. We argued until three. And then he left, just went in early to the station. I guess. I don't know. Maybe he has a girlfriend. Vic's idea about staying current wouldn't fly around here."

"Oh, Jessie." Rachel felt weighted down, as if a coat of iron had been draped across her shoulders.

Kevin wasn't a believer. Though he didn't outwardly resent his wife's newfound faith, he seldom attended church with her and the children. He had never darkened the door of the weekly Bible study Vic started a few years previously for the firefighters in his unit. Though the meeting times rotated around their work shifts, Kevin always had an excuse not to attend. Rachel knew her husband continued to pray for the younger man, but he didn't harp on him about coming.

Jessie went on. "It's never been this serious. I mean, we've been arguing a lot lately, but—" A sob cut off her words.

Rachel hurried to her side and embraced her. She let her cry it out. "Hon, Kevin's not the type to have a girlfriend."

"I would if I were him!" She drew a shaky breath. "I can't stop nagging!"

"Well then, you both have legitimate concerns. You know the schedule bothers him as much as it does you. Why don't you plan a getaway for just the two of you? A night downtown."

Jessie moved away, tore a paper towel from the roll, and blew her nose. "Easy for you to imagine something like that." She blew her nose. "Trust me, three kids tend to nip that idea right in the bud. I just can't do it all anymore. I don't even think I want to. If he—"

Rachel tuned her out. *Easy for you to imagine...because you don't have three kids.* Jessie hadn't heard the meaning behind her words, but they took shape in Rachel's mind. *As a matter of fact, you don't even have* one *kid.*

With a shake of her head, she quashed the thought. Her friend was upset. Ellen Hamilton had been upset, not to mention drunk. Their thoughtless words unintentionally shoved open a door Rachel did not have to walk through. Whether or not to expose her pain to the sunlight was her choice.

"Jessie!" she interrupted, somewhat exasperated. The subject of the Grays' marital discord wasn't a new one. "What do you want to do? Kick him out or work on it?"

"Kick him out."

Rachel caught her breath. "You can't mean that."

Jessie chewed her bottom lip and stared back at her.

"Jessie."

"Admit it, Rachel. Don't you sometimes feel like you're single?"

"No, because most nights we share the same bed. Of course I miss him horribly at times and really wish I didn't have to do some things by myself, but it goes with the territory. There's no getting around it. We make up for it when we can."

"Yeah, I know you two. If it's his day off and you have to teach and then go to your evening class, you both just stay awake half the night, catching up and getting *current*. I swear neither one of you needs sleep."

"You're getting off the subject. Why didn't you tell me you felt this bad?"

"I didn't know I did." She brushed at her eyes with an impatient gesture. "Don't worry, I'm not going to kick him out. I know it's not what God wants me to do, even if Kevin doesn't believe in Him."

"Maybe Vic can talk to him."

"And say what? Your wife is lonely? The kids miss you?"

"Yeah. He'll say it straight."

"No. Kevin should hear it from me. When I'm not screeching at him."

Rachel hugged her again. "Plan a getaway. We'll take the kids."

Jessie leaned back. "Rachel! You never take the kids if Vic's home. He hates babysitting."

She shrugged and blinked away her own tears. "So he can go visit his mother while I babysit."

~

The event Rachel most disliked doing without Vic was visiting his mother. Wanda Koski's demeanor could make the Mona Lisa wince.

The day the women first met, Vic ushered Rachel into his parents' home, the same humble clapboard two-story he had grown up in with his four brothers.

"Ma." He stood behind Rachel, hands on her shoulders, pride in his voice. Show-and-tell time. "This is Rache. Rachel Ruth Goldberg."

Shorter than Rachel's 5'6" by some inches, Vic's mother was a lean woman. Like opaque shrink-wrap, her skin stretched around bony angles with not one spare flap in sight. Her thin lips pressed together, making her mouth a small dash in the lined face. Her eyes were dark, unblinking.

Rachel knew in a glance that the shrink-wrap extended inwardly to Wanda's heart. And it spread outwardly, to the space directly before her, sucking air from the lungs of any who dared step near enough. No wonder Vic had let three months go by before taking Rachel home to meet his family.

The dash parted. "Vic said you were pretty."

She didn't emphasize the word "said." Rather, she stressed "pretty." *Vic said you were* pretty. A subtle disagreement with her son's opinion. Vic's fingers tensed on Rachel's shoulders.

"Mrs. Koski, it's a pleasure to meet you." She would confess the lie later, right after she asked the Lord again why it was He had brought this man into her life.

The dash curved upward, a tight parenthesis that would never crinkle her eyes. "Well, have a seat."

Rachel followed her through the spotless living room and sat on the worn couch.

Wanda wasn't finished directing traffic. "Vic, go out to the garage and take a look at your dad's lawn mower. It's giving him fits. He's at the hardware store right now."

"I'll wait for him."

"No, run along. I want to get to know your new friend without you interfering."

He hesitated.

Rachel smiled and winked in full view of his mother. At twenty-nine, Rachel had lived away from her parents' home for ten years. She had taught for six, earned her master's, was making car payments and renting an apartment. She could handle meeting this woman's terms and set some of her own in the process.

"Go ahead, Vic," she said. "This is female talk."

He grinned. His wonderful mouth must resemble his father's. "Ma, what's for dinner?"

Poor Vic. He was either in denial or hoping against hope. The scent of dinner had billowed through the screen door and assaulted her the moment they set foot in the front yard.

The parenthesis appeared again. "I'm baking a ham."

"Ma—"

"Mrs. Koski, that sounds absolutely perfect."

Perfect indeed. Even if Vic hadn't told her, Wanda would have guessed by Rachel's name that she was of Jewish heritage. Wanda's conspicuously nonkosher menu choice was a perfect expression of disapproval, perhaps even of disdain.

Rachel wondered which would count the most against her: her heritage or that she followed Messiah Yeshua. She suspected that the hurdles were going to be insurmountable.

There was not a woman on the face of the earth good enough for Wanda Koski's middle son.

⌒

"Vic!" Rachel nearly jumped into his arms as he walked through the back door Monday night. She nestled her face against his neck, muffling a squeal.

He laughed and hugged her tightly. "Mmm. Glad I'm home?" he murmured.

She knew he teased. Of course she was glad. His parents sat in the living room, waiting for him and dinner. With his fluctuating schedule, inviting them over was always a gamble. He might not make it home in time. Though his shift had ended at eight that morning and they had talked by phone, she hadn't seen him. His other commitments had kept him away all day. There was his meeting with Pastor Payton Wills about the Bible study Vic led. It consisted primarily of guys from his company. Vic regularly asked for Payton's direction. Then he'd gone downtown to help out with training a group of new guys, referred to as "probies," by putting them through a rigorous session of handling hose lines. Then there was the meeting with the battalion chief, which evidently had lasted longer than expected.

As his arms came around her waist now, she noticed the pair of black stilettos dangling from his hand. "Bryan must have delivered those?"

"Yeah. He stopped by the station yesterday and, of course, made a big deal out of them."

She laughed. "I don't think I want to hear what the guys had to say."

"Well, they may ask you about my shoe fetish. I owe Bry big time." Sniffing, Vic loosened his hold of her. "Do I smell what I think I smell?"

She nodded and whispered, "It's still her favorite."

His eyes widened. "It's her birthday." Mock dread underscored his statement.

Rachel burst into laughter and clapped a hand over her mouth. She shook her head.

"Mother's Day?"

She shook her head again.

He heaved his shoulders in an exaggerated shrug, his bushy eyebrows following suit.

Whenever he did that, Rachel heard his unspoken words. *Women! I'll never understand them. Especially my wife.* His attitude came from growing up with four brothers, no sisters, and Wanda.

"Dinner's almost ready." She tilted her head toward the living room.

He kissed her and loped off to greet Wanda and Stan. His mother wouldn't make the initial contact. Once when Vic had joined a family gathering late, Wanda planted herself between him and Rachel, more or less demanding his first hello. Gently but firmly he had pushed her aside, saying, "Ma, move. Please. I gotta kiss my wife." And then he had kissed Rachel, long enough for one of his brothers to whistle and howl. The woman had never again interrupted them.

Rachel hurried down the basement steps to retrieve the ham. A hot summer evening had been a ridiculous time to bake, even in the extra oven located downstairs. No matter. Nine years after they met, she was still working her plan to love Wanda Koski to pieces, even if it meant slaving over a hot stove to mash potatoes, stir gravy, and prepare a cream sauce for peas.

A short time later they gathered around the table in the dining area at one end of the living room. The kitchen had space for only a small table against the wall and three chairs.

"Rachel." Wanda's voice always carried an undertone of dissatisfaction, the timbre of an incessant talker who always had a better idea. "Ham? It's so hot tonight!"

Stan grasped Rachel's hand and squeezed it lightly as they bowed in prayer. "But, Wanda, it's your favorite."

Sergeant Stanislov Koski was easy to love. His heart stayed tuned to those around him. Nearly as tall as Vic, he had grown rotund since retiring seven years ago, making him one bear of a man. His voice still commanded attention, an appropriate attribute for a policeman. His features were an aged version of Vic with big ears, half-mast eyes, wide forehead, handsome rugged cheeks, and that wonderfully expressive mouth. Strands of gray wove themselves through the still-thick espresso brown hair.

Vic said the blessing. He tripped over a few words when he thanked God for protection and asked that He comfort a family and provide shelter. Rachel knew yesterday's fire lingered in his mind.

"In Jesus' name, amen."

"Amen," Rachel repeated and looked at him across the table, questioning with her eyes.

He nodded. The family was okay except for loss of possessions. The other men were okay. He was okay.

"Vic," his mother said, "did you have a long day? You know we'd be happy to come any other time when you're not off training or at a meeting or something." The comment was her stock conversation opener whenever they gathered for a meal Rachel planned.

"No such day exists, Ma."

"And besides, Wanda," Rachel intervened, "you're so busy yourself. How's the book club going?"

The subject changed before Vic began fussing at his mother, Rachel listened with one ear to what was wrong with the woman's book club. With the other ear, she tried to pick up on a tidbit that could be interpreted as a glass half full.

Except for her permed curls graying, Wanda hadn't aged a day in nine years. She read voraciously, played cards and bingo regularly, and still worked the morning shift three days a week at a neighborhood diner where she'd waitressed for 40 years. The shrink-wrapped woman had the stamina of an ox, an elephant's memory, and a mynah bird's penchant for repetition.

They would hear yet again how Stan wasted his time working as a greeter at a local discount store, what she didn't like about each of her other four daughters-in-law, how her ten grandchildren were spoiled beyond reason, and that her eldest was born nine and a half months after her wedding night. Did Rachel need any pointers? Wanda would shrug a bony shoulder and cock her head to one side, nonchalantly dispensing what she considered wisdom.

In between, Vic and his father caught up on their lives, and Stan in some way showed how he cherished his middle son's choice of a wife. Often he shooed Vic and Wanda into the living room while he helped Rachel clean up. Tonight he uncharacteristically communicated his opinion by ordering his wife to be quiet.

They were standing on the front porch when Wanda overstepped an unspoken boundary. In her capacity to overlook her mother-in-law's shortcomings, Rachel listened without comment to Wanda's familiar complaints, how Vic's bungalow was too small for children and they really should move into a larger house while interest rates were down. Rachel ignored Wanda's complaint that she was going to be too old to babysit for them. She even allowed her to crassly inquire if Rachel needed pointers. But tonight she went too far.

"Rachel." Even for Wanda the exasperated tone was turned up a notch. "You're not doing anything this summer. Why don't you find out what's wrong with you?"

The dam broke. The uneasiness Rachel had been struggling with since the reunion two nights ago engulfed her like a tidal wave and snatched away her breath.

Stan moved forward and faced his wife, partially obstructing her from view. He told her to hush in language Rachel had never heard come out of him. "We know they want to have kids. The rest is none of our business. I don't ever want to hear you speak of it again! Not one snide remark! Not even a hint! Not ever! Do you understand?"

Rachel heard footfalls on the porch steps and saw Wanda's small figure hurrying along the sidewalk, her plastic baggie of ham slices bouncing at her side.

Stan enveloped Rachel in a hug. "Rachel, I'm sorry. I've allowed her to interfere too much." And then he kissed her cheek, something he'd never done before. "Sorry, Vic." With that, he was gone.

Vic held her then, held her until air filled her lungs again. "I don't know why you keep inviting her over."

The funny thing of it was, Wanda's question echoed the same one she'd been asking herself for 48 hours.

*F*our

"Honey, you know why I keep inviting her over."

Rachel lay beside her husband in their dark bedroom and watched the brass fixtures of the ceiling fan twirl, blinking the streetlight's reflection. The cicadas hummed again, their song carried aloft on the warm night air seeping through the window screen.

Vic squeezed the hand that he held between them on the cotton sheet. "I know. You're loving her to Jesus. Trouble is, she thinks she knows Him because she goes to church. It's a hopeless situation! How can you keep putting up with her after all these years? I didn't have a choice growing up, but you do. You don't have to keep doing this just because she's my mother. We can see her on holidays."

"She needs regular reinforcement from us. She doesn't feel loved."

"How can she not feel loved? Dad's been there, day in and day out for forty-eight years! She has five sons who still live in Chicago and don't totally ignore her. Especially the middle one since his wife has a heart too big for her own good."

Rachel propped herself on an elbow and looked down on him in the faint light. "That's only because it overflows with all the love you pour into it."

"Yeah?"

She kissed him. "Yeah. Maybe your dad needs to do what you do."

"And what's that?"

"Send your mom flowers every single month."

He grinned. "Is that all it takes?"

She fell back down on her pillow. "Sometimes. Do you think they started out like us?"

"No way. Ma never could have resembled you."

"Maybe..." She hesitated to voice the words that had fluffed into existence with the mashing of the potatoes. "Maybe kids get in the way."

Vic remained silent.

Rachel splayed her fingers across her abdomen. Her womb. Empty except for the menses bloating her now. They came like clockwork. *You'd think we'd have figured out the ovulation thing by now...after 15 months of unsuccessful attempts to become pregnant.*

"Rache, even if you and I had five obnoxious boys in seven years, I'd still send you flowers on the twelfth of every month."

A tear slid from the corner of her eye, but she laughed. "Oh, Vic! You'd have to send them to the loony bin because that's where I'd be if I had five obnoxious boys like you all must have been. I don't know how your mother did it."

"Honestly, I don't either."

"So I'll invite her back again for dinner in four weeks or so."

He sighed and squeezed her hand again.

"Vic, are you too tired to discuss something?"

"No."

She knew he was. Though he had downplayed for his mother's sake the extent of the fire he fought yesterday, every fire pulled deeply from him. On top of that, he'd had a full day.

Clearly he was too drained to talk about what Wanda had said. Perhaps Rachel wasn't ready herself. The question—*Why don't I find out what's wrong with me?*—was a new one to her, an unfinished thought. At any rate, that wasn't the immediate dilemma.

"Something's come up with Jessie and Kevin. How was he yesterday?"

"Out of it. Couldn't point a nozzle worth beans." Vic's tone sharpened. He was a lieutenant now, the younger man's superior. "We didn't have a chance to talk much afterward. What's going on?"

Rachel told him about her conversation with Jessie, about their friends' midnight argument. "Tell me he doesn't have a girlfriend!"

"I seriously doubt he does. The guy's nuts about Jessie, even if he doesn't buy into her faith. I know some of the guys went over to Mojo's after Saturday night's game. The usual. A few beers, a few laughs. No big deal."

"No big deal except that she's left with putting three kids to bed by herself *again*. Oh." Her voice trailed off as the meaning of what she said began to sink in.

"What?"

"Is it the kids? Is that what's come between them? Like your parents? Jessie said she hadn't factored in three kids when he became a fireman. Maybe Kevin didn't either. Maybe he doesn't know how to handle them. Or how to fit them into his relationship with Jessie. Or—"

"Rache, calm down. They'll work it out. She probably just needs flowers once a month."

"But you don't go to Mojo's. Would you go if we had kids? Maybe you—"

"Rachel! I am not Kevin Gray and you are not Jessie or my mother."

"Oh, Vic, do you still even want kids?" The words tumbled straight from her heart onto her tongue, bypassing rational thought.

"Yeah!" No hesitation...but too automatic.

She sat up abruptly, switched on the lamp, and faced him. "Are you sure?

He blinked, his eyes growing accustomed to the light. "I haven't changed my mind."

Pressing a hand to her chest, she fought down panic and tried to lighten her tone. "Like the old story about the wife who asked her husband if he loved her?"

"And the husband said, I told you thirty years ago I did. Until I tell you otherwise, it's still true."

She bit her lip and nodded.

"Don't I tell you every month that I want kids?" His husky voice softened. "When I say things like, well, I guess it's back to the drawing board?"

"But after fifteen times?"

"Fourteen. I've only said it fourteen times."

She felt tears well. He knew. He had counted too. "Fifteen tomorrow."

Vic took her hand and pressed the palm to his lips. "Then tomorrow I'll say for the fifteenth time, let's try again."

And he would hold her tightly and ask God for next month.

"Rache, do you still want kids?"

"Oh, more than anything in the world!"

"Then that's what I'll give you."

Nine years ago, during their brief courtship, they assigned the subject of children to the negotiable list.

Negotiations on a variety of topics began two months after Vic Koski had walked into her classroom and turned her as well as her life upside down. Their late-night conversations took place at Myra B's Coffee Shop. Located approximately 16 minutes east of her apartment and 19 minutes northwest of his, the place had become their home away from home. Its old-fashioned red leatherette booths, dark-paneled walls, and plastic flowers offered a neutral ground for sussing out each other. Examining their aspirations, motives, opinions, and phobias had quickly become an intense process between them, as if a deadline had been set to determine their compatibility.

Rachel thought perhaps the feeling of an imposed time limit came because of their ages. At twenty-nine and thirty-four, they were weary of relational game playing. If their life views clashed, why prolong things? And then, too, by the second month, there was the physical attraction, its intensity unlike any she'd ever known. Which was why they chose Myra B's for their late-night conversations.

"Nonnegotiable." Rachel looked him straight in the eye. Twenty-five minutes before, she had shoved him out her apartment door and slammed it behind herself. Her heartbeat hadn't slowed yet.

Vic's sigh expressed annoyance. His heartbeat probably raced in tandem with hers. "I'm not suggesting we live together. I'm just saying that given how we feel, if things..." He waved his hands. "If things escalate, it's *natural.*"

"Well, I'm after supernatural or nothing at all."

"Supernatural?"

She nodded, still trying to regulate her breathing.

"What's that supposed to mean? I thought God created sex."

She pulled a Bible from her purse. They'd already covered their common faith. One week after meeting they had determined that they were both believers, having accepted Jesus as their Lord, as the only way to God the Father.

Rachel had walked in such faith since she was nine years old and had grown up accepting a nonnegotiable pact with Him: She would only marry a committed Christian. What fuzzed the picture now was Vic's young relationship with Christ. He didn't see things quite the same as she did. Though she didn't doubt that his life had changed, he'd only been a believer for about two years. Some notions were hard to readjust.

"Read this, Vic." She turned around her worn Bible. "See what I've underlined? Here." She flipped pages. "And here. All about not being physical before marriage. All about the woman's body belonging to her husband. God created sex for married people. It's a spiritual union, not only physical."

"I know all that."

"You know?" she cried.

"Bryan showed me those Scriptures and explained it all." His friend had diligently discipled him in those two years.

"Then...then?" Frustration garbled her thoughts. "Why?"

He rubbed his jaw and lifted a shoulder, clearly looking sheepish. "I thought that meant if she wasn't a Christian or if I didn't love her."

"Vic." She closed her eyes, blotting from view the man who could, with a certain gaze through those half-mast navy blue diamonds, annihilate every promise she'd made to her Lord about anything. To say nothing of his kisses... The desire he ignited in her terrified her.

"Vic." She tried again with her eyes open. "I'm a virgin."

He blinked. Color drained from his face.

The night ended badly. He didn't know what to do with an anomaly. She didn't know what to do with his past or with the new fire growing within her.

Over the ensuing weeks the subject became an uneven plank in the bridge they were building between themselves. They revisited it often, sawing here, pulling up nails there. Eventually he agreed that premarital sex was a nonnegotiable. She set nonnegotiable physical boundaries which, he said, tripled his time at the gym and introduced him to the benefits of frequent cold showers. In time, with tears in his eyes, he admitted how unworthy he felt to be granted the gift she offered. And, in time, she came to grasp the reality of Christ's forgiveness. From God's point of view, Vic Koski's slate was as clean as hers. The only choice was to align her point of view with His.

Four months into the relationship they discussed children.

"Negotiable," she said.

He hesitated and finally gave a half nod. "Negotiable."

"You're sure?"

He fiddled with his coffee cup, avoiding eye contact. "Sure."

"Come on, Vic."

"Okay." He set the cup down and met her eyes. "Right now I don't want any."

"I don't either. I'm perfectly happy teaching them and leaving them at school."

"I don't know if I'll *ever* want any."

"I don't either. So, it's negotiable. Right? Leave it up to God?"

"Right."

Later she would remember the sense that a shadow, for the merest of split seconds, had dimmed the sparkle in his eyes.

〜

At the age of twenty-nine she had led a full, deeply satisfying life that revolved around teaching, church, and her new
love. At twenty-nine she agreed to tacking motherhood onto
the negotiable list because it was not one of those black-and-
white subjects about which God unequivocally said yes or
no.

At twenty-nine, what did she know of biological clocks
and mysterious dreams?

At thirty-five she began to get an inkling.

The first dream arrived in technicolor, complete with stereo
sound and wide-awake scents, the most distinct being that of
baby shampoo.

She confided in her good friend Terri Schuman about it.
Terri sometimes worked the same shift as Vic. Though both of
them were trained as firefighters and paramedics, he majored
on fires and rescues while she attended to medical needs.

There were a few other women working out of the station,
but Terri was the first female to join Vic's unit. That she lasted
spoke volumes about her personality. She lived with her
boyfriend, partied hearty with the guys, and thought Rachel's
belief in God unfathomable. In many ways she was the
extreme opposite of Rachel. But that the two women related
so well was no mystery: They shared a pragmatic approach to
life.

Only after Terri came on board did Rachel gain a feminine
perspective of life at the firehouse. Terri described the first
time a victim died while she worked him, how afterward she
emoted all over the station, crying, wanting to talk it out. The
men offered little beyond stony stares and suggestions of
unfinished chores. One even said, "Stuff it, Schuman." Vic

handed her Bryan's phone number, referring to him as the unofficial part-time chaplain who took personal calls. Since then Terri "stuffed it" after a traumatic event and waited until the next shift arrived with another female emergency worker who gladly listened while she unburdened herself.

One sunny afternoon, the day after Rachel's odd dream, she sat with Terri on a set of bleachers, watching a Little League baseball game. Two of Vic's nephews played on the team. Their dad coached and Vic assisted his brother whenever his schedule permitted.

Rachel described the dream. "Not much happened, but I can't get it out of my mind. I was holding the most precious baby. I don't know if it was a boy or a girl, but there were Vic's navy blue eyes gazing up at me. And Vic rolled on the floor, kicking up his legs and howling like a little kid. I've never seen him so happy."

Terri grinned, her brown, thick-lashed eyes hidden behind sunglasses that enhanced the illusion she was a policewoman. She had short black hair tucked behind her ears, full lips, and the build of a model promoting exercise equipment. Rachel knew she'd feel as physically safe with Terri as with Vic in any sort of emergency situation.

Rachel went on. "I can't shake this warm, mushy feeling."

Her friend laughed out loud. "It's rather obvious what's going on. Your biological clock has begun ticking."

Rachel bristled at that assessment and gave Terri a withering look. The woman, younger by a few years, declared she'd been born without one hint of maternal instinct or whisper of desire to ever marry. She remained perfectly content dating Lee Reynolds, a high school teacher and football coach in the school district where Rachel taught.

"And what would you know about biological clocks, Miss Schuman?"

She laughed again. "My older sister. Same age as you. She hasn't had a dream, but she finds herself shopping in baby departments without knowing how she got there."

Well, she hadn't done that yet.

"So did you tell Vic?"

"It was just a silly dream."

"Right. No need to rile him up with warm, mushy feelings."

Terri's chuckles fed Rachel's growing discomfort, but her next statement totally unnerved her.

"You'll want to tell your grandmother, though. She understands things like this." Although she didn't believe in a personal God, Terri recognized that something of a deeper realm existed within Ruth Goldberg.

Rachel chewed a thumbnail. "Bubbie will say—" She gulped. "She'll say, 'Pay attention to your dreams. They're your love letters from God.'"

"That's your Bubbie. Powerful stuff."

Rachel nodded. "Yeah, well this letter is going to stay sealed inside its envelope."

Miss Control Freak, thinking she was in the driver's seat.

Five

Some weeks after Vic's high school reunion, Rachel carried
two white mugs full of fresh coffee onto the third-floor balcony of the vacation condominium. She set them on a small
square redwood table.

"Come here, baby." Vic grasped her waist and guided her
onto his lap.

Settling back against him, she curled up her legs and gazed
beyond the small balcony's railing. Early morning sunlight
crept across an unhindered vista of snowcapped Rocky Mountains, slowly displaying deep blues and purples in the distance. Below, across the road and through pine trees, the
reservoir in Dillon, Colorado, sparkled.

"This is so incredibly breathtaking."

"Mm-hmm."

She wrapped the terry cloth robe more securely around
herself against the crisp air. "Isn't it great to miss a week of
August humidity, even if it is cold enough to see our breath?"

He laughed. "It sure is. Coffee?"

"Thanks." She accepted the thick mug from him and
sipped. "Mmm. What's the station going to do without your
coffee?"

"Suffer immeasurably. Makes them appreciate me. What's
on the agenda for today?"

"Reading and napping at the pool. You can swim laps." They had arrived yesterday, renting a car at the Denver airport and driving up into the mountains. Breathing the thin air at 9000 feet took some adjustment. As they had done on previous visits, they would save hiking for later in the week.

"How about dinner at that French restaurant you liked so much last year?"

She twisted on his lap to look at him. "You remembered! You'd go, our very first night? Without one hint from me?"

"Yeah." He grinned. "And get it over with."

"Ha-ha. If you weren't so cute, I'd insist on going twice."

"If you didn't have me wrapped around your little finger, we wouldn't go at all."

She smiled. "You're wrapped around my little finger?"

"You better believe it."

"Okay, bud, what do you want?"

His infectious laugh chased away the hushed morning.

She clamped a hand over his mouth. "Shh."

He chuckled and she removed her hand. "Rache, you are such a teacher, always sniffing for underlying motives. What makes you think I want something?"

"Little boys have been buttering me up for fifteen years. You're the only one, though, who can afford to buy me a gourmet meal in a French restaurant."

"Well, I'm glad to hear that. But I didn't mean to butter you up. I really do like being at your beck and call."

She kissed his cheek. "I know."

"What I want is to visit the fire department. Do you mind if I skip the pool today?"

"Of course not."

"I didn't think so, but it is our first day."

"Meaning you'll have time to visit again this week."

"I think you know me too well."

Whenever they traveled outside of Chicago, Vic made it a point to meet other firefighters. His symbolic brotherhood encompassed the world. He had been known to spend an entire shift at a station where he'd never even previously met anyone.

She smiled. "And you know me. If I have enough reading material, I'll hardly notice you're gone."

"So what'd you bring?"

She had counted on him asking that question because he always took an interest in her activities. She set her mug on the table, leaned back against him, pulled a paperback from her robe pocket, and held it up for him to see.

He sipped his coffee, buying time. "Infertility, huh?"

"Mm-hmm." She laid the book on her lap.

The question his mother raised a few weeks ago had simmered long enough. *Why don't you find out what's wrong with you?* Now was the time to broach the subject, now when seven unencumbered vacation days stretched before them.

He set his mug on the table. "Fertility drugs and test-tube stuff. Tens of thousands of dollars."

She knew money wasn't the main issue. He would balk because to him, medically investigating conception smacked of not trusting God's hand. "Not necessarily drugs and test-tube stuff. People don't consider those things until they've exhausted every other avenue. Insurance covers many of the costs. All I want to know is why I can't conceive. There may be a simple, fixable answer."

"We've put it in God's hands. When it's time, He'll make it happen, not some doctor."

Rachel buried her face in the crook of his neck and whispered, "Talk with me, Vic, just talk with me."

Two Januarys before, soon after Rachel's thirty-sixth birthday, an emergency call set her biological clock's pendulum swinging so furiously it literally clanked in her ears at times.

The dream she shared with Terri recurred almost monthly, leaving her all warm and mushy for days at a time. Still, she was able to ignore the growing desire to have a baby and had never told Vic about the dream. All that changed one snowy night.

The fire was not a serious blaze, but it landed Vic in the ER just the same. When Rachel's phone rang shortly after midnight, her heart rocketed into a ragtime beat.

"Rachel, it's Terri. He's okay."

He's okay. A euphemism for "he's alive."

Before they married Vic explained that if the worst happened, someone would come to the house to tell her. Although he reiterated it would most likely be Bryan and the fire chief, the scene was so ingrained in her mind of a firefighter ringing her doorbell that she knew if Terri had arrived on her doorstep, she would have instantaneously surmised he was gone.

"But?" Rachel prompted. Obviously something wasn't okay, or else Terri would not have called.

"He slipped on the ice."

"He what?"

"Yeah. I think his arm's broken. He's at the hospital. I'm on my way now to pick you up."

"What was he doing?"

"They were out on a call in the middle of the ice storm. An abandoned car. Kids probably set it on fire." She mumbled a derogatory remark about juvenile delinquents. "Things were under control until he twisted around too fast and his legs flew out from under him. Are you all right?"

She blew out a shaky breath. "I will be."

Later, as she gazed down at her husband lying on a bed in a curtained cubicle of the ER, she heard the first clank of the ticktock.

Drugged as he was for the pain, his eyes were mere slits. No diamonds sparkled. His skin, normally the sanguine tone of an outdoor athlete, was washed out, the stubble on his jaw pronounced against the pallor. His espresso brown hair was matted where he'd no doubt perspired under his helmet even as ice coated the pavement beneath his boots.

From her standing angle, she could see the tips of his ears with their old scars. In his early firefighting days, before the Nomex hoods were standard equipment, encounters with 1000 degree plus temperatures damaged the vulnerable tissue. He always laughed, saying that if his ears weren't so big, they might not have burned so readily. They remained sensitive to heat. He avoided direct sunlight whenever possible...

She thought of those early days and how much smoke he had "eaten." Before the self-contained breathing apparatus had become readily available, he didn't have a mask to wear all the time. Even in recent years there were circumstances which he thought dictated that he remove it. When one of the guys couldn't hear his shout, he would lift it, ending up inhaling enough burning toxins to turn his mucous black...

Once after a fire he had taken his temperature. It was 106 degrees. Not that he was daily or even weekly in a fire, but 106 degrees? Bodies were not created to withstand such things...

Heart attack deaths ranked disproportionately high as the cause of death among firefighters in the line of duty. No wonder, in light of the extreme levels of stress their bodies were subjected to...

She looked at his large body draped haphazardly in a hospital gown, pulled the sheet more closely around him, and faced the unavoidable facts. Vic Koski was a hero of epic proportions, but even if he quit fighting fires tomorrow and avoided dying in one, he would more than likely die at a relatively young age from some disease induced by some contaminant he'd already encountered.

She wanted his baby.

After that revelation, Rachel waited until his cast had been removed from his arm before broaching the subject. She expected it would take him time to see her viewpoint. What she didn't expect was his total avoidance of the subject.

"Vic, let's negotiate."

"What's to negotiate? I'm not ready." His jaw would clench.

"You'll let me know when you are ready?"

His eyes narrowed.

Still, she didn't back down. "So that's the end of the discussion? Just like that?"

"I'll be in the garage."

Vic's response was highly atypical. In seven years no subject had been off limits between them. Never buying into the thought that wifely submission meant she should keep her mouth shut, Rachel pursued the subject, at times cajoling and describing the dream, at times tearfully begging. His reactions never varied from the initial one.

In those days, before her beloved grandmother lay in a nursing home unable to talk, Rachel sought the woman's advice.

"Rachel, Rachel." Ruth hugged her grandchild, rocking back and forth, murmuring a prayer in her native German language. "Since when did it become your job to change your husband? He is a godly man. Only Yeshua can whisper change into his heart."

"Oh, Bubbie." Though she Americanized the spelling, Rachel always addressed her with the Yiddish word for grandmother. "I pray every day he'll hear."

"And then you take him right back into your own hands again, don't you? You don't leave him with God, do you?"

"But Vic and I talk about everything except this!"

Bubbie waved a hand impatiently, swatting at the gnat of Rachel's silly words. "This ticking. What is it you call it?"

"Biological clock." Rachel fought back a sigh of exasperation. There were times when the old world clashed hopelessly with the new, when she knew Bubbie could not relate. What could an old Austrian Jew who met Christ in a WW II concentration camp know about biological clocks?

"God does not talk in loud ticktocks. Why doesn't your husband want children?"

"He only says he's not ready."

Bubbie slowly blinked her large eyes. Like Rachel's, they were a medium brown with a sprinkling of cinnamon. They took on a faraway stare Rachel knew well. The woman gazed inwardly, intent on seeing something that remained hidden to those around her.

"Rachel, your Vic needs healing. Come, let us pray."

They prayed that day as well as on subsequent days. Rachel eventually dropped the subject from her conversation with Vic and let God have him. One day they visited Bubbie together. Before leaving, the older woman asked Vic to sit on the floor beside her. Instead of holding his hands as she usually did when she prayed for him, she laid her hands on his head.

At first she prayed in German, perhaps concealing from him what she asked. In English she said, "Lord God, speak to him through his pain."

Later, on the drive home, he said only, "You know I love your grandma. And I say this with respect, but sometimes she sends shivers down my spine. If I weren't a believer, she'd give me the willies. I think she really has seen the face of God."

Not many weeks after, Vic called Rachel. "I'm at Memorial ER."

Her mind raced. *He's talking to me. He's talking to me. He can't be very hurt—*

"It's Teague. He's okay."

Firefighter talk again. The man wasn't dead.

"Rache, will you bring Lisa down here?" Lisa was Teague's wife. "And bring the boys."

"Is he...is he dying?"

"He'll be okay. Broken ribs, internal injuries. The side of a house fell on him. He was in the yard. Tree branches took most of the blow. He's conscious. Rache, the boys have to see him. Do you understand? Don't come without the boys."

Even at 3 A.M. on a school night, Rachel didn't question his insistence or his request. Much like the night Terri called her from the ER, the extraordinary ties dictated actions. Teague Michaels and Vic were family. By extension, so were their spouses. And their children.

The incident was an odd answer to Bubbie's prayer, but it cut to the heart of the matter and revealed to Vic why he avoided the subject of children. Within weeks he and Rachel negotiated an agreement about having their own.

Now in Colorado, as the sun slipped behind Buffalo Mountain and *l'escargots* were served at their table on the French restaurant's outdoor deck, Vic and Rachel began new negotiations. The talks were well under way by the time the *crêpes suzette* arrived.

Afterwards, satiated with delicious food, the vacationers quietly strolled the few blocks back to the condominium under a starry sky nearly close enough to touch. A short time later, they snuggled on the couch in front of a roaring fire which Rachel had built, sipping hazelnut decaf prepared by Vic.

"Honey, thanks for talking things over."

He smiled. "Hey, I learned my lesson. Why fight it? If I don't talk, Bubbie with her direct line to God will see to it my tongue is loosened."

"Do you think she still prays? Somehow, somewhere deep inside her soul?" The woman had lain for almost a year in a fetal position, uncommunicative.

"I think so."

"I do too. Otherwise, why would God keep her on the earth?"

"Rache, it's not like that other time."

She set her cup on the coffee table and reclined against a pillow on the couch's arm. Vic took her feet onto his lap. He was a good foot kneader, and she had walked to the restaurant and back in her stilettos.

For a while, as he gently massaged her feet and the fire crackled, they remained silent. No doubt he too was remembering that "other time" when the wounds of his childhood finally surfaced.

As far back as he could recall, terror had stalked him whenever his father, a policeman, was on duty. The day Stan Koski was shot, that fear was driven underground. Vic, at thirteen, became the terror himself. His mother dubbed him a "holy terror." From all accounts his brothers and Bryan shared with her, Vic grew into a bona fide misfit who left chaos in his wake and made more enemies than friends.

The Army and firefighting taught him to redirect his energies. He found legitimate ways to involve himself in terrifying situations. In essence he controlled his fears by facing them.

When Rachel tried discussing her desire for a baby, all the terror of Vic's childhood rose up. He couldn't name it or conquer it, and so he ignored it until Teague Michaels was injured. His friend's sons were twelve and fourteen. Vic's mind graphically replayed the day his dad was shot, how he learned about it from a neighbor lady, how he wasn't allowed at the hospital while his dad struggled in the ICU for two weeks, how no one held him and said things were going to be all right.

And then Vic understood his reluctance about having children. He argued with Rachel that there was no way he would bring into the world a kid who would live with the daily fear his father might be killed. Vic absolutely refused to be responsible for such a life.

Until God began to answer Bubbie's prayers for healing.

Vic stepped into the Michaels family, as did other firefighters. Teague's sons had several surrogate fathers while their own recuperated. In the process, Vic saw the antidote to his childhood terror: God's loving care became a living entity through members of the fire department. Any future child of his would never be left alone, and he would begin to teach that truth to him the day he was born.

Little by little her husband let go of his past. Neither of them would forget the day it vanished completely. He'd taken the boys to a Cubs game, arrived home late, and awakened her from a sound sleep. "Rachel!" he shouted, laughing hilariously.

"I want a dozen kids! Let's field a team!" And then, in her arms, he'd wept like a child.

Now he rested his hands atop her feet and turned to her. "It's really not like the other time," he repeated. "I want a kid with you. I do. I want to see a tangible form of our love. I just don't want to interfere with God's supernatural ways."

"Vic." She paused, recalling her grandmother's words. Had Rachel prayed about this moment? Yes. Was she jumping in ahead of God's timing? She didn't think so. "Honey, God can use modern technology."

"But why would He bother?"

"I don't know why. I just want one answer."

"The doctor said you should have conceived by now, and you want to know why it hasn't happened."

"Yes."

"And, hypothetically speaking, what if God says through modern technology that for some reason…" His voice trailed away.

"Vic, we may as well say it out loud. If for some reason He has allowed me to be barren."

"It's such an ugly word."

Barren. Infertile. Childless. Sterile. They were all ugly words. She hated them. She feared them.

And yet she resisted wallowing in such emotions. She shoved them aside and winked at him. "But you still think I'm gorgeous."

"Always. Anyway, if that happens, we stop there. We don't take drugs and have twenty-five kids at once. We don't let them mix up our…our *cells* in a petri dish."

Rachel wiggled her toes, mentally planting in her heels for the long haul. "Let's just agree on the first part for now. I don't understand all that other stuff either. How about we agree on one step at a time?"

He studied the fire. "And what does that mean?"

"Tests. They take time. A few months maybe. And..." Now she hesitated. He wasn't going to like this part. "And they have to start with you."

He whipped his head around. "Me?"

"It's the way our insurance works. You're the cheapest and easiest route. We have to rule you out first. Therefore, they begin with you."

"But *I* don't have a problem!"

"Oh? And where's the proof?"

"What do you mean, where's the proof?"

"Where's the child that proves you don't have a problem?"

He stared at her, speechless, his neck reddening.

Rachel swung her feet from his lap, sat up, and threw her arms around him. "Oh, Vic, honey." She laughed. "This isn't an attack on your masculinity. I *know* you don't have a problem in that department. You're my slayer of dragons, my knight, my gallant victor all rolled into one."

He hooked his hands around her waist. "Talk about buttering up."

She kissed his cheek. "What do you say?"

"I say Bubbie would tell you not to press."

"All right, all right. Will you pray about it?"

"You're still pressing."

"Vic!"

"How's the biological clock?"

"Still clanging."

"Unbearably?"

That was the word she had used two years ago. "No, but it's constant, what with all of our nieces and nephews and so many friends with children."

"And my mother."

"And your mother."

"But things are okay for now, while we're on vacation?" She nodded halfheartedly. "Mm-hmm."

"Rachel." His serious tone. "I'll pray about it. Good enough for now?"

She met the gaze of those navy blue diamonds reflecting the firelight. He wasn't really wrapped around her little finger, but he was crazy about her. He was devoted to her. And he loved her enough to be honest with her about his feelings. What more could she want...except the faith to know that if God desired to change her husband's mind, He would?

"I love you, Vic. Praying about it is all I need to ask of you."

Six

"Rachel?"

Sylvia Talbot's voice jerked Rachel from her reverie, and she swiveled her head around. "Sylvia!"

"Sorry." The principal of Franklin Elementary School threaded her way between the empty student desks clumped helter-skelter about the classroom. "I knocked, but you just kept staring out the window. Lost in thought?"

"A million miles away." Rachel sat perched atop her desk, bare feet resting on her cushioned chair. "Excuse the obstacle course."

"Rearranging?"

"Naturally." She smiled. "It's mid-August."

"We educators are creatures of habit, aren't we?" Sylvia returned the smile and leaned against a low bookcase built into the wall beneath windows that reached almost to the ceiling.

The school was vintage 1940s, three-story brick, windows that opened, no air-conditioning, waist-high registers that clanked like ghostly chains when the heat kicked on, asbestos tucked beneath gray stippled linoleum.

Rachel agreed. "We are, above all, creatures of habit. If we go to a year-round school calendar, I'm out of here. Vic usurped every other schedule of my life. I cannot possibly give this one up too."

They laughed. Though the day was hot and classes wouldn't start until next week, the ever-professional Sylvia wore a skirt, blouse, stockings, and pumps.

Rachel glanced down at her own shorts and T-shirt. "Sylvia, look at me. I don't know why I'm going for a degree in administration. I'll never achieve your aura."

"That's why I came in." She gave Rachel her signature glare, the one that left drug-dealing dads tongue-tied and gun-wielding mothers contrite. "We need to talk about your wardrobe."

Rachel burst into laughter. A tall, slender woman, Sylvia maintained her tight salt-and-pepper curls chin length, softening the sharp angles of her face. Her silver-rimmed glasses framed deep brown eyes. Her rich mahogany skin color attested to her heritage of a white mother and a father with mixed genes of African American and Native American. No one accused Dr. Talbot of being unable to relate to the concerns of minorities.

"Rachel, trust me, you have your own aura. You don't need mine. When does your fall course begin?"

"After Labor Day." She was working on her doctorate at the University of Chicago. "Did Jessie Gray call you yet?"

"Yes. She already signed up with the district office to sub and made an appointment to see me tomorrow."

"Good." Rachel had encouraged her friend to get back into teaching.

"Do you think she can handle Franklin?"

"She's got what it takes, though she hasn't been in the classroom for quite a few years. Right now she's dealing with some marriage issues, one of those bumps in the road. I told her teaching would get her mind off what she can't change."

"I trust your judgment. We may have a position opening up for the second semester."

Rachel's stomach lurched, an involuntary reaction to the news she suspected was coming. "Who's pregnant?"

"Michele." A second-grade teacher. "Three months. She's thinking of leaving after Christmas."

Rachel straightened her shoulders and forced enthusiasm into her response. "That's great! She's been wanting a second one for a while." *Like since springtime. Six whole months ago.* A wave of shame trailed the caustic thoughts. What a despicable, jealous woman she was becoming.

"Rachel."

She blinked and saw concern on her friend's face. They had worked together for 15 years with Sylvia as principal for 12 of them. Rachel had learned more from her about teaching than she had in all of her college studies.

"Do you want to talk, child?" Her voice could be as soft as a bird feather landing in the grass. Although nearly 20 years her senior, Sylvia treated Rachel as an equal, respecting her opinion, sharing matters for prayer, giggling with her over coffee. But there were moments, like now, when she slipped easily into a motherly role.

Rachel's vocal cords contorted. No sound formed.

"Honey, your room looked like this two days ago. You're not bubbling over with some new bulletin board scheme. You barely said two words at the faculty meeting. The Rachel Koski I know hasn't shown up yet, and time is running out. School starts in five days."

"If…" Her voice was a strained whisper, foreign to her ear, painful in her throat. "If I talk, I'll cry."

Sylvia touched her shoulder as she walked by. A moment later Rachel heard the door click shut. Her friend returned and handed her a small packet of tissues.

"There is nothing wrong with crying."

She yanked out a tissue and took a deep breath. "Oh, Sylvia! Compared to every little kid who'll file through that door next week, I don't have a *thing* to cry about!"

"Rachel, we all have our own sorrow. God understands that. And I understand that."

Like a surprise ambush, the tenderness of Sylvia's voice whisked right past Rachel's defenses. All the grief she had been tucking into the empty pockets of her soul rose up for release, and she burst into tears. Sylvia wordlessly wrapped her arms around her and rocked her in a hug. After some minutes, Rachel calmed and Sylvia released her.

"All right, child. We both know why you're hurting." Though they had talked only sporadically throughout the summer, she knew of Rachel's situation. "Tell me what's been happening."

"Well." Her attempt to smile failed. "I'm not pregnant."

The principal nodded and squeezed her arm. "And?"

Rachel took a shaky breath. How could she explain months of chasing an elusive hope through an endless maze? Rushing her words, she crammed the situation into a few sentences. "The doctor says she doesn't know what else to do. My hormones seem fine, but she doesn't have any experience in this area. She says it's time to see a specialist. And Vic refuses."

"Flat out?"

"Not exactly. He's praying about it."

"He's a good man."

"He is." She blew her nose. "But so far he refuses to get tested. He says God will take care of things."

"Well, there is something to be said for that."

"I know! Which confuses me to no end! But God gave us brains to use, and He gave us technology. Right? If it's for a good cause—" She shook her head. "This from the woman who always insists on the supernatural route! Am I nuts, Sylvia?"

"For wanting a baby and being willing to try some tests? No. But it sounds like things may be getting blown out of proportion. When I see you not functioning here at school, this desire is interfering with your life. I think that's called being anxious. Does Vic know that it's affecting you to this extreme?"

"*I* didn't know until just now!"

Sylvia sighed heavily. "You're stuffing all this inside. That's not like you. And the added stress can't be helping matters. Let it go, child. Just let it go."

"I don't know how!"

"Shh. You know how." She laid her hand on Rachel's shoulder and closed her eyes. "Father, hear Your daughter's cry and comfort her. Remove these anxious thoughts. Restore Your peace in her. I ask that You change Vic's heart. And I ask that You not let this create a rift between them..."

Like a healing ointment, her words saturated Rachel until at last they touched that place deep inside where the emptiness resided. She whispered, "Amen."

"And amen." Sylvia lowered her face until their noses were millimeters apart. "Rachel, don't let things build up like this. You know you can come to me at any time."

She nodded.

"I mean it." She straightened. "Your hands are going to be fuller than usual this year."

"How's that?"

"Rachel, you know I love you like one of my own daughters, but my prayer was self-serving. We have a, um, a situation." She hesitated. Sylvia never hesitated.

Rachel's stomach tightened again. When had she become so anxious?

"A new fourth grader. I just met him and his mother. He's a cha-r-r-ming boy." Sylvia smiled crookedly, clearly suggesting that the kid was a teacher's worst nightmare. "I know this is rotten timing. You're my first choice for him. Actually my only choice. A match made in heaven."

A sinking feeling nibbled at the fragile sense of peace she had just begun to feel. "Sylvia, one of the other fourth-grade teachers can handle him. You know the three charming boys already on my roster!"

"I'll pull out two of them. Yes, this one is definitely worth two. That's only fair. His name is Toby Meyers. You'll work wonders with him."

"But I don't need this—"

"Of course you do." Her crisp tone announced handholding time was over. She began weaving her way back through the cluttered room. "This will get your mind off what you can't change."

Her words echoed Rachel's earlier comment. Like a splash of cold water in her face, they got her attention. Maybe instead of smugly pointing out what Jessie Gray should do, she could start heeding her own advice.

∽

The early evening sun edged along its northwesterly descent, leaving the eastern window unattended. Rachel turned on a bedside lamp as shadows lengthened in her grandmother's private room at the nursing home.

She had left her classroom in its chaotic state soon after Sylvia's departure and driven straight to Bubbie's, about a 60-minute trip if it wasn't made during rush hour. That splash of cold water awakened her to what she needed. Bubbie couldn't talk, but she was no less Rachel's touchstone than she had ever been.

Ruth Goldberg lay as she had for months now, curled on her side, her face expressionless. Once in awhile a spark of life shimmered briefly in her otherwise dull eyes. Osteoporosis had ravaged her small body for years. When at last she could no longer bear the pain, the doctor prescribed different medication. Something went haywire.

She had aged almost beyond recognition. Her thin white hair was sparse, her cheeks shrunken where dentures were no longer worn, her cinnamon eyes more dominant than ever.

"Bubbie." Rachel touched her cheek, soft and downy as a newborn's. "Are you finished?"

In reply Ruth sucked again on the straw, her eyes never drifting from her granddaughter's face. The small carton Rachel held for her contained some superfortified, nourishing drink.

Rachel glanced around the plush room. Floral wallpaper, nice carpet, a handmade quilt, a Tiffany lamp, and family photos added comfortable touches of home. Cool air flowed quietly, maintaining a constant temperature, keeping the summer heat outdoors. Only occasionally did nursing home scents waft through the corridors. Her parents hadn't scrimped in providing for Bubbie.

The straw rattled in its carton.

"You drank it all! Great!" She dabbed a napkin at the corner of her grandmother's mouth and continued the one-sided conversation. "So anyway, Sylvia says I'm being anxious. She's probably right. Miss Control Freak here. Yeah, I know what you're thinking. Vic's been good for me that way, prying my fingers loose."

She cleared her throat, trying to rid her voice of its tremulous waver. "But I don't know, Bubbie. This situation is throwing me for a major loop."

She stopped talking and Ruth momentarily faded from view. Rachel gave herself a mental shake. Why did she keep going there? Why keep touching that knot of pain deep inside? That emptiness?

"Hey, let's call Vic." She pulled her cell phone from her purse on the floor and pushed the memory key for home. "He's off today, but you know how that goes. Class here, meeting there. He might be at the house—"

"Koski," Vic answered the phone.

"Hi."

"Hi, baby. Are you still at school?"

"No, I came up to Bubbie's. I'll stay a little longer, wait until the traffic winds down."

"Good idea. I should be home by ten." He chuckled. "Unless Bible study is like last week and the guys talk until eleven. Hey, you've probably got time to catch dinner at your folks."

Her parents lived only two miles away. "N-no. I'm...not up for it."

"What's wrong?"

She lifted a shoulder, shrugging aside the words she didn't want to repeat to him. She'd said them all in Colorado. "Long day. I needed a Bubbie touch." She wiped at the corner of her eye and smiled at her grandmother. "I don't know how to start school without her."

For 15 years Bubbie had come to her classroom the week before school started. Together they would pray beside each desk for the child who would soon be sitting in it.

"Rache, she'll still be praying."

She blinked rapidly. Where were all the tears coming from?

"Baby, I'm sorry. I know it's not the same, huh? Let me talk to her."

"Okay. Bubbie, Vic wants to talk to you." She leaned over and held the phone to the old woman's ear as she often did when Vic wasn't with her at the home.

As she watched, Rachel thought of the cyclical nature of life. Her grandmother must have carried on similar one-sided conversations with Rachel and her siblings when they were babies. Unable to comprehend, they simply gorged themselves on the rich feeding of her bountiful love. Now it was her turn to be on the receiving end. Rachel hoped she welcomed it, that it wasn't just headache-producing, nonsensical babble.

Suddenly Bubbie's eyes watered. Was she crying?

She pulled the phone back to her own ear. "Vic, she's crying! What did you say?"

"What I always say. I told her about my day and said I love her."

"Well, you struck a chord somewhere." She grabbed a tissue from the nightstand and blotted the tears now flowing sideways across her grandmother's face. "This is the most responsive she's been in months!"

"She always did like me best." His words exaggerated only slightly. "Tell her I'll visit this week. Whoops, I gotta go or I'll be late. Love you."

"Love you too. Bye." She responded automatically, intent on the phenomenon before her. Reaching for another tissue, she turned off the phone.

"Bubbie, why are you crying?"

Only silent tears answered her question.

A new soft spot in Ruth Goldberg's heart burst to life the moment she first laid eyes on Vic. Like granddaughter, like grandmother?

Rachel purposely had not revealed much about her new boyfriend to the family. She preferred to let them reach their own conclusions. Of course, only Bubbie's opinion counted. The woman was a permanent fixture in Rachel's life. In the midst of a Jewish household, Ruth taught her grandchild about Messiah Yeshua, her Savior.

Abe Goldberg put up with his mother's apostasy because his faith lay in the American dollar, not the God of Israel. And, after all, she was his mother. When he was two years old, she and his father had placed him in the care of relatives who fled Austria just ahead of the Nazis. His family found refuge in the home of friends in Chicago. Before his parents could escape, they were arrested. As a seven-year-old he finally met his mother again, saw her wrist with its crude numerical disfigurement, learned his father had been murdered in a camp. Despite her tales of so-called Christian miracles occurring in the cesspool of evil, he saw no evidence of a loving God in the world.

His wife, Bess, continued some of the orthodox traditions with which she had been raised. She more or less ignored her husband's attitude in the matter as well as the odd Bible in her mother-in-law's bedroom. Ruth helped Bess prepare the weekly Shabbat meal and maintain a kosher kitchen. Though she skipped synagogue and went to a *church*, the older woman wasn't a problem. In a home of seven opinionated people, she caused Bess no more grief than did Abe and their four children.

However, sparks flew at times due to Ruth's influence. Such as when Rachel announced at age nine that Yeshua was indeed the Messiah whose coming the prophets foretold. Or that month she dated an outspoken member of Jews for Jesus. Eventually, Bess flung her hands in the air and simply agreed with her other three children: Rachel and Bubbie were indeed two peas in a very strange pod.

For all its discrepancies, the household provided a solid base. Rachel learned the importance of hard work, the value of a dollar, how to cook and sew. Her attorney father taught her how to think on her feet. Her CPA mother taught her independence. Her brother, how to argue; her sisters, how to giggle.

And Bubbie taught her how meaningless life was without Messiah Yeshua.

By the time Rachel brought Vic home to meet the family, everyone had given up hope she would ever marry. She embodied a double dose of feminine strength and independence, the dominant traits of her mother and grandmother. Not exactly mate-attracting material. They hadn't envisioned the gallant Victor who could rescue her...

Poor Vic. Reminiscent of when Rachel faced his mother, he faced a wall of resistance. Though not in so many words, Abe asked how much firemen made a year. Bess's jaw literally dropped, her mouth hanging open for a full three seconds before she whispered loudly, "A *sheygets?*" meaning a non-Jewish male. Her older sister, Bits, raised her brows in disdain, revealing her question: *South* Chicago? Bram, older by a year and Rachel's childhood playmate, set his jaw, eager to test the guy's mettle. Younger sister Sarah, living in California, missed the whole event.

And Bubbie? Bubbie's face lit up. Fourth of July fireworks.

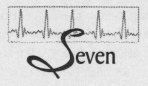

Seven

In the hazy shadows of an early September morning soon after the new school year had begun, Rachel lay on her side in bed, facing the nightstand. The clock radio's red digital numbers flipped to 5:03. A thermometer rested under her tongue, its stabbing point an irritation not only to her mouth, but to her entire being.

The instrument blurted three quick cheeps. With a loud sigh, she removed it and closed her eyes. *Lord, do I have to keep doing this?*

Just outside the open window there was a rustling in the bridal wreath bush. A bird trilled. Dawn was breaking.

"Oh, Father, the birds are worshiping You, and I'm taking my stupid temperature for the one hundred-sixty-something time in a row! What is wrong with this picture?"

Instead of pressing the thermometer's button to activate its nifty little light and reading yet another set of digital numbers, she set the thing on the nightstand.

Maybe she would quit.

There were six papers in the stand's drawer. On each was a photocopied grid with degrees listed vertically, ranging from 97 to 99, a normal range of body temperatures. Across the top were dates. The number one, however, referred not to the first of the month, but to the first day of her menstrual cycle.

If she hadn't pitched her Day-Timer years earlier, she would have by now. She'd had no idea such a peculiar calendar existed, let alone that her life could revolve around it. Between this system and Vic's one day on, two days off routine, there were days when she hadn't a clue what date to write on the chalkboard at school.

Every morning for the past six months she had reached for the thermometer first thing, being careful not to unnecessarily disturb any muscle not connected to that movement. In less than two minutes she read what was referred to as her basal body temperature. Then she pulled a paper from the drawer, dutifully marked the appropriate spot on the grid, and drew a short line to connect it with yesterday's reading.

By now she had six similar lines drawn. Her cycles were as predictable as the Cubs missing their shot at the series. The charts indicated daily ups and downs and then, at the same point of each month, a sharp rise. Aha! The mysterious, internal disturbance had begun. The egg was on its way. A pair of available X chromosomes all dressed up and waiting for the knight to arrive on his great white steed.

Rachel groaned and buried her face in the pillow. She was losing it.

The charts also provided blank squares for notes. Was she ill? Taking medication? Making love at prime time?

In the early days she unselfconsciously drew smiley faces. Yes! They were making a baby! Nowadays she scratched a check mark. The faces seemed puerile to her, a childish game she had outgrown. How could she reduce such an awesome gift from God to silliness? As a matter of fact, how could she reduce it to a check mark? How could she consider even *discussing* this most personal expression of their love with strangers, even if those strangers were medical professionals?

The phone rang. Vic always called her first thing if he was at the station. His shift ended at 8 o'clock, almost an hour after she left the house.

"Hi, Vic."

"Morning, sunshine. Taking your temp?"

"Mm-hmm," she mumbled, rolling over. "Can you put the 911 calls on hold and race home and make mad, passionate love real quick before I have to leave?"

He didn't reply, his wife-induced guilt palpable in the sound of his breathing.

Last month she had pointedly remarked they missed prime time due to his work schedule and proceeded to count how many months a similar timing had occurred. Not that a day or two one way or the other should make a difference. Not with a *healthy* couple anyway.

"Vic, I'm kidding."

"I can't tell anymore."

"That settles it then. The charts are history. The thermometer goes back into the medicine cabinet today."

"Rachel." His deep voice was weary.

"Hey, let's change the subject. How was your night?"

"Nonstop calls. Nothing major, though." He yawned. "I managed one forty-minute nap."

"My hero. *That slayer of dragons*," she sang softly, *"fresh from valiant deed. Come rescue me, O hero bold."*

He chuckled. "Can it wait until I get some sleep?"

They chatted a few moments and made evening plans for pizza and a video, a favorite Friday night activity when the schedule allowed it. Within minutes after hanging up, Rachel was drinking coffee and filing away the loathsome charts in the desk in the living room. She would keep them in the folder with her collection of notes about infertility. Just in case she wanted to show them to a doctor. Some day.

A feeling of dread crept through her like a vacuum cleaner drawing in whatever lay in its path. Rational thought, good intentions, the ability to see the first morning rays of sunshine, hope...

The mug slipped from her hand onto the desktop. Coffee sloshed over the sides before she steadied it.

"No!" She spoke aloud as she marched into the kitchen. "I am *not* going there. I refuse to wallow in self-pity." She grabbed a towel, marched back to the desk, and blotted the spilled coffee. "I *will not*. Lord, help me to not!"

The phone rang. She let it ring again, swallowing her desperate tone before picking up the cordless from its cradle on the desk. "Hello?"

"Rache, don't give up."

"What?"

"Just don't give up, baby. Don't give up *hope*."

"Oh, Vic! It hurts so bad to hope. It just gets knocked out of me month after month after month."

"But your hope keeps me going."

She heard the firehouse alarm sound on his end.

"Gotta go." The line went dead.

Your hope keeps me going.

"And you keep me going, Vic Koski." *Come rescue me...*

～

Later that day Rachel moved aside her lesson plan book, leaned back in her creaky wooden chair, and slid off her flats. She tucked the long skirt of her short-sleeved yellow cotton dress under her knees and propped her feet on top of the desk.

Friday afternoon, three-thirty, vacant classroom. Toby out of sight for two days. Heaven.

Before the first day of school, she had managed to move the desk to its August location: front corner, near the door. Across the room summer heat wafted through the wall of opened windows. They faced the blacktop one floor below. Student desks filled the center of the room, lined up in straight rows and facing hers. The arrangement was old-fashioned, but Rachel still felt it worked the best early in the year. The children needed to feel the full effect of her order. Once they were secure in that, she could loosen up, make beaver faces, and get creative with the furniture.

She smiled at the four roses and greenery in a large clear vase on the desk. One yellow, one red, one pink, one purple. If she had any doubts about today's date, the flowers told her it was the twelfth of September. They always arrived on the twelfth because on that date in May, she and Vic first met. Monthly, for almost nine and a half years now, he remembered the day that forever changed both of their lives by sending her flowers.

The sweet scent of roses altered the usual fumes of 24 energetic children cooped up for most of a late summer day in an old, non-air-conditioned classroom. Not that Rachel minded all that much. The odors of chalk dust, paste, construction paper, and books as well as the children made up her world.

Jessie Gray appeared in her doorway. "Hey!"

"Hey! Come on in. Pull up a seat."

Her friend sank into a student desk with a sigh, kicked off her shoes, and swung her feet onto the front edge of Rachel's desk. "Remind me to buy a pair of *real* shoes. ASAP."

Rachel smiled. After two weeks of frequent subbing, Jessie's cheeks had regained color, and her eyes again shone with the mischievous gleam that had been missing for a long time.

Jessie returned the smile. "Have I thanked you yet?"

"Once or twice."

"I'm having a ball here."

"It shows."

"Well, I don't know about that. Kevin hasn't seemed to notice yet, although I really am nagging less."

"But he is helping with the kids more, right? And not complaining."

"Not too much. Ah, Rachel. You and Vic are a tough act to follow." She nodded toward the vase. "Look at that. The entire school knows it's the twelfth because Mrs. Koski got flowers today from Mr. Koski."

She winced. "I laid a guilt trip on him."

"Rachel, you get flowers every month! I don't think you shamed him into it."

"No, really. He outdid himself this time. First off, when I left the house this morning, Harold the neighbor came over and gave me a rose from his garden. The red one. Isn't it gorgeous? He said, 'This is from Vic. I'd give it to you from myself, but you know Mildred. She'd skin me alive because one rose means I love you.' Bless his heart, I think he was flirting. The florist delivered the yellow one at ten, the pink one at noon, the purple at two."

"What do you think?" Jessie glanced up at the large clock on the wall. "White at four?"

"I don't know what to expect!"

"Good," someone rumbled from the doorway.

She turned to see Vic grinning, lime green tissue paper bunched around a white rose in his hand.

"I like to keep my woman guessing."

Rachel smiled as he sauntered toward her.

Jessie said, "Hey, Mr. Romance. Maybe you could give lessons down at the firehouse? I'll bake cookies for the occasion."

Ignoring her comment, he placed his hands on the arms of Rachel's chair, leaned over, and planted a serious kiss on her mouth.

Little Shirley Temple tap-danced right there on a Friday afternoon in her classroom.

"Hi," she exhaled the word.

"Hi." Those navy blue diamonds glittered.

All in her direction.

"Let me have the keys to your car?"

"Buddy, you can have whatever you want."

He grinned and handed her the flower.

"Thanks." She pulled open a desk drawer and found her car keys. "What do you want with these?"

"You'll see." He winked and turned. "Hi, Jessie. By the way, your kids and Kevin are outside."

"They are?" She swung her feet to the floor.

"They want to see where Mommy works. I think I heard something about a Friday night babysitter."

Jessie's eyes widened. She stared at him for one wordless moment before slipping on her shoes and rushing through the doorway.

Vic turned back to Rachel. "Kevin drove me over. I've got to move some luggage from his car."

"Luggage?"

"Well, an overnight bag." His mouth curved into that lazy grin.

Shirley tapped her little heart out.

~⌒~

The next morning Rachel and Vic lingered over a late breakfast. The restaurant window afforded a view of a wide sidewalk and sparse Saturday traffic along the main thoroughfare of Michigan Avenue.

Rachel speared her last bite of cheese and mushroom omelet. "What are we doing next?"

Vic reached across the table and took her free hand. His eyes were at their usual half-mast, his face relaxed. A gentle smile curved his mouth. "I now pronounce you completely cured."

She gave him a quizzical look and swallowed. "Of what?"

"Control Freak Disease."

"Hey, I threw out my calendar years ago."

"But I'd say we've scaled new heights. We're at the mountaintop now. Would you have ever allowed me to schedule a weekend without your input? Whisk you away from school, off to an unknown destination? Make hotel and dinner reservations? Not tell you a thing in advance? Pack an overnight bag for you?"

"No." She wrinkled her nose. "To all of the above."

"I rest my case."

"Am I that bad?"

"Were. Yes, you were." He winked.

"This has been the most fun I've had." She giggled. "Ever!"

They hadn't gone home yesterday after school. He'd literally whisked her away and driven to downtown Chicago. In spite of the duffel bag in the backseat, she really didn't believe they were spending the night until the valet parking attendant at the Marriott asked, "Are you checking in, sir?" and Vic had answered yes.

In the blessedly climate-controlled room, she curiously pulled items from the bag. His foray into packing feminine necessities delighted her. He hadn't missed a thing from black dress for dinner to capris for Saturday to earrings to facial creams to eye shadow. He said it was simple; he'd just emptied the bathroom cabinets.

"Vic," she said now, "what changed? What made you think I'd be ready for all this?"

"I noticed the thermometer missing from the nightstand. I probably wouldn't have, but since you mentioned it on the phone, I looked. And then I looked for the charts." He shrugged. "I realized what a tough thing that was for you to do. To let that go. I wanted to do something special to treat you. And then I saw this ad in the paper for a romantic getaway. The *Trib* works almost as good as the Bible sometimes in prompting husbands on how to treat their wives."

She smiled. "Thank you."

"You're welcome. So, Rache." He lowered his eyes. "How's your clock?"

She felt herself go still. "Ticktocking, clanging, and clattering. How's your prayer about getting tested?"

He met her gaze and gave her hand a brief squeeze. "I've asked Him every day since we were in Colorado what to do. Unless He zaps me with some new insight, I'm choosing *not* to go that route."

An involuntary wince scrunched her face.

"Rache, He's always met our needs, taken care of us. He'll give us a baby if and when it's time. He is our only hope. You taught me that, and I see it in you. Please don't give up just because I don't want to get tested."

"Vic, it won't go away. I want a baby so badly." Her throat tightened, cutting off further speech. That was all right. She had said all she needed to say.

"Sometimes." He paused, his voice a whisper. "Sometimes I wonder why I'm not enough for you."

A shock wave rolled through her. "Oh, Vic! You're enough! You're everything to me. A baby would—" She searched for the words. "A baby would give me *more* of you. He wouldn't be *instead* of you. I don't know how else to explain it."

He shook his head. "I guess it must be a female thing. Indecipherable. I'm sorry I don't understand better."

"I'm sorry for not seeing your side better."

His male side was as indecipherable to her. In the beginning his eagerness to have a child nearly matched her own. But that had waned, becoming more of an attempt to make her happy than a desire to be a daddy. Not exactly the best motivation for bringing a new life into the world. Though she had told him about that vivid dream, she no longer mentioned its occasional reappearance. Why add to his discomfort?

"Rache, you know our life is pretty full. I have to say I'm content with the status quo. Maybe God is telling us that's okay or that we need to focus more on what we are doing. Like we've talked, we could get involved as leaders with the young adult group at church. And there's always something else I could be doing with the firefighter's Bible study. Kevin's starting to ask about it. I feel that if I spent more time with him..."

She tuned him out. A feeling of defeat washed over her. She could find no fault with anything he said, but his words communicated just how little he cared about becoming a father.

"Hey, Rache. You're zoning out. I'm only trying to be positive here."

She nodded.

"Are you okay with it? With my decision not to get tested?"

"I don't know. You're either taking the high road of faith or you're just plain chicken. And if my hero is a chicken, then we're both in big trouble."

He studied her for a long moment. "Sounds like an impasse."

She sighed. She couldn't help it. "Yes, it does."

His handsome face dissolved into that of a little boy caught with his hand in the cookie jar. "But you still love me, right?"

"Of course I do!"

He grinned. "Then will you spend the day with me?"

She sighed again, but she had to smile. He always knew how to pull the plug on her frustration. "As you know perfectly well, Vic Koski, there's absolutely nothing else I'd rather do."

Eight

By mid-October, some five weeks after the surprise get-away, Rachel had concluded that impasses projected only the facade of a quiet standstill. In reality they teemed with activity.

Impasses were full of nooks and crannies where all sorts of unspoken words could be tucked away. They were like her soul with its pockets for stuffing unreleased emotions. Such words and feelings must remain tucked and packed away out of reach. To go to them was to touch the pain. And to touch the pain was to hear the clangor of that biological clock.

She had better things to do with her time. She couldn't serve God by lingering there.

Now she stood in the middle of her kitchen, unsure why she had entered it. The adjacent screened-in porch and their backyard overflowed with friends and family gathered to celebrate Vic's birthday. Vic insisted the public observance embarrassed him to no end, but she ignored his opinion. Three years ago she surprised him with a party on his fortieth. With everyone else's enthusiastic support, it had become an annual event in their home.

Midwest autumn days could either be cold and dank or so intensely gorgeous they left one speechless. Today rose to the high end of the beauty scale. Up and down the street and across neighboring backyards, trees flaunted their colors. Leaves of liquid gold and burnished scarlet touched a cerulean sky. Mild temperatures drew people outdoors, the brave in shorts and T-shirts one last time for the season, but most, like Rachel, in jeans and sweatshirts.

She glanced around the kitchen, turning a full circle, trying to recall why she had come inside. At least 35 adults and kids were waiting for the hostess to do...what? The gathering was always a potluck. Tables on the porch held a wide variety of dishes that Wanda was reorganizing. Vic and one of his brothers were grilling bratwurst and hot dogs. A rousing volleyball tournament was in full swing, the net set up as far from the grill as possible in their small, flat yard.

Ice? Buns? Forks? Ketchup?

The phone rang.

Rachel smiled to herself. Maybe that was why she was standing there, to answer the phone.

She reached the wall phone on its second ring. "Hello?"

"Rache? Hi!"

"Sarah!" Her sister in California. "Hi!"

"I'm sorry we missed the party."

They laughed, but Rachel knew her sister only partially joked. Three years her junior, they had grown close since leaving behind childhood rivalries. If not for the geographical distance, she would have been there at the party.

"Tell Vic happy birthday for us. I meant to call earlier this morning."

"Your timing is perfect. It's like having you here with me. Everyone is outdoors and I'm trying to remember what I'm doing in the kitchen. What do you think?"

"Chopped onions. They're in the fridge."

Rachel whooped and walked across the room to the refrigerator, the long coiled cord trailing behind her. "That's it! How do you do that?" She pulled out the plastic-covered bowl.

Sarah laughed. "Did Mom and Dad make it?"

"No. This year it was a golf outing at the club."

"No surprise there."

"None whatsoever."

Not that they disliked Vic, but Abe and Bess Goldberg mingled with the Koski clan only on rare occasions. Like at the wedding nearly nine years ago. Stan intimidated them. Wanda set her father's teeth on edge. Firefighters were too locker-room rowdy. Bryan, too *too* religious, especially when he wore that *collar*.

She unwrapped the onions. "Bram and family are here though." Having grown up with three sisters, their brother was intrigued with the five male Koski siblings and always attended, even on Christmas at Wanda's. "Sar, how are the kids?"

"Fine. Listen." Her voice bubbled. "I don't want to keep you, but I just had to tell you something before I burst!"

"What's up?"

"I'm pregnant!"

Rachel missed a beat, and in the span of that fractionated second something cracked. Those tidily packed words and emotions began seeping from their cubbyholes all at once. She sensed it happened even before she enthused "Congratulations," an automatic welling from the corner of herself where love resided for her little sister.

"Rache, please don't breathe a word to blabbermouth Bram. I'm only a couple months along, and I want to wait a few weeks before I tell Mom. Oh! Do you believe it? We had just decided we were two-and-through. We weren't even trying!" She giggled. "I mean, we were even *preventing*—Anyway, I had to tell you first."

"I'm so happy for you, Sarah. I love you."

"I love you too, sis. I'll let you get back to the party. Give Vic a hug. Bye!"

The room shifted, skewing itself in her vision. Rachel thought that odd because she hadn't taken a step. She felt the phone in her hand and went to hang it up. The floor wobbled. Wiggling lines replaced her peripheral vision. She clanked the phone onto its wall cradle.

Nausea engulfed her. A sharp pain shot through her stomach followed swiftly by another. Sweat broke out on her neck. Her breathing was irregular. Was she sick? She couldn't be sick. They were having a party. Now where was she?

Rejoicing with her sister.

Pitying herself.

Loathing her sister.

No! She shook her head again. Nonsense. Sarah loved being a mother, and she was excellent at it. One of the best nurturers Rachel had ever seen. *Lord, bless this new life in her.*

Now...

The nausea chopped her breath into eighth notes.

Onions. I have to get the onions.

Her fingers tingled. She walked out to the porch, clutching the small bowl. Wanda took it from her and said something, her voice garbled to Rachel's hearing.

She nodded, panting now, her fingers still curled as if wrapped around the bowl.

Sixteenth notes.

Where was Vic? She pushed open the screen porch door and stumbled over its threshold. Ahead, the green grass rolled like a giant wave on Lake Michigan. She stepped toward it, and the wiggling lines filled her vision.

"Rachel!"

The wiggling lines went black.

～

Calm voices penetrated Rachel's brain fog. Her hands still felt cramped and curled. Blue sky framed someone bending over her. She was lying in the grass. Fear swamped her, clammy fingers strangling every fiber of her being. She couldn't catch her breath.

"Time to wake up, Sleeping Beauty. That a girl."

A mewing sound escaped between panted breaths. It was all she could say.

"You're fine." Terri came into focus, her brown eyes intent on Rachel, her voice soft and steady. "You're just hyperventilating a little. Makes you lightheaded and your hands tingle. Try to relax. Nothing to worry about."

Terri's voice could mesmerize Rachel in a regular conversation. She felt the fear loosening its grip even though each breath continued to be a struggle. Now she felt her hand in Terri's. Fingers pressed gently against her wrist.

"We've got some oxygen coming. Can you tell me your name?"

"Rache..." She gasped out the syllable.

"You're fine, Rachel. Just fine. Relax. All right, we're going to elevate your legs."

She felt hands grasp her legs, lift them slightly, and gently lower them onto something soft. Something gripped one of her fingertips. It felt like a clothespin.

"Rachel, I'm placing this mask over your nose and mouth. Just breathe now."

A feeling of soft pressure settled around her nose and mouth. She flinched at the sudden confinement.

"Just breathe. I know, it feels a little weird. There you go. That a girl, Rachel."

Sweet blessed oxygen. She closed her eyes. Within moments her panting subsided. Something squeezed her arm and hissed. A blood pressure cuff? Voices murmured a string of numbers.

"Eyes open, Sleeping Beauty. You can nap later."

The mask was removed.

Terri hovered. "Better, huh? Tell me your name again?"

"Rachel." Her voice was throaty.

"Do you recognize me?"

"Terri. Where's Vic?"

"He's right here grading my performance as a paramedic. Can you tell me where we are?"

"My house. Backyard. It's Vic's birthday."

"Gold star, teacher. Do you remember what happened?"

"I don't know. All of a sudden I couldn't breathe."

"What were you doing when that happened?"

"I was…in the kitchen."

She sensed others around her and glanced to her right. The vertigo returned full force, nausea on its heels.

"Rachel, look at me. What were you doing in the kitchen?"

Wishing I were my sister. Tears sprang to her eyes. *Wondering why God doesn't give* me *a baby.* "I have to throw up!"

The shooting pains attacked her stomach again, and she drew up her legs. She felt hands rolling her sideways. She gagged but didn't vomit. Someone rubbed her back. A damp cloth was pressed against her forehead.

Terri came into focus again, her face practically level with Rachel's in the grass.

"Are you pregnant?" Her voice was low, keeping their conversation just between the two of them.

She squeezed shut her eyes and whispered. "No."

"When did you last eat?"

"I don't know." She looked at her. "Terri, I'm all right. Get Vic over here!" She heard laughter.

"I want to make sure you're all right."

"I'm all right!"

"I think you're stressed out over getting ready for today or something."

"Terri, can I please get up now?"

"Let's take it slow." She helped her sit. "Don't try to stand yet."

Someone else removed the blood pressure cuff. She accepted a fresh damp washcloth and held it to her mouth.

"Rachel." Now Bryan was in her face.

She groaned. "Paramedics *and* priests? What is this, my last rites?"

He grinned and touched her shoulder. "She's fine," he called out.

Laughter. Another voice joked loudly, "Too bad you can't say that for hubby here!" More laughter. "Koski, you look like you're going to keel over."

Vic growled something indecipherable.

Bryan chuckled. "He's coming. Can you hang on a minute longer?"

In reply she grasped his arm with one hand and Terri's with her other. "I thought *he* was a paramedic."

They helped her stand. She gritted her teeth against the dizzying effect.

"Rache." Vic finally reached her side. He slid his arm around her waist and led her away.

Rachel buried her face in Vic's chest as he guided her through the house.

Wanda's voice trailed behind. "Vic, she needs to eat."

"Yeah, Ma."

"She hasn't been eating. I can tell she's lost weight."

"I don't think—"

"Look at that sweatshirt. She's swimming in it!"

He guided Rachel onto their bed. "Ma."

"She's not taking care of herself. She runs herself ragged taking care of you and all those little kids. Going to night class." She clicked her tongue in disapproval and handed Rachel a glass of water. "Honey, you rest now. Don't worry about a thing in the kitchen. I'll take care of it. And Victor, you see to her. You're not paying attention. Running off to your Bible studies and whatnot classes."

"Okay, Ma, okay. Shut the door, please?"

Honey? Wanda called her honey? A lump formed in her throat as the door clicked shut. She sipped the water.

"Rache, you want to get undressed?"

She nodded and handed him the glass. "I just want to sleep. I'm sorry."

"Nothing to be sorry about." He found her nightie under the pillow and helped her change into it. Then he pulled back the covers.

She crawled into the bed. "I'm freezing."

He pulled the blankets around her and sat on the edge of the bed, rubbing her arm. "What happened, baby?"

"I don't know exactly. I just felt dizzy and sick to my stomach and I couldn't breathe."

"When did you eat last?"

"I had an apple for breakfast."

"That's it? It's four o'clock!" His voice wasn't as steady as Terri's. "When was the last time you drank something?"

"I had coffee."

"Rachel, no wonder you feel sick!"

"It's been a busy day."

"Every day is busy for you. And you probably *don't* eat right most days. Rache, you were hyperventilating, for goodness' sake! Something upset you. Did Ma say something?"

A tear slid from the corner of her eye. "Sarah called when I was in the kitchen. She's…pregnant."

His hand stilled on her arm.

"It's great." She was crying softly now. "And they weren't even trying!"

Vic laid down beside her and took her into his arms.

"I'm sorry, Vic. I'm sorry. I'm sorry I can't get pregnant. I'm sorry I can't handle someone else getting pregnant. I'm sorry—"

"Rache."

"I disrupted your party. I'm sorry you have to put up with me."

"Shh, Rachel. Shh, now. It's all right, baby. It's all right."

At last exhaustion overtook her, and she fell asleep to the consoling rhythm of her husband's voice.

∿

Rachel awoke at her usual time of 5 A.M. A corner of her mind noted an extra grogginess as she automatically stretched her hand through the predawn grayness to the nightstand.

The thermometer wasn't in its place on the top.

Still not moving from her pillow, she pulled open the small drawer and shuffled her hand around inside it. No thermometer there either.

From behind her, Vic touched her waist. "Rache."

"I can't find the thermometer."

"Rache."

Something in his voice stilled her hand. His tone was hushed, tender. He only spoke that way on the rare occasions when her independence couldn't quite carry her.

As her morning stupor faded, a familiar bone-deep weariness quickly overtook it. She wasn't taking her temperature anymore. She had missed most of Vic's party yesterday. Now it was Sunday, and he was on duty.

She rolled over to face him. "Hi."

"Hi. How are you feeling?"

"Okay, I think. Better. How long have I been sleeping?"

"Thirteen hours."

"Vic, I'm sor—"

He put a finger to her lips. "*I'm* sorry. Ma was right. I haven't been paying attention. Will you forgive me?"

She took hold of his hand. "For what?"

"For not noticing how affected you are with this pregnancy business. Why didn't you say something? Yell and cry and tell me what an idiot I am to say no to your one simple request?"

"You'd made up your mind. You knew my thinking. We were at an impasse. The subject was…too important to kvetch about. I was trying to wait for God to change you. Or me."

"Well, I'm it." His smile crinkled into a wince. "He scared me half to death yesterday. Go ahead and make the appointment."

She blinked. "Seriously?"

"Seriously."

They stared at each other, their hands held between them, a bird outside the window cheeping its first notes of a morning chorus.

"Vic, it'll be a hard, long haul." She had better lay it all on the line, give him one last chance. "From everything I've read and heard, the whole process is embarrassing, unpleasant, and expensive."

"That doesn't matter. I love you. Yesterday I saw Bryan catch you before you hit the ground, and I couldn't even move. Man, I thought I was in a nightmare. You know, one of those where your legs are made of cement. You were white as a sheet and not breathing right, and all I could do was stand there. Until somebody pushed me into a chair and jammed my head between my knees. I think it was Teague. He said we didn't need anyone else passing out."

She chuckled. "I guess it's because you don't play paramedic full-time?"

"No, it's because you're my wife. Maybe if we hadn't had a houseful of EMTs, I could have done more than tuck you into bed. I hope so. Rache, all I could think about was what if I lost you without having done the one thing you asked me to do. I'd regret it the rest of my life. Talk about not being current."

"Thank you," she whispered.

"Thank God. His timing is perfect. Like with Terri. She happened to have some emergency equipment in her car because she'd just come from teaching an EMT class. You would have been fine, but I would have taken you to the ER to have everything checked out."

"What else did I miss? Did everyone stay and have a good time?"

He leaned over and kissed her nose. "They did. You slept through quite a racket. Terri checked on you a few times. You sure had her worried. And Ma cleaned up the kitchen with a minimum of negative comments. Did the guys tell you what they were giving me?"

"No. What was it?"

"Shoes. A dozen pairs of *women's* shoes. *Used* women's shoes."

She laughed. "Heels?"

"Oh, yeah. Every pair. I hope Bram doesn't tell your folks I have a shoe fetish!"

Like two teenagers, they howled uncontrollably until sunlight filtered through the curtain. The laughter chased away predawn shadows as well as those that had lingered between them.

Nine

The evening after Thanksgiving, Rachel poured coffee beans into the grinder and pressed on the lid. Its loud whirring cut off the string of objections Vic had been spouting since they left the doctor's office 40 minutes ago. Hands on hips and drawn to his full height, he stood at her shoulder, glowering.

She released the grinding mechanism and poured the grounds into the basket. "Vic, calm down. Don't you think you're being slightly unreasonable?" Ridiculously childish better described her husband's demeanor, but Rachel thought it best to hold back the full extent of her opinion for the time being.

"No, I don't think I'm being unreasonable."

She elbowed him aside in order to reach the faucet and ran water into the carafe. "Intimidating me will get you nowhere fast, Koski."

"I'm not intim—Rachel, you can't understand! It's a guy thing. All right, there I said it. It's a *guy* thing."

She poured the water into the coffeemaker and punched the "on" switch. "Good. Now you can get over it. Be a man about it. Make it a *man* thing."

The doorbell chimed.

Vic stomped across the kitchen. "Isn't this dinnertime? For pete's sake, it's five-thirty!"

She followed on his heels, ready to protect the unsuspecting neighborhood child who probably stood on their doorstep eager to sell them a fund-raising candy bar.

Vic muttered his way to the front door. "Why is it they always ring the bell at five-thirty? They're as bad as phone solicitors. Like being at home makes us fair game." He flipped on the porch light and yanked open the door. "We don't want—"

Bryan O'Shaugnessy smiled through the glass storm door.

Vic pushed on the latch and stood aside as their friend walked in.

Rachel greeted him with a hug. "Hi, Bryan."

"Hi, Rachel. Vic."

Her husband merely nodded as he shut the door. Then he turned on his heel and lumbered to the hallway that led to the bedrooms.

Bryan looked at her while brushing snowflakes from his red hair. "Bad time?"

"He's doing his snarling bear act. Stay and keep me company?"

Bryan laughed and shrugged off his heavy winter coat. He wore what she referred to as his "uniform," a black jacket over a black shirt and white clerical collar.

"How about some coffee? I should warn you though, Vic didn't make it."

"Sounds great anyway. It's freezing outside."

They settled at the small table in the kitchen and chatted until Vic eventually reappeared. He helped himself to coffee before joining them.

"Sorry, Bry. We were in the middle of something."

"So I gathered." Bryan's green eyes flicked between the two of them. "You know, some couples actually come to me for counseling. Make appointments and everything. Care to talk about it?"

Rachel glanced at the wall clock and bit her lip. Years ago she had learned to give Vic a full minute before jumping in and taking control of a conversation. In the early days when his size intimidated her, it was her sharp tongue that daunted him.

He sipped his coffee. "It's personal."

"Vic, forget the collar. This is still me, confidant for nearly forty years. We have yet to draw the line on too personal."

Vic remained silent for a moment. "This is different. It involves both me and Rache." He looked at her, brows raised. "Your call."

"Hey, I have no problem confiding in Bryan. I think our intimate life is about to become an open book to a whole bunch of strangers. Maybe a close friend can help keep us centered."

Vic rubbed his hand over his jaw, not yet convinced.

"And," she added, "we could really use an unbiased opinion on this current situation."

He nodded. "Well, that's for sure. Okay. Bryan, you know we've started things at a fertility clinic. We just got back from my second visit—"

"Tell him the good news."

Vic's eyes narrowed at her.

She turned to Bryan. "The doctor says Vic's in great shape. So we can start on me immediately. Blood tests. Maybe an endometrial biopsy—no big deal, it's done in the office—if there's some hormonal imbalance. Next month Vic needs to go in one more time. The doc has to count his—"

Vic made a gurgling noise in his throat. "Rachel! You don't need to go into that much detail! Bryan doesn't want to hear a play-by-play description— How can you talk about that stuff like you're discussing the *weather*?" The tips of his ears reddened.

"Because now that we're at this point, those things *are* just like the weather! Totally clinical."

"Vic," Bryan said, "you'd be surprised at the stuff I hear. It might help if Rachel can say whatever she wants, out loud. Don't mind me."

Vic's cheeks were pink now as he eyed her. "Fine. Then tell him everything. Tell him exactly what that man is going to do to you."

"He's not a man, he's a doctor."

"He's a man, he's younger than I am, and he is not going to touch you!"

"It's not touching. It's performing *procedures!*"

"No difference." His eyes were slits, his voice snarling again. "Not one iota."

Now they were back to where they'd been when she'd turned on the coffee grinder. She turned to Bryan and raised her palms in a helpless gesture.

Their friend blinked a few times and cleared his throat. "Uh, is there a female doctor at the clinic?"

Rachel groaned. "It *is* a guy thing. Listen, you two. Male doctors have been around for ages."

"So?" they replied in unison.

"I don't get it!"

The men exchanged a glance before Bryan said, "It's the equivalent of Vic having a girlfriend."

"Oh, please. Give me a break, guys."

"Rachel, Vic cherishes you. I know it doesn't look that way because he's reacting like an uncivilized caveman here.

Perhaps it's that primal." Bryan paused. "The marriage union has made you two one. And then there's the writings of Paul in First Corinthians. That the husband and wife have rights over each other's bodies."

"Oh, sure. Bring up Scripture."

He smiled. "Besides that, we've got two against one here. If I were married, I imagine I'd feel the same."

"You would?"

He nodded.

Vic said in a quieter voice than he'd used all day, "There is a female doctor, but she's booked until after Christmas. We were anxious to get moving." He gazed at her.

They were at the beginning of a difficult journey. She suspected they faced unending choices and compromises. If they couldn't agree now, how would they ever get through this?

"Vic, if it's that important to you, I don't suppose waiting another six weeks will matter."

He shut his eyes and whispered, "Thank you."

～

Rachel sat curled in an armchair, reading while Vic and Bryan prepared a dinner of leftover turkey sandwiches in the kitchen. Ever since the incident at his birthday party, Vic had been pampering her whenever possible. He even rearranged his work schedule, which he rarely did, in order to spend Thanksgiving with her and his entire family at Stan and Wanda's house yesterday.

Her friends Sylvia, Terri, and Jessie urged her to accept all the attention he offered, adding that the more stress she cut out of her lifestyle, the better her chances were of becoming pregnant. Sylvia, radically enthusiastic about health, loaned her the book she read now. For years the principal had found fault with Rachel's thoughtless approach to what she put into her mouth. Certain that nutrition could play a role in Rachel's ability to conceive, Sylvia had put the book into her hands, an undisguised assignment from her superior. So far the book hadn't mentioned a thing about having babies. Besides, up until the point of fainting in the middle of a party, she had thrived on stress and antipyramid-style eating habits.

She closed the book and rested her head back against the chair. Why did she want a child so badly? *Lord, is this biological clock a figment of my imagination? Is the dream just the result of my imagination? Won't You please just take it all away if it isn't going to happen?*

What was so wrong with her life anyway? Her husband loved her. He was a great guy with a good job where he was liked and respected. Today he had taken a giant step toward pleasing her by making what was for him another embarrassing trip to a fertility specialist. Of course there had been some fallout, but he usually kept the caveman persona under wraps.

She loved her job, loved the wide variety of 24 students. She had nine nephews, eight nieces, and three unknowns on the way. Plenty of children to love.

Last month Wanda had called her honey, and yesterday she referred only twice to their lack of children. Her parents were wintering again in Florida; the distance eased the strain of that spiritually disconnected relationship.

She and Vic had a nice house. It would need a new roof soon, but the wiring and furnace were up to code and then some because, after all, she was married to a fireman.

Even Bubbie was fine in a way because Bubbie had always been fine. Rachel was sure her absolute trust in God carried her even now.

Absolute trust. Total lack of fear. Not an ounce of resentment toward Him for the horrendous, inexplicable events in her life. Bubbie used to say that what stood between her and the unknown was the face of Yeshua.

Rachel longed to emulate her grandmother. How far off the mark she remained! At Rachel's age of thirty-eight, Ruth Goldberg had lived in a foreign country for ten years, was the single mother of a seventeen-year-old, and was working in a bank. Her German accent infuriated many. Her Christian faith infuriated all of her relatives. And yet Rachel had never heard her speak a bitter word about those years.

At least she'd had her son. The one consolation Rachel didn't have. She could imagine facing anything if she had another person she could hold for the rest of her life, someone with Vic's navy blue eyes and big ears and infectious laugh. What she had instead was subtle but continual fear for Vic's safety. Her daily prayer for him since the day they'd become engaged was taken from Isaiah. *Should you walk through fire, you will not be scorched and the flames will not burn you.*

Fear. But that wasn't all, was it? Closing her eyes, she forced herself to let the thought come. Yes, she admitted it. She harbored a growing resentment toward him.

She shook her head. Could she be any further off the mark set by her grandmother?

Yes, Vic exhibited wildly thoughtful efforts on her behalf. She knew, though, his heart was not in it, not one hundred percent. His resistance today proved that it wasn't her imagination. For her sake he was trying, but he didn't really care one way or the other if he became a father.

Bubbie would say to give the fear and resentment to God. She would say that every time they came to mind, Rachel should envision herself wrapping them in newspaper like smelly old fish, rolling them up tightly, and setting the package at the foot of the cross. She would say all of life's rubbish disintegrated there.

Please, Lord? Take it away?

"Rachel," Vic called from the kitchen. "Can you come out here for a minute?"

Amen, she breathed as she set the book aside.

In the kitchen Vic and Bryan faced her, arms crossed, their backs to the sink.

She put her hands on her hips. "What did you break?"

Bryan chuckled and looked at Vic. "Mrs. Johnson."

"Nah. This teacher's even better than the one we had in fifth grade. Smells guilt a block away. Rache." He twisted his mouth and held out a white envelope to her. "We think you should see this."

She took the sealed envelope from him. It felt the weight of a card. She turned it over and read the looping feminine handwriting. *Mr. Victor Koski, c/o Reverend Bryan O'Shaugnessy, St. James...* And the return label. *Ellen Hamilton... Bettendorf, Iowa...*

Rachel looked up. "What is it?"

Vic shrugged. "Don't know. Don't want to know. It's, uh, the third one."

"The third one?" she exclaimed.

Bryan said, "Addressed in care of me. One came soon after the reunion. Another about the time of Vic's birthday. He read the first, not the second. We burned both."

She looked at Vic.

"It was full of hateful stuff."

"Be specific." Teacher tone. She couldn't help it.

Vic sighed heavily. "Quote: I could give you babies. I love you. I always loved you. I'm sorry I ever married Jay. Come back to me. Dump what's-her-name, and I'll make you happy again. Unquote."

"Eww."

"Exactly. No reason to put you or me through that. But if you want, you can open this one. I guess I'd feel better if you saw it for yourself."

Truly there was no reason to subject herself to the ramblings of a poor lost woman. Still, maybe there was something they should know. Maybe the note contained a threat. Maybe the woman was dangerous. Stranger things had been known to happen.

Rachel pried open the envelope and removed a folded card. It was pretty, with a sketch of irises. She flipped it open and read aloud the scrawled handwriting.

"My darling Vic. I'm waiting. You know what I have to offer you. You had it before."

She stopped speaking as she scanned the next sentence. It was obscene.

"Give me the matches," she ordered, slipping the card back into its envelope.

Vic handed her the box and smiled wryly. "My pleasure."

She stepped to the sink and struck a match so forcefully it snapped in two. She tried again and as the flame grew, held it to a corner of the envelope. "I have this strange urge to slip into a Wilma Flintstone dress and tie a turkey bone in my hair. And don't you dare laugh, Koski!"

He held up his hands in surrender. "I wouldn't dare, Cavewoman. I wouldn't dare."

Ten

The doctor folded her small hands atop her desk blotter. Behind her, a window framed a willow tree, its slender leaves dancing in the April sunshine. She cleared her throat. "Well, Rachel and Vic, we've reached a new beginning."

Sharon Mathis was a petite woman. Her delicate features, unencumbered by makeup or jewelry, were almost childlike. She wore her fine, light brown hair in a layered style. Her hazel eyes and soft voice communicated intelligence and a genuine empathy toward childless women, which Rachel thought surprising for a mother of three.

At their first meeting almost four months ago, her friendly demeanor revealed itself when she insisted they address her by her first name. Now, however, her entire being conveyed nothing but pure sympathy.

Rachel steeled herself. Sympathy was for dead ends, not new beginnings. She stared at the doctor's lime green silk blouse peeking out from under a white lab coat. The green matched the willow leaves, the color of late April, the color of new life.

Sharon went on. "My preliminary conclusions after last week's procedures have been verified. As always, there's good news slash bad news to the reports. The bad news..." She paused.

Vic squeezed Rachel's hand. She hadn't noticed he was holding it.

"The bad news is that you're in a minority. I can't find anything physiologically wrong with you. This happens approximately fifteen percent of the time. The good news is that there's no reason you cannot conceive."

Vic asked, "What's the new beginning?"

"Go home and relax. Let nature take its course. Or, as you say, let God take His. We've done every test under the sun."

Rachel felt a cold tight fist of pain in her chest.

Vic rubbed his thumb along her hand. "Are there any tests we should try again?"

"I don't think so, and I wouldn't recommend fertility drugs. You're both healthy. And Rachel, your eggs are healthy, you're ovulating, your hormones are balanced. I see no abnormalities in your uterus, tubes, or ovaries. There's nothing more to check."

The recent months played across the stage of Rachel's mind. Gray days. Christmas with the sound of children's laughter assaulting her senses like acid rock music. The countless 40-minute trips to the clinic through snow and ice. Appointments made and broken, bouncing around work and weather and fires. There were always more fires in the winter. Dropping her graduate course. Eliminating junk food from her diet. Blood test after blood test after blood test. Reporting to this woman practically every time she and Vic had intimate relations. Timing those relations to coincide with ovulation and a scheduled exam within 24 hours. Dye shot into her. Scopes inserted. An abdominal incision. Tubes inserted. Risking uterine perforation. Risking internal organ damage. Risking sanity itself.

"Rachel." Sharon handed her a tissue. She had risen from her chair and walked around the desk. She leaned back against it now. "I know this is more painful than all my poking and prodding."

"I feel like I've been to hell and back." She wiped her eyes. "And we could have bought a new roof instead."

Vic leaned over and kissed her cheek, his hand still tight around hers. "We didn't spend that much. So, Sharon." He turned. "Any suggestions?"

"Of course." She smiled gently. "As I said, relax. We should give more credit to emotions and mindset. They play a significant role. And there are a couple of things that may be difficult to hear, but I would be remiss in not opening the subjects. Keep in mind, you two are courageous troopers. It has been my pleasure getting to know you. In no way do I want you to feel guilty. You've given this your best shot. There's no more to be done except, perhaps, to consider these things."

She linked her fingers, hands resting below her waist. "Vic, you've indicated you're not in favor of adoption. That may be something to explore now. You can look into it without signing on any dotted line. I've had many, many patients who conceived after starting the adoption process. My unscientific opinion says there is an unidentified hormone lurking out there."

She shrugged and continued. "Rachel, you're an absolutely delightful woman, and I wish my children could have you for a teacher. You've been diligent in our efforts. I'm proud of your changed attitude toward nutrition and that you were willing to give up working on your doctorate for the time being. I know that was a difficult thing to do. Still, I sense a trace of...restiveness. What I'm about to say may sound a little radical. Just take it as a thought for down the road. You might consider a sabbatical, a leave of absence next fall. Perhaps for a semester."

Rachel stared at her. Vic remained quiet.

Sharon leaned over and placed a hand on the two of theirs still grasped atop the chair arm. "Please, give yourselves time to grieve, but don't give up hope. Think of this as a new beginning. I'll leave you alone now. You're welcome to stay in here as long as you need. Don't ever hesitate to call."

They murmured goodbyes as she left the office.

Vic released Rachel's hand and swung his arm around her shoulders. He kissed the top of her head. They sat that way in silence for a time, Rachel too numb to even cry much.

"Rache, we'll get through this."

She nodded against his shoulder and heaved a sigh.

"Ready?"

"Okay." She straightened.

Taking her chin in his hand, he focused those navy blue diamonds on her face. "I want to make love to you. I don't want to check the calendar first. I don't want to know what your temperature is. I don't want to think of it as a clinical procedure. I don't want to tell anyone."

"Oh, Vic, I'm sorry for all this."

"Shh. Don't be sorry. No regrets here." And then he kissed her as he had that very first time almost ten years ago to the date. Briefly. Sweetly. Chastely.

Perhaps the dead end was, after all, a new beginning.

~

On the twelfth of May, Vic entered Rachel's classroom carrying a single yellow rose and his firefighter's turnouts: helmet, coat, pants, boots, and air tank. He winked over the heads of 24 ogling students.

Vic's presentations had become something of a tradition in Franklin's fourth-grade classes. Rachel and the other teachers always scheduled her room last. Like that first time, he always lingered on through recess.

Leaning against the table in the back corner behind the students, she watched him now. The room size shrank, his large frame blocking half the front chalkboard. Between that and the stories he told in his deep voice, the children were mesmerized.

Even as he warned of the dangers of fires and of playing with matches, some boys asked for gruesome details of death and destruction. He discreetly sidestepped the issue. Toby wouldn't let it drop and persisted in commenting about burned bodies. Toby was still that thorn so neatly planted in her side last August by Sylvia. Rachel had looked up his name once in a baby name book. It was derived from the Hebrew Tobiah, meaning "God is good." She remembered enjoying a moment of comic relief after a particularly stressful day with him.

Now she noticed Vic's eyes narrowing, his laugh lines disappearing as he set his jaw. Not a good sign. She waved to get his attention. When he glanced her way, she made the beaver face.

He cracked up and the children joined in, not knowing what he was laughing about. Stumbling over words trying to get their attention back, he glared at her and blurted, "Hey, gang! Nobody's asked about the fireman's carry! Want to see it?"

If they had been older students, in middle or high school, the original tale of the fireman swooping Mrs. Koski off her feet would have become lore by now. They would have known to ask for the demonstration. If he had done it every year, they might have heard of it. But he had only done it that once. He asserted he had never before or since slung anyone over his shoulder during a community visit. She informed him it wasn't a fun thing and asked him not to do it again. He complied, and she had even begun wearing skirts on the days he visited.

Amidst boisterous clamoring, Vic now strode between desks to the back of the room. Rachel announced it was time to line up for recess, but no one heard her. She pleaded with her eyes for him to reconsider. He approached.

"Vic!" she hissed.

He only widened his eyes, waggled his brows, and bent over. "Just go limp. It's easier."

Well, at least she'd worn an ankle-length skirt.

Arms grasped around her thighs, he deftly lifted her, flipped her over his shoulder, and twirled around. Now he had the kids' attention. While the blood rushed to her head, he explained how rescuers sometimes had to carry people in this manner. Then he told them to line up for recess.

When he set her down, they stood at the door, noiseless until someone snickered.

Toby said, "Mr. Koski, you're in big trouble."

"You think so?" Vic asked.

"Mm-hmm. She only gets that red when I torque her off."

Rachel bit her lip to keep from bursting into laughter.

Vic replied, "What should I do?"

"You'd better say you're sorry."

Vic looked at her. "Mrs. Koski, I'm sorry."

She swallowed. "Apology accepted, but you have to miss recess."

The children giggled. She let them. By mid-May they knew how long her leash was. As did her husband.

When the bell rang, she sent them on with another teacher who would see they remained quiet through the halls.

"So." Vic rested his arm on the doorjamb above her head. "Is it Miss or Mrs. Koski?"

"At the moment it's *Ms.*"

"Not sure, huh?" He grinned. "Any chance then you'll have dinner with me tonight?"

"Oh, there's a slight chance. Very slight." She winked and turned on her heel.

Dinner was at the same restaurant where they'd gone when they first met ten years ago. He had especially chosen it to impress her. As if he had needed to impress her further...

She smiled at her handsome husband. He had gone home and changed into a tweed sport jacket and a silk navy blue tie, her favorite, the one that matched his eyes and sent Shirley Temple off on a tap dancing spree. Setting down her fork, she moaned. "That was so wonderful."

"But you saved room for dessert, right?" He speared his last bite of steak.

"Naturally. It's tradition. Ten years of tradition. Sylvia still can't believe we celebrate the day we met. Speaking of Sylvia, I asked her about Toby's background. She said his grandmother died in a fire when he was three."

Vic wrinkled his brow. "I thought as much. His interest went beyond little-boy curiosity. Maybe we could give him a tour of the station, help him get over his fear."

"Vic, you are such a Pooh Bear with these kids. I don't understand your aversion to adoption."

They had avoided the subject since leaving the doctor's office a few weeks ago. She felt strong enough to address it now and hoped he felt the same.

He shrugged. "Can you imagine living with a Toby?"

"But we'd want to adopt a baby, not a nine-year-old."

"In spite of Toby's experience, I still think there's an awful lot of genetics responsible for a kid like him. I'm forty-four, Rache. I'm not sure that at fifty-four I want to be responsible for a Toby."

"Maybe we could just investigate, like Sharon said. Not sign on the dotted line. Just start the process. Take my mind off me?" She ended in a hopeful tone.

"Maybe." He rocked his glass back and forth. "Have you thought about taking a leave of absence next year? At least the first semester?"

Now she shrugged. "I can't imagine what I'd do with myself."

"What you do in the summertime. All those things you don't get to do during the other nine months. Teach Sunday school. Take bubble baths and read. Organize that Bible study for the wives of the firemen in my group."

"I could join your mother's book club!"

He laughed at the sarcasm in her voice. "You could take a class or two, work on your doctorate in a more laid-back sort of way." He leaned forward. "Rachel, we can afford it. You don't have to work. We're the tightest tightwads I've ever met."

In truth his generosity flabbergasted her at times. "We are conservative in our spending."

"That too. Think about it?"

She winced.

"Rache, it's interfering with my work."

His tone was nowhere near accusatory, but his words had the effect of an abrupt stop of gale force winds against an unfurled flag. She crumpled.

"Oh, Vic."

"Just dumb stuff. Losing my focus in training exercises. Reaming out a probie who didn't do anything wrong."

"I had no idea it affected you so."

"I didn't tell you. The point is I don't function well if you're not right, baby. You're understandably stressed out. You look stretched to the limit, even worse than you did in October. But I don't know how to fix things for you without going totally against what I think is best for us."

Her emotions churned. There were no words to express the confusion.

"I don't want to force you into anything either. I just hope that you'll consider giving yourself a break from the classroom." His pager beeped, and he moved aside his jacket to read it. "It's your parents."

They stared at each other for a moment. Her parents never paged him. They didn't even have his number. Bram had his number. She couldn't imagine any reason he would give—

"Bubbie. Oh, Vic! It's Bubbie."

Eleven

They all congregated in the nursing home room: Vic; Rachel; her parents, Abe and Bess; her brother, Bram; her sister Bits. Bits's husband—in kind terms, a distant personality—was absent, as was Bram's sweet wife, who remained home with their toddler. Sarah, of course, was in California and nine months pregnant.

Bubbie had begun failing that morning, acting less responsive than usual, her vital signs dropping steadily.

Rachel sat beside her, clasping a hand, almost the only visible part of her not hooked up to a monitor or IV or wire of some sort. Even as she raged against letting Bubbie go, she sensed a peace beginning to envelope the little woman who had loved her so exquisitely.

Her grandmother's eyes fluttered open, and she gazed at Rachel.

"Bubbie, I love you."

The woman shifted her focus slightly, to above Rachel's shoulder where Vic stood. As on that day when he talked with her on the phone, her eyes filled with tears.

Vic leaned around Rachel and kissed the old woman's cheek.

There was a hoarse whispering. By the time Rachel realized what was happening, it was over. Had she seen and heard correctly? Had Bubbie actually *spoken* to Vic?

Bubbie closed her eyes, and all was as before.

"Vic!"

He knelt beside Rachel, his face awestruck. "She said it's time to go Home."

They stared at each other. Bubbie hadn't spoken a word in over a year.

Evidently no one else had noticed; their murmuring continued unabated.

"Abe." Vic stood abruptly and addressed her dad. "Let's get the doctor to unhook this stuff. There's no need to monitor. We're not resuscitating, right?"

Her dad, of medium build and appearing dazed, shook his balding head.

"She should be as comfortable as possible. Her Messiah Yeshua is waiting. We'll know when He takes her. It's time to tell her goodbye."

Rachel could only blink at him. He spoke in a tone she'd never heard him use before...one of authority, though different from what she called his fireman's voice. He sounded as if he understood things beyond human reasoning. Like Bubbie.

Shortly after midnight, Rachel and Vic sat on a chair against the wall. She was on his lap, the side of her face against his chest, her eyes turned toward her grandmother. Her parents sat on either side of the bed, holding Bubbie's hands. Her siblings sat quietly in the other chairs.

As far back as Rachel could remember, Bubbie taught her that the moment they died, they would literally see the Lord and He would welcome them with open arms. Rachel believed that with all her heart and, with great anticipation, imagined her grandmother being embraced at any moment now by her Savior. Still she cried softly, already missing Bubbie's presence.

Vic squeezed her hand tightly, and she began to sense a subtle shift in the energy of the room.

Bubbie was Home.

~

While other family and friends mingled in the living room and kitchen, Rachel and Vic sat in the den of her parents' colonial-style home. Bryan and Sylvia kept them company.

The room was comfortable with masculine furnishings and plush carpet. A blazing fire added a sweet coziness, a welcome tone on the evening of Bubbie's funeral. Record-breaking low temperatures added to the dankness of the rainy day. Although the service had been a celebration of Bubbie's life, Rachel imagined that the earth missed her presence.

She sat in one of the wing chairs flanking the fireplace, Vic in the other. Sylvia and Bryan occupied the leather couch facing the fire.

"Vic," Rachel said, "what do you call it when the smoke is so thick and dark you can't find your fire hose?"

"Losing your line."

"That's it. That's what I feel like. Like I've lost my line and can't find my way out of a burning building."

"Why, Rache? Because Bubbie was your line?"

She nodded. "Even when she couldn't speak, she represented answers because she'd always given them to me."

Bryan said, "That's a strong analogy coming from you. Not to diminish your loss or cut short your grieving, but your faith is stronger than the three of ours here combined. Which begs the question, what's the burning building you need to escape?"

"I don't know. Life, I guess."

His gaze pierced, and she couldn't look away. "Rachel, why is your life like a burning building?"

"Oh, I know it doesn't look like one! I have the most wonderful husband in the whole world. I have the best job in the whole world, but..." Her voice dropped to a whisper. "Some days I can scarcely breathe because I want a baby so bad."

She sensed their collective sigh. Old tune. New verse.

"Bubbie used to tell me a Jewish proverb: 'Pay attention to your dreams, for they are your letters from God.' It's still my dream to be the mother of Vic's child. It just won't go away."

Sylvia leaned toward the coffee table and set down her cup. "Honey, much as I hate to say this out loud, I think you should seriously consider what your doctor suggested. Take the fall semester off. At least take the summer off. Give yourself a long break from responsibility."

"We're planning on going out to California after Sarah's baby is born."

Sylvia shook her head. "I'm talking major time away."

Bryan said, "What do you think about going to a retreat center like I do once a year? Some place you could be totally alone."

"Aren't those places just for priests?"

"No. And you choose what you want to do. Fast. Read. Pray. Be counseled or simply be quiet."

Something in Bryan's voice resonated within her, striking a chord of possibility. She caught Vic's frown. Evidently Bryan did too because he turned to him.

"Vic, she needs a break."

"Granted."

"Don't take it personally. You can survive seven days without her."

"I told her to take next year off."

"This could be a good jump start to that. How about if I give you two some websites to check out?"

Her husband nodded.

Sylvia stood, smiling. "It's settled then. You have the principal's blessing and websites from the priest."

They all chuckled with her.

After helping her family put the house back in order, Vic and Rachel drove through the quiet midnight streets in silence. She felt exhausted.

"Rache?"

"Hmm?"

"How come I'm not your line?"

She watched the light and shadows play on his face as he drove, trying to decipher his question.

"Why can't I rescue you from the burning building of your life?" He glanced at her. "Shouldn't we be each other's lines to Christ when we can't find our way?"

She leaned across the console and rested her head against his arm. "Honey, you're so much my line, it scares me."

"Then why do you need time away from me?"

"Because at the moment we're in this building together."

"What's the *building*?" There was frustration in his voice, though he tempered it, speaking calmly.

"The building of being childless. Neither one of us can find the way out. If I don't find a way by myself, I'm afraid I will keep both of us in here so long that we'll suffocate."

"What do you want from me?"

"I don't know. The answer may all lie in my attitude, my acceptance of whatever God gives or doesn't give us without having to know why. I have to step away from everything and everybody here. Does that make any sense?"

He took a hand off the steering wheel and caressed her cheek. "Not really. I'm trying to hear you, but no, it doesn't make any sense."

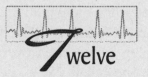

Twelve

Three weeks later, Rachel snuggled in Vic's arms, her ear against his chest, listening to his heart beat away the seconds like a kitchen timer. The ding would sound in 14 hours at the airport when they said goodbye.

She had finished the school year in robotlike fashion, feeling guilty that her usual year-end celebrations were relatively subdued. Not that the children could have known her efforts were different from other years. Within two days of their departure, she had set her classroom in order. An unprecedented shortness of time.

She and Vic had investigated retreat possibilities, but they hadn't found an appropriate one that offered space before August. However, her sister's mother-in-law broke an arm just days before Sarah gave birth and therefore had to cancel her plans to help. With two other little ones and an overworked attorney for a husband, Sarah was reading nanny ads during labor. Rachel, eager to prove to herself that infertility had not fatally hardened her heart toward children, offered to arrive as soon as possible.

And so, instead of kicking back for a few days at home, she hurled herself into a late-spring house cleaning marathon. Jessie and Terri volunteered to help. Each spent a different day scrubbing alongside her. Unwittingly they only increased her burden.

Though to a lesser degree than the previous year, Jessie still struggled with Kevin not being the perfect husband. Vic made a point of interacting more with him, trying to pave the way for him to join the firemen's Bible study. Vic had even consented to keeping the children overnight once. Jessie's faith still wobbled. She called Rachel her source of knowledge and wisdom, and mourned her leaving.

Terri on the other hand did not believe in Jesus Christ. She wasn't even sold on the idea of a living God. In the five years they'd known each other, Rachel did not pretend that she was perfect. However, now, at her lowest point in life, she felt the weight of not even being close to walking in an exemplary way of faith.

Besides letting down her friends, there were her in-laws. She invited Stan and Wanda for dinner along with Bryan as backup, knowing Wanda would listen to Bryan talk of time away and retreat centers, subjects Rachel herself could only intuitively grasp. No way could she explain her upcoming lengthy absence to her mother-in-law. And that inability compounded her burden.

Vic stirred beside her now. "Rache?"

"Hmm?"

"Have I loved you well?" Though he had declared his acceptance of her need to get away, an uncharacteristic hesitancy filled his voice.

"What do you mean?"

"I'm not sure. I guess I mean do you feel loved? Have I taken good care of you?"

She propped herself on an elbow and looked down at his face bathed in soft light filtering through the curtain from the streetlamp. "Yes and yes. Absolutely. Hon, I know this is confusing."

"I've let you down in this baby business." He hooked his hands behind his head on the pillow.

"How? You agreed to all the tests, and you held my hand through the major ones."

"But not the minor ones."

"Well, you were with me when we tried to make a baby." She gave him a half smile.

"Only if I wasn't working, didn't have Bible study, a class, or a meeting. Once or twice I totally forgot your reminder. Once or twice I even…" He stopped.

"Even what?"

He blew out a breath. "I even stayed away until late just to avoid the possibility."

"I know, Vic."

"You know?"

She shrugged. That feeling of defeat washed through her again. "I sensed it anyway. You've never really been a hundred percent sure you want to be a father."

He waited a beat before replying. "I guess that's true. I'm sorry. Will you forgive me?"

"You're only being you. There's nothing to forgive." The words were the right ones to say, but they echoed hollowly in her mind. She knew they didn't sink into her heart.

He unhooked his hands and hugged her. She laid her head upon his chest again.

"Vic, are you angry that I'm going?"

"Yeah, I'm ticked. Not at you, but at the situation. At the fact that I'm not enough for you."

"You are enough as far as is humanly possible."

"Seems like I should be more."

Yes, it did seem that way. And it seemed she should not want to be so far away from her husband for weeks on end.

How had her dream become a wedge between them?

In the quiet she listened to his steady breathing, to the rhythm of his heartbeat...less than soothing lullabies on this last night together.

∼

The next morning at O'Hare International Airport, Rachel clung to Vic's hand. Second guesses hammered in her head. Was the decision to leave him for such a long period of time a good one? The right one? A prudent one? Was she simply behaving like an immature adolescent trying to find herself?

He would join her in July, which was only next month, calendar-wise. Separation-wise, it would be the longest they'd experienced. She had been to her sister's in California without him. He had traveled twice to New York City after September 11 to help while she stayed home. There were other instances, but never for *six weeks*.

They sat near the security gate, a long, serpentine line in view, waiting until the last possible moment to say goodbye.

"Baby, are you okay? You're cutting off the circulation in my fingers."

"Sorry." She loosened her grip. "I think my pride at maintaining independence all these years despite being married has been false. I don't feel the least independent at the moment."

"You're one strong lady." He leaned down and kissed the tip of her nose. "On the other hand, I'm feeling so lonely already I'll probably go to Ma's for dinner."

"You could call Ellen Hamilton," she teased. "I'm sure she'd chat with you."

The notes had continued arriving sporadically at Bryan's office. At their request, he burned them.

Vic grunted at her poor attempt of a joke. "That's not funny."

"Sorry." She gulped a lung full of air. "Again. Guess I'm more than a little anxious about leaving."

He smiled, his half-mast eyes scanning her face like a thirsty man searching the desert horizon. "I love you."

She blinked away tears. She did love him so. How had it come to this?

"It's time," he said.

They rose to their feet as one, and he wrapped his arms around her. "I'm going to ignore your aversion to public displays of affection. In a big way."

He didn't wait for permission or protest, but simply lowered his head and kissed her. Intensely enough to send Shirley off tripping the light fantastic. Holding her close, he murmured, "Can't have anyone thinking my gorgeous woman is available."

Pressing her face against his neck, she inhaled the menthol scent of his shaving lotion. After a long moment, she reluctantly pulled away. "I love you."

"I love you. Oh!" He grinned, dug into his jeans pocket, and pulled out a small black velvet bag. "I almost forgot. This is an anniversary gift."

"Anniversary? Vic, you remember the twelfth every month but sometimes you forget we got married in December. This is *June*."

Holding the gift up beyond her reach, he removed the large shoulder bag from her arm. "It's a tenth anniversary gift from the day we met. I was going to give it to you that night at the restaurant when we were celebrating. Then what with Bubbie and all, I just never found a good time. And then I thought I'd save it for our wedding anniversary, but it seemed silly to wait that long since I already had the thing."

"Vic, what are you doing?"

He was stuffing the little bag into her purse. "I want you to open it later, on the plane. Sorry it's not wrapped. It was, but I know security dismantles wrapped gifts." He rezipped her purse and hung it back on her shoulder. "Make sure the guy sitting next to you knows it's from your caveman of a husband."

She protested. "Come on! I don't want to open it without you."

"Tough."

"What is it? Give me a hint."

"Okay. It's for our *tenth*, but it's not made of tin. And it's not a cookie sheet."

"What?"

"Those are traditional and modern tenth anniversary gifts." His voice resembled a British lecturer's. "I went with the alternate modern."

"I don't have a clue what you're talking about."

"I know." He grabbed her hand, and they walked to the now short line at the security checkpoint.

They waited in silence as the line crawled forward, its slow and steady pace much too hasty for Rachel's comfort. Her heart pounded, thundering in her ears.

"Hey, Rache." He whispered and touched the corner of her eye. "Try not to cry? You'll have me pushing my way through the gate up there to stay with you, and those guards are not going to like that."

She smiled and sniffed.

And then it was her turn.

They kissed briefly. As she inched forward, his callused fingertips slid along her palm, along her fingers. She moved to the conveyor belt and set down her handbag, catching his goodbye wink before she walked through the security frame.

On the other side, she turned and waved at her husband, who smiled and gave her a thumbs-up sign. The guard repeated an insistent, "Move along."

And then a new crowd swelled at the security entrance, hiding Vic from view.

It was time to go.

∽

With her seatmates finally settled on either side of her, Rachel rummaged through her large handbag. Where had he placed it? She began pulling out the contents. Book, magazine, wallet, cell phone, sunglasses... The security guard hadn't opened it, so there was no chance it had fallen out. She unzipped an inner pocket. Alongside a lipstick, her hand felt soft velvet.

She clutched it, haphazardly stuffing the other items back inside the purse, which she then shoved under the seat in front of her. The little bag obviously contained jewelry.

Rachel gasped as a delicate tennis bracelet tumbled from the black velvet. Diamond chips set in bright gold sparkled in her palm.

"Oh, my!" the woman in the aisle seat breathed. "How beautiful!"

"It is! I can't believe he did this."

"From your husband?"

"Yes."

"I saw you together in the lobby." Silver-haired, she spoke with a European accent and smiled kindly. "He is quite handsome. Rugged-looking."

"I think so."

"He must love you a great deal."

"Yes. Yes, he must." *But this bracelet is not what proves that truth.*

No, the bracelet only proved further that Vic was losing his touch.

She wrapped the diamonds around her left wrist alongside her watch. While the glittering piece complimented her rings, it made the everyday large-faced dial and dull gold stretch band look downright tacky. Her Day-Timer might have been pitched, but the durable watch was staying. She moved the bracelet and clasped it around her right wrist. There, that was better.

Except for her engagement ring and wedding band, she didn't pay much attention to jewelry. It was impractical for school and, besides, there was always some necessary item or charity to put money toward. Her mother had oodles of flashy stones, very few of them simple baubles. Bubbie's wedding band, of course, had been taken by Nazis, and she never remarried nor cared much for silver and gold...

The bracelet was exquisite. Like her engagement diamond, it was not ostentatious. Still...what must Vic be thinking? She was so utterly pragmatic and not frivolous. His gifts to her generally reflected that. Had she so thoroughly upset him that he had resorted to an extravagance she had never craved?

She studied her rings. The band matched Vic's: 14 carat, plain gold with a brushed effect. The diamond was octagonal in shape, three-fourths of a carat. Just right. As had been his proposal. Rachel smiled to herself, remembering an altogether different proposal.

They had been dating for about five or six weeks, seeing each other as regularly as their crammed, diverse schedules allowed. During that time she saw Wade Holden three times. He was an old friend from the church she had attended until she found one nearer her apartment. He lived north of the city. Through the years she occasionally met him and mutual friends downtown for dinner, a concert, or the theater.

Since Vic's entrance into her life, she joined that group for a concert, a date arranged months beforehand. When a movie they wanted to see opened, she went again with them. Both times Vic had been on duty. She didn't have to decide whether or not to invite him.

Then there came a week when Vic balked at her ballet suggestion and Wade enticed her with front row balcony seats.

Although she knew her heart was thoroughly tangled up with the firefighter, practical Rachel felt things had progressed too quickly. She accepted Wade's invitation, thereby gaining a false sense of control over her emotions regarding Vic. She could take him or leave him, a proper, manageable state just weeks into a relationship. Still, she was curious to see Vic's reaction. IIe maintained a cool demeanor and teased her about competition. Only after they were married did he admit to behaving like a snarling bear beyond her earshot.

Compared to Vic, Wade was physically medium. Medium brown hair, medium brown eyes, medium ears, medium build. Compared to Vic, he was nice and polite, which meant he cared about which fork to use, referred to his mother as *Mother*, and vacationed in Nassau. His meteoric rise as a corporate executive could be attributed to his driven personality. Rachel had always enjoyed his conversation.

She should have suspected something was up the night of the ballet. First off, the regular members of their group were not accompanying them. Second, Wade uncharacteristically insisted on picking her up, quite a number of miles out of his way. She had never minded driving herself or taking the train. That night he didn't exactly drive to her apartment. He arrived in a white stretch limousine.

Rachel liked the occasional dress-up affair. She liked the symphony and live theater. She liked gourmet dinners. She did not like being treated like royalty.

Her mother taught her how to be gracious, and so she smiled at Wade, limited herself to one snide remark which she murmured, and climbed onto the buttery soft leather seat. However, she drew the line at accepting a two-and-a-half carat diamond ring.

Poor Wade. Before they'd reached the Dan Ryan Expressway, he'd popped the cork of a champagne bottle and filled two goblets.

"Wade," she protested.

"Oh, just a sip. I think you'll like this."

While he gulped down his champagne, she examined her bubbling liquid and noticed something *solid* in the bottom of the flute.

"Rachel, I think we should get married. I am never going to find another girl who is as great as you are."

She stared at him. Where had that come from? They had never been a *couple*.

He took the flute from her hand, downed the drink, and deftly caught a diamond ring between his teeth. He dried it on a linen napkin and held it out to her.

"Two and a half." He smiled, his eyes glassy enough to make her wonder if the bottle wasn't the first one uncorked that evening. "What do you say?"

She stared at the ring. What rotten timing! Not because her heart was turned toward Vic—even without Vic in the picture she would not have said yes to Wade—but because the entire evening lay ahead. And there was a stranger up front in the driver's seat, casting surreptitious glances in the rearview mirror.

Still, what choice did she have? Say yes and change her mind after the final curtain call?

"Wade, do you love me?"

"Well, sure."

"And I love you...as a brother in Christ. I also like you an awful lot. Even my mother likes you, and you're not Jewish. But..." *But Shirley doesn't dance.* "But, I don't love you in a let's-spend-our-life-together sort of way."

He picked up the bottle and poured himself another drink. "Isn't this when you say you'll think about it?"

"I'm sorry. I had no idea. I...I really don't have anything to think about."

"Maybe you should. Take your time. I mean, we're a perfect match. You can move up north with me, come back to the church, find a school in the 'burbs. I imagine you'll want to keep teaching for a while. Before we start having kids."

Wade continued sipping as he reminisced about their past together and predicted a compatible future.

Rachel sat in horrified silence until at last, as they waited stalled in traffic near the theater, she blurted out, "I'm sorry! I just don't want to get married!"

He patted her hand. "Think about it. You can wear this if you like." He held up his hand where the enormous diamond sat on the knuckle of his little finger.

"Do you have a box for that?"

He patted his suit coat pockets, but came up empty. She took hold of his lapel, held out the coat, reached inside an inner pocket, and pulled out a ring box. After removing the ring from his pinkie, she stored it safely away in its velvet and stuck the box back into his pocket.

"Wade, you'll find someone. Off the top of my head I can think of half a dozen possibilities from your church alone."

"You're a good woman, Rachel."

"Thank you."

They eventually made their way inside the theater. After finding the seats, Wade excused himself. He never came back.

During intermission, too shaken to make her way home alone on the train, she found a pay telephone and called the only hero she knew to come rescue her. *I wait for the mighty hero of legends old. That brave defender of woman and child.*

Vic asked questions, exaggerating his enunciation of key words in her story. *Too much* champagne? *You turned down his* proposal? *He left you* stranded?

She could hear loud laughter in the background. Evidently, some of the guys were at his place, and he was letting them in on the conversation.

"Look," she said, "if I'd brought flat shoes along—"

"The Cubs are playing."

"Okay, fine. I got myself into this mess. Well, not exactly. But I can get myself out of it! I can! Excuse me for acting like a helpless female. I don't know what I was thinking. Goodbye."

"Rache!"

"What?"

"I love it when you act like a helpless female."

The volume of the background laughter intensified.

Tears of frustration burned in her eyes. "I hate acting like a helpless female!"

"I know, but I'm in the rescue business! Give me your location."

About 35,000 feet over Iowa...

Even in their early days together, Vic knew her better than Wade ever could have. He knew she didn't want a flashy diamond or a silly proposal in a luxurious limo. Why, oh why, was he now trying to rescue her with a piece of jewelry?

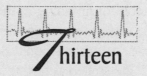

Thirteen

Rachel nuzzled the chubby folds of little Jacob's neck and deeply inhaled his freshly bathed baby scent as he slept in her arms. She kissed his cheek and whispered, "Thank You, Lord, for this new child." *And thank You for the love I feel for him...the joy I feel for my sister.*

Only God could sweeten the bitterness that had taken root during the long winter of infertility tests.

"Sarah." From the rocking chair, she glanced across the bedroom at her sister sitting on the bed. "I never saw Becka and Josh at two weeks of age. Jacob's cheeks are like gossamer, aren't they? And so downy. Bubbie's were like this."

They shared a sad smile.

Looking at Sarah was like gazing into a mirror. Same arched nose, large mouth, cinnamon eyes, and henna hair. Her sister, four years younger, was a bit shorter. There was more brown and less of a reddish hint in her hair, less thickness; she wore it in a longer style, the natural waves pulled back in a ponytail. And, too, a rosy glow of motherhood emanated from her.

"You look great, Sarah."

She waved her hand in dismissal. "Yeah? Check this out." She lifted her baggy T-shirt and patted the tummy covered with stretchy maternity pants.

"Comes with the territory, I guess."

Sarah's face fell. "I'm sorry, Rache."

"No, I'm sorry. That was a cutting remark."

"Well, mine was a stupid complaint. I wouldn't trade the extra weight and Jacob for anything in the entire world. And I know you wish you had the same problem."

"But it's not your fault that I don't. So stop apologizing and just ignore me." She smiled at her. "You know how I tend to blurt things out to you, even more so than to Vic."

Sarah giggled. "David is so glad my big sister is here to keep me in line."

"Let's hope you don't have to keep me in line. It has been a *long* winter."

"Anyway you look at it, you're a lot less strain on us than his mother, great as she is. And to tell the truth, I'm glad our mom isn't the granny type. I just hope you can relax here."

"Of course I can. You know how sometimes it's actually fun to clean up someone else's kitchen? It feels like that. Perfect place for healing." She glanced down at her nephew, now wriggling and emitting a tiny bleat. "Especially with this brand-new life. I think he's looking for you, Mama."

"Right on schedule, as in whenever he's awake."

Rachel stood aside, and Sarah slid into the rocker. After handing the baby to her, Rachel began to unpack. The contented sounds of Jacob nursing soon filled the softly lit room.

Sarah's sprawling ranch-style house followed the contours of a bluff in La Jolla and provided a distant view of the Pacific. The luxurious guest room was enormous with plenty of space for an armchair, ottoman, and television as well as the rocker David had carried in. Separated from the other bedrooms by the combined kitchen and family room, it was decorated in peachy colors and had its own private bath. A sliding door opened onto the flagstone patio that ran the length of the house. Through it she caught a glimpse of the setting sun.

"Rache, let me see the picture."

She had just pulled a five-by-seven framed photo of Vic from its padded nest in her sweaters. It had been snapped by a friend who hadn't slept through the birthday party.

"This was taken last October." She handed it to her sister.

"I still don't understand what you see in him."

Rachel laughed. The joke was a standing one. Hearing of the family's dismissive attitude toward Vic long before she met him, Sarah adopted their opinion, tongue in cheek, and mercilessly teased long distance. When she finally met him two days before the wedding, she knew, like Bubbie, he was tailor-made for her sister.

"Even at the ripe old age of forty-four, he still looks like your big dragon-slaying hero. He doesn't still call you baby, does he?"

"Yes, he does." She grinned. His nickname for her was the only thing Sarah took issue with against Vic.

She clicked her tongue. "It's so nauseatingly *macho*." She set the photo on the table beside the chair and lifted Jacob to her shoulder. "Rache, I still don't know how you do it."

Rachel slid open the mirrored closet doors and noted with amazement the empty space. Such a luxury compared to her house. "Do what, hon?"

"Live with the uncertainty."

Rachel stepped toward her sister and picked up the photo again. He did indeed look like a hero. His eyes laughed back at her with the intensity of a crisp, clear October sky. His face was scrunched like an accordion behind the grin. His broad shoulders promised safety. Why was it God had brought him into her life?

"Heroic lives are uncertain, Sarah, but Messiah Yeshua is for certain. Vic will be all right, no matter what."

"I still don't understand that."

Rachel set the photo back down and kissed the top of her sister's head. The topsy-turvy Goldberg household had wreaked havoc on the youngest child's spirit, which was probably why she lived halfway across the country from her family. The subject of religion set her teeth on edge. Her husband's childhood had been nearly as discombobulated. In the interest of community participation, they sporadically attended a Protestant church that didn't offer much challenge beyond finding a good parking spot on Easter.

She sat on the edge of the bed. "It doesn't make sense to our logical minds. My only explanation is faith. Vic is in God's hands."

"But Christian firefighters die."

"Of course. Being in His hands means when they die, He takes them Home to be with Him."

"But where does that leave you? Where does that leave you every time he walks out the door knowing he could very likely find himself in the middle of a fire sometime in the next twenty-four hours?"

The subject was nearly ten years old between them, but Rachel never tired of trying to help Sarah understand the reality of faith. "When I feel afraid, I have to ask the Lord to take it away. It's supernatural as well as a conscious choice to turn to Him." She noticed her sister's wrinkled brow. "What's wrong?"

"Yesterday..." She bit her lip. "Yesterday the doctor found a hole in Jacob's heart. Will your God fix that?"

Late that first night in California, Rachel sat curled in the armchair with the cell phone at her ear, talking to Vic. She tilted her wrist until the lamplight reflected off the diamond bracelet. It was beautiful. Impractical, but beautiful in a tasteful, understated sort of way.

Unlike his usual confident self, Vic sounded overly anxious about her reaction.

She tried to reassure him once again. "I'm going to wear it to bed."

He chuckled. "So you really like it?"

"Yeah, I *really* like it for the seventeenth time." And for the seventeenth time she bit back other words. *You didn't have to. Why did you? It's not me! And you're not acting like yourself!*

"I thought ten years called for something a little different. Especially after what you've been through. I hope this development with little Jacob isn't too wearing on you."

She had told him about the baby's heart. "There's nothing to be done for now except to wait and pray. It's not affecting him outwardly. The hole is tiny. The doctor is fairly certain it will grow shut on its own."

"But Sarah and David must be scared out of their wits. I'll pray for them. Rache." His voice grew eager. "You know, this could be how Jesus gets their attention. All of a sudden their life is no longer a cakewalk."

"My firefighting evangelist." Her tone lacked the necessary teasing note for such a comment. Why was she so on edge? Maybe she shouldn't have called him already. Maybe she needed more space than she thought. More time...

"I didn't mean to sound happy about what they're going through. To insinuate that now all they have to do is accept Jesus and everything will be hunky-dory."

"I know you didn't, Vic. I'm sorry. I'm just tired. They actually are having a very difficult time with this, and Sarah is asking more questions about God than she has in a long while. She seems to be listening in a different way."

Rachel chatted, putting distance between herself and her demeaning remark to Vic. He wasn't deterred.

"Rache, don't wear yourself out. You're supposed to be taking time off from responsibility. If things get to be too much for you, come home."

A mental image of throwing her hands in the air flashed in her mind's eye. He just didn't get it. She needed time off from home!

In spite of the sense that their conversation was unfinished, she ended the call. Annoyed with her husband. Annoyed with herself. Annoyed with life itself.

∽

Rachel soaked in a bubble bath. Located off the guest room, the luxurious bathroom was decorated in whites and off-whites. Gleaming mirrors, brass fixtures, and bright ceramic tile contrasted with fluffy rugs and towels. A now-darkened, one-way window afforded daytime views of luscious, large-leafed semitropical plants.

She had lit candles and dimmed the lights. Recalling the infertility specialist's words were small comfort, but she replayed them anyway. The doctor explained stress levels, how all situations—good and bad—carried varying value points. Rachel now added points for Bubbie's death. They increased a total already on the high end, what with infertility, medical tests, strained relations with her husband, a kid named Toby, above average mother-in-law discord, flying, being away from home...

Which meant something might break inside of her if she didn't slow down. Vic had been right in his assessment during their anniversary dinner. She was worse off than she had been in October, more tightly wound than a coiled spring.

Closing her eyes now, the scent of lavender wafting from the bubbles, she thought back to the early days...to a time when Vic understood her.

They had been dating for only four months when she knew at a deep, intuitive level they would marry eventually. No doubt about it. He had changed her life in a profound way. There was absolutely no going back. If he bowed out at that point, all color would be stripped from her world. Simple as that.

The pivotal word was *eventually*. Although the meaning of time had already lost its impact by that October, she was aware of the fact that five months had passed since they'd met. And five months was far too soon for *eventually* to have arrived. *Eventually* meant indefinite, but it allowed for some definite passage of time. It meant that some sensible inner voice would declare exactly when that time was up.

Vic heard the voice before she did and, once again, managed to sweep her off her feet.

Columbus Day was celebrated on a Monday. There was no school. The date was near enough to Vic's birthday that Rachel thought it a perfect day to surprise him at work. Not yet feeling a part of his unit's camaraderie, she didn't tell anyone she was coming. She just baked a triple-layer red velvet cake with thick buttercream frosting and drove to the station, praying he wouldn't be out on a call and that the alarm wouldn't sound for at least five minutes after she got there. She did so want to see the look on his face.

Her prayer was answered. Lunch was in progress when she arrived. Perfect. To her chagrin, forks clanked against plates and a dozen guys flew to their feet. They raced past Rachel without a word, Vic bringing up the rear. He grabbed her hand, the one not holding the cake carrier's handle, and pulled her along.

She remembered a flash of panic. He was taking her on an emergency call! His work fascinated her, intrigued her, invoked her respect, but there was no way she wanted to be any nearer than she'd been that one time as she'd watched him fight a fire.

Naturally, he had something unimaginable in mind.

The group had lined up beside the trucks and was facing her, 12 kneeling, grinning men. Rachel halted in her tracks. Vic dropped her hand, quickly joined them, and slipped to one knee.

They spoke in unison. "Rachel Goldberg, Vic loves you and we think you're the greatest. Will you marry us?"

Naturally, she was speechless.

Vic said, "It's a family affair here. We want you to be part of it. But you have to live with me."

Eventually had arrived. Tears sprang to her eyes. She covered her mouth with her hand and nodded.

The next few minutes remained a blur. She remembered bursts of clapping and congratulations and energetic shouts of joy and whistles. Someone relieved her of the cake as Vic scooped her up and twirled around. After kissing her soundly, he showed her a diamond ring which, she learned later, someone had retrieved from the office where it had been stowed two weeks before with hopes she would soon take him up on his invitation to stop by anytime. He promised to take her shopping if she didn't like his jewelry selection. She liked it.

Yes, Vic had known her well from the beginning. Unlike him, Wade surprised her with obvious nervousness and trappings that did not suit her. Vic surprised her with assurance, knowing only that he wanted to sweep her off her feet with a boundless expression of his love. He did so publicly and yet in the most personal of ways, welcoming her into his family.

The truth was he could not have bungled things. She loved him far too much for that to have been possible.

⌒

Rachel adored her sister's family. David Markham, her brother-in-law, wore his love for Sarah the way he wore his black hair: It was always in evidence and always a little on the wild and crazy side. That fact racked up major points in his favor. He was, as well, a kind and thoughtful man with a wired personality like Sarah's. In comparison Rachel felt calm.

Slender with dark hair and eyes, six-year-old Becka resembled her father. Four-year-old Josh looked more like his mother and aunt with reddish hints in his eyes and wavy hair.

Rachel easily fell into the daily rhythm of the Markham household. By 9 A.M. on her second day in their home, they all agreed David had hit his limit of playing Mr. Mom. She released him of his duties. Within the hour he'd packed up his attaché case and headed out to his law office, happy as a convict released months ahead of schedule.

That afternoon Rachel plunked baby Jacob into his car seat, ushered Sarah into the passenger seat, and, while driving their minivan, learned the routes to the grocery store, Becka's elementary school, and Josh's preschool, both of which were in session until mid-June. After picking up the children, she learned which streets led to the ocean. What else was necessary?

The mild sunny day beckoned them to La Jolla Cove, where a large grassy area provided plenty of romping space above the beach and tide pool areas. The coastline jutted out in the shape of a giant "J" before dropping back onto its meandering path south.

Rachel and her family sat on a blanket, munching cheese, apple slices, and cookies. Sunlight kissed the fresh scents of salty air and green grass. Endless blue-gray ocean stretched before them, the crash of its waves muted, its spray visible now and then. To the left, beyond their sight, sea lions napped on a sheltered beach they had reclaimed from humans. To the right, in the "J's" concave, long-distance swimmers performed laps out to buoys. As usual, no matter the day or time or weather, pedestrians strolled along the walkway perched atop the bluff and often paused at the railing to gaze out over the Pacific.

Like the brush of a butterfly's wings, the encompassing beauty touched Rachel ever so briefly somewhere deep inside of her soul. It left a distinct but elusive impression of hope.

⌒

Josh unwittingly did his best to stomp out that elusive impression. The little boy asked incessant questions about "Unca Bic," whom he remembered from the previous year when the family had visited Chicago. He begged Rachel on a daily basis to sit with him on the floor while he zoomed his large collection of fire trucks around her. He slept with a toy helmet. They made endless trips to the ice cream shop for "banilla" cones, Vic's favorite and now Josh's.

He intuitively placed the firefighter on a heroic pedestal, the same place Rachel used to keep him.

Josh's antics threatened to unnerve her. If the boy was nearby, Vic was at the forefront of her mind, reminding her that the knight no longer rode upon his great white steed.

~~

Sarah joined forces with Josh by asking tough questions. One Sunday afternoon the sisters lounged in the family room, sipping decaf iced tea while Sarah nursed the baby. David had taken the older children to the neighborhood club for a swim.

"Rache, are you avoiding Vic?"

She shrugged. "I just need a little space."

"But I know how you guys always talk at home. He's called me four times while you're out and says your cell phone isn't on. He leaves messages on our machine that make it sound as if you haven't called him back."

"I call him back, but you know how crazy his schedule is. Between that and the two-hour time difference, I sometimes don't catch up with him."

"The only time you called him *right* back was when he asked me to tell you that woman Ellen had died."

That had gotten her attention. The sudden death of his high school friend Ellen Hamilton stunned both of them. No cause of death had been listed in the newspaper. Vic felt guilty for not opening more of her letters. Rachel sympathized with him, but Bryan remained convinced the mail had only contained more hurtful verbiage.

"Rachel, did you at least thank him personally for the flowers?"

"Yes, I thanked him personally for the flowers."

"I can't believe he still sends you flowers every twelfth day of the month. So why don't you keep your cell on?"

"It's my time with the kids." *Or my alone time.* She had begun taking long, solitary walks at the beach, asking God what had happened to her dragon slayer, her knight. Was it just a natural progression after so many years together? Had she knocked the pedestal out from under him because he didn't fully support her desire to have a baby?

"Rache!" Sarah broke into her reverie.

"What?"

"What's really going on?"

She squirmed in her seat. She was Sarah's big sister, not the other way around. "I'm feeling...annoyed."

"*Annoyed?*" She lifted the baby to her shoulder and made a breathy *phew* noise of disbelief through her lips. "Yeah, right. Listen, sis, I grew up with you. If you're annoyed, you say so. You don't avoid."

"Well, this is different. Somehow."

She sighed. "How about we pretend I'm you and you're Bubbie? What would Bubbie say to you in this situation?"

She frowned. She really didn't like playing the little sister, but she owed Sarah an explanation for two reasons. One, they were close. And two, the accurate observations she'd made meant Rachel and Vic's self-acclaimed Christian marriage lay exposed to a critical eye. Ignoring Sarah's challenge would announce that believers didn't deal with real-life problems.

"All right." Rachel conjured up an image of their feisty little grandmother and listened for the thick German accent. "Vhat is your problem, little one?"

Sarah rocked, gently rubbing the baby's back. "I resent Vic for not wanting a baby."

Rachel's stomach somersaulted. "Resent..." The accent faded. She swallowed and wrapped her tongue around it again. "Resent is a strong vord. Did he not try as hard as you? Go to the doctor's appointments? Do as he was told?"

"He did, but he just wasn't *totally* into it. You know what I mean? And I blame him."

"It is not—it is not his fault."

"Then whose fault is it?"

"No one's, but God is responsible."

"Didn't we pray enough?"

"Of course you prayed enough. God answered no."

"Then I resent Him too."

"Then, little one, you are sick at heart." Rachel blinked back tears. "But you vill get better. God is in the healing business even when He says no."

"Where does that leave me with Vic?"

She hesitated. "Your love has not died, just your dream to have a child."

Sarah lowered baby Jacob and settled him against her breast. He began nursing again as she continued speaking from Rachel's perspective. "Maybe Vic and I should, like, redefine our relationship."

"Redefine?"

"Yeah. For years we were this cool couple dancing down Easy Street with plenty of time for romantic vacations and total commitments to our careers. Then we were this sweet couple trying to have a baby, working with an infertility specialist. Heartache of heartaches! Now we're this lost couple, very likely facing a childless future unless God intervenes. We need to let go of the word *lost.* Maybe replace it with some other adjective."

"Sarah," Rachel said in surprise, dropping the accent. "Is that how you've seen us?"

She looked up and met her sister's gaze. "Yes. Rache, I am so sorry you haven't been able to conceive a baby, but it is not a curse. It is not a stigma. It is not the end of the world. If you and Vic remain lost, then I'm lost because there's no one else who can show me the way like you two do."

The weight of her words multiplied the heaviness in Rachel's heart. Her little sister asked too much.

Fourteen

Four weeks after her arrival in La Jolla, Vic left a voice mail message that cut her to the quick.

"Rache, I have to tell you something while it's fresh in my mind. It won't keep!"

She recognized his upbeat tone. Either the fireman had just prevented a building from annihilation, or the evangelist had told someone about the Lord.

"I was praying about us." He chuckled. "Naturally."

The evangelist spoke.

"And it suddenly came to me. You know how I keep asking why I'm not enough for you? Well, I'm not supposed to be enough! That's God's role. That's why you had to get away from me, to find your place in Him again, like you were before we met. Totally dependent on Him. The frog told me."

Frog?

He chuckled. "You know that little ceramic one you had before we got married? It's been on our shelf all these years, but I haven't noticed it since I don't know when. While I was praying I saw it and remembered what you told me: fully relying on God. F-R-O-G. That was you."

He paused for a breath, and when he spoke again his voice was softer, his words less rushed. "Maybe I was interfering with

154

that relationship. Anyway, I just want you to know that it all makes better sense now, why you had to leave. Talk to you later. Love you, baby."

She shook her head and turned off the cell phone. "I suppose that was a nudge from You?"

Setting the phone down on the bed, she noticed her reflection in the mirrored closet doors. Her face appeared gaunt. She'd lost weight. What was it? The nutritious diet? Or the fear and resentment she'd allowed to take root in her heart over the past months? She didn't much care for her God, her husband, or herself.

And that left her feeling ashamed.

She wasn't ready yet to talk to Vic about frogs and separations.

⁓

Three days later, still not having talked with him, Rachel sat on a park bench, watching Becka and Josh play. An assemblage of slides, steps, swings, cubbyholes, and various bars made up an intricate piece of equipment, the likes of which would never be found in playgrounds near her home. It was painted in bright primary colors and, like everything else in the wealthy neighborhood, appeared brand-new and was always deluged in warm sunlight.

She clasped her hands tightly in her lap and took deep breaths. Earlier that morning she had been unable to find her diamond bracelet. With horror she realized she could not remember when she had last seen it. The more it interfered with cooking, cleaning, changing diapers, and playing with fire trucks, the less she had worn it.

She ranted and raved and cried and curled up in a fetal position, devastated at the thought she'd lost the jewelry.

Although she did not especially care for diamonds, the bracelet represented a slim thread of proof that Vic loved her mightily, that he would never give up on her. Her illogical, extreme reaction squelched the hope that she was anywhere near mending. No, she remained pathetically fragile, an adjective she despised, especially when used to describe herself.

Becka eventually found the bracelet behind the nightstand, her inquisitive mind and tiny hand doing the work a panicked Rachel could not even begin to tackle. Hours later she still felt in turmoil, alienated from her husband and God.

I'm sorry, Lord. I know You know what's best! But help me! Help me to accept that!

She had uttered the prayer for the first time on one of her solitary walks last week. Her words bounced like tennis balls against the iridescent blue sky with a hollow sounding *whunk*. Why didn't He answer?

Nearby voices rose in volume, above that of a park full of laughing, shouting children. Two young women walked over to a bench not far from hers. Eavesdropping was not a choice. Their loud conversation drowned out her own internal dialogue.

"I've had it with him! This was the last straw."

"At least he's home nights. Ron ships out on Wednesday for six months."

"At least you knew he was in the Navy when you married him. You knew what that entailed."

"And you knew Todd was a software genius with plans to change the world."

"But I didn't really understand what I was signing up for. Ninety-eight percent of him is consumed with work. The kids and I get what's left over. All I want is a little more time and attention. He could change his routine some, act somewhat interested in—"

Rachel stood abruptly and walked toward her niece and nephew, away from the plaintive tone, the woman's incessant nagging to remake her husband into something he wasn't created to—

I didn't really understand what I was signing up for...

"Yes, I did," she muttered to herself. "I *did*."

Vic had clearly laid out exactly what marrying him would mean. Firefighting was his life. His most intimate family was comprised of other firefighters who had even participated in his marriage proposal. He also lived freely in the realm of the Lord's passionate, unconditional love. To express that truth energized everything he did, not the least of which was the firemen's Bible study he'd initiated several years ago.

Yes, he loved her, but there were larger issues at stake for her hero. She was a moth drawn to the candle of his life already burning brightly with everything he needed. He didn't need a wife, then or now, let alone children. If anything, she had sidetracked *him*, especially in recent months, from his true self.

She had recognized he was a genuine hero ten years ago on the day they met. Even then she discerned somewhere deep within herself that heroes followed a higher calling. Dragon slayers spent themselves fighting evil. Fearless knights went home to the little woman only after the battle had been won.

Out of his love for her, Vic had tried to accommodate her. She hadn't consciously meant to run herself ragged and pass out on his birthday, thereby gaining his sympathy. Subconsciously, though, she manipulated him. He didn't share her dream to be a parent. By pressing him through the arduous months of testing, she was asking him to dismantle the essence of who he was. By withdrawing from him now, she was punishing him for simply being himself.

How could she have been so foolish?

She called out to the children, cutting short their playtime before the lament mounting in her lungs wailed forth right there in front of God and everyone.

⁓

When her tears dried, Rachel sat in the middle of her bed, knees drawn to her chest, and phoned Vic. He didn't answer his cell, but she left a message that he call no matter what time of the night. She tried their home number with the same result. At last she dialed the fire station. He was out on a call. She didn't know he was on duty today. Had she even lost track of his schedule?

Too distraught to do anything but wait for him to call her back, she crawled under the covers. An old fear surfaced, one from the early days of their marriage, the time before she had learned how to leave his safety in God's hand. What if he didn't come back? The words echoed. *What if he didn't come back?* What if she never got the chance to tell him how much she truly loved him? To apologize for what she'd put him through?

At last she fell asleep, cheeks still damp, Isaiah 43 still on her lips, the verse she had memorized nearly ten years ago and turned into a prayer for her husband. "Do not be afraid, for I have redeemed you; I have called you by name, you are mine. Should you pass through the sea, I will be with you; or through rivers, they will not swallow you up. Should you walk through fire, you will not be scorched and the flames will not burn you..."

⁓

The room was dark when the phone, tightly clutched in her hand, finally rang.

"Vic?"

"Hi, baby. Sorry it's so late."

She glanced at the red digits on the bedside clock. Eleven-forty. One-forty in the morning his time.

"We had back-to-back calls." His voice was pumped, the adrenaline flowing as it always did after fighting the battle. "The second was a three-alarm on an empty warehouse. Probably arson."

"Is everyone all right?"

"Yeah. What's up? You left messages all over the place. Is Jacob okay?"

He thought of the baby, even remembered his name. Vic, her hero, slayer of dragons, brave defender, gallant victor.

The fogginess of sleep dissipated as the afternoon's convictions charged again to the forefront of her mind. "Oh, Vic! I'm so sorry!"

"For what?"

"For everything! For trying to make you into something you're not. For not being satisfied with what we have, with who we are together. For sidetracking you from the important things in your life."

"Rache—"

"Let me finish! Everyone has been telling me, but it's like I was deaf. All Josh can talk about is Unca Bic, and he never stops playing with his fire trucks. He keeps reminding me you are my hero, and I'd forgotten. I'd forgotten, Vic! Sarah points out I'm not living by this great faith I claim I have. Even Bubbie reminds me God can heal anything. And then today, these two women were talking, kvetching right and left about their husbands, whining that the men weren't who their wives wanted them to be. And I'm sitting there thinking, oh, grow up. Your husbands are just being true to themselves. Maybe if you'd support them instead of fighting them at every turn—"

"Whoa, slow down, Rache!"

"Oh, Vic! Will you ever forgive me? I've been so distant and not just geographically. I've been undermining who you are. And I've been blaming you that I'm not pregnant!"

He let her ramble on until she'd exhausted her supply of pent-up emotions.

"Rachel, Rachel. There's nothing to forgive. We've been through a rough time of it. It's natural for you to blame me, especially since I wasn't totally supportive. Will you forgive me?"

"There's nothing to forgive."

"I think that means we're even." He chuckled. "I hope this means you're finally ready to see me?"

She began crying softly. There was nothing else she wanted in the entire world other than to see him.

His voice grew raspy as they talked for over an hour. "Rache, I thought I was losing you this winter."

"I know I gave that impression. I'm sorry."

"Maybe it was something we had to go through. To make us stronger."

"Maybe."

"What's happening with your ticking clock? And that dream?"

"The dream hasn't come back."

So vivid was that dream of holding a baby and seeing Vic laugh, she could remember the last time she had it: the night before the final visit with the infertility specialist. Perhaps it fled her unconscious mind along with the last shred of hope.

She closed her eyes. "The clock...it's still there." A deep sigh heaved her chest. "I want a baby. Oh, why doesn't He just take it away?"

"I think..." He paused. "I think He has something else in mind."

"Like what?"

"I don't know."

She heard an odd rhythm in his voice. "Vic, what's wrong?"

"Nothing's *wrong*." Again he hesitated. "I have to tell you about a...a development. But not over the phone."

Like a cloud that floats lazily beneath the hot summer sun, blanketing the otherwise bright earth in a shroud, a shadow inched its way across her heart. A stillness settled about her. "A development you can't talk about," she repeated. "Does that mean it's extremely good or extremely bad?"

"I can't say."

"Can't or won't?"

"Rache." Weariness laced his voice. "I can't. We have to figure it out together when I get there."

"Vic." Fear clutched her throat. "We always stay current."

For a moment only the sound of his breathing filled the ear piece. And then he said, "Gotta bend the rule this time. I'm sorry."

"But you won't be here for another two weeks!"

"Surprise. I'm coming Sunday."

"Sunday!" Relief flooded her. "Four days? No! It's already Thursday morning. That makes it three days! Oh, I'm so glad you're coming early."

"And I'm so glad to hear that. I still had doubts you were ready."

"I honestly don't know if I was ready before now."

Her words hung between them, their impact revealing how far gone she had been. "Vic, I never stopped loving you. There was never a doubt about my love."

"Thank You." He whispered it with such respect she suspected he wasn't speaking to her.

"Hon, I am stronger now than I was when I left home. I know I can handle whatever it is that's going on. Please don't leave me hanging even for three days. You never do this."

"This time I have to, baby. It's too involved of a subject. I'll see you soon enough. Okay?" His voice was fading. He was clearly exhausted.

We'll always stay current. That shadow hovered. "Okay. You better sleep."

"Yeah. I'm off tomorrow, but I traded shifts in order to get the vacation time. Which means I work Friday. The flight arrives at two Sunday afternoon. I'll call if anything changes."

"All right." She would keep the cell phone with her, its power on.

"I love you, Rachel. More than ever."

"And I love you, Vic Koski."

She waited to hear the dial tone before she regretfully pushed the "end" button. Blinking back tears, she plugged the cell into the battery charger.

Wide awake now, she slipped on a light robe and stepped through the sliding door. The patio flagstones were cool beneath her bare feet. The coastal humidity enveloped her in a luscious mantle of eucalyptus, gardenia, and a thousand other floral scents. A dense marine layer of moist haze obscured the stars. An occasional indistinct whoosh reached her ears as she stood facing the direction of the ocean far below.

Something wasn't right. Vic had never forewarned her like that, saying there was something to discuss but it had to wait.

He always did his best to explain what was on his mind. Why was he breaking his own rule?

Before her imagination inundated her with fear and doubt, she fixed her mind on the fact that Yeshua was the keeper of all knowledge. He knew what was going on with Vic.

A spark of hope ignited. Maybe, just maybe, he wanted to discuss adoption!

⌒

"What do you think, Sarah?" Rachel twirled before the full-length mirrored closet door.

"You look fantastic in both of them." Her sister sat nearby, contented Jacob settling in for a nap against her shoulder. "The black is striking, but I like the easy breezy style of this chartreuse one. And the color is absolutely perfect for us."

Rachel laughed. "You can borrow it."

"Yeah, right. Maybe in two years. *If* I exercise. You look great in it. If you can't keep both, I vote for this one."

They were in Rachel's room late Saturday morning, giggling like a couple of teenagers over her shopping spree. David had taken the older children to the beach.

"Okay, the green dress it is. Oh, check out these shoes." She went to the bed and opened another box. "Ta-da!"

"They match! Ouch! Those heels! Rache, you're going to hurt yourself."

"Vic will like them. Do you think he'll like my hair?" She turned again to the mirror and touched where waves used to be.

"It's only a teensy bit shorter, a perfect length for you."

"I can't believe you pay that much for every haircut. Anyway, what am I forgetting?"

Sarah held out a hand, numbering with her fingers. "Hair, dress, *and* shoes. Reservation for one night at the Hotel Del. Dinner reservations at The Top of the Cove tomorrow night. My car at your disposal."

"You're sure?"

"As Bubbie would say, stop with that question already! We'll be fine with one car on Monday. The kids and I have no plans to go out. Now, are you absolutely sure you don't want to stay two nights?"

"Yes. I went all out as it is. It's such a grand, gorgeous hotel and right on the ocean, the price is worth it. For *one* night. Okay. I think that covers everything."

"How about slinky nightie? I told you to get one."

"That doesn't mean I have to show it to you."

"Come on, Rache! You're living out my fantasy here. Let me see it."

She giggled and retrieved another bag from the bed. "Was that the doorbell?"

"I think so."

"Here." Passing by Sarah, she handed her the bag. "I am *not* trying it on. I'll see who's at the door."

She strode through the sprawling house. Its contemporary open style gave her a view of the foyer and front doors from the hallway even before she entered the living room. The wide, double interior doors stood open on the sunny summer day. Clear glass exterior doors revealed blue sky, the circular drive, lush vegetation…and a priest.

Bryan! Rachel smiled and increased her pace. She hadn't known he planned on being in town. Vic must have forgotten to mention it on the phone the other night. Why hadn't Bryan called? Maybe he—

The answer came, hitting her senses like a flash of lightning, a boom of thunder, the roar of tornado-force winds.

No one will call. Someone will come to tell you. The fire chief. And Bryan...Bryan will come...

She halted in the center of the room, covering her mouth with her hands and shaking her head.

Tears streamed from Bryan's eyes.

Sarah spoke from behind her. "Rachel? Oh, dear God—"

Time paused. Her lungs forgot to breathe, her heart to beat. Seconds stretched into eternal moments.

Sarah stood before her. Horror widened her eyes. Then it raised her brows, creased her forehead, distorted her mouth. She moved away.

Now Bryan filled Rachel's vision.

Air slammed back into her lungs, ripping away the breath it should have given. Like a racehorse bursting through the starting gate, her heart pounded. Its beats ricocheted violently, straining at the confines of her chest.

As her knees gave way, Bryan sank beside her to the floor, his shoulder catching her first sob.

Fifteen

Rachel had always imagined Vic's death would plunge her into a black hole, a numbing abyss that swallowed all sense of awareness, sight, taste, touch, smell, hearing... It didn't happen that way. On the contrary, horror intensified her faculties.

Still on the floor where she had first sunk, she huddled on her knees with Sarah and Bryan. Her sister held her from behind, around her waist. Feminine, motherly arms that cradled. Bryan's arms engulfed her. Big Irishman arms. Freckled forearms hidden under black sleeves. His jacket absorbed her tears, its summer-weight wool rough against her face. It smelled faintly of the cherry tobacco he liked to tamp into his seldom-smoked pipe. The edge of the price tag still attached to the new dress she wore scratched the underside of her arm.

Like some superficial refrain punctuating the stanzas of a bad poem, a prayer repeated itself. A senseless prayer really. Senseless because eons ago, in the murky cosmos where past, present, and future existed together, it had already been answered in the negative. *Lord, please don't ask this of me!*

She clutched Bryan's jacket, balling it up in her fists, and understood for the first time how her ancestors could rend their own clothes in despair.

Bryan hadn't yet said the awful words. What was the point? She knew Vic was gone.

Rachel looked up at him and choked out one word. "How?"

Sunshine flowed through the skylight in the ceiling above him. A pool of gold shone through his wild red hair and glistened in the flood of tears in his green eyes. His weathered face had aged.

"Later, Rachel. Just take one thing at a time. The details can wait."

Could it be worse than anything she hadn't already imagined at one time or another over the past ten years? "In a fire? Has his body been found? His *remains?* Tell me, Bryan!"

Sarah hugged more tightly. "Shh."

Bryan pressed her face against him again and began speaking in a low monotone, his voice scarcely above a whisper. "It was smoke inhalation."

Relief flickered momentarily. His body wasn't burned. *Should you walk through the fire, you will not be scorched.* He had always told her it wouldn't matter; he'd be getting a new body anyway. She disagreed. It mattered to her.

"An old office building caught on fire. Shawn Leonard got lost on the fifth floor, in heavy smoke. Vic went back in to find him. He saved his life, Rachel. He saved his life."

Bryan cried quietly with her, a silent tribute to the indisputable fact: Vic willingly sacrificed his life for another. Neither of them would ever question why he had made that choice. It was quite simply what made Vic Koski who he was.

"The rescue guys pulled Shawn into the stairwell. Vic got stuck somehow. They didn't know it until a few minutes later. They think cables fell from the ceiling, trapping him."

She clutched his jacket more tightly. Behind her, Sarah moaned.

"They got...they got him out in time. But his mask was gone. He'd been breathing toxic gases..." His shoulders heaved. "Terri called me right away. I called his parents. Took them to the hospital, about four this morning. We saw him... The doctor knew he..."

Fresh sobs broke, shaking him. With effort, he regained control. "I went straight to the airport. I called the hospital just now, from the taxi. He never regained consciousness. He died...thirty minutes ago."

~

When a wave of nausea hit, she stumbled to the bathroom and was sick. Then she curled onto the rug and wailed into a thick bath towel, scraping her vocal cords raw, stopping only when they refused to emit any more sound. Her body ached. She struggled to her feet and held onto the vanity until her wobbly legs took hold.

Lord, please don't ask this of me! Please!

Out in her bedroom, she found Sarah talking on the phone. She sat on the bed, near Jacob sleeping in the center of it.

Her sister said into the phone, "Hurry home, honey." She clicked off the phone, set it aside, and stood. Her eyes were swollen. "Rache, do you want to get out of that dress?"

Rachel looked down at the soft folds of the green dress. It wasn't even wrinkled. Nice fabric.

Sarah walked behind her and began unzipping. "Let me help. David will be here soon; he's taking the children to a friend's. Bryan's on the patio. A, um, San Diego fire chief came. Bryan explained the situation and begged off for you."

Rachel nodded absently. Because she was out of town, the Chicago Fire Department would have called the local department so that they would send someone to personally notify her. A spouse might hear the news from a stranger, but not from the television. *Thank You, Lord, for sending Bryan in time.*

With Sarah's hands guiding, she stepped out of the new dress. Perhaps the initial shock would shed itself with that act. At least she would not have to wear the dress again and think of what had happened the last time she wore it. She slipped into capris and a cotton blouse.

Sarah said, "A fireman came with the chief. He remembered meeting Vic at his station here. Just like Vic, huh? Making such an impression the guy recognized his name. He promised to come to the—" She burst into tears.

Funeral, Rachel completed the sentence as she cried anew in Sarah's embrace. Firefighters would indeed travel such distances to pay their respects...

Bryan sat outside in the shade of a patio umbrella. The noonday sun beat mercilessly against its bright coral top. Rachel sat on a cushioned chair and reached across the table for his hand, the hand that had undoubtedly touched her husband just hours ago.

He squeezed gently. His ruddy complexion had returned, as if he'd just scrubbed his face as she had. He'd removed his coat, revealing a short-sleeved black shirt.

He said, "I don't want it to go without saying. I am so sorry."

She nodded, studying the large-faced watch on his freckled wrist. He must not have changed it from central time because the hands indicated the time was about 2 o'clock. It must only be noon in California. When he rang the doorbell, the time must have been close to 11. Vic's death occurred 30 minutes before that, 10:30 California time. Twelve-thirty Illinois time. Half an hour from now, California time. *Lord, please turn back the clock—*

"Rachel?"

Noon. She'd known, then, for just over an hour. Just over an hour? She'd known for ten *years—*

"Rachel."

She started.

"Do you want to talk about going home?"

She took a tissue from a box on the table and held it to her eyes. Just like in the church sanctuary, where the pastor's wife strategically placed boxes to encourage worshipers to let the tears flow, whether from sheer joy or agony—

"Rachel."

"Okay. Home. Talk about home."

"I have us booked on a five o'clock flight. If that's too soon, we can take the next one at ten-thirty tonight, but it makes two stops and doesn't put us in until seven tomorrow morning. If we don't go right away, I think it'd be better to sleep here."

Sleep? Inconceivable. "I want to go now. As soon as possible."

"All right." He glanced at his watch. "We should probably leave here in a couple of hours. All right," he said again. "What can I do to help? Make some calls?"

The tenderness on his face took her breath away. She knew it would be there from now on, knew he would do anything for her and Vic's family. Bryan's own grief would express itself by loving others. Those Yeshua vibes she'd always observed in him were more palpable than ever.

"I need…" She tried to clear her throat. Her voice sounded like a stranger's, low and hoarse. "I need to talk with Stan and Wanda right away."

He nodded.

They sat in silence for a long moment, and then she said, "Sylvia. Will you call Sylvia? And…" she took a labored breath, "and tell her?"

"Yes. How about your family?"

"I think Sarah…" Her sister's hands had shaken uncontrollably when she unzipped the dress. "David will call them."

Another silence.

"Bryan, why was Shawn Leonard working with Vic?" Shawn worked opposite shifts from Vic.

"A vacation-related schedule change."

It happened. Guys traded times to accommodate days off.

The what-ifs began then. What if the regular firefighter had been there instead of Shawn? What if Shawn hadn't gotten himself into such a predicament?

She asked, "Whose place was Shawn taking?"

"Shawn? No, it was the other way around. I meant *Vic* traded a shift with somebody in Shawn's unit."

Her stomach lurched. The tears that had been continuously seeping now flowed again.

Vic died because *he* had changed schedules. And he had done so in order to be with her.

⌒

"Rachel, it's not your fault. You are not responsible for Vic changing his schedule. Don't go there."

She grabbed another tissue from the box on the table. Vic's words replayed. *I traded shifts…I work Friday.*

"Don't go there," Bryan repeated. "We have a loving heavenly Father who does not put us there."

She cried, inconsolable.

Lord, please don't ask this of me!

And thus she entered the second hour.

∽

The succeeding hours blurred while some moments crystallized.

David's hug. Such a lean man compared to Vic.

Crying with Stan on the phone. His rationalization for Wanda refusing to speak with her. Imagining the couple with Ty, Ed, Max, and Sig, Vic's brothers, there at the hospital, all standing around his bedside as he breathed his last.

Sarah, swiftly choosing clothes from the closet and drawers, expertly folding and stuffing them into luggage, promising to ship what was left behind. Rachel, sitting nearby, hugging the framed photograph of Vic.

Kissing baby Jacob's downy cheek.

Leaving packages for the other children in their bedrooms. While shopping yesterday, she had purchased impromptu gifts, a book for Becka, a fire truck for Josh.

Sarah, urging her to take one of the prescription tranquilizers Sarah used before the pregnancy. Rachel refused. If she slept, she would only have to wake up again and remember. Bryan pocketed the bottle, murmuring "just in case."

Waiting at the airport, staring at the diamond bracelet on her wrist. Seeing Vic, so *alive* in her thoughts.

On the plane, Bryan steered her into a seat. They were in first class. She questioned him with a glance.

"Stan's paying."

Oh, Lord, bless my father-in-law.

She blinked rapidly, wondering if the man was still exactly that, her father-in-law. If not, then what was he? What was Wanda? What were his four brothers? Was she still an aunt to their children? They were all there together now, in Chicago, with Vic. But she, his wife, wasn't. Nor was his lifelong best friend.

"Bryan, you should have been with him."

"No, Rachel, no. My place is with you. I promised him, you know."

She shook her head. She hadn't known. "What—" She bit her lip. "What did he look like?"

He took her hand into his. "Asleep. With a bunch of machines hooked up to him. A little soot on his cheek." He smiled softly. "Frowning. Like he was arguing with Jesus about His lousy timing."

∽

Silence settled about them. Under other circumstances she would have called it a companionable silence. At the moment it was something deeper than companionable. It was more on the level of intuitive understanding. If she didn't trust that Bryan sat there willing her to keep breathing, she did not know if she could take the next breath.

Somewhere over the desert she turned to him. "Every breath feels as though I'm exposing some enormous, gaping wound to air. It's like I've been sliced in two."

His own eyes filled again. "Rachel, you and Vic were one. You have been sliced in two."

∽

When Bryan turned the car onto her block, she saw her house, the windows bright, the porch lights on. As they pulled into the driveway, the front door opened, spilling out more light as well as Sylvia...and Jessie...and Terri. Mentor, fellow teacher, paramedic. Her dearest friends.

And thus began the first night.

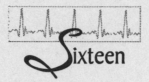

Sixteen

Pastor Payton Wills and his wife, Rosemarie, arrived with the dawn of the second day. Rachel watched them cross the backyard to where she sat on a lawn chair, her bare feet thrust into the dewy grass. Humidity thickened the early morning air. A handful of stars still winked in the navy blue sky.

Even if it weren't Sunday with an eight o'clock service pending, the couple would have come. In their early sixties with gray streaks in their brown hair, they were both unassuming in demeanor, always taking by surprise people who had heard their reputation as leaders of an energetic, cross-cultural church.

They spent the day.

"I've lost my son," Payton explained simply. The father of two grown daughters, he and Vic had shared an uncommon relationship, one that went beyond that of mentoring.

~

Late morning of that second day, Bryan accompanied Rachel through the worst.

The funeral home people said, "Wait. Wait until we've prepared the body, until it's in the casket."

"No." *I can't wait! I haven't seen him in nearly five weeks! I will not begin to comprehend until I see with my own eyes.*

Bryan added to her command, "Please."

And she lived through it. Perhaps God was, after all, still with her.

⁓

The horrifying initial moments with Stan, Wanda, and Vic's brothers followed. Rachel tried in vain to be swallowed up in that numbing abyss she had always imagined must exist for survivors at such a time. That place where stark details did not jump out and wrap themselves around one's soul.

The black cardigan that hung like a man's pajama top on Wanda's gaunt frame, enunciating a new frailty.

Stan's wide eyes and slack jaw, a shell-shocked expression totally incongruous with his usual policeman's visage.

The resemblance of Vic in his brother Ed's size...Max's ears...Sig's nose...Ty's smile.

Vic's absence intensifying as it always did at the family gatherings he missed.

Wanda's fingers dug into Rachel's forearm. "We should have done this *yesterday*, but no. You weren't even *here*."

Her sharp tone served as the jump start Rachel needed. Some emotional nuance shifted within her, sliding her into cruise control. There were specific tasks at hand. Yes. That was the focus now, not the living and breathing picture of tragedy before her.

They met with the funeral director and a liaison from the fire department, two absolute strangers who held the key to the Koski family's sanity. With it they unlocked a trunk load of formalities, a myriad of obligatory decisions. One by one, they steered the group through them in a compassionate manner.

Rachel leaned heavily on their expertise and avoided eye contact with her mother-in-law.

~

The evening of the second day, her older sister arrived at the house. Three years Rachel's elder, she was not as close to her as Sarah, and so she had waited on the sidelines until a more proper time before appearing.

"Rachel." Bits embraced her with long slender arms.

Originally named Elizabeth after their mother and called "Little Bess," the phrase had evolved to "Little Bits," which Rachel ultimately reduced to "Bits." Until this moment, that childhood chapter had been their strongest tie.

"I am so sorry, sweetheart. So very sorry. He was a good man." An air of efficiency quickly replaced her somber tears. Married to a bigwig of a giant corporation, she was, physically speaking, the most put-together woman Rachel personally knew. From her shoulder-length black hair and flawless skin to toned muscles and 24-carat gold around wrists, fingers, and neck, she was magazine cover material. And she majored on propriety, something Rachel lost sight of even on her best days.

"You'll need two black outfits," Bits announced and disappeared down the hall.

Rachel wished she could forgo the somber black and wear bright colors and stilettos.

"Rache," Vic had always said. "Death is just going Home. We'll take one step through an invisible veil, leave this life behind, and start living in heaven. Just imagine getting that first hug from Jesus! Man, I want my funeral to be full of laughter and every color of the rainbow."

But she could not comply. Her imagination shut down the moment she'd seen his lifeless body. Her attempts to envision a laughing, carefree Vic getting his first hug were futile. Instead, she perceived only the reality of the moment. The empty kitchen chair. The dried-out toothbrush. The robe hanging beneath hers on the bathroom door hook. The old loafers, size 12, waiting by the back door. The bed, far too large for one woman even once every three nights.

No. *I'm sorry, Lord. I believe, but I will not, I cannot celebrate this side of heaven.* She would wear black.

"Rachel." Bits entered the kitchen, a pair of black stilettos in one hand and a hanger bearing a black dress in the other. Her voice rolled compassion, chastisement, and inquiry into one tone.

The dress was the "little number" Rachel had worn to Vic's reunion last summer. "Yes," she answered the unspoken question, "that is the only black thing I own."

"Not a problem. I'll go shopping."

"I'll get you a check."

"No." Bits leaned forward and kissed her cheek. "My gift to you."

Such a blatant act of love from her sister caught Rachel unawares. For one fleeting moment she saw the hands of Yeshua liberally slather healing balm on her open wound.

~

Sunday night faded into Monday while Rachel sat on a webbed lounge chair in the backyard. The day's heat lingered, the air still heavy with humidity. Cicadas droned, crickets chirped, lightning bugs flashed, an occasional bat swooped overhead. Midnight stars shimmered in a navy blue sky, and she tried not to think about Vic's eyes.

Since returning from the funeral home, she had grabbed pockets of time to escape outdoors, away from a house too full of people and emotions. Either Sylvia or Terri must have dubbed it her "do not disturb" place because no one followed her out there. They probably thought she was praying.

She wasn't. Her prayer life shut down about the time her imagination shimmered to a blank.

Payton said, "Don't worry. There are hundreds doing it for you."

She wasn't so sure if that mattered.

The yard drew her, of course, because Vic was so proud of it. *Had been* so proud...

He loved mowing the grass, fertilizing and watering it until it felt as dense as a plush carpet. Flower beds had been added in recent years. Hollyhocks climbed the side of the detached garage that sat slightly behind the house. Gladiolas bloomed under windows. Hosta encircled the base of the oak tree. Annuals filled all the other available spaces.

Earlier one of Teague's sons had arrived to cut the grass. He'd blinked repeatedly when Rachel tried to pay him, explaining Lt. Koski had already done so, had hired him to care for the yard while he was in California.

She closed her eyes now, inhaling the scents heightened by the muggy air: alyssum, marigolds, pansies, petunias, and freshly cut grass.

Vic's fastidious side must have gone into overdrive. She'd noticed how clean everything was in the house, how orderly. Laundry hamper empty except for one shirt. Carpet vacuumed. The refrigerator had been nearly bare before the casseroles began arriving this morning. The newspaper and mail weren't delivered. He'd already stopped them. Yes, he was ready to leave, to join her...

Something nagged at the back of her mind, some thought violently shoved aside on Saturday at Bryan's arrival in California. She'd sensed it bobbing like a buoy, trying to get her attention, always disappearing beneath a wave of the present moment. What was it?

She had gone shopping on Friday, anticipating like a newlywed the imminent reunion with her husband. She had been so grateful at last to feel God's healing touch, to recognize that He was the giver of life, even if it meant infertility. Life held promise again, of what, she didn't know, but that was all right. Details did not matter at such points of renewal.

She didn't know… There had been something she did not know that day. It carried the feeling of something that could be avoided for a while, like an unpleasant medical test that would have to be faced eventually, but there was no need to worry in advance. What was it—

"*Nothing's wrong.*" She remembered Vic's words. They were some of the last he'd spoken to her. "*I have to tell you about a development, but not over the phone. We have to figure it out together when I get there.*"

When I get there…

She jerked as if a starting gun had exploded beside her. Her heart pounded against her ribcage.

～

"Bryan, do you have any clue at all what he was talking about?"

Rachel sat cross-legged on her bed, the cordless phone pressed to her ear and a thumb to her mouth. She chewed on the nail and listened to his breathing on the other end of the line. One A.M. The beginning of the third day. Conditions were not conducive to interpreting the nuances of how he breathed or how long he kept silent.

"Bryan!"

"I'm…trying to recall. Replaying conversations—"

"You would remember right off! It was *significant!* He would have said 'I can't tell her!' Did he say that?" Her voice rose above the sound of her heart thundering in her head. "Did he say anything like that?"

"He never said anything like that."

The thumbnail tore off between her teeth.

"Never. If something was between the two of you, it was between the two of you. You know how he was about the infertility testing. He told me everything, up to a certain point, and never out of order. You came first. That was his way."

She knew that.

"Rachel, I'm sorry I don't know. Maybe there's a clue there at the house. In his…his things?"

The silence hung again, suspending conversation. It was getting to be a common occurrence whenever they spoke.

"Have you asked Payton?"

"No."

"Call him."

"It's after one."

"You called me."

"I knew you'd be awake."

"Trust me, he is too."

~

"Rosie and I will come over."

"Payton! What is it? What couldn't he tell me over the phone?"

His fatherly sigh filled the line. "I don't know. I only know that he asked me to pray for something he needed to discuss with you. He didn't specify."

"That was all?"

"Yes. Almost the exact words he said to you."

She hopped from the bed and yanked open a dresser drawer. It contained Vic's socks. Rolled white athletic pairs, neatly folded dress argyles.

"He was devoted to you."

She swept her hand through the cottony stacks.

"Rachel, we'll come over."

"He broke his own rule, Payton. He broke his own stinking rule. And then he left me *not current.*" Socks spilled from the drawer onto the carpet. "How could he do this to me?"

Sylvia was there before she heard a step. "Honey, what is it?"

"I have to go through his things! I have to find out what he was talking about!"

"Rachel." Payton's voice in her ear.

She handed the phone to Sylvia and flung open another drawer.

~

Later that morning Rachel sat again in the yard. Because of the stifling heat, she'd moved the webbed lounge chair further back, under the shade of the oak tree. Its leaves filtered the sunlight and rustled in a faint, occasional breeze.

Vic had bought the house in August ten years ago, a few months before they married. They weren't even engaged at the time, but Rachel knew she could live with a kitchen that had a window above the sink overlooking a street full of tricycles, bikes, wagons, basketball hoops, and maple trees. For Vic, the majestic oak was the decision maker. It sat in a back corner where the alley ended and a green space for a new development began.

"Morning, Rachel."

She looked over her shoulder to see Bryan loping through the yard, carrying two large plastic tumblers probably filled with iced tea. Someone forgot to tell him about the "do not disturb" sign.

He handed her a glass. "Sorry to intrude. Mind if I grab a chair?" Not waiting for a reply, he loped back to the small patio and picked up a faded green resin chair.

As a matter of fact, she did mind. She retreated outside for only short periods when her polite facade threatened to crumble under the weight of others' grief.

Bryan lowered his bulk onto the flimsy chair and leaned forward, his elbows on his knees. Vic could never fit into that seat either.

"Get one of those wooden chairs."

"This is fine. Look, I *am* sorry to intrude."

She flinched. "I want to say you're not, but..."

"But I am."

"Why do I feel that way? It's so disgustingly self-centered. I hear this whining voice in my head. All I think of is me, me, me."

"It's natural right now. The pain—"

"No, it's not just right now. Think of last winter. That was all about Rachel wanting a baby. And taking off to California." Her voice took on a falsetto note as she mimicked having a two-way conversation with herself. "All about Rachel feeling sorry for herself, wanting to *find* herself like some angst-ridden adolescent. What about what Vic wanted? Oh, don't mind Vic. He'll do whatever you say because maybe he truly is wrapped around your little finger. You've so totally knocked the wind out of his sail, he can't even think straight."

She dropped the mocking tone. "Bryan, did I chase him away? Is that what he wanted to talk about? Did he find someone else?"

"Rachel." He shook his head. "I can't believe—well, yes, under the circumstances I can believe you'd say that. No. *That* I would have picked up on, even if he hadn't told me. You and I both would have picked up on it months, if not years, ago. Such a thing doesn't spring to life over one issue during a three-month time frame."

She traced a finger through the condensation on the yellow plastic cup.

"It's natural, Rachel. You need to grieve, and that's a very personal thing with not much energy left over for others."

"What happened to supernatural? What happened to my faith?" She looked at him.

His head hung as he toyed with the tumbler between his hands. "It's the same place as mine." He glanced at her. "It's like it's gone underground."

If asked if her heart could break any more than it already had, she would have replied no. Looking at her friend's face now, she realized that wasn't true. Hearts did not break in the same way a twig snapped off a tree. The breaking continued, almost in slow motion. She had heard about debridement, the agonizing process of removing burnt skin. It was more like that, an endless ripping away at an open wound. Without the benefit of morphine.

Seeing the sorrow on the face of her husband's best friend felt like that.

Bryan said, "I keep asking God why. I mean, I'm a priest. He should tell me these things. I have to know these things. And to think that I've actually counseled people, like I knew what I was talking about." He paused. "You know Terri's watching us."

She nodded.

"I have to remind myself that He did not promise we would not know pain. And in spite of it all, He is faithful, Rachel. He will somehow glorify Himself in this, and Terri will see that."

"I can't even say that. I want to tell Terri that he's alive, that he's happy. But then I feel like who cares? I'm a walking dead person who cannot imagine ever smiling again. And that brings us right back to pure selfishness."

Long silent moments passed. She stared at the trunk of the oak and sipped the cold tea, wondering if she could ask for morphine instead of caffeine.

"Rachel, Sylvia told me you talked to Payton and went through Vic's things last night. And found nothing."

She shrugged.

"I thought of something." He noticed her expression. "No, I'm sorry. I didn't mean to get your hopes up."

She hated being so readable.

"I don't think it's related. It's just a conversation that came to mind. He told me about Ruth's last moments."

She thought back to her grandmother's room at the nursing home. Her family gathered around her. Vic kissing her cheek. Bubbie *speaking*. "She said something to him."

"About going Home. You both thought, of course, that she spoke of heaven. That it was time for her to go. Vic." He paused. "Vic heard more or imagined he heard more. He asked my opinion. She said, 'Time for *you* to go Home.'"

Rachel stared at him.

"They say Kennedy dreamt of attending his own funeral shortly before he went to Dallas. I think Vic knew. Not the time or the place or the how. Not so he would worry or try to prevent what wasn't preventable."

"Then why? He lived every day of his life with that truth before him. He always kept in mind that he could go Home at any moment, and he was ready."

"Maybe, if your Bubbie really said that, maybe there was a pocket of fear somewhere in him, and he needed to hear directly that God truly did have a place for him."

"But why didn't he tell me?"

"Like I said, he wasn't sure he heard correctly. At any rate, would your fears have dissolved if you'd known?"

"Hardly. I guess that answers my question why he wouldn't mention it. But you don't think that was what he wanted to talk about?"

"No. There was nothing to talk about."

More long quiet moments ticked away. A small breeze cooled the perspiration at her neck.

"Bryan, his death didn't...didn't...surprise me."

A sad smile crinkled his red-rimmed eyes. "Me neither."

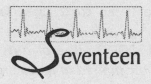

Seventeen

Sylvia, Jessie, and Terri took turns spending the night with her, sleeping in the spare bedroom.

Rachel did not sleep. She took fitful naps between midnight and dawn, waking countless times with a pounding heart, knowing exactly where she was and what had happened. She was afraid a deep sleep would erase that knowledge. When she awoke, she would have to begin assimilating it all over again. Three steps forward, four steps back. Maybe five.

Tuesday night was Terri's turn. They sat down in the kitchen. A few wives of the firemen from Vic's company had just left.

Rachel stifled a yawn. "I'm going to make some coffee. Do you want some?"

Terri dropped her caring paramedic's expression and nailed her with the look that Rachel always thought belonged on a cop.

"No coffee for you or me. It's after eleven." She went to a cupboard and pulled out a medicine bottle. "Bryan left these."

"I don't want Sarah's prescribed tranquilizers. Isn't that against the law? Besides, I don't want to wake up groggy and start the—the *process* all over again."

Her friend sighed and sat back down. "Rachel, you won't make it through the next two days if you don't get a good night's sleep. I'll be picking you up off the ground again."

She blinked in reply.

"Have you ever been to a Class One LODD funeral before?"

Rachel winced. *LODD…line of duty death. Class One death…includes those injured at an emergency incident and later die as a result of those injuries.* She'd spent the past two days learning details conveyed by a funeral coordinator assigned by the department to work with her. The event would not be a simple two-hour visitation, a 30-minute church service, a hearse, a couple of limos for the immediate family…

"No, I never went with Vic to one."

"It's an endurance test, and you're not ready." She was definitely in cop mode. "Let's see." She read the label. "These are fine. Just your common, low-dose nighty-night pills. It says 'do not operate machinery.' No problem there. 'Do not take if pregnant or nursing.' I know you're not nursing." She looked at her. "Any possibility you're pregnant?" Her voice had softened.

A deluge of pain swamped Rachel. Waves of shame, anger, frustration, and defeat flushed her skin, jumbled her thoughts. Memories darted through her mind. Vic's birthday party. Terri, her face sideways in the grass, asking that very same question. The infertility doctor. The all-consuming desire to hold a child that had Vic's big ears, his infectious laugh. The cruelty of that dream being snatched away in a heartbeat.

Terri touched her hand. "It's the fourteenth. When did you last start your cycle?"

"The…the…" Her mind refused to focus. "It comes like clockwork, every four weeks. Around the fifth or sixth."

"So you had it last week?"

She shook her head. "I had it last month, soon after school was out. It was different. Kind of light. I blamed it on stress. I mean, stress never affected it before, but then I'd never left my husband before."

"You didn't leave him."

"Somewhere deep inside I did, though I knew it was temporary."

"Well, however you want to phrase it... And now this month... Your stress level has got to be off the charts. But still..." Terri's brown eyes conveyed a thought neither wanted to say aloud. She set aside the bottle. "Sylvia left some special herbal tea, supposedly it promotes a good night's sleep. Will you try some?"

"All right." The unspoken thought tiptoed around her mind like a kitten prepping a spot in which to settle. She felt its warm breath. "Terri, is it possible?"

Her friend looked thoughtful. "My younger sister had the same experience with both her kids. Thought her cycle was off for one reason or another. She was three months along before she realized she was pregnant."

"But still, she didn't have a major issue with her husband, did she? He didn't die."

"No. No, he didn't die."

"It's probably the stress."

"Probably."

The kitten stilled, flattened its ears, and darted off.

⁓

Wearing the new black dress her sister had purchased and a strand of her sister's genuine pearls, Rachel stood near the casket, again grateful that not a hair of Vic's thick brown hair had been singed. Except for his five o'clock shadow, his coloring was a surrealistic shade. But his body was clothed in his navy blue dress uniform, buttons twinkling on his broad chest.

To her left, on the other side of Stan, someone lingered with Wanda. Her father-in-law touched her shoulder. "It's satisfying."

She exchanged a tiny smile with him. It was her first since Saturday morning. "It is satisfying."

Everywhere she looked there were flowers. The room smelled like a greenhouse, its damp air heavy with the scents of potted plants and blossoms: lilies, carnations, mums. Lined up the other side of Wanda were Vic's brothers, all four of them resembling him in some way. His large ears, his strong chin, his height, his mouth. Scattered about were her parents, Bram and his family, Bits and hers. Sarah was missing because no one wanted the baby to fly, but David was there with Josh. The little boy had grasped an idea beyond his age and insisted on saying goodbye to Unca Bic.

Behind the casket four flags were displayed, those of the United States, Illinois, Chicago, and the Chicago Fire Department. Directly across from her stood an honor guard member. Just outside the double doors were two more as well the fire chief.

As expected, the line of mourners extended out through the funeral home's front door and down the block. The visitation was scheduled to last from 12 noon until 7. Vic belonged to the community and the community came. His immediate family included thousands in a nationwide brotherhood, many who would travel great distances to attend. He had made personal friends in New York City, traveling there twice after September 11. If at all possible, they would honor him with their presence. At five o'clock the walk-through would occur, when all the firefighters present would pass by.

Stan went on, "I had no idea so many people knew my son. And we haven't even seen the guys yet. Mostly we've seen church people." He paused, looking down at the floor, obviously trying to get his voice under control. "They all tell me things like he was a real-life Jesus to them. And then that whole slew of teenage boys talking about his camping trips and how their lives haven't been the same since. I-I never understood his faith."

Rachel squeezed his arm. What was there to say? She wasn't so sure she understood it anymore either.

The line moved again, and he became distracted.

Bryan kept urging her to take more breaks, to sit, but something energized her. Perhaps it was those stories which she too had been hearing, accompanied by the hugs of fellow believers. Perhaps it was the compassion poured in her direction from not only friends but from total strangers. Perhaps it was the full impact of Vic's life all lumped into one afternoon. Perhaps it was the beautiful formality that so overtly recognized her hero as a hero.

Whatever the source, she had been given much and was being sustained through the nightmare. Unlike Wanda.

She glanced now beyond Stan to Wanda and felt an overwhelming desire to hold her, to loosen the shrink-wrap that held her emotions staunchly in check. She had yet to shed a tear in Rachel's presence. That wasn't right. The two most important women of Vic's life should comfort one another. *Lord, help me make the first move.*

Had Rachel been too mouthy during the funeral planning? While Wanda nitpicked about everything from chrysanthemums to the pastor's sermon, Rachel asserted her role as wife, at times ungraciously. *For this reason a man shall leave his mother...* There were certain things she knew about Vic that Wanda could not know. His faith had changed him in radical ways that the woman refused to acknowledge. Rachel had the last say, and in so doing she handed her mother-in-law one major grudge on a silver platter.

Rachel went behind Stan and politely excused herself to someone who was speaking. "Wanda."

Wanda turned and Rachel enveloped her in her arms and held tightly, refusing to let go. At last she felt a shudder go through the narrow body and heard the weeping begin. After a few moments, Rachel looked down into her face.

"Wanda, I love you." Even as she spoke, she knew she said the words out of obedience, not emotion.

The small woman's eyes narrowed. "You think that makes everything all right? You killed my son! If you'd been here where you were supposed to be, this never would have happened. I will never, *ever* forgive you!"

Rachel backed away, the hissed words resounding in her head.

Once again Wanda Koski had managed to reach deep into the secret places of Rachel's heart and yank out that which haunted her most.

∾

"Sylvia, I'll be fine tonight. Please, go home and sleep in your own bed." She linked her elbow through her friend's as they walked slowly across the nearly deserted parking lot of the funeral home. Twilight had settled, the visitation going long past what had been scheduled.

"Nonsense. There's no one waiting for me there." Her twin daughters were grown with families of their own. Her husband had left her when they were babies. "Besides, I promised your sister I'd be there in the morning to make sure you pour your feet back into those pumps. And I know you. If I don't stay, you'll be up and ready by the crack of dawn, wearing that new black suit and your brown oxfords."

Rachel didn't reply to the gentle teasing. Sylvia and Bits had connected right off the bat. They would see her through the details of propriety. Since Wanda's lashing out, she was only going through the motions.

"Mrs. Koski! Mrs. Koski!"

They stopped and Rachel turned to see people approaching, a couple and three small children. The man wore a fireman's uniform.

"Mrs. Koski." He stretched his hand toward her.

They had never met, but she knew him. She felt herself gawking, surprised to see such a fresh, all-American face. What had she expected? An evil Simon Legree? Someone easy to despise? *I'm not responsible, Wanda. This guy is.* "You're Shawn Leonard."

"I'm sorry."

She put her hand into his.

"This—this is my wife, Jody." He sniffed.

The petite woman resembled him, late twenties, cute, dark blonde hair, cheeks dimpled even without a smile.

"And our children. Zak, Cammie, and Seth." Three smaller versions of the parents. Three cherubs.

"Mrs. Koski," Jody whispered.

She saw then in the dim light the tears streaming down the young woman's face.

Of course Vic would have known. He knew the personal business about everyone at the firehouse. Within 60 seconds of meeting someone he asked to see family photos. It was a given that he had seen this family. He had undoubtedly asked Shawn about them that day, probably by name.

Vic assessed emergency situations rapidly. As a lieutenant, he eliminated unnecessary risk to his men. Though he never told her, she understood that if he had a choice, he would be the one to attempt to rescue a fellow firefighter. And if he'd known the cost of that choice? Hands down, he'd still go in. Because Shawn Leonard was, above all, a father with children at home who may very likely, as did Vic, worry about their daddy not coming home from work.

The knowledge almost, but not quite, canceled Wanda's attack.

Jody spoke around an obvious lump in her throat. "We wanted to express our sympathy away from the others. And to thank you. Mrs. Koski, we are so grateful. So very grateful."

She spread her arms wide and drew the young couple close to herself. "Call me Rachel."

Eighteen

"A voice was heard in Ramah, sobbing and loudly lamenting: it was Rachel weeping for her children, refusing to be comforted because they were no more."

Rachel awoke to the sound of her own sobbing, the Bible verse echoing as if someone had spoken it aloud. And then she felt the telltale signs.

She wasn't pregnant.

Never had been.

Never would be.

"Rachel!" Sylvia opened her bedroom door and hurried to her side. "Rachel, shh, it's all right."

She scrambled to her knees, jerking at the covers and crying loudly. "It's not all right! Don't say that! It's never going to be all right again!"

Her friend sat quietly on the edge of the bed. Sylvia was praying. Even in her disoriented state, Rachel knew that.

"Oh, Sylvia!" she sobbed. "Why is God doing this? I can't go on. I'm done. I quit!"

Sylvia took her into her arms. "Shh, child, shh."

"Vic's gone! There is nothing left of him! *Nothing!*"

Time slipped away as she wept and ranted and raved, growing hysterical. From some small corner of her mind she sensed herself watching herself, unable to control what was happening.

"Shh." Sylvia rocked her, like a mother soothing a little girl. "You're all right. Shh. You're all right now."

When at last the shuddering slowed, Rachel wiped her cheeks with the sleeve of Vic's T-shirt, which she had been wearing as pajamas all week.

Sylvia rubbed her back. "Okay now?"

Too winded yet to speak, she gave a half nod.

"The city's about ready to memorialize that big hero of yours. Come on now. Vic needs his woman by his side. We'd better get you ready."

Rachel stared at her. Vic needed her? The words deflected the approach of another wave of despair. Yes, he needed her by his side. "Do I have to wear the pumps?"

She laughed softly. "Yes, dear, you have to wear the pumps."

∽

Stan stood up. "I need a smoke."

Rachel slid her black stockinged feet into the pumps. "I need some air."

Waiting for their appointed time to enter the sanctuary and signal the beginning of the funeral, other family members scarcely glanced up as Stan and Rachel left the small anteroom. She led him through a back door and into an enclosed courtyard, far from the commotion occurring in front of the church. Thousands of pieces of apparatus from all over the country lined the streets, ready for the procession to the cemetery. Mourners packed the sidewalks. Family, friends, fire department officials, city dignitaries, and Chicago firefighters streamed into the building. The Church of Hope's maximum seating of 1800 would be reached today.

Midmorning sun rays peeked around the steeple. As if out of deference to the crowd's comfort, the weather had turned from its extremes of earlier in the week. It was not a typical July day. It was, rather, a gorgeous day. Perhaps someone had prayed.

Stan struck a match and squinted as he lit his cigarette. After a moment he said, "You look especially nice today."

The comment would have remained unspoken in the presence of Wanda. Rachel wondered if his earlier greeting of a hand clasp meant he would no longer hug her in front of his wife either.

"Thanks. New clothes. Compliments of my sister." She smoothed the fitted silk jacket across her rumbling stomach.

He touched the corner of his eye. "The shades are a perfect accessory."

"Terri's glasses. Contemporary version of a veil, I guess." In fact, her eyes were mere slits. No amount of drops or creams or makeup alleviated the blotchy puffiness. Terri said the reflective lenses hid what the world did not need to see, the face of tragedy. "Do I look like a cop?"

He gave her a grim smile. "No. I don't think anyone would take you for a cop."

The morning's hysteria still pounded in her chest, reiterating her failures in a staccato beat. "No, probably not. I imagine it was even kind of hard at times to take me for a fireman's wife." She bit her lip and turned away.

More than likely, Stan had not overheard Wanda's diatribe yesterday at the visitation when she'd laid the responsibility for Vic's death on Rachel, but surely that was not the first time his wife had uttered her thoughts on the matter. The truth was, if Rachel had been at home, had not run away to California, this retired cop would not be standing beside her with his own red-rimmed eyes, grieving the loss of his middle son.

"Stan, I am sorry. For everything."

He exhaled loudly. "What's done is done." As he walked behind her, he patted her shoulder. She heard his retreating footsteps, the click of the church door being opened, its closing swish.

So. She had lost her father-in-law too.

~

Rachel sank onto a concrete bench, the weight of a memory closing in. She and Stan had met in this same courtyard nine and a half years ago. Did he remember?

The date was December 29. Her wedding day. A foot of snow had fallen during the night, soft blankets of plump flakes drifting earthward and inviting neighbors to romp in a midnight wonderland. Rachel and Vic, along with Sarah and her husband, David, played in the front yard of their house where Vic was already living. They plopped on their backs into the drifts, fanned arms and legs to create a host of angels. They rolled enormous globes of snow and created a bride and groom snowman couple. Only Wanda and Bits worried that the city plows would be unable to clear the streets in time. As if Vic would even consider postponing the event...

By early afternoon traffic flowed unencumbered. Someone had even scooped the church's courtyard, piling the snow into six-foot banks around the edges. No north wind gusted into the enclosure, and the mounds of white fluff were left to glisten silently in brilliant sunshine. The winter day was every bit as gorgeous as any in summer, the high of 24 degrees notwithstanding.

Thirty minutes prior to the scheduled ceremony, to the chagrin of Bits, Rachel wrapped her long woolen coat over her slip and white stockings, stepped into the white pumps and fled the dressing area. She needed air, away from the free-for-all taking place there between Bits, Sarah, their mother, Bubbie, and Wanda. The clamorous exchange of opinions drained the room of oxygen, not to mention sanity. Nothing escaped their notice. Her dress, hair, makeup, and choice of music were particularly favorite topics. Maybe she and Vic should have followed Plan A and eloped.

She found Stan outside, no overcoat, appearing slightly ill-at-ease in a tuxedo and smoking within the confines of an unfamiliar church.

"Stan, can I have one of those?"

He smiled. "I think you're teasing."

She inhaled a lung full of frosty air. "Maybe. What do you think? Did we move too fast? Oh!" The word was a long sigh. "This is hardly the time to ask *that* question!"

"It's natural to be nervous on your wedding day, but no, I don't think you moved too fast. You two were meant for each other." The phrase was a mouthful for the usually reticent man. Vic physically resembled him, but he'd picked up his penchant for talking from his mother, not Stan.

Taken aback, she asked a rhetorical question. "You really think so?"

He smiled, the mirror image of Vic, his face folding along accordion lines. "I wouldn't say it if I didn't mean it."

She knew that.

"I never said it to my four other sons' wives. With Vic." He shrugged. "You've made a major impact on his life. It shows. He's...he's settled."

"If this is settled, I don't want to see unsettled! Here we are, getting married a mere nine months after we met, like some gestation term. Not that I didn't know early on he was the one. I mean, it's like I always knew that." Unfinished thoughts tumbled into coherence and poured glibly from her tongue. "The thing is, he seems to be in a hurry about everything he does, as though he's following some invisible timetable. He's aware of passing moments, like they're limited. Which of course they are, for everyone. But who counts them? Well, Vic counts them. Stan, will we grow old together?"

In reply, he ground out his cigarette with his well-polished shoe on the patio stone and enveloped her in a bear hug. After a long moment, he said, "I'm a cop. He's a fireman. I don't know. But I do know you're perfect for him. I know I'll be proud, in about half an hour, to call you my daughter-in-law. As a matter of fact, I wish you were my daughter so I could walk you down the aisle."

From that point on, Rachel and Stan shared a soft spot for each other. He lost some of his reticence and actually conversed with her. She kept him supplied with the fireball candies he craved. She trusted that Stan Koski would always be there for her no matter what.

Evidently she'd been mistaken.

~

"Rachel." Bryan's voice.

She blinked and saw a profusion of marigolds and multicolored petunias at her feet, bordering the courtyard's stone walkway.

He touched her shoulder. "It's time."

She looked up at him from her seat on the bench. His reddish brows were curved and slightly raised, like crescent moons over dark-circled eyes that pleaded for the nightmare to end, for slumber to come again. When was the last time he had slept well? Creases lined his forehead. In spite of the difficult road he had chosen to travel, his worn face had grown smoother through the years. God's hand erasing the years the locusts had eaten. But not today.

"Bryan, do you blame me?"

He sat beside her, his black cassock folding with him. "Rachel, you know I don't."

"Not even subconsciously?"

"Of course not. God is in charge, not you—"

"But maybe if you did, like others do, then we could all just leave it there and not struggle with *why* it happened."

"What others?"

She waved a hand in the air. Surely she didn't have to name names.

"They're grieving. Perhaps it is easier to accept Vic's death if we can lay the responsibility on one person. The other choice, to know that our loving Father did not prevent it, is too big to wrap our minds around at this moment. We all need time. Don't try to figure it out today." He pressed his thin lips together. Not quite a smile, the familiar expression signaled the close of his homily.

She turned away and shut her eyes, waiting for the infiltration of the calm that always emanated from him. The day loomed before her, its toll on her physical energy just the tip of an iceberg of what it would cost her to endure.

The funeral would last nearly two hours. Following that was the procession to the cemetery. With the entourage, that trip would take hours. All those pieces of apparatus waiting out front only began to describe what was involved. There were drummers, bagpipers, a color guard, the gleaming red-and-silver fire truck bearing the flag-draped casket, the family limousines, the streets lined with thousands of community members, people paying respect to a man who had protected them for 24 years... And then there was the cemetery. Two fire trucks would be parked there, two ladders extended between them holding aloft a large American flag... The American Legion... A 21-gun salute...

Calm escaped her.

"Bryan." She heard a note of panic in her voice, felt it in her heart that pounded again. "I can't do this alone. Stan needs to support Wanda. My mom needs my dad. David's hands are full with Josh. Bram has his family. Payton—"

"What makes you think I won't be next to you through the whole thing?"

Puzzled, she stared at him. Right now inside the church there sat, in assigned seats, the fire chief, the *mayor*, firefighters, families from Vic's battalion, the Koski and Goldberg extended families, all the faculty members from her school, the superintendent, former students. The procession was not a willy-nilly parade: Every vehicle and walker held a designated position. During the service, Bryan would speak, one of many orators. He was, therefore, to sit on the *left* side, not on the *right* side with family. He would not ride to the cemetery with the widow and parents in the family limousine. By necessity the funeral was a highly organized affair.

She replied, "Protocol."

He smiled softly. "Protocol, schmotocol. I promised Vic, you know."

~

Rachel balked at the sanctuary entrance, clutching Bryan's arm as if it were a lifesaver that kept her from sinking back into the sea of hysteria. Every pew was packed. Uniformed firefighters filled the entire left half.

She had balked in much the same way nine and a half years ago as she rested her hand in the crook of her dad's elbow and surveyed the church. Their small wedding plans had evolved to the point of almost filling the pews that day too. A Christmas tree soared to the ceiling. The platform overflowed with red and white poinsettia plants. Evergreen garlands draped the altar.

Rachel loved and respected the man beside her. Abe Goldberg was honest and fair, a hard worker. Not affectionate by nature, he doted on his mishmash of children at arm's length. Physically she resembled him. He wasn't much taller; his eyes dominated his face; his thick wavy hair required a stylist as opposed to a barber to keep it under control. Although she knew he always shook his head in skepticism over her choices, he had eventually been won over by Vic. The clincher was when Vic actually asked Abe for his daughter's hand in marriage, promising to financially take care of her. Abe knew the phrase was relative, but the fact that the young man addressed the money issue struck a chord. Abe began planning the wedding on the spot.

Holding his arm, Rachel balked for the space of a heartbeat as she spotted the handsome man in the black tuxedo waiting for her at the end of the white-carpeted aisle. What did the hero see in her? Such a plain Jane of a teacher. With his good looks, sense of humor, and confidence, he could have had any beautiful exotic woman. True, he was rough around the edges, but that was the sort of thing that attracted some females.

That sort of thing didn't attract her mother, however. Rachel thought it was those rough edges that repelled Bess even more than his non-Jewish heritage. However, when Wade Holden married another woman three months after Rachel rejected his proposal, Bess must have concluded the fireman was her daughter's best bet because he was, in fact, her only bet. But honestly, did the wedding have to take place on the *south* side of Chicago?

Yes, it did. Rachel loved her church, both the building and the people. Located not far from her school and not far from Vic's firehouse, it was a formal edifice which had belonged to a mainline denomination whose congregation had moved to the suburbs. The Church of Hope, bursting at its temporary seams in a rented hall, purchased the building and breathed life back into the old stone walls. Pastor Payton Wills led a lively flock that impacted the community.

As her roots grew deep into her new neighborhood, Rachel wearied of the weekly drive north to her and Bubbie's church and longed for fellowship closer to home. She accepted Sylvia's invitation to The Church of Hope and instantly felt at home.

Vic's reaction had been the same. While Bryan faithfully discipled him, he struggled to fit in at their childhood church where his mother still judged his every move and misunderstood his newfound faith. Soon after he began regularly attending church with Rachel, he had made more friends there than she had in five years. He and Pastor Payton, 15 years his senior, became fast friends; a mentoring relationship developed.

Yes, their church was the only choice for the wedding... the only choice for a funeral.

"Rachel," Bryan murmured now, breaking into her reverie. "Ready?"

No, but then she never would be ready to say goodbye to her husband.

His best friend squeezed her hand. "Come on. Vic's waiting for his gorgeous wife."

⌒

In the early evening, Rachel sat in the limousine, Bryan still by her side as he'd promised. On her other side sat Ed, Vic's oldest brother, the one who most resembled him in humor and breadth of shoulders. She faced the backs of Wanda and Stan, who occupied the center bench seat along with Max, Vic's next oldest brother, the one who most resembled their mother in wiry features.

She pressed the tri-folded American flag tightly to her breast, a vestige of the honor bestowed on the former soldier, the fallen firefighter lieutenant. Earlier, in the church, when she had first taken her seat in the front pew, her pastor left his chair behind the pulpit and came down around the casket to speak with her.

"Rachel." He leaned toward her and whispered for her ears only, "The circle is upstairs praying. Solely for you."

An image blotted out Payton's face before her. She saw herself being carried by unseen hands. A floating sensation overwhelmed her. The group he referred to was the Anna Circle, women who devoted hours to praying for the needs of church members.

Now, speeding along in the limousine, the miles multiplying themselves between herself and the cemetery, she remembered the women whose faith had surely borne her through the day. The floating sensation diminished, shoved aside by an ironic thought. The Anna Circle was named after the 84-year-old New Testament prophetess who saw the baby Jesus. Rachel could now join the group even though the youngest was at least 68. Age didn't matter. The criteria was a praying heart...and being, like Anna, like Rachel, a widow.

Ed broke the silence, speaking quietly beside her. "The neighbors are putting together something at the house. We're heading there now."

"You're not staying at the church? They've got enough food—they're expecting all of us. Family and friends."

Wanda jerked her head halfway around. "Those aren't our people." The words were the first she'd spoken to Rachel since the day before, during the visitation.

"But they're Vic's people!"

She whipped her head back the other way, an indistinguishable growl rumbling in her throat.

Ed went on. "Some of the guys from his company are coming. You're welcome to come. Later. After. You know."

Rachel stiffened as she struggled to comprehend. Protocol prescribed that things were not yet finished. The closest of family and friends would linger a while, drawing one more draught of sustenance from each other and the meal. It wasn't right that Vic's family should leave.

You're welcome to come. As though she were an afterthought, an acquaintance. Not a family member who had spent the last ten years in their homes, sharing meals and laughter, giving their children birthday gifts. His words weren't even an invitation. They weren't: *Will you come? We'd like you to come.*

The limousine pulled into the church parking lot and came to a halt. Doors opened. The seat in front of her cleared. Doors slammed shut.

Ed kissed her cheek. "I'm sorry." And then he was gone.

Sorry for what? For leaving? For snubbing protocol? For snubbing her? For snubbing *his brother,* whose laughter still echoed somewhere in the walls of this church building?

Or sorry that she was responsible for Vic's death?

"Rachel." Bryan's voice was tight, his face flushed nearly the color of his hair. "I'll see you inside."

She grasped his arm as he flung one leg through the car door. "Let it go."

"No, not this." He completed his exit and shut the door.

She leaned her head back against the seat and closed her eyes. If only she could sleep. Sleep for an entire year. She'd heard that was how long it would take...to get used to...the situation. To adjust to living without him.

Not even a week had passed. Four and three-fourths days in which life itself felt like death. Only 360 and a fourth more to go.

Nineteen

On the afternoon of the twenty-first day, Rachel sat on a high stool at the workbench in the single-car garage. Greasy automotive and lawn mower scents hung in the humid air. A gentle summer rain pattered on the rooftop and behind her on the raised door. It plopped on the driveway and on Vic's pickup, which she had backed out of the garage. The day after the funeral, two of the guys drove the truck home from the station. Since then she had kept it locked in the garage, out of sight, out of mind.

The place was Vic's domain. In her frenzied midnight search for a clue as to what he wanted to discuss once he met up with her in California, she had given it only a cursory glance. The stark display of neatly hung tools and the shelves and drawers full of whatnots and widgets offered no help. Not that she knew what she was looking for, even now.

The rain had nudged her from the quiet house. Vic often spent rainy afternoons piddling with this whatnot or that widget. Guy things that seemed as pointless to her as creating bulletin board displays seemed to him. Sometimes she would wander to the garage, take him iced tea. More often than not he sat on the stool, singing, his head bopping and his shoulders jerking in time with music that blared from the radio.

She snapped it on now. Heavy metal rock music resounded against the rafters, and she quickly lowered the volume. His taste in music had always puzzled her.

A calendar caught her eye. It hung from the Peg-Board next to a hammer. At least his taste in garage art hadn't run the sleazy gamut. She recognized the aerial view of the Rockies. Last year in Colorado on a shopping day while he hung out at a fire station, she had bought the 16-month calendar for him.

Why hadn't she thought of the calendar? It was nothing like a Day-Timer that other men might keep, but she knew he wrote on it. There were *some* things he scheduled.

She hesitated. Inside the house she hadn't done much except eat and sleep as best she could and write thank-you notes. Friends still came by. Bits had even made the trip twice. One of the guys from the station or one of their wives stopped in every single day. She sensed it was hardest for them. She was the poster child for what could happen. Who wanted to gaze on that? Jessie and Terri scheduled outings and dragged her along, sometimes with Jessie's kids. Faithful Sylvia was a daily source of comfort on the phone if not in person.

The dresser drawers and closet she had ransacked that night were straightened by Sylvia. Her friend reassured her there was no timetable to follow. His clothing could wait for whenever she was ready.

Her brother-in-law David had organized the desk drawers she'd left in disarray and even did lawyerly things like find the will and take care of insurance matters. She had managed to keep up with monthly bills, a chore she and Vic had shared.

The garage felt almost foreign, which was probably why she had entered it. Now, however, staring at the calendar, she thought the place felt more personal than his pillowcase, which she had yet to launder.

She unhooked it from the board.

"Mrs. Koski?"

She spun around to see a man standing in the open doorway. The overhead light shone on his fresh young face. Shawn Leonard.

"Sorry."

"It's okay. Hey, you're supposed to call me Rachel."

"Sorry."

She sighed to herself. The guy was going to spend his entire life being sorry. "Come on in." She pointed to another stool.

"I tried calling." He slid onto the seat. Though nowhere near as tall as Vic, he had an athletic build. "I got the message that the number had been changed and it's unlisted."

"Oh, sorry." Now she was sorry. As she would be for the rest of her life. "Terri said she posted it at the station. You must not have noticed. I'm trying to let everyone know. The calls." She shook her head. "I couldn't take one more sales call for 'Vic Koski.' And there were several hang-ups, no message left on the machine." Annoying and eerie. "There was an acquaintance who'd been out of town and hadn't heard..."

But the clincher had been something altogether different, too painful to vocalize. A woman from the reservations desk of a resort in Los Angeles called to say that the honeymoon suite was now available if Mr. Koski still wanted it. Vic must have planned to surprise her—

"So I changed the number." She shrugged. "How is your family?"

"Fine. You know, we're still, like every day, so grateful."

She nodded, ashamed at the twinge of envy.

"Can I, uh, I mean do you mind if I tell you about…about that night?"

Her heart felt as if it spun around, instantly knocking her emotions off kilter. The facade of calm she was learning to hide behind slipped.

"I mean, only if you want. It just seems right that you should hear it. From me."

She hadn't lost control now for at least a week. Not total control, anyway. Her sleep was usually a string of catnaps. If she sank deeper, she awoke into a split moment of airy lightness as if she still trusted in God. And that was unbearable.

Struggling to regain her composure, she stared at him. Such a fresh young face. At the most he was twenty-seven years old, too young for the responsibility he was carrying about. If he ever smiled again, he would no doubt have dimples like his wife.

"Shawn, I don't blame you."

His Adam's apple bounced, and he fiddled with the ball cap in his hand. "That means an awful lot to me, ma'am. Father O'Shaugnessy said you didn't." He glanced at her. "He took me to see Mr. Koski, the lieutenant's dad. They both wanted to hear the story. Father O didn't think you were ready at the time. He thought maybe now…"

Bryan with his Yeshua vibes held one of the few slender threads holding her world together. She couldn't bear to trust God, but she had to trust her friend's opinion.

"Let's go inside."

⌒

"It was a six-story office building." Shawn sipped from his mug. "Great coffee, by the way."

The kid was way too polite. Rachel assumed he could not have lasted at the station for the past three years by being so. More than likely it had something to do with sitting across the room from the widow of the man who died saving his life.

She set her own mug on the lamp table beside the recliner and pulled her cardigan more tightly around herself. Seventy-five degrees and she couldn't get warm.

Shawn went on. "It's an old brick place. Pretty. You know how they are. The stairwells and hallways are full of twists and turns, nooks and crannies." His shoulders heaved. "Sprinklers out of date and not inspected."

She watched the young man's eyes drift to some point within himself, heard the pitch of his voice edge upward. In spite of the outcome of the fire he was describing, he'd slipped into what she had long ago dubbed "fireman's zone." Adrenaline flowed anew as a soldier recounted the battle.

"I followed the lieutenant in with Michaels and Greer. Command radioed that smoke was spotted in a fifth-floor window, so we hiked up there trying to find the fire. The hall was filled with thick black smoke. As soon as I put on my mask, I knew I was in trouble. I started coughing. Greer heard my SCBA leaking."

He referred to the self-contained breathing apparatus, the cylinder of oxygen firefighters strapped onto their backs. Twenty to 30 minutes of sweet air flowed into their masks while black smoke swirled around their heads.

"Ma'am, I've been in two serious fires, but nothing like this. If it's any comfort, the smoke Lieutenant Koski took in would have rendered him unconscious almost immediately."

In other words, he hadn't suffered too much? How much is too much? One eternal minute of knowing—

"He told me to get out, gave me a little shove toward the exit. It was the middle of the night, pitch-black with smoke.

We'd only gone in ten feet or so." He hung his head and low-ered his voice. "But I couldn't find my way out. Went right past the stairwell door."

"Shawn."

He looked at her.

"One time." She paused, gathering the scattered remnants of calm about her in an effort to speak coherently. "One time Vic tried to explain a situation he'd been in. I kept suggesting things like, 'but why didn't you do this or that?' Finally he said he would just show me. It was night. We turned off the lights in this house. He had an SCBA here for some reason. He strapped it on me, and then he put electrical tape over the mask. That's when I started to freak out. Then he turned the radio up to simulate how loud things are between roaring flames and gushing hoses and firefighters yelling above it all." The experiment had haunted her for weeks. "I couldn't find my way out of my own kitchen."

Appreciation lit his eyes. He nodded. "I ended up wander-ing around wrong corners, getting farther and farther away from the exit. The smoke lessened as I got back into another wing, which is the only reason I lasted as long as I did.

"In the meantime fire was found on the floor below us. By then the second company was getting the hoses up there. The lieutenant went down to the lobby looking for me. Nobody had seen me. He figured it out." He gulped his coffee. "They told me he started running, yelling out he knew where I was. He was four, five minutes ahead of rescue. Nothing against them. The janitor who called in the alarm said nobody was inside."

Up and down five flights of stairs three times. Even in the excellent condition Vic kept himself, that would have required more from his SCBA, shortening its allotted time.

Shawn went on. "My PASS wasn't working either. You know, the alarm we wear that goes off if we're motionless? Unbelievable. It was like somebody assigned all the dud equipment to me that night."

Deep inside, where the facade would never reach, Rachel's voice screamed, *Didn't you check it? And who should have caught a leaky SCBA?*

Another voice whispered, *Rache, baby, equipment is not infallible. Even if everything checked out—*

"I did test it. And activated it. I'm sorry, Mrs. Koski. He would have found me sooner. Gotten himself—"

"Shawn, we can't go down that road."

He took a deep breath and straightened his shoulders. "He found me faster than anyone could have. Obviously he figured out I was in the other direction of the stairwell door. I don't know how far in I was. When I came to, there was the lieutenant staring down at me, grinning, holding his mask to my face. I guess I woke up enough. He put his mask back on and hauled me down the corridor. I was coughing and barfing."

She grabbed a tissue from the box beside her coffee mug and pressed it to her face.

"Mrs. Koski, he was amazing. No hose to follow out. The light on his helmet just bouncing back at us. He had to have been counting steps or something. Never missed a turn. I remember hearing somewhere along the way his low-air signal going off. The rescue guys caught me in the doorway. Then I passed out again."

When Rachel drove on the expressway and came upon an accident that slowed lines of traffic, she never had difficulty turning her face away. She skipped lengthy newspaper descriptions of heinous crimes. She didn't watch violent television shows or movies.

She wanted to run now from the horrifying scene before her but there was nowhere to bury her head.

Shawn lowered his voice. "I came to in the ambulance. We hadn't left yet. I knew he should be there because he *would* be. You know? That was Lieutenant Koski. I kept looking, trying to talk, shoving the EMTs out of my face. The heat, you know, had swelled things pretty much shut." He touched his chest. "But I got the lieutenant's name out. That's when they realized he wasn't with us."

He paused for a long moment. "Later they told me things must have fallen on him just as they got me through the doorway. Wires and cables from the ceiling. The fire had gone up inside the walls. Probably something stunned him. Then his feet got all tangled up in those lines. With all that smoke and carbon monoxide. His tank out of air. If only..." Shawn's voice trailed off.

Yes, if only.

⌒

Three steps forward and two steps back. Rachel understood that was the process. Shawn's visit, however, increased the reverse direction to at least four. She was in the hole. An already barely functioning awareness shut down even further.

"Shawn, would you mind putting Vic's truck back in the garage?"

"Not at all."

While he did that, she turned off the telephone ringers, lowered the volume on the answering machine, turned off lights, shut window blinds and curtains.

He came back in through the back porch and handed her the keys. "That's a great pickup."

"He's had it forever." *Had it. Had had it.*

"Yeah. That's why it's so great. Perfect for hauling whatever. Kids can't hurt it. Bet he loved it."

Now even her tongue refused to work.

"Well, I'll go. Look, if there's anything I can do, please call. Jody and I owe you everything."

With a wave of her hand she shooed him and his compassionate blue eyes out the door and locked it behind him.

It was only five o'clock in the afternoon, but she crawled into bed, fully dressed. The nightmare of Vic's final moments hung like a heavy cloud in the house, pressing down upon her. Much like the smoke must have borne down on him, choking life...

Dear Lord, please let me sleep this time. Please.

The prayer was her first, as was the 12-hour respite that followed.

Twenty

Rachel hung up the phone and stared at the kitchen wall clock. In 40 minutes she would pass a milestone: the precise moment when four weeks ago Vic breathed his last.

Terri poured herself another cup of coffee. "I can't believe you bother to call them."

"They're my in-laws." She shrugged and joined Jessie at the table. "It's just something one does, I guess, in this situation. You'd do the same thing."

"Not if they treated me the way they treat you." Terri shook her head and clucked her tongue. "No, sirree. Trust me, they do not deserve it. Do *they* ever call *you?*"

Jessie answered for her. "Stan called that one time to ask what she was doing with Vic's new-last-year winter jacket. Were you here, Terri? He said Ty could use it. Of course, you know Wanda put him up to that. Who else would think of a winter jacket in July?"

Terri sat down. "Or mentally pick through your son's things a week after you buried him? That call does not count."

They both turned to her. Clearly they knew Stan and Wanda never called her. She said, "It doesn't matter. What matters is it's the right thing for me to do anyway."

217

Terri said, "That's your doormat faith talking. At least it's talking again."

"Christ is not a doormat. Just compassionate."

"So that's what you're trying to be? Because you're a Christian and that's what you're supposed to do? Be compassionate?"

"Faith isn't about supposed to." Her reply was automatic. After 30 years of trusting in God and His Son, she had an explanation on the tip of her tongue for everything. Everything except for what happened three weeks, six days, twenty-three hours, and thirty-five minutes ago. Forget an explanation. She wasn't even sure she *trusted* anymore.

"So why do you do it, Rachel? Why do you call that woman twice a week just to get snubbed by her?"

Vic's voice came to mind. *"I don't know why you continue to invite my mother over."*

She bit her lip. Since that first prayer a week ago for sleep, she had gotten into the habit of whispering the name of Yeshua at night. Hardly a prayer. Hardly the habit of continually speaking to Him in her mind, which she had been doing consciously since high school. She felt as if she had been turned upside down and shaken like a saltshaker, emptied of all that made up Rachel Koski. How could that be? Would He ever fill her up with faith again? With trust? Was it His move or hers?

"Rachel, I'm sorry. Just tell me to shut up."

"It's okay. I guess I don't know why I do it."

Jessie said, "It must make you feel good, though. They're grieving, and you're trying to go through it with them."

She lifted a shoulder. "I don't really feel anything when I do it." Emotions were emptied, scattered across the countryside with the rest of the salt.

"Well, I think it's noble of you."

Terri exchanged a look with Jessie. "Doormat. Both of you."

Rachel noticed a subtle shift in the atmosphere. "What's going on?"

Again the other two glanced at each other. Jessie answered, "Nothing. Well, some things, but you don't need to be bothered."

Terri said, "Maybe she does need to be bothered. It might be good for her to hear that other people have major problems too. That the rest of the world did not come to an end. As a matter of fact, I think it's time she stopped feeling so sorry for herself."

Jessie gasped, her eyes bulged. "Terri Schuman! What an awful thing to say!"

"What's so awful? It's the truth. If Rachel can't take it, then I vote we lock her up and throw away the key because she ain't ever coming back." She crossed her arms and leaned sideways in the chair, a smirk on her face.

Nausea tingled in Rachel's throat. She went to the sink, flipped on the faucet, and splashed cold water on her face. What had she said to Bryan weeks ago? All she could think about was herself. About Vic. About his absence. *Me, me, me.*

She grabbed a towel and held it to her face, fighting back tears. Evidently bodies came equipped with an endless supply of saltwater, unlike trust and acceptance and goodness.

She looked up at the clock. "In twenty-six minutes it will have been only four weeks."

Terri walked over. "Need a little cheese with that whine?" She wrapped Rachel in a hug and squeezed tightly. "So how much time do you think you really need? I mean, we're missing you something fierce, lady."

While they munched on sandwiches prepared by Terri, Rachel's friends discussed the men in their lives. Things had been brewing for months.

Jessie frowned. "We can't talk without arguing."

"At least you see each other long enough to argue," Terri said. "Granted, Lee and I aren't married, but we've shared the apartment now for eighteen months. We struggle with the same day in and day out issues you're talking about."

Rachel let the comment slide. After one heated discussion last spring, they had agreed to avoid the subject of Lee Reynolds except in the context of totally innocuous areas. Like what he ate for dinner.

Rachel had cautiously relayed gossip she'd heard within the school district community: Lee was seeing someone else, another teacher. Terri confronted him. He denied it. She then accused Rachel of trying to break them up, of mandating her own outdated moral standards. Perhaps there was a hint of truth to that. Still, she accused Terri of foolishly ignoring the truth. In the end their friendship withstood the exchange.

Terri went on now. "Lee's never home when I am. And this is summertime! No school! Even with football practice already underway, you'd think he'd have more time available to hang out with me. It's so obvious. We're just going in opposite directions. Which I suspect really started with that other woman."

"Other woman?"

Terri glanced at Rachel.

Terri was admitting that she knew! She'd always known then. Had she been too proud to admit it? Or too fearful of losing him?

"Last year," Terri explained to Jessie. "Something was up. Something not right between us. Like he was holding back. Some woman called a few times. He said she was the new history teacher. He was late a few times. He said the new teacher needed help." She shrugged. "I never met her because he's never invited me to faculty outings in three years of going together. Mystery woman. I don't know how far things went between them. I always think I would have known if it was more than a crush."

"And now?"

"Supposedly she changed schools this fall."

"But the two of you haven't really recovered."

Terri blew out a breath. "I never thought of it that way, but yeah, you're right."

"Well, Kevin is totally tied up in everything outside the home. I don't care so much since I'm busy teaching now. But the result is we're going in different directions too."

Jessie and Terri continued their discussion, comparing notes on the men's inattention.

Rachel listened, wondering again if she and Vic would have been there. Come to think of it, they were there. Not connecting when they talked. Not really living together those last six weeks. Focused on infertility and doctor appointments and making love based on a *schedule*. That really wasn't the correct term for trying to make a baby—

Terri shook her arm. "Hey, we need some Rachel input here."

She struggled to organize her scattered thoughts. "The old Rachel would say you need to pray for harmony. And I still think that's true. But the new Rachel says." She paused. "The new me says: Imagine if Kevin and Lee were to die tomorrow. What would you do differently today?"

Later that afternoon Rachel returned to the garage. Vic's calendar lay on the workbench where she had left it a week earlier when she and Shawn Leonard had gone into the house.

She sat down on the stool and stared through a sunny side window. There was a flower box attached on the exterior, full of red and white petunias.

Suddenly a furry body pounced onto the box amidst the flowers, startling her. It was a gray squirrel. He sat back on his haunches and went still except for his twitching muscles and wiggling nose. Then he turned his head toward the window-pane and appeared to be staring right at her.

She smiled.

He cocked his head, a look of amazement on his face.

And she giggled.

He bounded off.

"Well," she said aloud to herself. "A red-letter day. First smile. First laugh. First listening to someone else's problems instead of my own."

Maybe tomorrow she would return to church. Maybe afterward she would offer to watch the Gray children in the evening and encourage Jessie and Kevin to go out to dinner. Maybe on Monday she would find Vic's down jacket and take it to his parents' house. Then maybe she would start hoping again.

Sylvia talked of hope. She read to her more of the passage from Jeremiah, beyond those words that haunted Rachel the morning of Vic's funeral. *A voice was heard in Ramah, sobbing and loudly lamenting: it was Rachel weeping for her children, refusing to be comforted because they were no more.*

"Yes, it's true," Sylvia said. "Rachel wept. But," she pointed a long finger to the verses that followed, *"Cease your loud weeping, shed no more tears.* And here. *You shall leave descendants after you.*" Her face lit up. "Rachel, think of all the lives you've affected in your classroom. Those are your descendants, child. Your tears will dry and you will find hope again in the work He's given you to do."

"But first," Rachel said aloud now to herself in the garage, "I have to search one more time." Like a carrot on a stick, the mystery dangled out there just out of reach. The desire to know what Vic was thinking in those final days obsessed her. The new development he'd wanted to tell her about was her last touchstone with him. Shouldn't she know exactly what that was?

The calendar seemed, like his wallet, the most likely place he would write down anything. Vic was an auditory learner and didn't need the printed word to drive home knowledge. Firefighting manuals and the Bible comprised his reading list. Occasional questions from study booklets and Payton's sermons fueled the men's study he led.

She opened the calendar to January. There on the eighteenth he'd written her name in his bold hand with capital letters. He never forgot her birthday, so it wasn't as a reminder. No, he wrote it because he would have seen his note every day that month and prayed for her more than he usually did.

She smiled. For the second time in one day.

A sobering thought struck her. She'd lost the prayers of Bubbie and Vic, all within a two-month time span. *Hundreds are praying for you.* Payton's words came to mind. Yes, hundreds. But were they still praying, four weeks later? And did they have any idea of what she was like? Of her needs? Bubbie and Vic knew her better than she knew herself and prayed accordingly.

A chilling sensation settled in her chest. Who would cover her now? Those hundreds, most of them virtual strangers? She doubted it. Not in the same way. She felt exposed, unprotected, beyond vulnerable.

"Dear God," she whispered.

She began flipping through the months, through breathtaking photographs of the Rockies, through the winter and early spring where he'd circled the twelfth in red and diligently wrote in doctor appointments and his schedule. A quick thumbing revealed the twelfth was noted through December. The anniversary of the day they met, the day he always sent flowers.

She went back to study June, the month she'd missed for the most part. Her departure date was noted, as were his shifts and softball games. Bibles study, its meeting time and day different every week, floating around work and training seminars but never canceled. She turned to July. A big smiley face filled the twelfth...the day he was to arrive. His schedule the previous week had been crossed out and rewritten...the days he'd rearranged in order to change his vacation time...there was still a smile on the twenty-first, his original due date in California.

And then it caught her eye. July fifth. Something in pencil, not his usual conspicuous large letters in blue or red ink. She lifted the calendar and peered closely.

Fiona. A phone number followed.

Who was *Fiona?*

⌒

"Bryan, who is she?" Fear and rage mangled Rachel's voice into a demanding screech. She had lost count of the times she'd asked the question of him since arriving at his study a short time ago.

Her husband's best friend, the only person on the face of the earth who had the answer, walked around his large desk and pressed her back into the chair. "Rachel, please. Calm down. Vic would never cheat on you. He adored you. I have no idea who Fiona is, but she could not have been between you."

"Of course she was! He wanted to talk about something that came up. But not over the phone! And then he dies. According to his calendar, she came up in July. She will always be between us!"

"Let me call the number. It's an Illinois area code. Downstate—"

"No!"

"Rachel." His tone was exasperated.

"I don't want to know."

"Well, maybe I do! Go sit in the sanctuary if you don't want to hear the truth." His voice hardened enough to grab her attention.

She cried then and curled up into the winged back leather chair. Bryan handed her another tissue and sat again behind his desk.

She'd driven straight to his church, speeding through neighborhoods and yellow lights, steering with one hand while she called him with the cell phone. Even if he hadn't answered, she probably would have come. The only other option was to remain at home where she knew she would have broken something. She'd had enough sense to realize it would have belonged to Vic and she would have regretted it later.

Bryan picked up the phone, and, reading from the calendar she'd flung onto the desk earlier, touched the keypad. He watched her as he listened, his face unreadable. After a few moments he disconnected and repeated the procedure. Then he gently set down the receiver.

"The number is no longer in service."

Twenty-One

The following week Rachel and Jessie sat cross-legged on the living room floor surrounded by cardboard boxes and piles of clothing, books and magazines on firefighting, men's toiletries.

Jessie folded a pair of Vic's jeans. "You're absolutely, positively sure about this? It's not too soon?"

She nodded. "It's such a waste to have all these clothes of Vic's lying around here when others could use them. And once school starts, it's hard telling when I would get around to sorting through his things."

"Well, I guess you do need to move on."

"The only other choice is to just curl up and die myself."

Her friend winced.

"Jess, talking straight about it is okay. Terri was right to give me a kick in the pants. You can mope around in a daze for only so long. Life must go on."

Rachel hadn't told Jessie everything. Terri's kick was just the first step. Finding that woman's name written on the calendar was the second. Bryan's fruitless phone call was the third. Anger burned away the dross of brokenheartedness. The pain remained, but the flames of anger were blackening the edges of depression. She had to get on with life.

Jessie said, "You sound mad. But they say anger is part of the grieving process."

"Yes, that's what they say."

The trouble was, she thought she'd already gone through being angry at Vic. This anger had nothing to do with him dying.

"Rachel, since we're talking straight..." Jessie fingered a strand of hair, clearly uncomfortable with talking straight. "Does this mean you've accepted the, uh, situation?"

Accepted that he bailed out on her? Accepted that he'd refused to tell her something in a timely fashion? Accepted that someone named Fiona stood between them? Accepted that God allowed it all?

"No!" She swallowed her restive tone. "No. I don't think so. Unfortunately. I have to get on with life, but I can't seem to envision myself coherent in a classroom full of fourth graders."

Jessie blinked and held up a black sweatshirt, a small University of Chicago emblem on the front. "What do you want to do with this?"

Maybe she should just go back to college full-time. Work on her doctorate and not think about nine-year-olds.

"Rachel?"

"Huh?"

"The sweatshirt. What do you think?"

"What do *you* think?"

"It looks new. Firehouse box. If the big guys don't want it, maybe Teague's oldest would like it." Jessie folded it and tossed it into a nearby box. "Terri keeps asking me where God comes into it all."

"Mm-hmm." She suspected as much. "And what do you say?"

Jessie pulled another pile onto her lap. "I know I haven't been a Christian for very long, but I think I should have the answer. Trouble is, I don't."

Rachel hugged a navy blue T-shirt to herself and closed her eyes. What did she know? When all was said and done, what did she really know? "God is inscrutable."

"His thoughts are way higher than ours. But He sent Jesus, and *He* wasn't all that inscrutable. He said He was the way and the truth and the life and that no one gets to the Father except through Him. And to love your neighbor as yourself. Pretty straightforward stuff."

Like the faint rustle of someone softly walking by, Rachel heard the sound of hope. She looked at her friend. "So we love. And we hold the hand of Jesus and let Him lead the way."

"Yeah!" Jessie's smile faded. "Aren't you doing that?"

"No." She didn't have to ponder that question.

"You've always done that. I watched you live that way for years. Rachel, that's why I'm a Christian. *You're* why I'm a Christian."

She sighed heavily. Had she been faking it all this time? The rubber should have been meeting the road right now. "I know He's there. Here. I just haven't been connecting."

"Well, what are you waiting for?" For someone unaccustomed to straight talk, she prodded with the best of them.

"I think you've been hanging out with Terri too much."

Jessie grinned. "You didn't answer my question. You know, maybe He's just waiting for you to get down on your knees, girl."

"What? And give up all this denial and anger and depression? Not on your life. I like living this way."

"Your sense of humor is returning. This is a good thing."

The doorbell rang. Rachel climbed to her feet and teased, "Isn't it time for you to go pick up your kids or something?"

Jessie laughed.

Rachel crossed the room. Through the screen door she saw a massive bouquet of mixed flowers. It blocked the face of whoever stood there. Her chest tightened. How many more plants and flowers and condolence cards could she accept?

A young man peered around a fern. "Mrs. Koski?"

"Yes." She opened the door.

"These are for you." He handed her the white ceramic vase. "It's heavy. Got it?"

"Yes. Thank you."

"Have a good day. Oh, almost forgot." He pulled a business-size envelope from his shirt pocket. "This goes with it." With a wave and a smile he headed down the sidewalk.

The door swished shut behind her as she turned toward Jessie.

"Oh, Rachel, how gorgeous! Here, put them on the coffee table." She moved a stack of books to the floor as Rachel set down the bouquet and envelope.

"I should put some water in the vase."

"Don't you want to read the letter first?"

"You go ahead." She stepped to the kitchen doorway.

"But I know who they're from."

Rachel stopped. Some vague thought nagged at the back of her mind.

Jessie grinned. "It's the twelfth."

She twirled around.

"Everybody knows Mrs. Koski gets flowers on the twelfth."

"But." She held a hand to her mouth. "Did he pay ahead? No. He never sent such a huge…" She shook her head.

"Rachel." Jessie picked up the envelope from the table and walked over to her. "Here."

She didn't need to open it. "They didn't."

"They did."

"Was it Terri's idea? Or yours?"

"Nope. Kevin said it just sort of evolved as they were all sitting around one night at the station, wondering what to do for you."

"They've already done so—" She covered her mouth again, pressing back the cry.

"Come on." Jessie pulled her over to the couch and sat beside her. "Open it."

An image flashed. Vic and about a dozen coworkers on bended knee, proposing to her. She truly had gained a family that day.

Breaking the seal on the envelope, her hands trembled. What more could they do? She pulled out a sheet of paper and read the first typed line. "The Firefighter Spouse's Prayer, Koski Version."

Jessie elbowed her. "They didn't think the original fit either."

She had opposed the reading of the prayer at the funeral because it mentioned *children* being proud of their daddy. "I can't read it."

Jessie took the page from her and cleared her throat. "The table's set with Rachel's world-famous leg of lamb and latkes. The in-laws will soon arrive, looking for ham. Old Vic once more disappears with a hope of keeping a kid alive. Stuck at home, the schedule all awry, Rachel might just sit down and cry. But she knows that's no help to Vic, which he explained in nauseating detail long before he popped the question. Yes, she knew the drawbacks when she walked down the aisle, knew his job might be his final fate. Yet with God's help she still remains Victor Koski's faithful mate." Jessie wiped tears from her own cheeks. "Hugs and kisses, Truck and Engine

Companies blah blah blah. And look, they've all signed it. Oh, my goodness. Is that the sweetest thing ever or what?"

Rachel smiled through her own tears. They didn't blame her. They really didn't blame her.

⌒

You killed my son! If you'd been here where you were supposed to be, this never would have happened. I will never, ever forgive you!

Wanda's accusations echoed in Rachel's head as she sat in her car outside the Koski house.

At some cognitive level Rachel understood that her mother-in-law attacked out of a hideous grief and the words should be forgiven and forgotten. And though she still blamed herself, Rachel knew she needn't because when all was said and done, God was in charge and God knew what He was doing. Period. End of story.

But that cognitive level shifted like the deck of a boat on Lake Michigan in the middle of a storm. The ability to plant her feet in its reasonableness eluded her. She could not grasp the ability to dwell there.

Vic's winter jacket lay on her lap. She touched the forest green fabric puffed with down. It rustled under her fingertips. She'd given it to him on his last birthday.

To have Wanda accuse her was not a new thing. Though the woman sprinkled her conversation with subtle digs before the wedding, it wasn't until after that she hit her full on with the undisguised verbal jabs.

"You know, Vic was perfectly happy at Bryan's church. After all, it's our family church. The one he and Bryan grew up in. Do you think he really wants to go to your church?" Wanda crossed her arms and slightly lifted her chin, a signal

Rachel had not yet come to recognize as the donning of a suit of armor and taking hold of the sword.

They sat in Rachel's kitchen on a cold January night just a few weeks after she and Vic had returned from their Florida honeymoon. Although thick snowflakes were stacking up on the windowpanes, Stan had gone outdoors to scoop them from the driveway. At the rate they were falling, his efforts were no doubt a losing battle.

Vic, evidently in the throes of marital bliss, felt moved to invite his parents over to celebrate his new wife's birthday, his gallant attempt to promote familial camaraderie. He planned to cook. As a matter of fact, his famous pot roast was in the oven and luscious scents wafted throughout the house. He, however, was at the fire station. Just as his parents knocked on the front door, he answered the phone. They had left their house early, cautiously driven through snow which the plows couldn't keep up with, and arrived two hours early. Vic yelled hello and goodbye, and he promised to be home as soon as possible. With all the emergency calls, he was needed at the station.

Rachel answered her mother-in-law's question. "Yes, I know he wants to be at Church of Hope. It's been his church as much as mine from the first day he walked in. People sometimes change, Wanda."

"Well, obviously men change when they want to please a woman. They'll do just about anything for a little you know what." In that characteristic way of hers she shrugged a bony shoulder and cocked her head as if to say *you may not believe it, but I know it's true.*

Rachel felt her face go hot.

"It's just such a shame, splitting up the family. All my other boys go. Bryan's young, but he's a good priest. Why can't

you leave your church? You left your other one. The Jew one."
She sipped her coffee with an annoying slurping sound.

Rachel's entire body went hot. That she recognized.
During her early encounters with irate parents who blamed
her for their child's failures, she felt just such an internal heat
wave and spouted off words that Sylvia later made her retract.
She'd learned to listen to her body's signals, count to ten, and
ignore what they said. With Wanda, she made it to seven.

"Wanda, it's nothing against Bryan or your church. C.S.
Lewis said that Christianity is like a huge mansion. All the
rooms are decorated differently. One might be done in an
eclectic style. Another in Victorian. Or Queen Anne. Another
in stripes and plaids. Another in purple. The point is, some
people are drawn to purple, some to Queen Anne. The how
of worship doesn't matter as much as our individual personalities. Vic feels he fits better in our church."

"Why don't we throw those buns in the oven? If you've got
a can of green beans, we can just eat those with the meat.
Poor Vic having to work. We should have fixed the potatoes
and carrots for him. Too late now. I'll go get Stan."

Late that night, when a weary Vic climbed into bed, Rachel
asked him, "Did you marry me and change churches just so
we could sleep together?"

He paused, a look of astonishment on his face. "Huh?"

"Your mother said—"

He burst into laughter and fell backward onto the pillows.
He laughed until tears rolled down his cheeks.

After that, Rachel did her best not to take Wanda's criticism
personally. Dertermined to win her over, she parried the
verbal attacks with a prayer, a turning of her cheek, and
laughter.

Her prayer life had disintegrated last month somewhere
between San Diego and Chicago. She didn't perceive that she

had another cheek to turn. And the entire situation was certainly no laughing matter.

⌢

A thumping on the windshield startled Rachel. She looked up to see Stan peering through the open passenger window.

"You coming in or are you going to sit out here all night?"

"Stan, I didn't kill him."

Her words broke through the cop exterior he'd ducked behind the morning of the funeral. She had even heard it in his tone when they talked on the phone. Now, something flickered in his eyes. Tension eased away from his jaw, relaxing the mouth. It nearly resembled Vic's again, a picture of contentment. Nearly.

"Rachel. I know that."

She looked toward the windshield and bit her lip.

He walked around the car and opened her door. "Why don't you come inside?"

"I don't want to upset Wanda anymore than I—"

"She'll probably stay in her room. But I made a pot of coffee. Come on." He grasped her elbow, helped her out, and let go. His physical touch did not progress to what used to be standard fare between them: a hug.

"Uh, I have a box." She opened the rear door.

"I'll get it."

A moment later they went up the walk, side by side. She carried the jacket. "Has she gone back to work yet?"

"Yeah. Yesterday and today. And a friend got her to the book club the other night."

"That's good."

He grunted. "You been going through his things?"

"Mm-hmm."

"That's good."

His two words of approval were like the last drops of water from a canteen in the middle of the desert. What she desperately wanted was an oasis complete with a waterfall and palm trees: a hug from the man she could have easily called "Dad."

Inside the house she laid the jacket on a chair as he set the box on the floor. She followed him into the kitchen and sat at the table. He poured two mugs of coffee and joined her.

They talked for a while, a trace of their old familiarity creeping in now and then. He told her about his work as a greeter at a discount store, how not a day passed that someone didn't stop and talk to him about Vic. She told him of her plans to do some work in her classroom later in the week. She did not tell him about the calendar.

"Stan, I want to sell his truck to one of the guys."

He nodded. All his sons had pickups, as did he.

"To Shawn Leonard."

He froze.

She went on. "Vic should have waited for rescue to go in for him, but he didn't. I think he didn't because he knew if he waited, three little kids would grow up without a father."

Stan pressed his lips together.

"He acted like his own father would have." She reached across the table and touched his hand briefly. "The kids are all under five. Shawn works a second job, and they have one car. His wife doesn't work. You know what firemen make." She didn't mention that she was going to sell it to him for a dollar. She didn't need her father-in-law's approval on that, only her husband's. Without a doubt he would agree.

Stan cleared his throat. "I suppose they have a sick dog too?"

"Maybe." A smile tugged at the corners of her mouth. "And his mom's in the hospital recovering from major surgery."

"Dad's in a wheelchair?"

"Mm-hmm."

Stan's eyes twinkled. "His mother-in-law is probably about as helpful as a bump on a log."

They exchanged a quick grin.

"Rachel, it's a good idea."

"Thank you."

She sensed a movement on her left.

Wanda entered the kitchen carrying a denim blue cotton sweater. She must have found it in the box of Vic's things left in the living room. "Who's this for?"

"I thought Ed might like it."

"Humph."

Even the shrink-wrap sagged on the woman's small body. Rachel wondered yet again how her teddy bear of a husband could have a mother so totally devoid of tenderness.

"I see you brought the jacket. Ty could use one."

"He's welcome to it."

Wanda made her humphing noise again, laid the sweater on an empty chair, and went to the refrigerator. "It's time to cook supper."

Rachel stood. "Well, I need to leave. Thanks for the coffee."

Her head bent inside the refrigerator, Wanda said, "What are you going to do with that tent?"

"Our tent?"

"Vic had that before he married you."

"He had a smaller one. We replaced—" She clenched her teeth.

Stan walked over to the coffeepot and touched his wife's shoulder. "Wanda, give her some time."

She straightened. "It's not like she's going camping by herself. Sig's boys want to go, but he can't afford to buy everything and then just have it sit if they decide they don't like it."

Rachel felt as if she were suffocating. "They can have it. It's up high in the garage. I can't get it down by myself. Tell Sig to come this weekend. Bye." Not waiting for a reply, she left the kitchen and walked down the hallway.

Stan caught up with her at the front door as he placed a lid on a mug. "One coffee to go, coming up. *Good* coffee."

The gesture caught her off guard. It spoke of years of teasing about which Koski made the best coffee. By everyone's admission, including her own, she came in last. Vic and Stan tied for first place. She let out a heavy breath.

"Oh, I miss his coffee."

"Figured you did." He winked and handed her the cup. "Take care, Rachel."

It was very nearly an oasis complete with a waterfall and palm trees.

Twenty-Two

As the ceiling lights flickered on, Rachel surveyed her vacant classroom. The gray stippled tile shone from its summer waxing, unmarred yet by little shoes coated with playground dirt. Student desks and chairs were bunched into the back half of the room, inverted ones atop right-side-up ones. Metal legs pointed like a still-life chorus line of upside-down caterpillars. Vic always dismantled the stacks.

Behind her, Terri inhaled loudly. "Man! The smells!" She sat down on a corner of Rachel's desk. "They take me right back to fourth grade. I guess some things never change."

Oh, yes they do. Everything under the sun changes. The scents as well as the scene before her were unfamiliar because she now perceived them through the knowledge that Vic was gone. Her stomach hurt as she tried to imagine teaching with that knowledge. No, nothing would ever be the same again.

"Okay, Mrs. Koski, let's get started. What do you want me to do first?"

"Well." She looked around. "Wherever you see a bookshelf or cabinet, unload it and clean it."

"I thought you had custodians."

She crossed her arms. "I'm a little particular."

238

"Okay, okay. I know. I volunteered for whatever you needed." Terri slid from the desk and tilted her head. "I'll start in that corner under the windows. Hey, can we have some music?"

Rachel watched her stride in that confident way of hers. "Sure." She went to a cabinet behind her desk and pulled out a radio, wondering again if Terri's presence was a good idea.

Not that she really had a choice. Her friend hadn't asked if she could tag along. She simply announced she would tag along.

While Jessie and Sylvia still called often, their visits had gradually lessened. They had returned to their regularly scheduled busy lives. Terri, on the other hand, had become somewhat of a shadow. Between her 24-hour shifts she had three days off, quite a bit of which she spent with Rachel.

Bryan's words replayed. *Terri's watching us.* And Jessie's. *Terri has questions.* She was curious. *What will these Christians do now?*

Rachel didn't mind the sense of living in a fishbowl before her friend. Christians were human, they cracked under pressure. They were devastated by life's blows, those horrors that passed through God's hands. She would not hide those facts from Terri anymore than she had ever hidden her belief that her joy and purpose in life came only from a relationship with Christ.

What she minded was Terri's egging her on, subtly pressuring her to take steps forward. A part of Rachel resisted. Wallowing in a daze was by far the preferred state. It had become her comfort zone, and she was in no hurry to leave it.

She set the radio on her desk and plugged it in. Terri's taste in music resembled Vic's, at the opposite end of the spectrum from her own preference for classical. Maybe they could compromise.

She turned the radio on and immediately recognized the station she and Vic had compromised on last spring when he helped her pack up the room. The words of the song playing stopped her cold.

"*When your life falls apart, trust His heart.*"

"So, Rachel," Terri said loudly over the music and the thumping of books being piled onto the floor. "I've been thinking about what you said."

Trust His heart.

"You know, the other day when Jessie and I were griping about the guys."

I can't see His heart. This burden is too heavy. It's too heavy, God!

"Remember?"

You could try talking to His heart.

Terri stood before her desk now. "You asked us what we'd do differently if we knew Lee and Kevin would die tomorrow. Shall I use these paper towels and cleaning spray?"

"Yes."

"So." She sashayed back to the corner. "I cooked. Oh, yes I did."

The lack of homecooked meals was Lee's major complaint against Terri. Of course, her friend's response was to show him where the kitchen was located.

Terri attacked the shelves while she talked, squirting the spray until a fine mist gathered about her head. "Cooked up a storm, as a matter of fact." She rubbed the towel across the shelf as if to wipe the grain clear off the wood.

Rachel walked to where her friend crouched before the shelves. "And?"

"And it wasn't too bad. I tried that lasagna recipe of Jessie's. From scratch, no less."

"Terri. You're skirting what you really want to tell me."

She winked over her shoulder. "And I talked calmly. Told him no matter what, I would forgive him. He didn't know what hit him. He admitted the other woman was real and told me more than I needed to hear, but we discussed the whole thing. As well as our future, including the possibility of marriage."

Rachel wasn't sure she heard correctly.

"The goofy thing is..." Terri tore off another paper towel and fiddled with it, her eyes lowered. "I never would have attempted replacing my anger at Lee with love and forgiveness. Not if Vic hadn't—" Her voice cracked, and she covered her face with the towel.

Trust His heart.

Rachel knelt and enveloped her in a hug.

His heart. God loved Terri. Did He love her to such an extent that calling Vic Home was the only way to get her to look up?

Lord, You ask too much!

If Vic had known, would he have agreed? Yes, of course he would have. Even as the Son had agreed.

∽

"Rachel!" Jessie's ecstatic voice shouted from the answering machine. "Teague got Vic's Bible study group going again and Kevin went this morning! Then he came home for lunch! Now he took the kids to the park! And he's talking about trying church on Sunday!" She giggled. "Keep praying!"

Standing in the center of her living room, the whir of the machine rewinding on the desk behind her, Rachel took a shaky breath.

"Well, Lord, why don't You just hit me over the head?"

She hadn't felt all that steady since comforting Terri in her classroom several hours ago. Stoic Terri, who never shed a tear in public and swore that rampant hormones were a figment of the female imagination, cried uncontrollably. After that, her friend made quick work of cleaning the bookshelves and flipping desks right side up. Then she insisted they stop for pizza on the way home. Rachel managed to accomplish a few tasks, but she could scarcely string two cohesive thoughts together, not to mention words. Sentences were hopeless. Terri didn't seem to notice.

Or maybe she did notice. Yeshua's love was palpable, a living presence clicking the scattered bits of her life into place like puzzle pieces. The imperfect expressions of two women didn't matter. What mattered was that a transcendent love enfolded them like a mantle.

Trust His heart.

When was the last time she had prayed for Terri? When was the last time she had prayed for Kevin, the guy Vic especially longed to reach, a man's man whose stolid demeanor surpassed Terri's? *When was the last time she had even prayed?* Bubbie taught her life was nothing without prayer. Jessie was counting on her prayers. Terri needed her prayers whether she understood that or not. Vic had always depended on her prayers.

She knelt beside the couch, that mantle of love doing its work. Absorbing her pain. Siphoning out her feelings of guilt over Vic's death. Dissolving the anger she harbored against the Almighty. Turning uncertainty and doubt inside out. Burning away impurities until only gold remained, the essence of her faith, more brilliant and solid than it had ever been before Vic entered that burning building.

~

Rachel walked into the sanctuary, and immediately her sight homed in on the back of Sylvia's head full of salt-and-pepper curls midway up the left center section. After a slight hesitation, she walked directly to that pew. The courage to glance around at the gathering crowd failed her. She made it to Sylvia's row without making eye contact or identifying a single person. That she made it at all was a major accomplishment. With her heart thumping in her throat, she stepped past a family.

She had come to church only twice since the funeral, both times sitting near the back exit and scooting out as soon as possible. Avoiding sympathetic stares and hugs had been her only goal. Not much of a motivation to show up on a Sunday morning.

"Rachel!" Sylvia's face beamed and her eyes sparkled. She hugged Rachel as she sat down beside her.

"Hi."

A man leaned around her friend. His resemblance to Sylvia was remarkable. Tall, more salt than pepper hair but just as curly, dark eyes, an obvious mixture of cultures in his facial lines.

"Rachel, this is Harrison Robbins. New assistant superintendent." Sylvia still beamed. "Harrison, this is Rachel Koski, one of my fourth-grade teachers."

He held out his hand and smiled. "How do you do?"

"Nice to meet you." She received his firm handshake, and then he retreated back behind her friend.

Sylvia touched her arm. "Honey, did you get to school yet?"

"Friday afternoon. I heard you were playing hooky."

"Is that what they told you?" Sylvia scowled and shook her head. "My staff. Tsk, tsk."

Rachel knew she teased because her smile continued unabated through the scowl. What was going on? "So where were you?"

"Child, we are here to worship, not gossip." She cut her eyes in the direction of the new superintendent. "Harrison hadn't had a proper tour of downtown yet."

Rachel rounded her mouth in an exaggerated O.

"He's a believer," Sylvia said sotto voce. "Widower." Her brows went up as the congregation stood and began singing.

Dr. Sylvia Talbot had a crush on the new assistant superintendent of schools.

Rachel's vocal cords felt like dry sticks rubbing together. They weren't likely to produce a musical note. If she hadn't been in the middle of the row in the middle of the church, she probably would have succumbed to a sudden desire to flee.

Deep in the recesses of her mind she heard the tinkling of a warning bell. Bubbie had taught her how to hear it. She hadn't listened for it in a long while. It meant something was awry, something at odds with the Holy Spirit.

Envy. That's what it was. She was jealous of Sylvia being excited about this Harrison Robbins. Her dearest, oldest of friends who hadn't been loved by a man in 30 years, who'd raised two daughters on her own after being abandoned by their father.

I'm sorry, Lord.

A larger wave of envy hit her as she thought of Sylvia's twins. And then the faces of Jessie, Sarah, Bits, and countless others filled her mental screen. Mothers, every last one of them. The thing none of them could understand was that if their husbands died tomorrow, at least they would be left their children.

Sylvia tugged on her arm, indicating she should sit down with everyone else. She sat.

Maybe she had come too soon. Pushed herself too hard. *Father, I'm not ready. Just let me crawl back into a hole where it doesn't hurt so much.*

On Saturday she had straightened the garage. The week before, after finding Vic's calendar with the mystery woman's name on it, she had literally torn the place apart, emptying drawers onto the floor, shoving aside cans and whatnots that lined the shelves. Nothing had offered up a further clue to Fiona's identity.

Praying again at last on Friday night had given her courage to enter the garage. No, that wasn't quite it. She hadn't asked for courage. She hadn't asked for anything. She had simply let her Savior love her. He filled her with an intuitive knowledge that she wasn't alone. Of course, Bubbie had long ago described how she lived through the war, how she emigrated to a new country, how she became reacquainted with a son who scarcely remembered her and spoke a foreign language. Rachel hadn't the ears to hear her grandmother's lessons until she herself lost a husband and, in less time than it took a heart to beat, her world disintegrated.

Now as she sat in church, she focused on Christ's love. Though she missed the entire song service and string of announcements, the despicable emotions she had welcomed far too easily began to fade. A soft peace pushed aside envy for those other women's situations and a seething anger at Vic's betrayal.

Sylvia nudged her. She looked up and saw her friend smile softly, nodding toward the front.

Shawn and Jody Leonard stood at the altar with Payton. The pastor said, "I'd like to introduce two new members of our family."

Rachel felt as if thunder exploded in her ears. She couldn't hear his next words. Panic-stricken that she would burst into loud wailing, she tore her gaze from the scene up front.

And then she saw the others scattered about the crowded pews. There was Kevin sitting with Jessie. And Steve and Duke? They were firefighters with Vic's company. Their families almost filled an entire row. And Alice! Alice Koski, the wife of Vic's brother Ty.

Rachel took hold of Sylvia's hand and squeezed it tightly. The evidence before her was too much to comprehend. As far as she knew, except for Jessie, they were all there for the very first time. Well, the first time not counting the funeral.

Shawn's voice resonated through the sound system. "As you all know, he saved my life. But he did more than save my physical life. Lieutenant Koski died for me, and now it's like I've got a new set of ears. I can hear what he was always telling us guys. That Jesus died for me."

The thunder clapped again.

Thunder? Perhaps it was rather the echo of God's voice welcoming Vic Home. "Well done, My good and faithful servant."

∿

At Rachel's request, Bryan met her for coffee early Monday morning. She chose an upscale place in a new mini-mall not far from his church or her school rather than her and Vic's old favorite, Myra B's Coffee Shop. The entire city of Chicago was a minefield of memories waiting to explode and shred to pieces her flimsy grasp on reality. She avoided the particularly hot spots like Myra B's. All she could handle for the time being were house, school, and, as of the day before, church.

Bryan carried two steaming mugs of coffee to the booth where she waited. "Way too many choices here. Hope the flavor of the day is okay with you. They didn't accept my order for two simple black *coffees*."

She returned his smile as he sat down. "How are you?"

"Better now that I see you smile. I think that's the first one in some time. How are *you?*"

She held out a hand and wobbled it.

"Looks like great progress."

"It is. Bryan, I'm sorry I've been avoiding you since I went crazy in your study last week. I think I held it against you that Vic kept something from me. I needed you to know who this Fiona is."

"Understandable, Rachel. And I'm sorry I've been avoiding you."

She raised her brows.

"Yeah, I have been. I could have called you too, you know."

"I guess I didn't notice that you hadn't."

"Good. Sounds like you've been busy then."

"It's been a full week. I'm starting to hear that still small voice again."

Some of the exhaustion left his ruddy face. He said softly, "I can't tell you how glad that makes me feel."

"Yeah? You should feel it from this side."

He grinned. "Tell me about your week."

She brought him up to date. About the bouquet from the guys. About Stan's warming. About Terri and Lee. About herself praying again. About Shawn and the others in church.

"Praise God." He sat quietly for a moment, as if digesting it all, a look of satisfaction on his face. "You know Jim? He was in church yesterday. Rachel, they've all been going to the Bible study Vic started. Teague asked me to help him with it."

Her throat closed, and she choked out, "Bryan, is this why?"

"We can't know that." Tears filled his eyes. "We can only thank God for Vic's influence."

"And yours and Payton's. The words you spoke at the funeral left for no room for doubt as to why he was the way he was."

"Ah, they all knew that before. They can only begin to comprehend it now. Vic laid the groundwork."

That was what Shawn had said. She stared out the window, waiting for the tearful sensation to pass. Would the desire to cry at the drop of a hat ever go completely away? She didn't think so.

"Bryan, why have you been avoiding me?"

He sighed. "It hurt too much."

"I'm sorry."

"It's not your fault. And then that woman's name and number completely unnerved me. I'm sure he's innocent of any wrongdoing except breaking his promise to stay current with you." He shrugged. "But there it is, an unknown haunting us. How are you handling it?"

"When it gets the better of me, I talk to God until my nostrils stop flaring. I'm usually awake from two until four in the morning."

"You know he would not cheat on you. He would not."

His words loosened the thread of doubt that often constricted her heart. "I take you for granted. You're the closest thing I have to Vic. Now you know what the poor guy put up with."

His attempt to smile failed as miserably as did hers. "I think we're both still more fragile than we want to admit. I don't mean to discourage, but are you sure you shouldn't take the semester off?"

She shook her head. "When I was in the classroom on Friday, I finally felt a sense of purpose again. Just a trace, but it was there."

"All right. I trust Sylvia will watch for signs and tell you if you need a break. I'm recognizing my own signs of burnout. I need some time away. I'm going to a retreat center."

Her hand shook as she set the mug on the table, betraying the rush of panic. He was always incommunicado on his retreats. "For how long?"

He touched her forearm. "A month. But I'm not going until you feel settled in your school routine."

"Oh, Bryan! Who knows when that will be?" Though she wanted to cling to him until the hurt went away, she knew better. "Go now. As soon as possible."

"I was only his friend. You were his wife. You still come first. How about if I leave in time to be back for his birthday? We can start some sort of new tradition. Dinner or something. Maybe with Stan and Wanda."

She wrinkled her nose. "Yeah, right."

"Have you forgotten? Our Father is in the business of changing hearts."

Yes, their Father was in the business of changing hearts.

As she drove from the restaurant, Rachel was struck with the thought that if not for Vic's changed heart, none of them would be where they were at that moment in time, least of all herself. If he hadn't turned his heart toward God, they never would have married in the first place. She doubted they would have even gone out that first time.

If not for his changed heart, there would not exist that particular firefighter's Bible study and prayer group. Jessie wouldn't be in church. Kevin certainly wouldn't be. Nor Shawn and Jody, or Alice, or those other firemen, Steve, Duke, and Jim. Terri would not be interested in forgiving Lee.

Strange to think that every single one of those developments were rooted in a fire. Bryan included the incident in his eulogy at the funeral service.

Though Vic had abandoned his forays into illegal activities while in the Army, he still lived a wild and crazy life as a firefighter. His off-duty hours were spent partying, driving fast, racing speedboats, skydiving, and rock climbing. If danger wasn't on the agenda, neither was Vic.

He spent less time than ever with Bryan, his best buddy since the age of four when they'd picked all of Wanda Koski's green tomatoes and thrown them at other neighborhood children. They had gone through boot camp together. Somehow along the way, Vic discovered firefighting and Bryan discovered religion. Go figure.

Then there came the day of a house fire, over 12 years ago now. By the time Vic and his company arrived, the two-story frame was fully involved, a 3000-degree flaming torch. The fire, electrical in origin, must have smoldered for days in the walls. There was little the firefighters could do except keep it from spreading to nearby homes. The house burned to the ground. At least the owners were out of town and no one was hurt.

Vic, nicknamed "Curious George," returned to the scene with the fire inspector, eager to sift through ashes and learn the cause of such devastation. What he found instead, buried beneath the ashes and unrecognizable charred clumps, was a Bible. Totally intact. Totally untouched by flames or heat or water damage.

That moment changed Vic's life forever. God sprang into reality. And his friend the Episcopal priest would have the answers to a growing fear that Vic Koski's life was as meaningless as an ash heap.

Those at the funeral who personally knew Vic knew the story. He never tired of telling it.

But, Rachel now suspected, that day when Bryan told it they would have heard it as if for the first time. They would have heard it in a different way. With new ears. Finely tuned ears that were only capable of hearing when hearts were broken.

$\mathscr{T}$wenty-$\mathscr{T}$hree

Rachel paused beside one of the 24 vacant student desks. It was the first one in the first row nearest the door. Taped across its top, in the right-hand corner, was a rectangular piece of manila paper. With black marker in bold cursive letters large enough to be read across the room, a name had been written: Deshawn Baker.

Vic had always been impressed with the symmetry of her handwriting. She said if he practiced penmanship nine months of every year of his life, he too could write legibly.

"Knock knock."

She looked up to see Sylvia at the door. "Hi, boss."

"Hi." The principal leaned against the doorjamb. "So, how are you doing, two and a half days into it?"

"Well, today I heard, and I quote, 'Yo, Mizz Koski! Pay attention. You're zoning out on us.' That about sums it up." She shrugged. "The focus comes and goes."

Sylvia smiled softly. "It's early yet. Who said that?"

"I'm not sure," she murmured and moved down the aisle. "He is mouthy, but smart. Potentially cute personality if I can rein him in soon enough. Here." She stopped beside a desk and touched the name card. "Juan. Yes, he was Hispanic."

"Rachel."

She heard concern in Sylvia's voice and turned. "What?"

"You didn't remember his name?"

"I can't remember *any* of their names." She made a sweeping motion with her arm over the desktops. "I've had to resort to these idiot cards."

"It's only the second full day—"

"I haven't used them since my first year. I've always had their names and simple alphabetized seating chart memorized before I ever laid eyes on them. By the second day I could match names with faces. Oh, Sylvia! I'm letting them down! I don't belong here!"

Her friend was at her side now and pulled her into a hug. "Shh. You're not letting them down, child, and of course you belong here."

She leaned her forehead on Sylvia's shoulder. Hugs. That was what she missed the most. Vic was a hugger. Morning, noon, and night his teddy bear arms held her, his large chest blocking out the world's horrors, his kisses on top of her head reminders of the happiness he brought into her life. When she fretted as she did now, that only egged him on to hug more. Correction. Toward the end of spring, her fretting hadn't egged him on to more hugs. It had egged him on to buy a diamond bracelet.

"Rachel, join me for dinner tonight. I should say us." What sounded like a giggle escaped her. She cleared her throat. "Harrison and I are trying out a new Thai place."

Fingering the bracelet at her wrist, she raised her head and lightened her tone. "You two are getting to be an *item.*"

"Friends." Her sparkling eyes belied the term.

Rachel whispered, "You are attracted to each other. I watched him watching you while you were talking to someone else."

"Hush."

"What do your girls think of him?"

Sylvia patted Rachel's shoulders. "They enjoyed his company Wednesday night at dinner downtown."

"You went out Wednesday night too?"

"Celebrated the first day of school. Tonight is, well, Friday."

"Time to celebrate the end of the first week of school."

"Yes, well, whatever. Will you come?"

"Thank you, but no. Jessie invited me over too..."

"But you declined. Would you come if it were just with me?"

"Probably." She shook her head and exhaled noisily. "Then again, maybe not. There's just no getting around it, Sylvia. This is the first Friday night of the school year without Vic. I have to go home and get through it one minute at a time. Actually, I think I'm up to one quarter hour at a time." She smiled. "Besides, I have some homework. Memorizing names and faces."

"Honey, you're allowed to relax."

Relax? As in drop the burdens of childless widowhood, insurance quagmires, and the mystery woman Fiona? "The word no longer exists in my vocabulary."

"It'll return. Someday when you're not looking for it."

⌣

Saturday, September twelfth. Two and a half weeks since school started. Nine weeks to the day since Vic's death.

Rachel hadn't replaced that Day-Timer she'd pitched so many years ago. She didn't need it. A sixth sense had taken hold in her brain like some atomic clock that tracked the passage of time without batteries or winding or her authorization to do so.

The thing even provided a *schedule*. Without making a conscious decision, she knew when it was time to sort through Vic's clothes, visit her in-laws, prepare for school, sell his truck. She had balked at Terri's pressing her into emotional arenas she'd just as soon bypass, but even those succeeded in getting her eyes lifted elsewhere and off of her own misery. Evidently Terri was a dancing molecule that kept that atomic clock ticking.

Now on this Saturday afternoon in September, she knew it was time to move Vic's exercise equipment from the spare bedroom. He had been finishing off an area in the basement, tiling the floor and paneling the walls, in preparation to move it all down there and turn the bedroom into a nursery. She didn't know yet what she'd do with the room. No doubt that internal planner would let her know.

She had invited the Leonards over to help. While Shawn and his five-year-old, Zak, figured things out, she and Jody sat at the kitchen table. Cammie and Seth, the two younger ones, quietly played on the floor with a variety of brightly colored toys.

Shawn entered through the living room doorway, a screwdriver in his hand. "Mrs. Koski, are you sure—"

"Shawn, please! I'm only twelve years older than you!"

He scratched his blond crew cut. "Yeah, but you're still the lieutenant's wife."

Widow, she silently amended. But that was splitting hairs. His point was Vic had been his superior and, therefore, by extension so was she. Forever and always, evidently. "But I'm also your friend and Jody's." She gestured to his wife sitting beside her at the table. "My name is Rachel."

He nodded. "Anyway, are you sure about this, ma'am? You could get quite a bit of money for the lieutenant's stuff. Our treadmill at the station isn't anywhere near as nice, and his weights—"

"Exactly. The department can't afford those things. If Vic had thought of it, he would have added to his will: Give it all to the guys. Trust me, Shawn, I certainly don't use it."

"But you're sacrificing a ton of money! And you just gave us his truck!"

"You paid for that."

He shook his head, clearly exasperated at her convoluted thinking.

"Listen, both of you, I have an excellent job. On top of that I'm receiving insurance benefits, and my expenses have been cut at least in half. This will sound horribly flippant but the truth is, my husband ate an awful lot and though he was generally frugal, he was better than Santa when it came to buying me gifts. And besides, I am convinced this is what he would have wanted."

With a start she realized that she had passionately spoken of Vic in the past tense without bursting into tears. Even jokingly about his food intake. Some atom must have jumped, pushing the timetable into the section titled, *I can talk of him fondly in regular conversation with people I don't know very well.*

Jody said, "It's like Jesus, isn't it?" Her voice was soft. Cheerleader cute like Jessie, she wasn't as spunky. "I mean, His gift to us is free. All we have to do is accept it."

Rachel smiled. "Yes. That sums it up perfectly. I'm glad you have a truck to haul it away in."

Shawn shifted his glance back and forth between them, as if figuring out how to contend with the thought processes of two women. "Okay." He left the room.

"Wachel?" Cammie stood at her elbow.

"What, sweetie?" She pulled the three-year-old onto her lap.

And just like that those atoms whirled again, stirring up a flame and rekindling an old warmth. It was time to notice little ones again. She couldn't remember the last time she'd played with Lexi, Kevin and Jessie's youngest. Thirty minutes ago the Leonard children had walked into her home, their presence scarcely registering in her mind. There were two new Koski nieces, both at least eight months old by now, whom she had not seen since they were born. She had not checked on little Jacob out in California since school started.

"Cammie!" her mother gently reprimanded. "You should say Mrs. Koski."

Rachel winked over the little girl's head. "She's the only one listening to me. She should say Rachel. Or Wachel. Or Aunt Wachel." She lowered her face to Cammie's. "Do you want some milk or apple juice?"

"Milk, please!"

"Is that all right with your mommy?"

Jody nodded. "Rachel, can I ask you something really personal?"

How personal was really personal? Grief had redefined the word personal. After publicly living her worst nightmare, no subject seemed too personal or off limits. "Of course."

"Well." She smiled almost nervously. "You said we're friends. And you said Cammie can call you 'Aunt.' I was wondering, uh, well, we've been talking with Pastor Payton, and he suggested I pray about a mentor. You know, an older woman. I mean older in the faith mostly, not so much agewise. Someone who could teach me the Bible and how to be a godly woman. Would you consider doing that?"

Mentor? Rachel opened her mouth to immediately dispel the notion that she was mentor material, but something made her close it. She was getting better at not spouting off the first thing that popped into her head. Grief was responsible for that too.

But teaching the Bible? That was Vic's gift. And how on earth could she tell a young woman how to be a wife when she had, more or less, left her husband? Even temporarily? And how to be a *mother?* Now that was a laugh.

Jody went on, "I know it's probably too soon after the lieutenant's, uh, uh..."

"Home going. That's what he liked to call it." She blew out a breath. Those atoms definitely hadn't skittered into mentoring territory, but she said, "I have to think about it."

The young woman's dimples deepened. "And I'll pray about it."

Maybe Rachel was the one in need of a mentor.

~

"Jessie?" Rachel thought she had called the Grays' number, but the giggly woman didn't sound like her friend.

"Rachel! Just the person I want to talk to. Kevin, don't you dare walk out of this room!" Her tone teased.

She heard Kevin's garbled voice.

"Rachel." Jessie was back on the line. "What are we supposed to do? He's got some training seminar lined up all next week, but it's our anniversary. He doesn't *have* to go to his thing. They'll do it again in November. But I made reservations downtown for all night and the grandparents have agreed to keep the kids, if we split them up. Does the Bible really say I have to keep my mouth shut and submit to whatever decision he makes?"

"Rachel." Kevin's voice in the phone now. "It does, doesn't it? That's exactly what Payton said last week."

"He did not!" Jessie again. "Go on. Shoo. Let me talk."

There was a muffling noise and then laughter.

Oh, Lord. They're kissing, and I'm sitting here listening to it.

"Okay, Rachel." Jessie, serious now. "So what do you say? Keep my opinion to myself? Cancel the reservation and the babysitters?"

"Why are you asking me?"

"For goodness' sake, you lived with a fireman for ten years! You've been a Christian your entire life! Who better to ask?"

She closed her eyes. *Would you be my mentor?* "Jess, Payton talked about nagging. You can express an opinion, just try not to nag while you're doing it. The rest, I don't know. Pray about it."

"You can't give me a straighter answer than that?"

"No. Living by faith is not a cut-and-dry, question-and-answer sort of deal where everything makes sense." *If it were, my husband would be laughing right here beside me, being silly on the phone, and kissing me. Oh, Lord, it's still too soon. I want to crawl into a hole, not mingle with people!*

"Oh. Okay. Guess I can work on that. Did you call for something?"

No, I don't think so. Rachel spotted the three small plastic tumblers in the sink. Cammie had used one for milk. Seth drank apple juice out of another. Zak, mimicking his dad, had opted for ice water. She should have given him a real glass. He could have handled it. He was a mature little boy.

"Rachel?"

"I, uh, I was wondering if Lexi could come over and play. Maybe spend the night? Aunt Wachel is lonesome for her company."

"How soon do you want her?" The grin in Jessie's voice nearly crackled the lines. "She packed a bag the minute she heard you were back from California."

That old warmth flared again. Maybe it would catch hold this time.

⁓

Rachel greeted Terri at the back door. "Hi. Come in. Want some coffee?"

"Yeah, thanks. Hey, I'm sorry I haven't been around much lately." She shoved her sunglasses on top of her head and tapped her hip. "Getting bleacher bottom sitting at all those football games."

"That'll be the day." The woman ran the equivalent of a marathon every week. "How's the team doing?"

"Great. Which makes for one happy coach and one happy home. How are you doing? Good grief, what are you doing? *Cooking?*"

Rachel smiled at her messy kitchen. "Lexi's coming over. She likes spaghetti and meatballs. And chocolate chip cookies without the chips. But I baked some with chips. I'll give you a plate."

"Rachel, you're cooking."

"All the casseroles are gone."

Terri tilted her head, clearly not buying the answer. "I said you're *cooking.*"

"I'm hungry. Ravenous, as a matter of fact."

Her friend thrust a fist into the air. "Yes!"

"I guess it's time to eat."

"I guess so."

Terri helped herself to coffee and sat while Rachel continued browning meatballs. "Rachel, I've been wanting to tell you something." Her tone indicated something was bothering her.

What was it? Dump Your Troubles on Rachel Koski Day? *Attention, everyone! She's making progress. That means she's fair game.*

She turned off the burner and washed her hands. "What?"

"Can you sit down a minute?"

"Sure." She sat.

"I don't want to hurt your feelings."

A mirthless laugh croaked in her throat. "I can't imagine anything hurting anymore than it already does."

"I'm sorry."

She waved aside the unnecessary apology. "What's up?"

Terri fidgeted in her chair and with the coffee mug, uncharacteristically ill at ease. "We had grief counselors around the station, you know, right after. I thought I talked everything out. This sounds ridiculous, but I was so angry. I was angry at the other rescue guys for losing track of Vic. I mean, I know how pitch-black and loud the whole situation was. Sixty firefighters here and there, but—" She caught her bottom lip in her teeth and held it there for a long moment. "I was angry that I was working on Shawn and couldn't go in for Vic. I was angry at him for—" Now she clapped a hand over her mouth and closed her eyes.

Rachel reached across the table and took hold of her other hand. "For dying. I know. I still am, at least twice a day."

"What do you do?"

"Talk to God until it goes away." Her answer wouldn't make sense to Terri. "Sometimes I wish Vic were here just so I could smack him."

She nodded. "The problem is, I think I've accepted everything as well as I can at this point in time. But I'm still mad at him. Royally ticked off. And I just figured out why."

Rachel blinked, not really sure she wanted to hear what was coming. Some skeleton in Terri's closet? Maybe she knew who Fiona was!

"Vic never invited me to his Bible study."

"What?" Relief and disappointment tripped over each other, trying to get the upper hand on her emotions. She wasn't sure what Terri was talking about.

"He never invited me to his weekly group. We rescued people together, fought fires together, socialized together, ate meals together, slept together, in a manner of speaking. But he only invited *guys* to his study. And I always felt hurt. Not that I would have admitted it. I don't even know that I would have gone, but man! What was the deal? Wasn't I good enough?"

"Oh, Terri! Good enough had nothing to do with it." She squeezed her hand and let go. "My guess is he didn't invite any of the women in the entire battalion."

"There aren't many of us, but I never asked around."

"You know how conservative he could be. Sometimes it was as much a counseling session as a study. Things got real personal between the men."

"More personal than me taking off his shirt to see how badly his arm was broken and checking his vitals?"

"Yeah, more personal than that. Now this might scare you off, but sometimes we hold hands in church and pray in groups. He never liked it when another man held my hand. In his study group, the guys prayed and hugged and cried and soul-searched and shared their innermost man thoughts. I know he thought men and women don't mix in such a deeply personal setting. It's too tempting to develop intimate relationships with someone you're not married to."

Terri sniffed and glanced around the kitchen. "I can't say that I'd much like to hear the innermost confessions of a bunch of testosterone-laden souls." She smiled crookedly at Rachel. "Thank you. That helps a lot."

"You're welcome."

Rachel thought about the scene she had described. That was Vic. And Payton. Their pastor, in his younger years, made it a rule not to counsel women of similar age or younger behind closed doors. Vic held his opinion, that relating in such an extremely personal way with the opposite sex was to sign up for temptation. Had something happened to change his mind? Had he somehow backed into a tempting situation with this Fiona person and—

"Rachel, I think your way of believing is beginning to make sense to me."

Terri's words jerked her back to the present.

"There was always something different about you and Vic. Still is about you, of course. What you're going through." She shook her head. "I'm thinking maybe I should investigate things. I don't have a clue where to begin though."

Rachel knew what was coming before Terri said it.

Her friend went on. "Church is the logical starting point, but you're right. The place intimidates me. They'd probably want me to wear a skirt. And hold hands and pray out loud?" She shuddered as if the thought sent a chill through her. "I was thinking maybe you could teach me."

After Terri left, Rachel stood at the kitchen sink scrubbing the iron skillet. That atomic clock was clicking audibly now, much like the biological one had a lifetime ago. Jody, Jessie, Terri, all looking for a little guidance by someone who'd walked the road before them. Third time's the charm?

A florist's van stopped at the curb in front of her house.

September *twelfth*. The date was September twelfth.

After a few moments, the driver climbed out, a bouquet in his hand, and walked toward her front door.

She released a breath she didn't know she was holding. Vic's friends hadn't forgotten her.

God hadn't forgotten her. If He loved her so much, how could she not love Him back?

Twenty-Four

"I read the book of Job last night." Terri pinched her sleek warm-up pants at the knees and sat down on the couch, tucking a leg underneath herself.

Rachel smiled as she settled into an overstuffed chair. Her friend's pragmatic approach to life naturally spilled over into her investigation of God. Now in late November, over two months since she suggested Rachel teach her, Terri was an earnest student. She accepted nothing at face value. She wanted second opinions on Scriptures and scriptural support for doctrine. Rachel gave her a Bible; Terri bought two other versions. Always a voracious reader, she diligently worked her way through Rachel's theological books and spent a small fortune at a local Christian bookstore.

"Why Job, Terri? It wasn't in the workbook."

"Everybody knows the man was dealt the worst hand imaginable. I was curious to see what really happened because, when Vic died and you weren't pregnant, I thought of Job. I think you lost more than he did really."

"But he lost *everything* except his wife. Even his health was gone."

"You can be so literal at times. I think he lost the most meaningful parts of his life, like you did. The main point is he didn't curse God. I don't think you have either. Not as far as I can tell anyway. Have you?"

Had she? She had blamed God for not intervening. She had given up on praying for a time. She wondered if she hadn't started praying again, would Terri, Jody, and Jessie have prompted her into this mentoring role?

By late October a Bible study of sorts had evolved. Jessie and Jody insisted there were other wives who felt much as Terri had: left out. How come the guys had a group? Reluctantly Rachel agreed they could meet weekly in her home. They worked around Terri's schedule, which often coincided with the times of those firefighting husbands.

She balked, though, at preparing lesson plans and assignments, even informal ones. Her formal ones for school were all the challenge she could handle in that department. Jessie came through for them. She found a study booklet geared toward women, ordered copies, and suggested they simply work through it together. If the goal was to get them studying the Bible and talking about it, the booklet approach was succeeding. Five women had just left her house after a lively discussion on wifely submission. It was their fourth meeting, and they eagerly scheduled the next. As usual, Terri stayed behind.

She answered her friend's question. "No, I haven't cursed Him. But…" She hesitated. Terri hadn't declared that she was a believer, though her conversation indicated more and more that she believed the Bible was historically true. Rachel didn't want to confuse her.

"Rachel, you've always been up front with me. If God is real, nothing you say can mess up what He has in store for me."

How could she argue with that? "I'm not sure if I…*trust* Him anymore. It's like I'm shell-shocked. Jumpy at the slightest movement, always expecting another explosion. Payton says it will go away. In time." How much time? Evidently more than four months.

Next week was Thanksgiving, a tornado on the horizon. It had already touched down and was approaching, churning her emotions like bits of debris in its path. There was no escaping its inevitable arrival and the total chaos it would bring on the holiday. She knew all this for a fact because the same storm had just blown through last month the week of Vic's birthday. Her parents had invited her to spend the day with them, as did Jessie, Sylvia, and Terri. She saw no reason to share the storm. She planned to simply stay home and weather it alone.

Terri said, "But you still believe in Him?"

"Oh, yes. I could never not believe in Him."

"But what difference does that make then?"

"I know Vic is alive. I will see him again."

"Something to look forward to. But what about right here and now?"

She blinked. What about right here and now? The answer should have been on the tip of her tongue. Joy, peace, an intuitive knowing that life would make sense again. Well, there they were. On the tip of her mental tongue. But they weren't quite in the center of her heart from which she could speak.

"Rachel, I've always admired you. I look at you and see one gutsy lady. First of all, you married a firefighter. Second, you stand up in front of a bunch of fourth graders day after day, year after year. Not to mention that crazy thing you did facing the kid with the knife. Third, you're exactly like your grandma. My point is, I think you and your grandma could face anything all by your independent little selves and come out the other end stronger than ever."

She shook her head. "Our personalities only make us look like that. Bubbie said she would have arrived in America a bitter old woman at the age of twenty-eight if it hadn't been for Christ. He gave her the ability to forgive the soldiers who killed my grandfather. He gave her a joy of life, an unshakable peace, and the strength to move on even without her husband beside—"

Rachel fixed her eyes on Terri's, letting her own words sink in.

After a moment Terri said slowly, "She had a son."

Rachel nodded. Was that what kept her grandmother going? No, of course not. She knew her Bubbie better than that. A child could not account for the exuberant, faithful life she had lived. "That wasn't the deciding factor for her joy and peace and strength."

"So you're saying it was Christ?"

She nodded again.

"Then He'll do the same for you, right? In time. I bet He didn't zap your grandma overnight with all that abstract stuff. Which means what in the here and now?" Back to her original question.

"Terri, I know I look like I'm functioning all right, but on the inside I'm not. In the classroom I'm not, not really. I don't know if I'll make it through the school year. But in the here and now…He gets me out of bed every day."

Her friend smiled crookedly. "Hey, it's a start."

"Three steps forward, two steps back. It used to be three steps back. Or four."

The doorbell rang. Rachel got up and walked across the living room.

Terri said, "Are you eating well?" She asked her that question at least once a week.

"Yes. And did you notice? Only two cups of coffee during the study." She smiled over her shoulder and then pulled open the front door.

Through the glass partition in the storm door, she saw a woman and pushed that door open. A gust of cold, damp air immediately chilled her.

The stranger standing on her porch was quite young, under thirty for certain. She wasn't beautiful, not even pretty in a conventional way. But something about her narrow face mesmerized. An almost ethereal glow. Skin like velvety rose petals. A mouth with corners curved slightly upward as if that were their perpetual location. Rachel had seen the face before, if only in her imagination. It was a fairy-tale face, suitable for some lovely, extraordinary creature.

Her hair appeared dark, covered for the most part by a light blue knit hat. She was slightly taller than Rachel. A black woolen coat obscured her figure...except the front where she grasped the lapels together. Beneath that the coat flared open...revealing that she was pregnant. Quite pregnant.

Rachel knew who she was.

The girl spoke. "Is Vic here?"

A great rushing noise whooshed through Rachel's mind. Crashing sounds echoed, as of doors and windows slamming. She felt a vague notion that everything was shutting down. Her vision blurred.

"Vic." She stopped long enough to acknowledge a sickening desire to blurt the words triumphantly, words that would surely cause the stranger excruciating pain. Tit for tat. An eye for an eye. So be it. "Vic is dead."

The enchanting face crumpled.

Rachel whispered, "Are you Fiona?"

The girl nodded.

There was no more to be said. Rachel's knees buckled, and she let the blessed darkness overtake her.

~~

Time grew confusing again, as it had the day Vic died. There was no connection between its passage and reality. She was unaware even of what she did or said.

Later—minutes? hours?—she opened her eyelids. They felt as if lead weights sat on them. The room was pitch-black except for dim light from the streetlamp hitting the backside of the curtains. She lay in bed, under the covers, on her back. She never slept on her back. Rolling to her side, she read the illuminated digital numbers on the clock. Three-seventeen.

Her movements felt constricted, and she realized she wore street clothes. She touched her arm and felt the softness of her sweatshirt. Those fleecy yellow sweats Vic said made him want to cuddle her.

Vic.

Go away!

The furnace kicked on with a thump. A moment later warm air billowed up from a nearby register.

There was a thickness in her head, a fuzziness keeping lucid thoughts at bay. She closed her eyes, searching for that black hole again. She had found it at last, that place of numbness where nothing could touch her. She wasn't sure how she had climbed into it, but she knew she was staying put. Perhaps her family would place her in a hospital. That would be fine. Professionals could look after her needs so family and friends would no longer be bothered.

Friends. Family.

No, Lord. I don't want to go there.

Terri had helped her into bed. She remembered that much. From a corner of her brain she had watched herself grow hysterical, appalled at the unrestrained behavior she couldn't rein in. Her friend urged her to take one of Sarah's sleeping pills. Rachel hadn't resisted.

There had been loud crying, hers and...*Fiona's*. Terri, a shadowy figure grasping arms, leading, propping feet, serving water. Her paramedic's voice commanding gently.

What did the dispenser of emergency aid know? The situation was not a crisis that would pass with time. Vic Koski's fall from grace split her world in two. His death had broken her, but now *everything* was broken. There would be no healing.

The woman was so young. But...beguiling. Fragile. Attributes no one in their right mind would use to describe Rachel.

Not to mention *pregnant*.

She flung back the covers and slid from the bed. In the bathroom she found a note taped to the mirror. "Rachel, if you read this after 3 A.M. and the sun isn't up yet, take this pill." An arrow pointed down to the vanity where a tiny tablet sat beside a glass of water. "You need to sleep more. Check on you later."

Rachel needed no more encouragement. She followed the directions.

~

"Rachel." The high-pitched tone of Terri's voice on the answering machine eclipsed her capable personality. "I hope you're still asleep and skipping church. You need a break, girl. Whew! Why didn't you tell me what was going on? Well, obviously you didn't know everything or else you would have. I checked on Fiona. She's doing okay, considering the circumstances."

The machine went quiet for a long moment, as if her friend paused to compose herself.

"I gave her your unlisted number." Terri's voice had risen another notch, not at all composed. "Of course, she had tried to call months ago but couldn't get the new number. I think you both need some space today, some time to recover. There'll be plenty of time later...I'm at the station if you need me."

Rachel picked up the phone, called Sylvia, and waited for the beep. "Sylvia, I need a sub for Monday. I need...a day off. Maybe two. Thank you."

She sank onto the couch.

Hours later, when the late afternoon shadows lengthened, she still sat in the same place, not having moved, not having stopped asking the question: Why had Terri given that Fiona woman her unlisted phone number? At last the answer came to her. So simple it was laughable. So monumental it pressed her to the edge of that black hole.

Terri had given the number because the baby was Vic's. Consequently, that child was entitled to money.

~

Early that evening the phone rang. Rachel let the machine pick it up. When the childlike voice began speaking, she clicked on the cordless.

"Hello. It's me."

"I'm sorry to bother you." There was a snuffling noise. "I have to...to go home tomorrow. I live in Iowa. Can we talk a little now?"

Physically Rachel hadn't moved from the couch all day. Emotionally she remained in the hole. Yes, she could speak from there, from the center of numbness. "All right."

"Did he tell you about me?"

"Yes and no."

"I'm so sorry. Your friend Terri said he didn't get to California. He wanted to explain in person. Before we met." She was crying.

"Things don't usually go as we hope they will. Do you need money?"

"Money? No."

"I realize you're entitled."

"I don't need money."

"All right. Well, there's nothing else to discuss then. Goodbye." She clicked off the phone.

Rachel unplugged the answering machine, the cordless receiver, and the kitchen phone. In the bedroom she couldn't reach the plug behind the bed. Therefore she yanked it loose.

Vic's betrayal was worse than his dying. She was alone now, totally alone. No one could go through this with her. Absolutely no one.

She felt awful. She climbed into bed, still wearing the fleecy yellow sweat suit.

∽

Late Monday afternoon a pounding on the front door awoke her. She pulled the covers over her head. It didn't dull the scrape of a key, the click of the lock unfastening. The week leading up to the funeral, Terri made four copies of her house key. Now Terri, Sylvia, Jessie, and Bits all had one. *Just in case.* Like she was some pathetic invalid who needed constant attention.

"Rachel?" Terri's voice.

"In here."

Her friend entered the bedroom. "Kevin told me Jessie's subbing in your room. I called and called. You look awful." She sat on the edge of the bed and pressed the back of her hand to Rachel's forehead. "A hundred and one point five."

Her eyes and throat burned. But then, why wouldn't they? A fire had started deep within her and spread everywhere. She'd estimated the temperature much higher.

"Are you chilled? Achy?"

She couldn't nod her 20-pound bowling ball of a head. "Mm-hmm."

"When did it start?"

"Don't know."

"It's going around. Did you see Fiona today?"

The fire hissed now in her ears. She mumbled in the negative.

"It's best you wait. You wouldn't want to expose her to an infection. She has more than enough to deal with. Did you talk?"

"Sunday."

Terri grinned. "This is just so awesome, I can hardly believe it. You know, the more I think about it—"

"Awesome?" She kicked off the covers and nearly knocked Terri to the floor as she brushed past her. "Awesome?"

"Yeah. I mean it's one of your stranger-than-strange happenstances. Who would have thunk it, huh? Is this what you call a gift from God? You should stop pacing and get back into bed."

"A gift from God?"

"Well, you know. It's Vic's baby, so to speak. Not exactly the way you planned—"

"Terri!" Her voice shrilled. "Vic Koski has an affair with a snip of a girl and you call it a gift from God? Like maybe she's some sort of *surrogate?*"

"Vic had an affair? No way! Not in a million years. With who? What are you talking about?"

"Fiona! The name on the calendar!"

Terri grasped her wrists. "Rachel, calm down. You're not making any sense."

"*You're* not making any sense! Vic got what's-her-face Fiona pregnant!"

"Who told you that?"

"Nobody! Nobody has to! I drove him away! He—"

Terri pulled her into a hug and pressed Rachel's face against her shoulder. "Listen to me! Listen to me! Shh! Fiona *Victoria* Gallagher is Vic's daughter. Do you hear me? She's his *daughter.*"

Rachel gulped a breath and looked at Terri. Her friend was crying. "His daughter?"

"Yes. She's carrying his grandchild. That makes you, Rachel Koski, a stepmom and a stepgrandmother-to-be. All in one day."

Rachel covered her mouth with her hands, still gasping for air. It was beyond comprehension.

Terri wiped at her eyes. "Your Jesus is more real than the nose on my face."

Twenty-Five

With both hands clutching the steering wheel, Rachel sped west on I-80, the November landscape a blur of flat browns with gray edges. Tomorrow was Thanksgiving, and she was on her way to some small Iowa town she had never heard of before Monday night. Hulking semis clattered and clanked in front, behind, and beside her car. A claustrophobic feeling seized her.

"Oh! Get out of the way!"

At least her voice was back. She wouldn't be in the car right now if Terri had not dragged her to the doctor. After one look at her throat he pronounced she had a strep infection and gave her an antibiotic without waiting for the culture to confirm his diagnosis. Her fever broke Tuesday morning. On Wednesday, over 24 hours later, she pronounced herself no longer contagious. Terri cautioned her to give it another day; Fiona was in an extremely vulnerable situation. But how could she wait to see her again face-to-face? Rachel had inflicted enough damage.

But what if she *was* still contagious? What if she exposed her to the infection? What if she gave Vic's daughter strep throat?

Relax, Rachel. The voices of her friends echoed. *Just calm down. Deep breath now.* Terri, Sylvia, and Bryan had repeated such phrases ad nauseam since Monday night. No wonder she couldn't get the words out of her head.

But they were impossible words! How could she calm down? Her loathsome treatment of Fiona Gallagher was unforgivable. Doubting in Vic's faithfulness was unforgivable. Refusing to trust in the Almighty was unforgivable.

But of course her despicable behavior was all forgivable. "Lord, I'm so sorry. I am so, so sorry."

Bryan said grief wore many faces, including even lack of faith in God and in the integrity of a trustworthy husband. Rachel wondered how long she could continue to blame her life on grief. She was beginning to miss herself almost as much as she missed Vic. She was also beginning to fear that like Vic, her old self was long gone.

"Oh, *move*, you stupid truck!"

Monday night Rachel had laughed and cried and grown anxious with Terri. She tucked away the image of the sane paramedic alternately sobbing, laughing like a wild person, and chewing a fingernail. Her unprecedented behavior was something to ponder later.

Rachel's fever spiked to 103 degrees and a flaming throat extinguished her voice. She refused to go to the doctor until they had tracked down Fiona's number. Their clues were a few stabs in the dark. Evidently the girl had moved from the downstate Illinois phone number written on Vic's calendar before she had acquired a new number. She had said "Iowa" to Rachel. To Terri she mentioned her husband's name. Rachel felt certain she was the daughter of Vic's high school girlfriend, Ellen Cunningham Hamilton, the woman who sent him mail with a return address of Bettendorf, Iowa.

With the atlas opened between them on the couch, Terri called Information.

"Yes," Terri said into the phone. "I think the city is Bettendorf, Iowa. Maybe Davenport." She studied the atlas. "I need the number for Danny Gallagher. Dan, Daniel, whatever."

Waiting for the operator to gather information, she said to Rachel, "You didn't notice her ears? Vic's. No question about it. And her eyes, same deep midnight blue, heavy lids. Same color hair too. Real short, tucked behind those big ears."

She croaked hoarsely, "I wasn't paying too close attention." No attention whatsoever. She'd been far too busy jumping to wrong conclusions.

From the moment she had read Fiona's name on Vic's calendar, her mind was made up that the unknown subject he took to his grave concerned a girlfriend. Which made sense considering how she'd pushed him away. The scenario was easy to imagine. While she was in California, some chance encounter had put him in a vulnerable situation. One thing led to another. No doubt he planned to ask for her forgiveness.

"Nothing?" Terri said into the phone. "Well, try some others...I don't *know* which city. All of them in Iowa! There can't be that many— Look, who's paying for this phone call? If I had a computer in front of me right now, I'd do this myself. It's a family emergency!"

Rachel nudged her and pointed to the map. "Try these."

"Okay." Terri lowered her voice. "Try Clinton...Iowa City...Muscatine...Maquoketa... M-A-Q-U-O..."

Rachel studied the finer print and pointed.

"Try Le Claire...Eldridge..." Terri whooped. "She said 'bingo.'"

They called. A machine answered. Rachel refused to leave a message. Her apology had to be in real time.

Back at the house after the visit to the doctor, Terri called in reinforcements. Bryan and Sylvia soon arrived. They continued trying Fiona's number to no avail until after 9. By then Rachel's voice was totally gone and her nerves frayed beyond sensibility. Terri became her spokeswoman.

"Fiona, this is Terri Schuman. How are you?" Pause. "Preterm labor? What did the doctor say?" Another pause. "Mm-hmm. I see. Well, stay in bed and take care of yourself. Uh, listen, I'm at Rachel's. She told me about hanging up on you. There's been a major misunderstanding here. She had absolutely no idea who you were. No idea whatsoever. You see, Vic never had the chance to tell her."

Rachel mouthed, "I'm sorry. Forgive me!"

Terri went on. "Really. She saw your name on his calendar and jumped to crazy conclusions— Well, she wants to tell you about it personally, but now she's got strep and laryngitis. She's apologizing profusely here and asks that you forgive her."

Terri covered the mouthpiece. "She's crying."

As one they held their breath. Sylvia squeezed Rachel's hand. Bryan closed his eyes and paced.

"Nice to meet you, Danny." She whispered to the others, "Husband."

After another moment, Terri said, "Sure. No problem." And then she repeated the story to him. "She really is a nice woman. Actually, the nicest I know."

In her soothing paramedic's voice—not the one she'd used with the Information operator—Terri paved the way. At last she grinned and an audible sigh went round the room.

On Tuesday afternoon Rachel talked briefly with Fiona. Although the young woman graciously accepted her apology,

Rachel sensed things would remain unfinished until she could see her in person. Fiona must have felt the same because she invited Rachel for Thanksgiving dinner.

She accepted without thinking. What was there to ponder? Every situation in her life paled by comparison to the existence of Vic's daughter.

At last the semi in the left-hand lane moved ahead, leaving a space. Rachel zipped into it.

She waved to the trucker she passed on her right as well as the one filling her rearview mirror. "Eat my dust! I can't be late for Thanksgiving at my stepdaughter's!"

⌒

Three hours and 20 minutes from the time she left home, Rachel pulled into a subdivision about 15 miles north of the Mississippi River. The area was flatter than what she'd driven through on the Illinois side, and the wind whipped unabated across the plains.

Her fourth right-hand turn off I-80 put her in the Gallaghers' driveway. She cut the engine and sat.

What if this is all a hoax? Or a coincidence?

No, it couldn't be. Terri, Sylvia, and Bryan all agreed with her. There were too many indications pointing to a strong likelihood that it was true. There was Vic's admission that he'd had relations with Ellen Hamilton at the end of their senior year, now 26 years ago. There were Ellen's accusations at the reunion, blaming Vic for her miserable life. Later there were her attempts to communicate with him through the mail. Last but not least, for goodness' sake, there were Fiona's *ears*.

Rachel had thought of calling Stan and Wanda. But the emotions clinging to that idea had overwhelmed her to such a frightening degree that Bryan urged her to hold off. Taking one step at a time was the wiser course.

Now she removed the key from the ignition and studied the house. It was a two-story, white with green shutters, with neatly trimmed shrubbery and an oak tree on the side that had some brown leaves still clinging, flapping in the wind. A June and Ward Cleaver home if there ever was one, a house begging to be filled with children. She glanced around the cul-de-sac. Basketball hoops, bicycles, tricycles, and wagons. Upper-middle-class. How could a young couple afford it?

The front door opened. Unsure where to begin, she hesitated before climbing out of the car. A young man waved to her. He wore a winter jacket and blue jeans and carried a duffel bag. Fiona appeared then, wearing the blue knit cap and that large coat that didn't quite fit around her middle. Again Rachel was struck with the almost gossamer appearance of her face.

They met on the sidewalk.

"Rachel." The man shook her hand. "Hi. I'm Danny. We're on our way to the hospital. Mind driving?"

Fiona gave her a wan smile.

"Oh my gosh! Is it time?" Rachel asked as she led them to her car.

Danny shook his head. "No. We're not due until early January. There have been...problems. The doctor wants to observe her for a day or two." He helped Fiona into the backseat, and then he joined Rachel in the front. "Hang a right on the highway."

Rachel glanced over her shoulder. "Fiona, I am so sorry."

The young woman nodded absentmindedly and grimaced.

Danny said, "It's okay. Sorry for the crazy welcome." He smiled. He was a lean, good-looking guy with medium brown hair, longish and curly. "Perfect timing though. I'm in no shape to drive."

"And you think I am?" Three days' worth of self-torment packed a wallop of emotions that now spilled over onto the two strangers sitting in her car. "I treated my husband's daughter worse than I'd treat a *dog*. I had myself believing he had a *girlfriend*, which was totally insane and demented. He never deserved even a hint of such an accusation! I've spent the last three and a half hours yelling at truck drivers and wondering what on earth I could do to ever make it up to you!"

Fiona leaned forward and touched her shoulder. "You came, Rachel. You came."

She turned long enough meet the young woman's eyes. Navy blue diamonds. No doubt about it.

~

A new guilt washed over Rachel as she paced in the waiting room. *She* was the cause of Fiona's distress. Four days ago she'd informed the girl that her father was dead, and then she inquired in the rudest tone imaginable if she wanted money. Money! At a time like that! Vic would have been so hurt, so horribly disappointed.

When was it Ellen had died? While Rachel was in California. Early June? Poor Fiona! She was suddenly an orphan. But what about the dad she had grown up with, Ellen's husband? Where did he fit into the picture?

A new thought struck, and she stopped her pacing. What if something happened to the baby? The baby! *Father, please take care of that baby. There has been enough death and heartache in this family.* She closed her eyes and began to pray in earnest for the little one she had been imagining in her arms since Monday night. *Is this the one of my dreams, Lord?*

"Fiona Gallagher's stepmother?"

Rachel opened her eyes. Across the room a nurse stood just inside the door and glanced around. She repeated what Rachel thought she'd heard. "Fiona Gallagher's stepmother?"

People filled many of the stuffed chairs and couches, anxious lines written on every face and slouched shoulder. No one paid the nurse any attention.

With a start, Rachel replayed the nurse's words. As if in a classroom, she raised her hand. "That's me!"

"They're asking for you."

They were asking for her, not by name but rather by role. A new role. She'd just been adopted.

For the first time in recent history, Rachel Koski grinned.

Fiona turned her head on the bed pillow and smiled. "Rachel, come listen."

Struck by the enormity of the moment, she hesitated. Like the winter coat she'd worn, Fiona's hospital gown was pushed aside, revealing a basketball-sized abdomen. A grinning Danny leaned over her, a stethoscope in his ears. Beside him a small woman in a white jacket held the circular end against Fiona's skin. It was an incredibly beautiful sight.

She walked over to the bed. "Is everything all right?"

The doctor nodded. "Things appear stable. But," she shook her forefinger at Fiona, "you're staying put tonight. You've put too much stress and strain on this little one. He didn't want to drive to Chicago and bake pies and stuff a turkey."

"I haven't stuffed it yet," Fiona protested mildly. "You can't do that until tomorrow."

Rachel asked, "You know how to bake pies?"

Danny removed the stethoscope and straightened. "She does, from scratch even. None of those ready-made crusts in our house."

Rachel stepped beside the pole holding an IV bag. She touched Fiona's hand, carefully avoiding the tube taped to it. "You're just like your father. Vic always made the pies for the Koskis. From scratch." The thought crossed her mind that she didn't know who was baking them this year. The last time she and Stan talked, the subject hadn't come up.

A tear trickled from the corner of Fiona's eyes. "Tell me all about him?"

Rachel nodded and accepted the stethoscope from the doctor. A few moments later she heard it: an indistinct thump-thimp, thump-thimp, a tiny steady sound amidst louder whooshing noises that threatened to drown it.

Oh, the world in that little heartbeat! Vic's genetic code winding its way through the young mother and continuing on into the unborn. Vic's navy blue eyes and big ears and infectious laugh. His propensity for baking pies and for heroism. His life continued in the here and now where Rachel could touch it. *Thank You, Father. Oh, thank You!*

Rachel sat beside Fiona's bed. Night had fallen. They'd sent Danny on home. After all, someone had to stuff that turkey in the morning. The young woman rested on her side, fluids still dripping into her system. The doctor mentioned preterm labor. Rachel didn't understand the situation, but there had been too much else to discuss.

They had covered the basics. Rachel explained the misunderstanding, which stemmed from the note on Vic's calendar.

Described their infertility, how she alienated herself from him, and her grief was a painful process. But they had to know that although Vic was human, he was a real-life hero with an integrity she never should have questioned.

Fiona said she was an only child, and yes, Ellen Cunningham Hamilton was her mother. The summer after her high school graduation, Ellen told Jay Hamilton, her college fiancé, that she was pregnant, letting him believe the baby was his, and they soon married. Fiona was born two months early, supposedly, and weighed over seven pounds. Her mother insisted the middle name be "Victoria," a name her dad wasn't too fond of. The day she learned about genetics in biology class, her deep brown hair, blue-black eyes, and above-average height puzzled her, but she asked no questions of her blond, tawny-eyed, short parents.

Fiona and Vic never met in person, never even exchanged photographs. "He wasn't quite sure how to proceed. He kept saying 'my wife needs to know first.'" They had talked four times on the phone between late June and July tenth.

She became a Christian during high school. A friend took her to church, and there she met the two loves of her life: Danny and her Savior.

Rachel wondered at the completion of it all. Had Vic known about his daughter, he surely would have prayed for her soul. Did God answer such prayers, unspoken because of lack of information? Bubbie would cup Rachel's cheeks and playfully chide her for such a question. "Stop with the what-ifs already!"

Before Danny left, Rachel had slipped out to the car, turned on the heater, and called Terri and Bryan with her cell phone. They were cautiously ecstatic. As was she. In her mind, the grin expanded to Cheshire proportions.

Some latent mama bear awakened the moment she heard that tiny heartbeat. Which explained why ten minutes ago she had given her car keys to a near stranger and insisted she wanted to spend the night in a recliner in a hospital room.

Fiona stirred in the bed, like Rachel, too jazzed to sleep. "I had my tonsils out when I was six and my appendix when I was twelve. My mother never spent the night with me in the hospital."

Fiona's tone wasn't a whine. Rachel doubted the girl had a complaining bone in her body. Vic would have adored her.

Clenching her teeth, Rachel mentally braced herself against a fresh onslaught of grief. This had been happening since Monday, as if she experienced his death all over again because he was no longer Vic the firefighter, husband, son, and brother. Now he was Vic the father. Fiona added another dimension to his life. Hers was another life maimed by the loss of him.

Perhaps Rachel was in the way now. "I've been known to bully my way into situations and make people uncomfortable. Presumptuous is my middle name. I don't need to stay. I'll be perfectly fine at the motel down the street. Really."

"No, please." She paused. Her voice was childlike, soft, and she seemed not to speak without first considering her words. She had a college degree in art. Her personality revealed her artistic bent: She was aware of everything around her. Rachel thought she must see details that the untrained eye missed.

Fiona smiled. "Please stay. It's nice being cared for. You're not presumptuous; you're a natural nurturer. Thank you for staying."

Rachel blinked back tears. *And thank You, Lord, for the privilege of nurturing my husband's child.*

A nurse peeked into the room, frowned, and with a shake of her head turned away.

Rachel ignored the hint. Fiona was explaining how she found Vic.

"Mom dropped hints. She was drunk most of the time. That's what killed her by the way, mixing alcohol with sleeping pills. Anyway, she'd say things like my dad wasn't really my dad. I always took it to mean that he'd divorced her and more or less checked out of my life. I don't blame him really. She was impossible to live with. I never went without anything materially. He gave us enough for a down payment on a house as a wedding gift. Mom's family has money too. She set up a trust fund for me, so Danny and I are rather well off."

And Rachel had offered her money!

"But my parents were both distant emotionally."

"When did they divorce?"

"I was thirteen, in middle school. After she died in June, I was going through her things and found a letter addressed to me, telling me the whole story of her...affair with Vic. How she and Dad didn't see each other those last six weeks she was in high school so she knows I wasn't his. She told me how good-looking Vic was, but how his dad was only a cop and he was a hoodlum and things never would have worked if she'd married him.

"When I showed it to Dad, he said he'd always suspected as much. He hired an investigator who specializes in uniting adopted children with their biological parents. He located Vic and talked to him first. When Vic agreed to talk to me, the man gave us his phone number and address. Danny thought it was my pregnant hormones gone wild, but I think it was the

Holy Spirit prompting me to get on with it. I couldn't get him out of my mind. We were still living in Champaign while Danny finished up his degree." She smiled. "He was on the ten-year plan."

That explained the Illinois area code and the disconnected phone number.

"I had just lost my mother. We were in the process of moving back to this area, trying to find a house. I had a million things to do, but all I could think about was this stranger. So I called him."

Thank You, Father. "What was his reaction?"

"He was guarded and didn't tell me a lot about himself. I didn't even know he was a firefighter."

"And so you paid no attention to a story about a Chicago firefighter losing his life."

"None at all. I doubt I even glanced at a newspaper all summer. Vic said you and he had been married almost ten years and didn't have any children. He told me about his faith in Christ. He was full of questions, naturally. He admitted it was a real possibility I was his, given his history with my mother, but he wasn't convinced."

"I imagine he was feeling some remorse over his actions. In his mind, although he didn't know about you, he would see it as abandoning you." Rachel smiled. "If he'd only seen you in person, he would not have doubted."

"I look that much like him?"

"You look that much like him. In the ears anyway. And your hair and eye coloring. Somewhat through the chin, though your face is decidedly more delicate. Tomorrow we'll look at the photo albums I brought." She kept to herself how she eagerly awaited the moment when Fiona would laugh. Today hadn't been a laughing day. "You should rest now."

She reached over for Rachel's hand. "It's so sad."

She nodded and gently squeezed Fiona's hand.

"I think he liked me."

"I know he did, Fiona."

"The last time we talked he sounded hopeful. He said you were his best friend and the love of his life. He had to tell you first. He just didn't feel right about meeting me before that. He said he would call from San Diego, by late July. He didn't. We moved the end of August. I called him."

"And found the number unlisted. Fiona, how devastated you must have been!"

She lowered her eyes briefly. "But it's over. And you've come. And I will meet him in heaven."

Rachel stood, leaned over, and hugged her. "Yes, you will, honey. You will."

Twenty-Six

There was a rhythm to the Gallagher household that mesmerized Rachel the moment she stepped through the front door, long before Danny's Thanksgiving dinner prayer in which he said, "Thank You for bringing Grandma Koski into our lives."

After the "amen" she sat very still, pressed her hands into her lap, and fiddled with her diamond bracelet. Muted strains of a Vivaldi concerto reached her ear. The delicious scents of roasted turkey and sage stuffing and warm yeasty rolls saturated her sense of smell. She waited for her heartbeat to return to normal.

Fiona said, "Rachel, will you be our baby's grandma?"

Danny added, "Technically you are his or her stepgrandma. We thought we could drop the technicality."

"Oh my. You've only just met me."

They grinned and Fiona said, "You spent the night in a chair in the hospital. That kind of says it all."

Her aching body reiterated the fact that she'd slept in a rock-hard recliner. At the house they'd shown her the guest room with its private bath. As elsewhere, the furnishings were sparse, but the shower was hot and the towel fluffy. She imagined she would accept their offer that she stay with them and sleep in the cozy-looking double bed which, Fiona said, was purchased with her and Vic in mind. That was before his daughter knew he was 6'4".

Though they hadn't had the time yet to fill the rooms with furniture, artwork adorned the walls and shelves. Included were many framed watercolors by Fiona. Reflecting her work, pastel hues graced the walls, carpets, and furnishings. Sunlight streaming through large windows heightened the calm, airy effect.

A shiny black piano and intricate sound system dominated the living room. An electric guitar was propped on a stand in the corner. They attested to Danny's passion for music. An eccentric in the eyes of his family, he'd earned a degree in music composition. As predicted, he didn't do anything with it except continue performing at church. He worked where he'd always worked: his dad's car repair shop. Fiona said his other passion was tearing apart engines.

"Rachel?"

She blew out a noisy breath. How did one express the refining of a dream? She'd wanted Vic's baby. Instead she'd been presented with a daughter only 14 years her junior and a grandbaby. Why not her own baby? Why not Vic at her side? If their child now lived in their little Chicago bungalow with or without his daddy, would Rachel have spent the night at the hospital nurturing a woman who had never known the reality of that word?

No. More than likely not.

Lord, why?

Bubbie's voice echoed, *Stop with the whys already! Just let Him love you.*

She looked at her new family. "I would be honored to be a grandma to your child."

They grinned at her.

"There's a hitch, though. We already have one Grandma Koski in the family." And in the form of Wanda, one was certainly more than enough. "What would you say to incorporating a little Yiddish into the Gallagher family?"

Their grins widened.

"Call me Bubbie?"

They were delighted with the suggestion.

~

Later that evening they sat in the living room eating Fiona's excellent pecan pie. There was so much to learn about each other, so many years to cover, so many different life paths now converging. Questions and answers and stories hadn't ceased through dinner preparations, eating, or cleanup.

"Then you're saying I was a convenient excuse?" Rachel teased. They had just explained how they weren't close with Danny's family and preferred to spend the holiday at home.

"More or less." He smiled. Danny was three years older than his wife with hazel eyes that danced whenever he looked at her. It was easy to imagine the energetic young man playing his electric guitar and singing upbeat tempos with his band, who, she learned, performed only when the crowd was predominantly under thirty. That left out Sunday mornings.

He said, "We could have gone to my sister's for Thanksgiving, but things are always a bit awkward. You noticed how neither of my sisters or my mother came to the hospital."

Fiona added, "Danny, that's just their way." She turned to Rachel. "He works with his dad, but other than that, the Gallaghers don't get together very often. Besides, we're a little too offbeat for his mother's taste. I mean, we bought a piano instead of real furniture."

Danny laughed. "That's not it. Mom's still miffed at you for wooing me out of Illinois. She thinks of Iowa as a foreign country."

Fiona wrinkled her nose and turned to Rachel. "Or we could have gone to my dad's, but that's way too awkward. His wife is nearer my age than yours, and they're not interested in children."

Rachel asked, "What about your mother's family in Chicago?"

"Mom was an only child too. Her parents live in Arizona." She lifted a shoulder. "They always send a card on my birthday. So do my Hamilton grandparents from Florida, though I suppose they might disown me now."

Danny reached over and took his wife's hand. "Our family is really at the church. We did have invitations for dinner, but after you called, well, there wasn't anything more important than meeting you. Thanksgiving seemed the most appropriate day."

"It was indeed the most appropriate day. I was, to put it mildly, dreading the first one without Vic. His birthday was…" She bit her lip. The pain diverted her attention from thinking about the abyss she'd fallen into on that October day. She requested a sub, wept with Bryan at the cemetery, and spent the rest of the day home alone blubbering. "Anyway, thank you for getting me through this."

Rachel too had received invitations, from Sylvia, Jessie, and even Bits. Not, however, from Stan and Wanda, who always hosted the Koski gathering. She hoped that they too had found a drastically different way to spend the holiday and take their minds off the hole in the family. Maybe they could think of him working, as he had often enough through the years.

As a gift for the Gallaghers, Rachel had made an eight-by-ten copy of her favorite photo of Vic in his dress uniform and framed it. Fiona hadn't let it out of her sight all day, carrying it from room to room, indecisive of where to keep it. Now seemed the time to introduce her to the other relatives.

Rachel said, "Well, I don't know if you're ready yet, but you have a whole slew of family members in Chicago."

"Really?"

"Mm-hmm. Vic had four brothers. That means you have four uncles, four aunts by marriage, and thirteen cousins ranging in age from eight months to twenty-two years old. You're the oldest of the group."

Fiona blushed like a child on Christmas morning. "Oh my goodness. Danny! I have cousins!"

He grinned. "A baker's dozen!"

"And," Rachel said, "you have a Grandma and Grandpa Koski," *who I desperately hope will welcome you as I do,* "whom you are about to make great-grandparents. Do you want to see pictures of everyone?"

"You have pictures of all of them?"

"I do."

Fiona began laughing.

At the sound of such sheer delight, Rachel let go of the heavy sorrow she'd been dragging around for over four months. She forcefully willed herself to stop asking why Vic missed the moment. And then she joined in the hilarity. Fiona's laugh was an incredibly infectious sound.

Just like her father's.

⤙⤚

Saturday morning Rachel said goodbye to her newfound family. The reluctance to leave surprised her. She felt as if she'd just spent three days enfolded in a warm cocoon and now some outside force was ripping apart the silky layers of protection.

She and Fiona stood in the foyer and hugged each other tightly.

"Rachel, can't you stay one more day?"

"My thoughts exactly. But no." They smiled at each other through teary eyes. "I have to tell Stan and Wanda, and, just like Vic, I don't want to do it over the phone. It's not right to keep them waiting, even though they don't know they're waiting!"

"And you'll come back in two weeks for the baby shower?"

"I wouldn't miss that for the world."

"Even if you have to meet the relatives?"

"I'll bring Great-Grandma Koski for protection. She'll whip them into shape."

Fiona giggled. "I hope she comes. Thank you for everything."

"Thank *you* for everything."

One more hug and she made herself walk out the front door. Danny was across the street talking to a neighbor. He walked toward the car where he'd already placed her bag.

The day was windless. Her breath fogged the air, but the sun shone brightly from a clear blue sky. Fields surrounded the small neighborhood, brown and barren after the season's corn harvest. Still they exuded the promise of new life. Two miles down the road was the small town which contained all of life's necessities: library, grocery store, gas station, hair salon, barbershop, two restaurants, park, fire station. The setting entranced her.

"Rachel." Danny smiled, squinting in the sunlight. "You've changed her world. I don't know how to thank you."

She sniffed and waved away his compliment. "Enough already. You two, make that you *three,* have changed mine."

"Will you pray for her?"

"Of course I will."

His face grew somber. "She didn't tell you about this preterm labor complication. Hers is a high-risk pregnancy."

Rachel couldn't read his expression. She swallowed her pride. "I don't know what that means."

"It means her and the baby's health, even their very lives, are at risk. The symptoms started in September. She spent eight weeks in bed and probably should have stayed there."

"Why does such a thing occur?"

"Her doctor can't find a physical reason, like an infection. Fiona doesn't smoke, drink, or use illegal drugs. Which leaves..." He kicked a rock. "Stress."

"She's certainly had more than her fair share of that this year." Losing her mother, learning her dad wasn't her dad, finding Vic and losing him were all natural turns of events in the course of a lifetime. Tragic but not preventable. Rachel's input, on the other hand, was shameful and needless.

Danny said, "Stress. It's such a ubiquitous word."

"And beyond our control. Thursday morning the doctor said the baby was fine. I have the sonogram picture in my pocket to prove it."

"Still, there's so much that could go wrong. If the baby came now—"

"Danny, listen to me. My Bubbie always told me to pay attention to my dreams because they were my letters from God. One time, even before I consciously wanted a baby, I dreamt of holding one. It was one of those dreams where you wake up and you're not sure you were asleep. I actually looked around the bed, certain there was a baby there some-where. It wasn't long after that Vic got hurt. That was when I began to want a baby. It became a conscious dream then, and I trusted the Dream Maker."

"God?"

She nodded. "When Vic died, I lost that trust. In the past three days, I've found it again. Your baby will be fine. Do you want to know how I know?"

"Sure."

"The baby in my dream had ears just like Fiona's."

The euphoria accompanied her east on I-80. It remained well past the bridge spanning the Mississippi and on past the Geneseo exit. She sang and worshiped the Lord, amazed at the rebirth of trust, a development she hadn't recognized until she spoke it to Danny.

Near LaSalle-Peru, she laughed out loud.

Near Ottawa, she wondered if Vic had fathered other children.

The euphoria dwindled.

Near Morrison she asked herself why Vic hadn't told her on the phone. It wasn't as if she hadn't known he'd been promiscuous. Didn't he know how much she loved him? That she would accept his own child no matter what the circumstances?

That she would accept his ability to conceive with another woman?

Well…maybe not.

By Joliet the flood of euphoria had slackened off to a mere trickle.

Of course it would have hurt. Nothing like she hurt now, but then widowhood was in a class by itself. No situation could ever induce that depth of sorrow. Yes, learning that he'd had a child with another woman would have ushered in a painful time.

But hadn't she apologized enough during that last conversation? She'd admitted to pushing him away, to blaming him, to trying to make him into something he wasn't. She told him how wrong she'd been, asked his forgiveness.

Lord, I want to talk to him so badly. What did he think of Fiona? Of the situation? He would feel guilty, but he knew what to do with his guilt. She remembered how upset he'd been with Ellen at the reunion. Had she told him that night?

No. No way. Vic would not have kept that from Rachel. He had spilled his heart to her afterward. He would not have held back.

Perhaps his guilt was more than he could accept forgiveness for. After all, this went way beyond shoplifting, breaking and entering, cutting school, vandalism, drunkenness, sleeping around, and just generally putting his parents through hell. Not only was there Fiona, there was Ellen, probably begging for help through the mail the last months of her life, and he'd ignored her when he could have, perhaps, extended some consolation.

Rachel concluded he would have needed to see her in person when he told her. She remembered how at times, when they sat across from each other at Myra B's Coffee Shop, he would tell her things.

"Vic, I don't need the sordid details. Really. Christ forgives you. I forgive you."

"No, Rache, you have to hear this one."

"But why?"

"Because I need to see in your eyes that you forgive me for breaking into the high school principal's house and stealing two bottles of whiskey, three six-packs of beer, and one hundred seventy-five dollars."

Etcetera, etcetera.

"Vic, you should have a record a mile long. How in the world did you never get caught?"

"That was the easy part. Dad always said crooks were compelled to brag about what they did. Eventually the cops heard. I simply kept my mouth shut."

He'd made up for that after they fell in love.

Yes, he would have needed to see the forgiveness in her eyes when he told her about Ellen and Fiona. And the baby.

The baby.

Rachel smiled. "I forgive you, Vic Koski. I forgive you with all my heart."

Twenty-Seven

At 12:45 that afternoon, Rachel pulled into a shopping center parking lot, cut the engine, and dug the cell phone from her purse.

"Please, please be available."

A moment later, he answered. "Bryan O'Shaugnessy."

"Bryan. Hi." She heard the relief in her own voice.

"Rachel! Where are you? *How* are you?"

"Evergreen Plaza. And I'm good. Great, as a matter of fact."

"I've been so anxious to hear more."

"I know. I'm sorry I didn't call again. It was all just too incredible. Are you busy now? Silly question. Of course you are."

"Nothing that can't wait."

Yeshua vibes. The man would drop anything if someone needed him. "I have to tell Stan and Wanda, as soon as possible. Now, if possible."

"This Fiona is for real then?"

"She's for real."

"Okay. I'll meet you at their house. Twenty minutes?"

Just like that. "Uh, they don't know I'm coming. I-I'm sorry. I'm getting cold feet. Will you call them first? Tell them we'd like to talk to them?"

"Of course."

"Of course. Oh, Bryan. Thank you!"

"You're welcome. Did you just get back in town?"

"Yes."

"You don't want to go home first?"

"No. This can't wait."

"All right. I'll call you back on your cell in a couple minutes. Bye."

"Bye."

Suddenly she felt ravenous. She reached for a brown paper bag sitting on the passenger seat and removed the lunch Fiona and Danny had packed for her. Turkey-and-pickle sandwich, an apple, a small bag of homemade chocolate chip cookies, and a box of apple juice. She carefully peeled the plastic from the bread. As she savored her first bite, a gentle feeling enfolded her. The cocoon spun itself around her once more.

You don't want to go home first?

She shook her head. Nope. She'd just come from home.

～

"Coffee will be ready in a minute," Stan announced as he closed his front door behind Rachel and Bryan. "Just lay your coats there." He indicated a ladder-back chair, and then he smiled sheepishly. "Where you always put them."

They followed him into the kitchen, the common gathering place for family powwows. Not that he knew a powwow was coming, but Rachel was grateful for the familiar environment. The living room was used for Wanda-decreed formalities.

While Rachel and Bryan sat at the worn maple table, Stan rummaged in the cupboard and pulled out four coffee cups.

The men engaged in small talk about Thursday's football game.

Stan said, "I'll tell Wanda you're here." He left the room.

Bryan flashed her a smile. She latched onto the encouragement behind it like a lion tamer clutching a chair to wield off the animal's swinging paws. Was the tamer's action merely defensive or was there an offensive motive behind it, provoking the creature to excess?

Lord, remove any offensive way in me.

The lioness entered the kitchen ahead of Stan. Wanda clearly resented the summons. Though Stan hadn't greeted Rachel with his customary hug of bygone days, he had looked her in the eye and said hello. Wanda pointedly ignored her.

"Bryan." She went to him as he stood. They embraced. "How's your mother?"

"She's well, thanks."

"You tell her I said hello."

"I'll do that. How are you?" He held her hands between them.

"Oh, so-so." Uncharacteristically, she did not recite a litany of minor physical ailments or bemoan the latest bit of news regarding a friend or grandchild. Like Rachel, she'd been leveled. Most complaints were no longer worth the breath it took to mention them.

"I missed you at church this week, but I understand."

She nodded and sat down.

Rachel said, "Hello, Wanda."

Her response was indecipherable. At least it was an acknowledgment that her daughter-in-law was in the room.

Stan served them coffee and sat down.

Bryan cleared his throat. "I'm not quite sure how to prepare you for some surprising news."

Wanda gurgled a harumph in her throat. "I suppose *she's* getting married."

"Oh!" Rachel cried out. "My goodness no!" A look of panic crossed Stan's face, compelling her to add, "No! What a horrible thing to imagine!" Let alone say out loud.

Wanda said, "Well, you know darn well you can replace him. We can't."

Rachel envisioned herself shaking that chair in the direction of the lioness. Defensive reaction. Purely defensive. She entwined her fingers on her lap, squeezing until they hurt. Defensive could be just as offensive as an intentional slap. *Oh, Lord! All I ever wanted to do was love her to You!*

Bryan leaned forward, his jaw set. Evidently he'd heard enough. "Vic has a twenty-five-year-old daughter."

So much for preparing the Koskis.

Wanda gasped; her face paled. Stan flopped back in his chair as if shot by a stun gun.

Bryan explained the story, everything from last year's reunion encounter to what escapades he remembered Ellen joined in on with him and Vic during high school. He mentioned the mail and the mysterious name on the calendar. Sensitive to Rachel, he skimmed over her wild deduction about that. He described Fiona's visit and her confession to Terri after Terri had helped Rachel to bed.

He looked at her now. "Rachel just got back from visiting Fiona and her husband. I haven't heard the details yet."

Stan and Wanda remained speechless and continued to listen while Rachel told Fiona's story of how she contacted Vic, of their phone calls, of Vic's last conversation with Rachel hinting at the news.

Wanda blinked. "Hogwash."

Rachel took a paper from her purse. "This is a copy of the letter she found in her mother's things. Ellen clearly states that Vic was the father, that he was the only one she was with at that time."

Stan took it from her.

Wanda said, "Doesn't prove a thing. She probably wants money."

"They don't need money. Ellen and her ex-husband both came from wealthy families. Fiona could live off the trust fund her mother left."

"You saw bank statements?"

"Well, no. But I stayed in their lovely house and got to know them."

Stan asked, "Why didn't Vic say anything? He would have told Bryan."

Bryan shook his head. "Not necessarily. Something like this, I can imagine him wanting to tell Rachel first. I mean, in essence he was telling her that she was a stepmom. Major surprise."

"Or maybe he just didn't believe it," Stan said. "Is there any proof?" He rattled the paper in his hand. "This is the ramblings of a drunk."

Now Rachel leaned forward and lowered her voice. "She has Vic's ears. And his eyes, the heavy lids and deep blue."

Wanda said, "So do a lot of people."

"Why don't you want to believe that she's Vic's flesh and blood?"

"Vic would never let something like that happen. If he got a girl pregnant, he would have married her." Wanda wore rose-colored glasses when it came to viewing her middle son's youth.

"But what if he didn't know about it?"

"I can't believe any girl would not tell him. He was a good catch. Though *you* might not think so."

Now Rachel perceived herself the lioness as the hairs on the back of her neck rose.

Fortunately Bryan intervened. "I remember Ellen Cunningham as a spoiled rich brat who would lie her way out of any situation. She got engaged to this older guy at Christmastime of our senior year. He was at some college out of state. She hung around with our group, but her future was already mapped out. I don't think she was serious about Vic."

Wanda said, "I still think it's hogwash."

Exhaustion fell on Rachel like a sudden rain shower. Her strep infection, the emotions of the week, and the long drive finally caught up with her. She had said what she needed to say. "It's a lot to take in. I know." She stood. "It took me a while. Just think about it?"

Stan nodded and held the letter out toward her.

"You keep it. I don't need it. I'll see myself out."

Wanda's words caught up with her in the kitchen doorway. "Why do you want us to believe this?"

Rachel turned. "Fiona's pregnant. You're going to be a great-grandma in January, Wanda. I thought you would want to know."

Wanda's face reddened. Anger? Excitement? Grief? Maybe all three. Whatever it was, it stopped her tongue.

Rachel knew she and Stan needed time. "Next time I'll bring her picture."

Stan raised his brows as if in expectancy. And Wanda did not say as she expected, *Don't bother.*

Rachel took their response as a positive sign.

⌒

Sunday afternoon Rachel sat at Jessie's kitchen table. Kevin had headed out the door some time ago. The three children played in the basement, their voices muffled by the closed stairway door. Remains of leftover Thanksgiving food stuck to dishes scattered about the table and countertop. Mashed potatoes and gravy solidified alongside green bean casserole on the dinner plates. A lettuce salad clung limply to the sides of a bowl. Pieces of rolls hardened to stone consistency. Still, Rachel and Jessie sat.

As the story unfolded, Jessie's eyes grew wider and wider. "Wow. Unbelievable."

"I'm sorry I didn't have a chance to explain what was going on."

"Good grief, you had a few things on your mind. Not that I was glad you were sick, but I was grateful for the two and a half days of subbing in your room."

Her friend had spent nearly as much time teaching her class as had Rachel this semester. "And I was grateful to have you there. The kids know you, which eased things for me. I didn't give school much thought." Come to think of it, she hadn't given school any thought since a week ago when she'd asked Sylvia for a substitute.

"Wow," Jessie repeated. "It really is unbelievable. This is like one of those bizarre stories you read about in the newspaper. You just know someone is up to no good, and you can't believe the people fell for their line in the first place."

"You don't believe Fiona is for real?"

"Well, sure. I guess. Maybe." She frowned.

"Jess, what would they be after?"

"Money is the usual goal."

"They don't need it."

"Do you know that for a fact? Maybe they borrowed the house. Maybe they owe tens of thousands in credit card debt."

"I didn't ask to see their credit report."

"Of course not."

"Scam artists go after vulnerable, wealthy people."

"Vulnerable like widows?"

"I may be a lonely widow, but I'm not senile or wealthy! You read too much trash. They're a lovely young couple about to become parents. She's Vic's daughter, who desperately wishes she'd met him."

"People can look like a lot of things they're not. Did you meet any of their relatives? Their pastor? Friends?"

"No, no, and no, except for a neighbor. Fiona was ordered to stay in bed, though she did get up for Thanksgiving dinner. She spent eight weeks in bed this fall. By now everyone knows what that means. No company."

"But they let you come."

"She wasn't in bed when I arrived. Friday Danny worked, she stayed put, I cooked and cleaned. That night we looked at my photo albums again."

"Maybe they want a free nanny who does housework. If you say you're moving to Iowa, then I know we're in trouble."

"Jess, you're missing the point. This is my stepdaughter. We connected. We want to be in each other's lives."

"And that's wonderful. All I'm saying is to be careful. You are in one of the most vulnerable stages of life you'll ever be in."

Rachel sighed. So far her euphoria wasn't all that catching.

Twenty-Eight

Late Monday afternoon, long after the students had left school for the day, Rachel walked unhurriedly down the deserted hallway. Grief taught her the sanity of slowness, of limitations. In bygone years she had regularly bitten off more than she could chew and then some, filling her days with nonstop activities and people. Much as she loathed to admit it, the act of coping eclipsed all those old energies.

After leaving Stan and Wanda's Saturday afternoon, she'd gone home and fought new monsters sprung to life by the visit. Her in-laws obviously resisted the idea of opening their hearts to Vic's daughter. Rachel doubted she had the wherewithal to combat that. And Bryan! Bryan had been so nauseatingly diplomatic he'd all but disappeared from the landscape. Without his support, she was treading in deep water.

She carried home their disappointing reactions, a shroud of wet cement that replaced the Iowa cocoon. The feeling intensified the moment she opened her back door. The emptiness reverberated more loudly than ever.

Like Goldilocks she tiptoed through the rooms and critiqued furnishings grown unfamiliar during her absence. Who lived there? A faint scent of apple spice potpourri hung in air chilled from a thermostat set low through four winter days. The bed loomed Papa Bear size.

At that moment her womanly facade crumbled to the floor. Only a little girl was left to absorb the changes.

She carried her overnight bag into the spare room and eyed the two twin beds. They'd been purchased to fill the void created by the removal of Vic's exercise equipment.

Rachel sighed. The bed nearest the window appeared just the right size.

And so, instead of calling Jessie, Sylvia, Terri, and her sister Sarah as she had euphorically planned earlier in the day, Rachel hibernated.

Sunday's equally disappointing encounter with Jessie convinced her that friends and relatives had to be taken in small doses. People had been telling her for months now to take life one day at a time. They had no idea of the pace of one *hour* at a time. Now it seemed one person at a time was all she could handle also. And so after leaving Jessie's, she again hibernated. It helped that Sylvia had not been in church that morning, and that Terri left a message on the answering machine. She had gone to Chestnut to ski, but she could hardly wait to hear all the "Iowa details." How about an early dinner on Wednesday?

Now, on Monday, it was Sylvia's turn. Rachel found the principal alone in her office.

~

"Incredible story, Rachel. Simply incredible!" Sylvia leaned back in her chair, a faraway look on her face.

Rachel glanced around the cramped office chock-full of cabinets and mounds of files. The desktop was clear except for the blotter, a covered crystal candy dish, and a double five-by-seven frame featuring her twins. The photos were taken two years ago. Graduate degrees in hand, Natalie and Alicia wore graduation caps and gowns and wide grins.

I could work on my doctorate from home.

She looked at her friend and mentor. "Incredible as in 'wow' or as in 'unbelievable'?"

Sylvia sighed. It wasn't an audible sigh, but Rachel knew the look. A slight tightening of the crow's feet as she slowly removed her silver-rimmed glasses. Two dark brows perfectly arched, neither raised nor vying for space above the bridge of her nose.

"Sylvia, Fiona is for real."

"I'm sure she is. I'm sure she's as lovely as you describe her and that she sincerely believes Vic was her father. But the situation demands we believe the twenty-six-year-old story of an alcoholic."

Now Rachel sighed, as loudly as her aching chest allowed.

"Honey, stress and the mind are powerful forces within us. We can't always consciously control them. Fiona wanted a father who could undo the damage done by a dad who abandoned her and her mother."

"She found a Father in God. She just wanted closure on the note Ellen left, on her mother's memory."

Sylvia held up a palm, graciously halting Rachel's argument. "And you wanted Vic's child more than anything in the world. Fiona is in desperate need of a mother. She's never really had one and, apart from Danny, has no family support whatsoever."

"She has his features."

"I believed my husband loved me. When he slammed me against the wall, my mind said it was an expression of his love."

"It's not my imagination or gross sense of unworthiness that tells me Fiona is my stepdaughter! Sylvia, please, meet her. Come with me to the baby shower on the twelfth. We can stay in a motel. I'll pay."

An eyebrow went up. That meant a number of things, not the least of which was the recognition that Rachel was whining. It also encompassed the phenomena of December. The next three weeks preceded Christmas break, peak season for obnoxious student behavior and frazzled teacher nerves. Sylvia clearly had a million and one other things on her mind than going to a baby shower in Eldridge, Iowa. Come to think of it, that millionth-one thing was more than likely Harrison Robbins, the superintendent who appeared to quickly be approaching the status of Boyfriend, capital B.

The eyebrow went down and Sylvia's principal demeanor softened. She leaned across the desk. "What if I'm right?"

"I don't want to know if you're right." She shrugged. Ostrich behavior, another grief lesson. *Ignore for the time being what you can't handle.*

"But you'll think about it?" the wise loving mentor asked. Rachel nodded. *Tomorrow. Or the next day.*

◜◞

Bryan called Tuesday night. "Rachel, I'm concerned."

She pointed the remote at the television and lowered the volume. "About what?"

"About this new business."

Why couldn't he say Fiona's name?

"Maybe we got our hopes up too high."

Rachel squirmed around in the recliner. The chair had grown to Papa Bear size too, but unlike the bed, it comforted her to rest in it. She could play ostrich from the seat, watching a string of senseless sitcoms, snuggled beneath a navy blue terry cloth robe big enough to be used as a blanket.

"Bryan, why do you say that?"

"Probably because I never trusted Ellen Cunningham Hamilton. She was capable of inconceivable deception."

"But you know it could have happened just as she said."

"Yes."

"Then what?"

"I don't know."

They were silent. She reflected on how they could be quiet together for long periods the way she and Vic could. Like families could. Bryan had been closer than a brother to Vic.

She said, "Maybe you think Vic would have known deep down. And that he had an inkling of the truth when Ellen cornered him at the reunion, but he chose to ignore it just like he did her letters." A flush radiated up her neck. "Maybe you're so disappointed in him that you don't want to believe Fiona."

"That's not it. I don't think he had an inkling. And even if he did, it wouldn't lower my esteem of him. I loved him beyond measure when we were hoodlums. That doesn't begin to describe what I felt for the man he'd grown into."

Rachel's anger disintegrated, and then she heard it. Bryan was crying.

He said, "If Fiona is for real, then she missed out on knowing him, and *he* missed out on knowing her." His voice was halting, his words sputtered out between sobs. "And that hurts too much, Rachel. That just hurts too much."

Bryan had never broken down with her before. He'd been her rock through the whole thing. She hadn't taken him for granted, but then neither had she asked who his human rock was, the one who gave him that safe place where he felt the freedom to cry.

She gripped the phone as if it were his hand and whispered, "I'm here, Bryan."

Vic's terry cloth robe absorbed her own tears.

~

"Terri, thank you for not fighting me on this." Rachel speared a tortellini with her fork.

"Fight you? Why would I do that? Fiona is Vic's flesh and blood. Of course you should be part of her life. What's to fight?" She took a bite of crusty garlic bread.

Rachel looked around the small dimly lit restaurant. When her friend suggested dinner, Rachel purposely chose Mario's because it had been a favorite of Vic's. He enjoyed the casual ambience, complete with cozy booths, red-checked tablecloths, candles stuck in old wine bottles with layers upon layers of melted wax, and an overpowering scent of garlic. He said the faded posters of Italian towns had decorated the rough paneling since he was in grade school.

"Hey." Terri swallowed. "You okay?"

"Yeah, I am." She smiled and gently slapped the hand Terri held up in a high-five sign. "Vic loved this place. That Bolognese was his favorite. And he always ordered extra garlic bread."

"The guy could eat like there was no tomorrow." Halting a forkful of Bolognese halfway to her mouth, she raised her eyes, a look of panic on her face. "I'm sorry! Dumb saying. Really dumb."

Not really, Rachel thought. No tomorrows meant only *now.* Heaven would be like that. Life should be like that, lived in the moment without thought for tomorrow. "Vic lived his life like that, always in the moment, not anxious about what tomorrow would bring."

"Matthew six. Towards the end of the chapter."

Rachel froze now, a bite of pasta poised in front of her mouth.

Terri shrugged a shoulder nonchalantly. "Don't worry about tomorrow. Every day has enough problems of its own. Or something like that. Which reminds me, I'm off on Saturday. Do you think we can get the group together for Bible— What are you grinning at?"

"Terri Schuman, you just quoted Scripture."

"So?"

"So nothing." She put the pasta into her mouth.

"About Saturday. Will that work for you?"

Rachel nodded.

"Great. I'll let the others know. I hated missing last week." Her eyes widened. "Just think of all that's happened in a week! Lee can't get over it. I can't get over it. So who's fighting you on it? Let me guess. Wanda."

"Stan's not too thrilled about it. Jessie thinks it's all a scam. Sylvia thinks it's my imagination. Bryan would rather not consider the possibility. Sarah's leery. Bits is appalled, like it's a scandal. Mom thinks I'm going to ask my nephew Josh to give back Unca Bic's helmet. Dad ordered me not to put anything in writing. I don't get it."

"They're just afraid."

"Of what?"

"Of you getting hurt again. Let's face it, this is going to disrupt your life. I believe in a good way, but still a disruptive way. If you get hurt, they get hurt."

"They're afraid, then."

"Mm-hmm."

"And I thought I was the ostrich. Terri, how come you're different?"

She grinned slyly and they laughed.

Rachel said, "I know, I know. Your brother says it's because he dropped you on your head when you were three months old. But really. Why aren't you telling me to slow down? Is it because you met her?"

"It goes beyond that. If we were talking about a man, I'd be blocking your path. Way too soon for that. But this is Vic's daughter. Circumstantial evidence? Sure. That didn't slow Vic down though. I think the minute he believed her, he was on the horn, changing his schedule."

"I think so too. If her story made no sense to him, he wouldn't have changed his shift or vacation time. You know how he disliked disrupting the schedule on such short notice. Nor would he have bothered to mention there was something to talk about. Right?"

"Exactly. And besides the fact that I believe Fiona is his daughter, I'm not telling you what to do because you're a courageous woman of faith. You should be stark raving mad after what I've seen you go through. Instead you're cooking spaghetti for Lexi and planning another trip to *Iowa*. Nothing is going to shut down Rachel Koski. Like the Bible says, who do I need to be afraid of? God is my fortress."

"Where does it say that?"

"Psalm 27."

"Terri, are you a Christian?"

"If you mean do I believe Jesus is God's Son, that He died for my sins so I don't have to, and that He's living in me because I asked him to, then yes, I am a Christian."

Rachel felt her brows go up and her jaw drop.

"How could I ignore all that stuff at his funeral? Bryan and your pastor talked so plainly about Vic's faith and eternal life. And I thought well, shoot, if Vic and Rachel are going to heaven and that's how you get there, then sign me up, God. I wasn't sure that took. I mean, I didn't get zapped or anything.

But between your Bible study and the books I've been reading, I think I've got it wired. I mean, I *know* I do. The Holy Spirit in me tells me I do! Rachel, are you *ever* going to stop crying at the drop of a hat?"

Friday morning Rachel stood at her kitchen sink, staring out the window and munching on a bagel topped with peanut butter. Worship music played softly on the radio. Shafts of the rising sun's rays split through the bare trees behind the neighbor's house across the street. Winter solstice would arrive in just a few weeks, the shortest day of the year. When that night ended, the days would begin growing longer again, a promise that spring was on its way even at the beginning of winter.

Time was a strange thing indeed.

"What's it like, Vic? Not having any time constraints?"

Talking out loud to her husband did not feel strange. He was always there in her mind. She couldn't imagine him ever not being there. Sometime during the past week her mental monologues directed at him had become vocal. The house echoed less that way.

A car slowed on the street. Stan's. He turned onto her driveway and parked. When was the last time he'd been to the house? The week of the funeral? He had asked about Wanda's sister riding in one of the limousines. A silly request that didn't necessitate a visit in person or her opinion. Perhaps the question was simply a reason for him to stop by.

She met him at the front door. "Good morning. Come on inside."

"Morning. Do you have any coffee?"

"I have hot brown liquid."

He unzipped his jacket and smiled. "That'll do if you have a minute. I know you've got to get to school."

"I've plenty of time." She'd been ready for 20 minutes and didn't have to leave for another half hour. Except during her bout with the infection, sleeping long and well wasn't her forte. Sitting in the predawn living room was more her style. At least she had stopped pacing away those hours. Perhaps one of these days she would pick up a devotional book again.

In the kitchen Stan accepted a cup from her. They sat at the table.

He asked, "How's school going?"

"About as lousy as this coffee."

"You don't want to sugarcoat that answer?"

He hadn't missed a beat. As if a feather grazed the surface of her skin, Rachel felt the wispy sense of a tickle. Stan's question was a standing joke between them. It had originated before she and Vic married, at a Koski gathering. One of the grandchildren misbehaved in a particularly obnoxious way, and Stan turned to her and asked, *What would you do, Miss Teacher?* Without thinking, she described to the entire family in succinct detail exactly what she would do. She'd laid the blame for the young boy's behavior solidly at the feet of his parents. The room went silent. Stan asked about sugarcoating to break the tension, and then he proceeded to agree with her. A debate ensued, two against everyone else except Vic. Her boyfriend only grinned.

She said to Stan now, "No reason to sugarcoat it. If I never set foot in my classroom again, it would be too soon." She drew quotation marks in the air with her fingers. "*They* tell me it'll get better. How are things at the store?"

He shrugged a shoulder and grimaced. "They cut back my hours. No big deal."

She knew there was a story behind his nonchalance. "Why did they do that? I thought you were their ace security guy."

"I tackled a shoplifter in the parking lot."

"Ouch."

"Well, you know, if they'd let me carry my gun, I wouldn't have to get so physical. One clean shot in the leg would have stopped him, no problem."

She laughed until her sides hurt.

He joined in. "At least they haven't fired me yet."

Their laughter faded slowly. It still bubbled in her throat when she said, "Thank you. I really, really needed that."

"Yeah, me too. So anyway." He rapped his knuckles on the table, announcing a change of demeanor. "I came by to see what you think about DNA testing."

She searched his eyes. "What do you mean?"

"This Fiona person. Let's get proof."

"How involved is that?"

"I ordered a kit. You just use the enclosed cotton swab and swipe it inside the cheek. Seal it all up and bring it back to me."

"What about...?" She didn't finish the question. Obviously there were no live cells for Vic.

Stan's eyes focused over her shoulder, and he spoke toward the refrigerator. "We talked about storing his DNA. It seemed a smart thing to do after September 11. You know, if we had to identify remains... He said it wasn't necessary."

That was news to her.

He paused before meeting her gaze. "Forensics can work with a hairbrush, but some experts don't think it's as accurate. I want to go with this mail-in kit. They use a parent's DNA. His genotype can be reconstructed from mine."

"And that will prove one way or the other if Vic is Fiona's father?"

He nodded.

Doubts assailed her. What if the Gallaghers *were* scam artists? Even if they weren't, what if the whole thing was a figment of Ellen's delusions and Rachel's imagination? What if Fiona *wasn't*— No! *Don't go there*. What Stan offered was a major concession for him and Wanda. The first step to their acceptance.

She stood, went to the counter, and picked up a packet of newly developed photos. "I want to show you something." She set the pictures before him and sat back down.

He shuffled through the stack until he came to a close-up of Vic's daughter. Then he paused and studied it. "She's got the ears."

"And you know what's funny? She doesn't try to hide them at all. See how short she wears her hair? Almost like she's proud of them."

"Hmm." He set the pictures aside and looked at Rachel. "This and the letter are circumstantial evidence."

"But enough to convict."

"You never know what a jury's going to do. If we can nail down the proof, we nail down the proof. We don't go with circumstantial."

"Okay, okay. I'll work on it. Hey, I thought you were supposed to be retired, Mr. Cop."

"Why would I retire when I can get paid for tackling punks in parking lots?" He stood to leave.

She walked with him to the front door, reluctant to end their conversation. "I'm going back to Fiona's Saturday for a baby shower. Did Wanda receive her invitation?" Fiona had asked for the address.

"It came." He zipped his jacket.

"Will she go with me? I'll get us a nice motel room."

"I'll ask, but I don't think so."

One step at a time, Rache, one step. The early morning visit had been a giant step. "Stan, thank you for coming by."

"You're welcome. I'll get the kit to you next week." He placed his hand on the doorknob. "Well, try not to bark at those kids of yours."

"And you try to stay on your feet today." She met his eyes. The moment was awkward, but Rachel knew in the blink of an eye that if she didn't make the first move, the awkwardness was never going to go away. She took a step, slipped her arms around him, and laid her head against his chest.

When he didn't respond, she fought down the urge to apologize. He needed the hug. It didn't matter whether she got one or not. She was doing this for him.

And then he lifted his bear arms and wrapped them around her. They stood in silence for a long moment.

"Take care of yourself, Rachel."

"You too."

He left without another word. But of course there was nothing else that needed to be said.

$\mathcal{T}$wenty-$\mathcal{N}$ine

The following week Rachel watched the six o'clock Thursday evening weather report while she unwrapped a frozen pizza and placed it on a cookie sheet.

"There's a fifty percent chance of rain Friday night. There's a slight chance that may turn to freezing rain by early Saturday morning."

"Well, fifty-fifty and slight chance sounds certain enough to me." She slid the baking sheet into the oven, set the timer, and picked up the telephone.

A moment later Jessie's voice came on the line. "Hi, Rachel." Caller ID. Surprising a friend was impossible anymore. "Did you catch the forecast?"

"Yes." She didn't even have to tell Jessie why she was calling.

"You'd better stay home." There was a smile in Jessie's voice.

"Or leave town early."

"That was my second thought."

"If I go at lunch time, that'll be early enough. Do you mind subbing just half a day tomorrow?"

"Not at all. See you about 11:30?"

"Perfect. The kids have been asking for you."

She laughed. "I already said I'd do it."

"Thank you." *And thank you for not trying to talk me out of this again,* she thought as she hung up the phone.

Saturday was Fiona's baby shower. Jessie still held reservations about that whole situation. Whenever the topic came up, she discouraged Rachel. At least she was willing to sub for her.

The students truly did ask about her often. Understandable, given the fact that as of the first of December they'd spent half the semester with her as their teacher. Literally half. Rachel had counted up the days. Not that Sylvia or any other administrator called her on it. After all, she was a new widow. These things took time.

She herself found the statistic appalling. If she'd heard of a teacher showing up half-time, she'd render a scathing opinion about the detrimental effect on the children. Still, there was nothing to be done about it. She had lived through five months without Vic. She had found her way back to her knees and into the loving arms of Messiah Yeshua. She ate regularly, albeit frozen pizza three or four times a week. She laughed on occasion. She thanked God fervently for Terri's new faith and prayed fiercely for Wanda's change of heart.

And yet there were times when she wasn't sure how she could take another breath, much less function as a teacher.

Last month when Rachel had missed days in a row, Sylvia gave her permission to dispense with going through the channels and simply contact Jessie herself if the need for a substitute arose. By now the class belonged to Jessie as much as to Rachel. Team teaching wasn't in the contract, but that was exactly what they were doing. Of course it went against protocol, but everyone understood. After all, she was a new widow. These things took time.

She picked up the phone again and pressed Danny and Fiona's number. They would be delighted to hear she was accepting their invitation to come a day early.

She grinned, imagining a scene Fiona had described to her the other day: Danny leaned over Fiona's abdomen and announced, "Bubbie's coming!"

Yes indeed, Bubbie was coming.

Driving west on I-80 under a smoke-gray sky, Rachel pressed the cruise control button, catching the speedometer at 70 miles per hour. She turned up the radio volume in a vain attempt to put her mind on cruise control and let another voice be in charge for a while. Some voice that didn't carry the persistent tone of a death knell.

Today was Friday, December eleventh. Five months to the date. Tomorrow it would be 22 weeks. At least she had stopped counting in days and hours. That was something, wasn't it?

The cell phone rang and she reached for it. For a split second she considered not answering. Vic was forever warning her of the dangers of driving and talking at the same time. Then he would give her the latest grim statistics, the high percentage of accidents that occurred while doing so. The guy obsessed over safety issues...

She glanced at the caller ID display. Bryan. He always called on the eleventh, the monthly anniversary of Vic's death. This would be his fifth such call. He was her lifeline. She lowered the radio volume and pressed the talk key.

"Hi, Bryan."

"How are you doing?"

"What? No hello?" They had to move beyond temperature taking on the eleventh.

"Hello."

But then these things took time. "I'm a basket case! If Stan were sitting here, I'd ask him for a cigarette."

"And what would you do with it?"

That brought a smile to her face. "You always ask the difficult questions."

"It's my job. Where are you?"

"I just passed Joliet."

"You're going to Fiona's today?"

"The weather forecast spurred me on. Not to mention the date. Jessie came in to sub. If she hadn't shown up an hour early, the place would have been in complete, total chaos. I'm not so sure it wasn't already. I don't even know if I'd recognize that condition anymore."

"Because of the date, right? I thought things were going fairly well otherwise."

"Things are going fairly *okay*. We can't use the word 'well' to describe anything about my life yet."

"'Yet.' That's a good sign."

"Yes, I suppose so, but this morning was like one of those three steps forward, four steps back scenarios. Jessie came early to the classroom because she knew the date would throw me for a loop. I guess I tried to ignore it and got preoccupied planning this trip. That worked until I woke up at three-thirty this morning. Things went downhill from there. How are you doing?"

"Fairly *well*. God is gracious." His voice soothed. "Keep that in mind, Rachel. At the forefront."

She let his words sink in. "I'll try."

"Can you drive while I pray?"

"Oh, Bryan, I'm sorry for being so negative! I'm sorry you have to call every month on this date and pray for me."

"This will pass, Rachel. Until then there's no reason to be sorry. Just watch the traffic. Heavenly Father, impart Your unfathomable peace to my sister in Christ."

He went on, the connection cutting in and out. It didn't really matter. She knew that, like God, Bryan was there.

∽

As she crested the final tree-covered Illinois hill, the mighty Mississippi came into view. It was a magnificent site, liquid gun-metal gray with scattered whitecaps stirred by a strong northwest wind. It flowed beneath the interstate bridge, a flat broad structure with no overhead ironwork. On the other side Iowa waited, its trees sparse, its hills less steep and soon flattening out, its promise of respite beckoning.

Rachel thought of her ancient ancestors. How must the Israelites have reacted at the sight of their Promised Land? With a surge of adrenaline? A shout of praise? A hush of awe at the powerful mystery of the Almighty? A quickening of hope? A whispered prayer that it was for real, that truly joy and peace and new beginnings lay on the other side?

All of those responses flashed through her as she sped along the bridge. The overcast sky parted in the distance over Iowa, and sunlight broke through, luminous shafts bursting upon the barren winter landscape.

"Lord, I'm not really looking for a Promised Land here on earth, am I?"

∽

The silken threads of the cocoon began weaving themselves around Rachel even before she reached the end of the bridge. By the time she pulled into the Gallaghers' driveway, the world was a soft, warm, snugly place.

As she got out of the car, a young woman across the street called a hello from her front door. "Can I help you?"

"I'm Rachel," she said loudly, hoping that was enough. Explaining she was the widow of Fiona's newly discovered biological father was a bit of a mouthful to shout.

"You're Bubbie!" The woman laughed. "Fiona's expecting you. I left the front door unlocked. Go on in. See you later!"

Bubbie. Rachel smiled to herself. Yes, she rather liked the sound of that.

She hesitated only briefly before letting herself in. After two weeks of daily phone calls with Fiona, she knew the little family's routine by now. At three o'clock in the afternoon, Danny was still at work and Fiona was still in bed per the doctor's orders.

As before, the house instantly enveloped her, breathing fresh air into her soul.

"Fiona?" she called softly from the bottom of the staircase.

"Rachel! Come on up!"

A moment later she entered the master bedroom, hurried to the bedside, and embraced Fiona. They giggled like two girls suddenly released from a dreary day at school.

"Oh, Rachel! Thank you for coming!"

"It's my pleasure. Thank you for inviting me!"

As she sat in a nearby overstuffed chair facing the bed, Fiona settled back amidst a mass of pillows. Naturally on the pale side, she appeared even more wan. That ethereal presence Rachel had first noticed in her hadn't diminished, though. She wore a pale blue sweatshirt, a puff of cloud beneath finger-combed espresso brown hair and navy blue diamonds.

Rachel said, "Your neighbor spotted me and told me to let myself inside."

"Ali. She looks out for me. They all do, everyone on the street. Danny hasn't had to cook dinner in two weeks."

"That's wonderful. But is he getting tired of chicken casseroles?"

She grinned. "A little."

"I'll cook tomorrow night, okay? Vic's favorite, roasted lamb and latkes."

Fiona clapped her hands. "His favorite. I'd like that. Do you need to go to the store?"

"No, everything is in a cooler in my trunk."

"You are amazing. Do you have Wanda out there too?"

She laughed. "No. I'm sorry. She didn't make a last-minute decision to come. Maybe next time. Now how are you?"

She gestured at the bed, its colorful patchwork quilt nearly covered with books, papers, remote controls, and a laptop. "I'm not bored anyway. I can read, watch television, listen to music, send email, and draw, all without stepping foot out of bed. I only miss my paints. Danny hasn't figured out how to rig up something for them." A smile didn't quite lift the corners of Fiona's mouth. "The truth is I'm too terrified to be bored."

Rachel went to her side and hugged her tightly again. "Fear can be a good teacher," she teased. "It's probably what keeps you in bed."

"Yeah, it does." Her voice was muffled against Rachel's shoulder. "How did you do it? I mean apart from God I don't know how you're doing it now, but I really don't know how you lived with a fireman. Weren't you scared all the time? I'm so afraid of losing this baby."

"Honey." Rachel sat back and cupped Fiona's chin. "After the year you've had, of course you're shell-shocked. I didn't live through your experience, but I was scared. I had to train myself not to live in fear of the worst that could happen. I let Vic go every day, put him in God's hands every day. When those fearful thoughts came, I imagined wrapping them up in newsaper like smelly old fish. I'd hold out that bundle." She lifted an arm. "And ask God to please take out the garbage. My Bubbie gave me that image."

"It's like the Scripture that says to take every thought captive to Him."

"I thought it said garbage."

Fiona grinned.

Rachel smiled in return. Those days were nothing compared to losing her trust in Him after Vic died. But the young woman didn't need to hear that story. Not yet anyway. Evidently Fiona still trusted. Would that change if the baby were to— No. *Don't go there.*

"Fiona, it's all about living in the grace of the moment."

Saturday morning Rachel watched Danny take apart a daybed upstairs, carry it downstairs, and reassemble it in the living room in preparation for the baby shower. The rooms in the Gallagher house were large and airy. The master bedroom had enough space to accommodate today's small group, but Danny thought the ladies would be more comfortable downstairs. And so he took apart the daybed. Fiona could recline on it, thereby technically remaining in bed.

"Rachel," he said as he hefted the mattress into place, "Fiona is so much more relaxed since you got here."

"It works both ways." *Yesterday morning I was a basket case. By three-thirty I was giggling with my stepdaughter. Thank You, Lord.* "Danny, I'll take care of the bedding."

"Okay." He grinned and quit struggling with the fitted sheet. "I'll bring in the kitchen chairs, carry Fiona down, and then I'm out of here before the decorating crew arrives."

"This is sweet of them to move the party here."

"Guess they didn't have a choice if they wanted her to attend." He laughed.

"I suppose not. Danny, can I ask you something before you bring her down?"

He sat on the bed. "What's up?"

"You know my father-in-law, Stan, is a retired policeman." He nodded.

"Well, he's into concrete proof of things and would like to do DNA testing with Fiona."

"That's great!"

"Really?"

"Yeah. She and Vic talked about it. He said something about home kits. She was all for it. I think she still has doubts. If you'd known her mother, you would know why."

"What did Vic say about it?" Though she wanted to grill Fiona with questions about her conversations with Vic, she hadn't yet.

"He offered to pay for it. He said it would be the smart thing to do legally."

"Legally! Oh my goodness. I know I offered money but I hadn't thought— The insurance company may owe her!" What an ostrich she'd been!

"That doesn't matter to her."

"I think I knew that, but I'll check into it. Danny, what did Vic sound like? Did he believe the story?"

"I got the feeling from what Fiona said at the time that he *wanted* to believe it."

Oh, Vic! He would want to believe it for only one reason: his wife.

The doorbell rang and Danny went to answer it. Rachel pondered his words, imagining Vic's tone of voice. Cautious, Fiona had said. And now hopeful had been added to that description. There had probably been some resentment toward Ellen as well as guilt aimed at himself for not opening the later mail she sent. His daughter heard the mixed bag of emotions communicated over telephone lines without benefit of seeing his face.

How Rachel missed his face—

"Rachel, this is for you." Danny handed her a long white rectangular box. "And look at this. It's for Fiona." In his arm he held a white ceramic cache pot. It contained a green plant and sticks displaying pink and blue ribbons and tiny mylar balloons that read "Baby."

She smiled. Was Terri behind this? Rachel hadn't wanted to tell everyone yet. After all, she was still getting used to the idea, and she was way ahead of her family and friends in accepting the situation. But Wednesday night at dinner she'd given Terri permission to tell Teague. Telling one firefighter was like telling the entire battalion.

Not bothering to read the card, she announced, "It's from the guys. Vic's company."

"You're kidding!"

"Open the card." She looked down at her own box and hesitated. *You know it's the twelfth because Mrs. Koski gets flowers on the twelfth.* They hadn't missed one yet. In August she'd received the enormous bouquet. Special month, that first one. September, October, and November flowers were more similar to Vic's, small bouquets of carnations or daisies with ferns and baby's breath.

Now she knew she was looking at a box of long-stemmed roses.

"Rachel, it is from his company! How did you know?" His eyes widened.

"Vic always sent me flowers on the twelfth because we met on May twelfth."

He let out a whistle that clearly stated he was impressed. "Can we keep that between us? I don't think I could live up to that romantic standard."

She smiled. "I'm...I was the envy of many. And now the guys send me flowers. I told my neighbor to be on the lookout for the florist truck today."

"Man, that's some brotherhood. Why don't you open them?"

Because I am so tired of bawling. With some trepidation she lifted the lid. There they were, a dozen long-stemmed yellow roses. Why such a special remembrance this time?

She picked up the card.

Congratulations, Grandma! With love, Aunt Terri and all the uncles.

Late that night as she lay in the guest room in a bed that was just the right size, snuggled under a comforter listening to the sound of a wintery wind bluster across the barren fields, Rachel knew beyond a shadow of a doubt that Bryan's prayer had been answered. An unfathomable peace filled her, a feeling that went beyond that of the cocoon. The silken threads staved off attacks. The new sense of peace worked from within, pressing aside deep hurts, filling their vacated spots with a soothing presence.

She had caught a glimpse of it last week when shopping for a gift for Fiona and Danny's child. In the past few years, dread always accompanied her into a store's baby department. Her stomach twisted, and she raced almost breathless through the task of choosing a gift. Nothing like that occurred last week. As she fingered a miniature white sweater she was struck with the thought that she was thoroughly enjoying herself. But then, why not? In essence she shopped for Vic's daughter, the mother of his unborn grandchild.

In the past, shopping didn't hold a candle to attending a baby shower when her heart would pound in her throat and her mind blanked hopelessly during inane games related to baby names, baby toys, baby clothes, baby paraphernalia, and nursery rhymes. That didn't happen at Fiona's shower. It simply did not happen. Again, she thoroughly enjoyed herself and even won first prize in one of the games. Even Fiona's tiresome in-laws could not detract from the flood of gratitude that she was a part of it all.

Who could have imagined that in the middle of an Iowa cornfield she would lose her despair over infertility?

Thirty

Rachel sighed loudly in defeat. "I quit. This is just not going to happen."

She sat perched atop a stepladder in the hall, a small area off her living room that framed the bathroom and bedroom doorways. Her upper body poked through the hatchlike opening into the dim, musty attic.

"No way. Not this year."

The problem wasn't pulling the Christmas tree box across the attic floor planks to the opening. Even manhandling it down the ladder was not an insurmountable task. The other boxes, full of ornaments, posed no problem either. When her and Vic's December schedules conflicted and threatened to push Christmas decorating into January, she had accomplished the project alone, without Vic's help.

Without Vic. Period. *That* was the problem now.

"No way," she said aloud again. "Maybe not even in this lifetime."

A smile tugged at her mouth. What an absurd thing to say! Her grandchild was about to be born. Just that morning before she left Iowa she had laid a hand on Fiona's abdomen and felt the kick of a tiny foot. Of course Christmas would happen again in her home in this lifetime. That child would know what Grandpa Vic liked about the holiday because Bubbie Rachel would show him or her.

Rachel and Vic celebrated their first Christmas together before the wedding on the twenty-ninth. Because he was working Christmas Eve and his family always gathered the next day, he suggested a quiet dinner and exchange of gifts at their new house on the twenty-third. She arrived totally unprepared for the scene that met her.

Vic had transformed the living room into a winter wonderland, complete with the green tree now stored in the attic. Of course he avoided real trees given the number of blackened ones he'd seen through the years. But he went all out with colorful, old-fashioned balls, silver garlands, and hundreds upon hundreds of twinkle lights. Single electric candles glowed in every window. They lit six real ones in brass candlesticks, an early wedding gift, and ate his pot roast sitting on the floor next to the coffee table.

She opened his first Christmas gift to her: a miniature porcelain chalet, the first piece of an Alpine village. He opened his gift from her: an electric train set. Like two kids they giggled in delight. A tradition was established. In subsequent years the village grew, the train elongated, and nieces and nephews yammered to visit, delighted as Aunt Rachel and Uncle Vic.

"But not this year." She sighed again, more in resignation now. The memory of silken Iowa cocoon threads floated through her mind.

"Just not this year," she repeated. "I'm not up for it. And that's perfectly all right under the circumstances."

Brushing attic dust from her hands, Rachel heard the doorbell ring and went to find Jessie at the front door.

"Hi, Jess. Come on in. Mmmm. Sugar cookies with frosting?"

Her friend hugged her with one arm. "Yes, they're for you. Hey, I'm glad you're here. I want to hear all about the baby shower!" She handed her the plate and shrugged out of her winter jacket.

Rachel set the cookies on the coffee table. The plate was colorful porcelain in the shape of a snowman with a black hat and red cheeks. It was the only visible Christmas decoration in her entire house. She sat in the overstuffed chair. "And I suppose I should say 'I want to hear all about your day with my class.' But I don't really care to hear about it."

"Oh, everything went fine." Waving a hand in dismissal, Jessie plopped onto the couch and began to detail lessons, recess, and misbehavior.

Evidently Jessie had not heard her exact words. Rachel truly did *not* care to hear about her class. Disloyal as the concept sounded, the students no longer registered on her "of-interest" scale. That disconcerting fact had surfaced during the drive home earlier in the day, revealing itself in direct proportion to the shedding of cocoon layers. She suspected that she had known it at some deeper level for some time. Facing that knowledge, however, had taken the stark contrast of experiencing a new life in Iowa.

Though she shrank from blaming yet another development on grief, she admitted that the process quite possibly was not yet finished. *These things take time.* Grief still worked in her soul, robbing her of familiar ways. Teaching no longer consumed her. Now even the desire to decorate for Christmas, a small thing that always gave her great pleasure, had vanished.

Jessie said, "So? How did it go? Tell me about the DNA saga, the stroller, the friends and family. Did you meet any obvious scam artists?"

"Jessie!"

"Kidding." She glanced at the ceiling and then looked at her again. "Sort of."

Her friend's disbelief threatened to snip what remained of those silken threads of comfort. "Maybe you want to wait until the DNA test results are in?"

"She agreed to do the test?"

"She was more than happy to give up a few cheek cells to the cause." *Maybe I'd better count to ten.*

"Rachel, I'm only looking after your best interests."

"I know. I'm sorry for my tone." She blew out a breath. "What happened to your mollycoddling approach?"

Jessie opened her mouth and quickly closed it, cutting off what was probably a smart-aleck retort. She regarded Rachel with gentle eyes and said quietly, "Do you still need that?"

"Yes!" *These things take time.* But how *much* time? "No! I don't want that."

Jessie didn't look convinced. "I have no clue what you're going through. You seem so strong."

"Strong?" She leaned over, grabbed the plate of cookies, and set it on her lap. "Let me show you how strong." She peeled off the plastic. "Are there a dozen here? Nice large cutouts. I could polish off six in no time." To prove her point she took a bite. Butter and sugar melted in her mouth. "Jess," she said around a mouthful, "these are fantastic."

"Yeah, well, you don't need six in one sitting." Jessie's teacher voice was in tip-top shape.

Rachel swallowed and straightened the plastic over the cookies. "Yes, ma'am. Anyway, I dropped the DNA kit off at Stan and Wanda's about noon today."

"What did they say?"

"Nobody was home." Fortuitous timing. She wasn't prepared yet to talk with her mother-in-law. That dialogue definitely had to wait until after the test results. "I left it on the kitchen table. So, back to Iowa. Fiona is still confined to bed. Danny is such a sweetheart." She described how he had set up the bed and carried Fiona downstairs for yesterday's baby shower. "Later he brought home a real Christmas tree, a little one, and we decorated it last night in their bedroom!"

"Really?" It was less a question of disbelief and more a hint she wanted to meet the guy.

"Yes, really. Fiona loved the stroller. Their friends are wonderful, real, down-to-earth, and extremely supportive. Most of them were from their church. And I cooked dinner last night for the three of us, which they thought was great."

"You didn't mention family."

"Mm-hmm."

"Mm-hmm what?"

"Oh, Jess, you know how in-laws are. They're in a different category. I only spent a couple of hours with them."

"Does that mean you spent a longer time with the friends whom you just described as wonderful and supportive? Or does that mean they weren't wonderful and supportive?"

She winced. "Answer B. Insensitive magpies. Oh, that sounds so spiteful."

"You've never spoken spitefully about Wanda." Jessie shrugged. "You said magpies. Plural?"

"Danny's mother, Luanne, and two sisters, both older than him. They were all nice enough. Very nice. But self-centered." Again she winced. "You know the type. They show well. They're attractive, smiling, generous with their gifts, involved in church and community. But when you listen carefully, you hear them talk only about themselves. Luanne did say she was sorry to hear about my husband. It was evident she thought it an odd situation that I would be there. She asked three times about children. 'And you never had any children?' I wanted to say well, we had six but had somehow misplaced them."

Jessie laughed.

"I could tell they wore on Fiona, poor thing. They acted absolutely oblivious to her condition." Rachel felt her ire rising again. The more those three women dominated the gathering, the less Fiona smiled and the paler she grew. "I finally called Danny on his cell phone and threatened that if he didn't get home in ten minutes and carry his wife back upstairs, I'd call 911 and get a fireman to do it. He made it in time. I didn't verbalize my opinion that his family was at fault. He and Fiona are incredibly nonjudgmental and uncomplaining about them."

"Like you with Wanda."

"But Wanda never walked all over me!"

"Only because you never let her."

"You don't understand. This woman could subtly crush the spirit right out of Fiona and smile the whole time she's doing it."

"I guess a couple of hours was long enough to form an opinion after all. You're a little bent out of shape, girl."

Rachel realized how unreasonable she sounded and shook her head. "Let's hope I was too hasty."

"Remind me to sic you on my mother-in-law. She gets particularly impossible at Christmastime. Hey, shouldn't you be getting ready?"

"For what?"

"For the faculty Christmas party." Jessie stood and pulled on her jacket.

"I'm drawing a blank."

"It's tonight."

"It is?"

"Yes. It starts in an hour. A reminder notice was in your mailbox at school. And I can tell by the look on your face you've totally forgotten. Rachel, I can't sub for you at this thing."

"Of course not. I wouldn't ask you to." She lifted the plastic wrap and pulled out another cookie. The desire to mingle with coworkers and their spouses and to fake enjoyment ranked even below hauling out Christmas decorations. "Well, I'm sure they won't miss me." She took a bite.

Jessie pressed her lips together and gave her a compassionate, mollycoddling look. "They'll miss you, but they'll understand. These things take time." She leaned over and hugged her.

～

As the last of her students filed out the classroom door on Tuesday afternoon, Rachel heaved a sigh of relief and murmured, "Two down, three to go." She referred to the countdown of days before Christmas break officially started.

Within minutes she donned her coat and switched off the light. As she shut the door and turned the key she imagined locking in a heavy burden of guilt. There wasn't anything to be done now about the afternoon's free-for-all euphemistically referred to as art class. And those papers to grade? They could keep her tied to the desk until midnight. But who said they had to be completed tonight at her desk? Any midnight would do. Next week over Christmas break. Timing wasn't that crucial; fourth graders didn't care. Any desk would do. Any chair. Why not the recliner at home? Cookie in one hand, red pen in the other.

Grief lesson number 27: rationalize until a comfortable solution is reached.

She drove to a large shopping mall long before the appointed time to meet Terri there. The extra hour allowed her to savor a cup of coffee in the bustling food court area and ponder the woeful Christmas season.

Sunday night Terri called from the station, eager for Iowa news. Rachel bubbled over with highlights of her visit. Her friend commented that she sounded so *happy*. The wonderment of that statement silenced them both for a long moment. Was it another lesson in grief? Get involved in someone else's life until you forget to notice your own?

What if the DNA test came back negative?

Rachel shook off that line of thinking and pulled a small notebook from her shoulder bag. Terri had asked if she'd meet her at the mall and help solve a shopping dilemma. Now Rachel thought about her own shopping dilemma: 20 nieces and nephews. Thirteen celebrated Christmas, four celebrated Hanukkah, Sarah and David's three celebrated a hybrid combination. Rachel could not dismiss the children as she had Christmas decorations, the faculty party, and paper grading. She couldn't even dismiss them with a gift of cash. Gifts from Uncle Vic and Aunt Rachel carried a reputation for being extremely cool.

She read through her list of names, ages, sizes, and what she called "bents," a combination of interests and personalities. Much of the information carried over from previous years, though she phoned her sisters as well as Vic's sister-in-law Alice for current information. After all, three babies had been added within the past year, and she hadn't exactly been on top of her game. The women told her not to be concerned, but she insisted. She reminded herself of how she had betrayed her class throughout the semester, not so much in ways they would notice but in other ways, not the least of which was failing to regularly pray for them. She wasn't about to disappoint the children related to her as well.

But could she possibly accomplish that goal without Vic's help? They had always taken time to brainstorm about the gifts. She possessed only a fraction of the creativity without the two of them working together.

Lesson: Get involved in someone else's life.

Think of the children anticipating an extremely cool item.

Think of God as the source of all creativity, of His imagination available for the asking.

Think of buying gifts for your stepdaughter and stepson-in-law.

Think of the grandbaby!

∽

"I hope I'm on that list."

Rachel looked up from her notebook to see Terri standing beside her. "And what would you like for Christmas, little girl?"

Terri gave her a brisk hug and sat down at the table. "I think I already got it." She giggled, and then she grinned so broadly her eyes shut.

Terri wasn't a hugger, especially in public. Nor was she a giggler. Nor was she prone to grinning. She was a compassionate paramedic who radiated warmth through her skillful hands and thoughtful speech that put victims at ease, a woman who worked doubly hard to gain respect in a world dominated by men. There hadn't been a place for hugging, giggling, and grinning.

Rachel smiled. "What did you get?"

Suddenly tears welled in her friend's eyes. She didn't cry easily either.

"Terri?"

"Lee invited me to his faculty Christmas party. He said he *wants* me to come."

Rachel's breath caught. She knew the significance of what her friend had just said. The annual gathering included spouses and significant others. Lee resisted including her in such things. He would mention it in an offhanded way a day or two before it was scheduled, not giving her enough advance warning for her to get off work if necessary, downplaying her need to socialize with people who had nothing in common with her.

In a typically scorned woman response, Terri insisted she didn't want to go anyway and didn't invite him to her work parties.

"Terri, what did you say?"

"I said yes." Her brown eyes sparkled.

Rachel smiled. "What do you think happened?"

"God answered my prayer. Not that I asked specifically for this party, just for Lee's change of heart. Some clarification on where we stood with each other."

"You've captured his attention with your respectful behavior and quieter spirit."

"Which is precious in God's sight. First Peter." Terri grinned again. "Have you really seen that in me?"

"Most definitely."

"He is real, isn't He?"

"Yes, He is real. So let me guess the shopping dilemma. You need something to wear to the party?"

"A dress. A knock-Lee's-socks-off dress."

"I think you've already knocked his socks off."

"It's going to be an extra-special night."

"There's this red dress in a Marshall Field's ad. You'd look perfect in it."

Terri reached over and slapped her hand in a high five. "This is why I called you."

Get involved in someone else's life.

"Rachel." Terri bit her lip, somber now, and gazed at her. "The night has to be extra special because if he doesn't agree to getting married, I'm moving out."

She stared back at her, speechless.

Terri's eyebrows rose, giving her a look of bewilderment. "It just seems the right thing to do."

Rachel nodded.

"Anyway, I wanted to ask you something. Remember you asked me and Jessie what we would do differently if we knew Kevin and Lee would die soon?"

"Yes."

"What would you have done differently?"

She glanced away. "You and Bryan."

"Me and Bryan what?"

"Ask the tough questions."

Terri smiled apologetically.

She blew out a breath. "I could have ignored the fact that my infertility was the most painful, confusing, faith-toppling thing I'd ever faced. I could have pretended I was not at the end of my rope and needed to run away to California. But that would not have been loving Vic well because I would not have been taking care of my relationship with God, which is the thing that supersedes all other relationships. And..."

She paused, fingering the diamond bracelet. She had never said her next words aloud, words that came quietly to her while wrapped in that Eldridge, Iowa, cocoon late Saturday night. Words that soothed the despair over Vic's absence in his daughter's home.

"What is it, Rachel?"

"I don't think if I'd stayed home from California Vic would be alive today. I don't think God would lay that kind of responsibility on my shoulders."

Terri didn't reply for a moment. "Then there's nothing you would have done differently?"

"Oh, I would have kvetched less stridently. Kissed him longer at the airport."

"You two had a wonderful marriage."

She nodded, ready to return to getting involved in someone else's life. "We should get to the store before they sell out of that red dress."

"How can I ever thank you?"

She knew her friend referred to something deeper than a shopping expedition. Vic's death and Rachel's response had made all the difference in Terri Schuman's life. "God is responsible."

"But you let Him be so. Thank you."

"You're welcome, Terri." She smiled. Her heart hadn't burst in two. Her friend knew Yeshua as Messiah. "You're so very welcome."

Thirty-One

Rachel turned down party and open house invitations right and left. *'Tis the season to be jolly.* Not true. Not this year. Perhaps another lifetime.

One request overrode her stock answer of "No, but thank you." She stopped in at a restaurant where Vic's department gathered to celebrate the season. She declined to stay for the buffet dinner and simply made the rounds, greeting everyone individually, thanking them for the monthly flowers, for their continued friendship and support. And then she left. Though it did not show on any face nor taint any spoken word, her presence disturbed the atmosphere, dampened the hilarity of the brotherhood that deserved a night off.

Two nights before Christmas, she accepted one other invitation. Bryan asked if she'd join him, Stan, and Wanda for dinner at Mario's. Since dining there with Terri, the restaurant posed no threat. She'd already faced down visiting a favorite haunt of Vic's and survived the experience. The thought of eating across the table from Wanda, however, nearly gave her indigestion before she set foot in the place.

She met them there, in the crowded entryway. Bryan hugged her. Stan followed suit. Like some mega antacid, his action instantly checked the assault on her stomach. While

Rachel gave Wanda a quick hug, the smaller woman stood stiffly, arms at her side. At least she hadn't pushed her away or slugged her. Another soothing antacid. Maybe Rachel would be able to eat pasta after all.

They sat at a table for four, each on their own side, a better arrangement than a cozy booth. Bryan, the consummate priest, embarked on a humorous story designed to put them all at ease.

Stan reached across the table and touched his arm. "Excuse me, Bry, but there's something first off I gotta tell Rachel."

Of course the question was on the tip of her tongue, but she hadn't the courage to ask it.

Stan turned to her and answered it. "The test results aren't in yet. Holidays and all. You know how it goes."

She nodded. Relief and despair played tag with her emotions. A melting sensation flowed through her limbs.

"Okay," he said to Bryan, "go on with your story."

Before he could reply, Wanda said, "Vic loved this place."

Rachel felt the sudden ignition of a connecting spark with her mother-in-law. "He told me you celebrated special events here. Birthdays. Anniversaries."

"We held my parents' fiftieth here in the back room. It was always a real family place. Not like today's fast-food joints. Not like one of those hoity-toity places either where the food is supposed to look like art but it's really just a few bites stuck on a plate three-fourths empty. Then they push you out the door." She glanced around. "Here you could sit back and relax, let your food digest. The kids ran loose and nobody minded. Looks like it hasn't changed."

Rachel smiled to herself. In a way she missed hearing Wanda's view on things, not her half-empty syndrome but her unique slant that only 69 years on the earth could add to one's perception.

Beneath Wanda's crusty exterior was a steadfast foundation: She would love and defend her family against all odds. Until Vic's death that included every daughter-in-law. The intent of her criticism was alwasy to prod them on to something better.

The older woman was light years ahead of Luanne Gallagher, who displayed none of Wanda's familial loyalty. Fiona was worse off than Rachel had initially thought when it came to mothers-in-law.

Stan touched his wife's hand. "We need to bring the grandkids here."

"Why did we stop coming?"

He shrugged a shoulder. "The family got too darn big. Sig's wife doesn't eat pasta. Ty was never crazy about it."

"Besides that, the boys were always too busy." She still referred to their adult sons as "the boys." "Let's bring the youngsters, a few at a time."

"Night out with Grandma and Grandpa?"

"Yeah. Maybe we could group them by birthday months." They nodded, their hands clasped atop Wanda's menu.

Rachel realized a significance in the moment. Her in-laws were not just planning future events—they were suggesting the resurrection of an old family tradition. She saw a softness between them that hadn't existed before Vic's death. Perhaps it was the dim lighting, but even Wanda's shrink-wrap appeared smoother than a few weeks ago, her eyes brighter. Stan seemed to sit taller again, his chest filling out the red sweater Vic and Rachel had given him one Christmas. Were they beginning to move forward?

A friendly young waitress came for their order. Without opening the menu, Wanda asked if they still served Bolognese.

After the girl left, Rachel said, "Was that Vic's favorite when he was little too?"

The harmless question hung like a cloud over the small table, and Rachel felt a sudden chill. Had she crossed some invisible line? Evidently it was Wanda's prerogative to introduce the subject of her son, not Rachel's.

She fought back a mounting belligerence. He was her *husband!* She would speak of him with tenderness and compassion and with all the joy he had brought into her life. She would measure her words no longer.

Swallowing that nasty tone and lowering her eyes to the tabletop, she said softly, "He sometimes ordered two servings."

Wanda's tightly clenched fists uncurled slightly, "And extra bread *and* Neapolitan ice cream for dessert."

Rachel looked up and made the first real eye contact she'd had with Wanda since that night at the funeral home.

Wanda said, "He started that when he was nine years old. Remember, Stan?" She glanced at him and turned back to Rachel. "We thought he'd be sick, but no. Slept all night and bounced out of bed to help Ed deliver newspapers early the next morning. That's when I knew he was going to be bigger than his dad some day."

The women exchanged a smile. Their first in a very, *very* long time.

∽

The evening progressed. Now and then they shared a laugh. Now and then tears were hastily blinked away. They talked of Vic's childhood. They skirted other topics.

At one point Bryan and Rachel were left alone at the table. He returned to one of those topics.

"So what are you doing for Christmas, Rachel?"

She smiled. "Waiting for the baby."

"The Koskis didn't invite you." It was a statement, not a question.

"No, but it's all right. My parents invited me to join them in Florida. Terri invited me to ski in Colorado with her. Sylvia invited me to her house. I'll probably go to Sylvia's. She and I need to talk shop." She paused before opening one of those other topics. "Oh, Bryan. If I were graded as a teacher, I'd deserve a D minus this first semester."

"It was too soon after..." The unfinished phrased hovered between them.

"It was too soon," she agreed. "I should have taken the time off like you suggested."

"We all agreed you had to try it. It seemed the best way to get on with life."

"It did at the time, but now I see I was avoiding reality." She shrugged. "Whew! At least we've come a *little* ways, haven't we?"

"Oh, we've come a *long* ways. Look at me." He pointed toward his face. "I'm smiling."

She returned his smile.

"A month from now we'll be doing it more often. You'll work up to a B minus by spring at the latest."

She grew somber. "I'm...I'm not going back this school year. There are about three weeks left of this semester after the break. Jessie could easily take over. I'm hoping the school board will hire her full-time. I asked her if she was ready. She and Kevin had already talked about the possibility; they're both ready."

He studied her face. "You've made up your mind."

"The kids are paying for my grief, Bryan. That's just not right. They shouldn't be the ones to have to work me up to a B minus."

"Does Sylvia know yet?"

"No, that's the shoptalk I mentioned. I better tell her before she fires me."

"That bad, huh?"

"Oh yes, that bad."

"What will you do?"

"Visit my grandchild often."

"And the DNA test?"

"It doesn't matter. God brought Fiona into my life for some reason. She needs a friend, a mentor. You know what she said recently? That Mary might have been a young teen when she gave birth to Jesus, so my being only fourteen years older doesn't preclude my status as stepmother." She grinned. "Stepmother is way above mentor."

"Way above." He returned the grin. "I'd like to meet her and Danny someday."

"And what if the test comes back negative?"

"It doesn't matter. I think they're your adopted family. I want to meet them."

She felt a rush of gratitude. "Oh, Bryan! Thank you for sticking by me even when I don't make any sense."

He winked. "I promised Vic, you know. I'm always here for you, Rachel, no matter how bizarre your plans are."

⌢

The four of them walked outside the restaurant and halted near the Koskis' car parked curbside. Falling snow glistened in light cast from a streetlamp. The flakes were minuscule, nearly invisible. They floated gently earthward, melting the instant they touched the sidewalk.

"White Christmas?" Stan asked.

"Maybe!" Rachel heard the note of hope in her own voice and was taken aback. Hope? Where had that come from? In two days she'd wake up alone on Christmas morning and pretend Vic was at work. Then she would try to accept reality. And then she would make it through the day. Somehow. No, not somehow. By the grace of God.

While Bryan exchanged goodbyes with Stan and Wanda, Rachel tilted her face up and proceeded to catch snowflakes on her tongue. The hope bubbled now. Unmistakable. And what was that? Joy clinging to its coattails? *Joy?*

The thought had scarcely formed before the words flew through the night air. "Wanda, come with me to Iowa next week."

Conversation stopper. They all stared at her.

Rachel went on hurriedly. "Fiona and Danny would love meeting you. They don't have much planned for the holiday, of course, since she's confined to bed. That baby shower was just too much for her. I said I'd wait until after the baby was born to visit again, but we talk every day and they insist I'm no bother. We could go for a day, spend the night in a motel. There's a nice mall not far from where they live. We could check out the after-Christmas bargains and then come home." She stopped only because she was out of breath.

They all three continued staring at her. Bryan's eyebrows rose, as if in surprise. Stan's face was stoic, unreadable.

Wanda appeared...curious. "What day?"

"The twenty-ninth." The reply popped out with no forethought whatsoever.

Wanda gazed directly at her, full eye contact. She understood. Rachel had always been a strong woman. If the Koskis did not include her in their Christmas plans because her presence would only intensify their grief, that was all right. She could make it through Christmas. The tenth anniversary of her marriage to Vic, on the other hand, was a different matter altogether.

Stan said, "What about the DNA test?"

Rachel turned to him. "Stan, does it matter? Does it really matter? What if it comes back positive and a wonderful opportunity was missed waiting for some stupid scientific results? They're just people, just hurting people like us. And if I have to spend the twenty-ninth by myself, I may lose my mind!" She didn't hear the hysterical edge to her voice until she felt an increasing pressure on her elbow.

Bryan squeezed it again.

"I'm sorry!" she cried. Briskly she hugged each of them. "And here I thought I was doing so well! Bye. Call me. Please. Take care."

Not waiting for a response, she rushed down the sidewalk toward the parking lot. The snow had grown thicker and became a blur before her eyes. Who cared about a white Christmas? It meant dangerous driving conditions, snowplow drivers working through the night, and heightened risks for emergency personnel hustling through the streets. It meant shoveling her none-too-short driveway. Or struggling with the old heavy snowblower which Vic had purchased secondhand and which always needed his special touch to keep the engine purring. Or calling someone for help. Or just staying home until the spring thaw.

That was it. She would stay home. Home, where she couldn't disturb anyone. Home, where grief could remain a private thing.

∽

Rachel awoke in the twin bed with a smile on her face Christmas Eve morning. She had dreamt of the baby. It was the first time since before she'd gone to California. Like before, she couldn't determine if the chubby-cheeked bundle was a boy or a girl, but he or she cooed and smiled. She touched a downy cheek and awoke, a warm, heavy sensation fading from her arms.

"Oh, Lord, I'm sorry for fussing last night! You gave me a glimpse of hope and joy, and I tried to shove it down Wanda's throat, which of course smashed it all to pieces. Why do I do that? Father, it's an old prayer but I ask it again. Please help me love her to You."

Enough with the looking at your feet already! Bubbie's voice. *Just keep your eyes on Him and you can walk on water.*

Bubbie said something like that whenever Rachel complained that she had done everything she could but God hadn't answered a prayer. And what was her point? Ruth would smile, pat her granddaughter's cheek, and say, "It's not about *you* doing anything."

"Lord, do I try too hard with Wanda? Okay, You do it. I'm here. I'm available. But You do it. You love her to Yourself. Yes," she whispered, "You love her in Your own way."

Rachel noticed the bedroom was too bright for six o'clock in the morning. That meant there was snow and plenty of it, whitening the world the other side of the curtains. She smiled. The kids would be ecstatic. "But, Lord, I can't stay home. I have grocery shopping to do and gifts to deliver. Please get me out of the driveway!"

Without turning on a lamp, she climbed from the bed and pushed aside a curtain. The backyard was a winter wonderland.

Later, while sipping her first cup of coffee in the kitchen, she listened to the radio. No snow had been forecast, but eight inches had fallen during the night. No more was expected. She smiled at the audacity to attempt to predict such a fickle thing as weather. And then she frowned.

Eight inches meant the snowblower. Shoveling it would take her until noon. She couldn't think of a neighbor to ask for help. Vic had been the one to help the elderly neighbors. The young men all had families and were too busy.

She heard a snowblower start up and went to the sink. An unfamiliar pickup sat out front. Snow sprayed from a noisy blower inching its way up her driveway.

Imagine that.

When the hooded figure pushing the blower neared the side window, she caught a glimpse of a young man's face. She didn't know him, but she knew who he must be. She went through the back porch, pushed the door against the piled snow, and leaned out into the cold. He stopped a few feet from her and turned off the blower.

"Good morning, probie!" she called. He would be the new guy in the department, sent over for extra duty on his day off.

He grinned, his cheeks rosy in the frosty air. "Good morning, ma'am."

"Would you like some coffee?"

"Uh, no thank you, ma'am."

"You've been warned."

"Yes, ma'am. I mean no, ma'am."

She laughed.

"I mean I don't drink coffee."

"How about some tea? Hot chocolate?"

"Hot chocolate would be great, ma'am."

"I'll get it ready."

"Thank you, ma'am." He restarted the snowblower.

Back inside the kitchen, Rachel poured milk into a pan and set it on a burner. She would prepare hot chocolate the way Vic liked it best. And she would add to her grocery list

Italian bread, salad fixings, and ingredients for lasagna, enough for her two largest pans, enough to feed a group of firefighters who would be working Christmas Day. It was about time she did something for that side of her family, which so diligently continued to care for her.

Thirty-Two

Thanksgiving Day had taught Rachel another grief lesson: Stay busy. She took it to heart on Christmas Eve.

After chatting with the new firefighter, Tommy, while he drank the hot chocolate, she plunged into the day. It became a whirl of activity punctuated with brief crying episodes and glimpses of hope. She bought groceries early in the morning, and on her way home she stopped at Ty and Alice's house to deliver all the gifts for her Koski nieces and nephews.

Alice had been attending church regularly, sometimes with Ty, Vic's youngest brother. The same age as Rachel, she had initiated a rapport with Rachel the day Vic introduced them. That relationship had deepened over the past couple of months as she began to open up about her spiritual needs.

Now when she saw Rachel standing at her door with an armful of gifts, she burst into tears. Naturally Rachel followed suit. As they wiped their eyes and unloaded more gifts from the car, Alice apologized profusely, something she had been doing on every Sunday for the past month. She felt personally responsible for being unable to sway Wanda's refusal to include Rachel in the traditional family Christmas Day gathering.

"Alice," she blubbered and paused to compose herself. Just inside the front door she glanced around, soaking in the sights and smells. Evergreen, twinkle lights, gifts piled under the tree, scented candles aglow, four stockings hanging from the fireplace mantle.

"Rachel, I'm so, so sorry." Alice wiped her eyes. She was a blue-eyed blonde, petite, with a shy disposition that prompted Rachel through the years to pray she would not be mowed down by the overbearing Koski clan. Her decision to attend Rachel's church was a major step in defiance against their mother-in-law.

Alice asked, "Will you stay for a cup of coffee?"

"No, thank you. I have to prepare food for Sylvia's potluck tomorrow. And I'm making lasagna for the guys at the station."

"Homemade? From scratch? For all of them?"

"Yeah." She smiled. "They used to like it. Anyway, hon, don't worry about Christmas. It's okay. Really."

"Are you sure?"

She winced. "Truthfully? It feels like my stomach is in a vise. But I realize no one is angry at me or holds me reponsible." Vic's brothers and their wives called her routinely. Not two days passed that she didn't hear from one of them. In the past few weeks even Stan had called twice just to check in with her.

Alice shook her head. "But Wanda and her matriarchal pose! Forever ruling the emotional roost. Why is it we all still kowtow to her?"

"Oh, Alice, we can't be too hard on her now. We need to offer her major allowances. I cannot begin to comprehend how deeply her sorrow must run. Losing a son? I don't know. I think it must be worse than losing a husband."

Fresh tears sprang to Alice's eyes. "It's not that I don't love Ty, but if he died, I could go on if for no other reason than the kids' sake. If I lost TJ or Steffi, though, I think I'd just lay down and die myself."

Rachel nodded. Given the fact that she had no personal experience with bearing a child, her thoughts were pure speculation. Alice's words confirmed them.

Hours later, when she finally tumbled into bed, Rachel replayed the conversation. Yes, the Koski snubbing still hurt. Silly and childish perhaps, but it was there.

"Forgive me, Father. Help me to forgive them. Help me to let it go."

As in the early morning, the snow lay outside the bedroom window, piled in the backyard, on bushes, and the neighbor's roof. Even through closed curtains its presence brightened the room. The clock's digital numerals read 12:17.

Christmas morning had arrived.

She smiled.

Yeshua was born. Forgiveness entered the world and nothing, absolutely nothing, was ever impossible.

"Merry Christmas, Vic."

Not many hours later Rachel parked at the fire station. Tommy, the probie, was busy sweeping salt from the sidewalk. He hurried over and opened the car door for her.

"Merry Christmas, ma'am."

"Tommy!" She climbed out. "I thought we settled that yesterday. Call me Rachel."

He grinned sheepishly. "Need some help?"

"Yes, please." She pointed to the car, its seats filled with foil-covered pans of lasagna, plastic-covered salad bowls, and long loaves of Italian bread.

He whistled and began unloading. "Is this all for us?"

"Merry Christmas, Tommy."

She noted how young and fresh his face appeared, and she suddenly felt matronly. Not old, but mature, as if she'd put on new skin.

The Bible verse from Isaiah came to mind, the one she always prayed for Vic. *Should you walk through fire, you will not be scorched and the flames will not burn you. For I am Yahweh, your God, the Holy One of Israel, your savior.* Perhaps the prayer had been for herself as well. Lieutenant Koski's widow walked into the fire. It scorched, but only her old self, only that old skin destined for debridement. Without the peeling away of those layers, new skin would never have a chance to grow. And she needed the new because it stretched around a maturing faith which the old could not have housed.

Yes, she had walked into the fire, and she had emerged on the other side. She understood that now.

Inside the firehouse she exchanged holiday greetings and hugs with Vic's brotherhood, friends who would always be closer than family. Most of them had been there ten years ago, down on bended knee, proposing right alongside Vic. Someone handed her a cup of coffee. Someone put away the food. No need to give baking instructions. They knew their way around a kitchen.

Teague sat with her at a table. "You look good, Rache."

She smiled crookedly, mentally completing his sentence. *You look good considering.* She was long overdue for a haircut. In spite of horrid eating habits, she'd lost weight, leaving her face haggard in appearance. She refrained from checking to see if her socks matched. At least she'd changed from sweats into a decent pair of wool slacks.

"Thanks. How's everyone here?"

"Okay. Morale's picking up slowly but surely. Still, there are times." He turned away, blinking rapidly. "He left a big hole." Teague sniffed discreetly and smiled at her. "We had big hopes that at least one of the two probies knew how to make coffee. No such luck."

She laughed with him.

A short while later she left, feeling like she did on the twelfth of every month: deeply cherished. In essence Vic had just given her a Christmas gift.

~

The phone rang as Rachel shut the kitchen door.

"Hello?"

"Rachel, it's Danny. We're at the hospital!" His voice was breathless. "It's coming."

"What?"

"The baby!"

The baby? It was too soon!

He went on to explain in garbled, out-of-sequence phrases that Fiona had gone into labor. There was no turning back now, no stopping it this time.

"I'm on my way."

"It's Christmas! You don't need to— This may take a long time."

"Like I've got something more important to do? Give me the hospital's phone number."

After hanging up, Rachel sank onto a chair. Her hands were shaking. "Oh, Lord. It's too soon. It's too soon! But You know what You're doing. Keep them safe."

What was it she had decided about Wanda? To back off? To let God love her without Rachel's interference?

"Father, You started this. It's her great-grandchild! I'm interfering and I ask Your blessing!"

She dialed the Koskis. Stan answered.

"Stan, hi. I'm coming to get Wanda. I'll be there in half an hour. The baby is on its way."

"Rachel?"

"Yes! Your great-grandchild is going to be born any minute now! They're at the hospital! Tell Wanda to get packed, a few days' worth. And don't you dare mention the DNA test." The bossy sniping resounded in her head, and then she heard his stunned silence. "I'm sorry."

He chuckled. "For what? You always used to talk to me that way. I guess you still love me after all. We'll see you when you get here."

Thirty minutes later, rolling suitcase at her side, Rachel stood in the living room and reviewed a mental checklist. Draperies drawn, timer set for the lamp to go on and off, heat turned down, door locked. Something nagged for attention. Had she left a task unfinished?

Except for furniture, the house hardly appeared lived in. Missing, of course, was her usual clutter. Vic had been the neat one. It came from folding hoses just so and inspecting equipment and following procedure and always correcting safety infractions. Keeping that fire engine shiny. Watching over a probie until he got things right. She was precise when it came to schedules and children showing respect and grading papers, but she didn't pay much attention at home to placing her things in their proper places. He sometimes asked her if she knew the purpose of closets and cupboards.

That was before. During the past five months she had begun to pick up after herself. Constantly. Another grief lesson: preoccupation with life's insignificant details.

She did a slow 360 degree turn, taking in the hallway and the kitchen doorway, searching for what nagged.

"It doesn't feel like home anymore."

Not like home anymore. She felt wistful at the thought and yet relieved at the same time. The nagging eased as a new understanding emerged into her consciousness.

Her heart wasn't at home. Her heart wasn't in her classroom either, nor with the students. Her heart wasn't even in Chicago. Where in the world was it?

The answer surfaced.

"For goodness' sake, Lord. *That's* where it is?"

~⌒

Stan opened the door before she knocked and said, "Give me your keys. I'll get your stuff out of the car. We're taking my SUV. It does better in the snow."

Rachel stared at him.

"Come on, come on, we don't have all day."

"You're going?" She stepped inside.

"You don't mind, do you?"

"Of course not. I just had no idea you'd care to—"

"It's a harebrained scheme, but I'm not about to let my frantic daughter-in-law drive my frantic wife across the state on Christmas Day with snow in the forecast."

"You sound a little frantic yourself, Sergeant Koski. What happened?" She gasped. "You heard from the DNA people!"

"You always gotta bring that up. No, I did not hear from the DNA people. I just thought—" He clamped his mouth shut and picked up a suitcase. "Give me the keys."

She pulled them from her coat pocket, handed them to him, and held his hand. "Just thought what?"

His shoulders heaved in a quiet sigh. "I just thought a drive sure beat sitting around Max's house missing Vic."

She stood on tiptoe and kissed his cheek. "Thank you."

"Yeah, yeah."

Ten minutes later they backed out of the driveway, Rachel in the rear seat of Stan's big trucklike vehicle, Wanda up front, her small frame nearly swallowed by the large seat.

Wanda chattered nonstop, reporting in great detail her conversations with each of her boys. They totally understood her decision to leave, excited that the first great-grandchild was about to be born. She then complimented Rachel on the nice gesture of delivering gifts to Ty's house. Following that was a litany of what she had bought the grandchildren.

Stan and Rachel scarcely were able to get a word in edgewise.

Which was par for the course when Wanda wasn't in Grinch mode.

Rachel smiled to herself. *Thank You, Lord.*

$\mathcal{T}$hirty-$\mathcal{T}$hree

The three of them were ushered into the birthing room, a pretty space with chintz curtains, a gingham-checked cushioned rocker, and ruffled bedding. Rachel went immediately to the bedside to greet Fiona while Stan, Wanda, and Danny introduced themselves.

"Rachel! Thank you for coming." She hugged her fiercely with one arm from her prone position on her side. "Bubbie."

Rachel smoothed back the young woman's damp hair. "Wouldn't miss it for the world. Neither would the great-grandparents!" She stood. "Wanda, Stan, this is Fiona."

Wanda clasped Fiona's hand in both of hers. "It's like looking at Vic if he'd been a girl."

Stan said over his wife's shoulder, "Vic was never *this* pretty. Hello, Fiona."

Fiona giggled.

Rachel breathed a prayer of thanks. Four for four. Terri, Rachel, now Stan and Wanda. Who needed DNA testing? She hugged Danny. "How are things?"

"The doctor says it'll be a while yet." His Adam's apple bobbed, and he literally wrung his hands.

"You don't look so good, Dad."

Stan clapped his shoulder. "He needs a smoke. Come on, Danny, let's go outdoors. Leave the ladies to handle things here."

"I don't smoke."

"But I do, and I haven't had one in four hours thanks to two bossy females in my car." His hand still on Danny's shoulder, they left the room.

The man exaggerated the time. He'd driven as if in pursuit of some criminal on the run, shaving 20 minutes off the trip. Rachel slid onto a chair and watched in fascination. Fiona appeared to stare at the ceiling while she and Wanda breathed in synchronized pants.

A moment later Fiona said, "Thanks. Danny was getting tired out."

Wanda hooted and sat on the edge of the bed. "Men. They don't know the first thing about hard work. I can keep you company for a while. I've been through five of these you know. Just work with the pain. That little one will be out sooner or later."

"But it's too early. By four weeks!"

Wanda clucked her tongue. "Not to worry. Your dad was five weeks early. Weighed nine and a half pounds. Like pushing out a bowling ball—oh! You don't want to hear about that right now! But imagine if he'd waited five more weeks. He was my favorite, you know."

Fiona smiled. "He was?"

Rachel laughed to herself. *Told you so, Vic!* He never believed her when she suggested such a thing.

Wanda continued. "We shouldn't really have favorites. I never let on. But he was the spark plug. That kid gave me every gray hair I ever had. Of course I put a rinse on it now, so you can't see all of them. I swear he came out kicking and squalling. Didn't really stop until he married Rachel. She settled him down. Well, as much as possible anyway. Neither one of us could stop him from going into burning buildings. That was just what he did. He was a real hero, you know."

Wanda was off and running, taking a break every four minutes to breathe in that special way with her granddaughter. Rachel didn't have to say a word except the ones she prayed to her Father.

Early that evening, about four hours after they'd been ushered into the birthing room, the Koskis were ushered out of it. Fiona's was a high-risk pregnancy. She and Danny were moved into a sterile delivery room before things were too far along. Rachel doubted there were ruffles or gingham checks in it.

While Stan drove to a nearby motel to register for them, the women sat in a waiting area. The hospital was new, and the room had a comfortable couch they sank onto.

"Wanda, I am so glad you came. You made all the difference for Fiona. I didn't have a clue what to do. And Danny was a basket case."

In that characteristic way of hers, she shrugged a bony shoulder and cocked her head briefly.

Rachel smiled. "It *was* a big deal."

"Well, the poor thing needs someone, doesn't she?"

Danny's mother had stopped by; a collective sigh had gone round the room when she left after a few minutes.

"Yes, she does."

Wanda nodded. "Can't imagine how Danny came from such a *negative* woman. She vacuumed all the good energy right out of that room, didn't she?" The question was rhetorical and she chattered on, not waiting for an answer.

Rachel hid her astonishment as best she could. Her mother-in-law was indeed light years ahead of Luanne Gallagher. If the DNA test came back negative, Rachel figured Stan would not bother sharing that news with his wife. She'd never believe it. She had latched onto Fiona as easily as had Rachel.

Imagine that. They had something in common. *Now, Lord?* She took a deep breath.

"Wanda, I want to say something, and I hope you don't mind too much."

"I suppose you want to get all touchy-feely-mushy. I'm just not that way. Never have been."

"Why not?"

Again her little shrug. "My family was too big, I guess. You know, eight kids and all. After my dad ran out on us and my mom lost touch with reality, we were too busy working. No time for that silliness when you have to put food on the table."

"When did your dad run out on you?" Rachel had never heard that part of Wanda's story.

"I was thirteen. Oh, he'd come back now and then, when he needed a place to sleep."

"My goodness, you never had a real childhood, did you?"

"No, I suppose not. But I turned out fine."

Well, there was fine and then there was fine. She was obviously still a wounded soul. "God loves you, Wanda, more than your parents could."

She pressed her thin lips together.

"That's what I wanted to tell you. Sometimes the thought takes some getting used to."

"If He loves me, then why did He take away my son?"

"I don't know. We won't know until we get to heaven and can ask Him face-to-face. But I do know lives are being changed since Vic died. And that was Vic's whole reason for getting up in the morning, to let someone know that Jesus loved them and could change their lives."

"What lives?"

"Terri's for one. She believes in God now and reads the Bible."

"She didn't believe in God before?"

"No."

"How can someone not believe in God?"

"It happens. They don't see Him at work, but Terri saw Him at work in Vic's life. And Kevin, Jessie's husband. He goes to our church now. So do Steve and Duke, with their families. And Alice. She didn't grasp it at your church, like Vic didn't for some reason. Who knows? We're all just different. And have you seen Jim? Bryan says he's been attending your church."

She nodded. "He's been coming every week."

"Teague says three new guys have been coming to the Bible study Vic started. I know God could have reached these people in other ways besides Vic's death, but the point is Vic made a huge impact on a lot of people. Some of them didn't catch on until they sat at his funeral. And," she took another deep breath, "I've changed."

"Why would you have to change?"

"I didn't really trust God. I was always wanting to control things. He's more real to me than He ever was in my entire life."

Wanda crossed her legs and snorted. "That's nice."

Okay, Lord. I'll be quiet. And then she began to pray for Fiona and the baby.

"Why would He love me?"

Rachel started.

"I'm a grouchy old woman."

"God loves all His creation. And you're only grouchy because your parents, like everyone's, were unable to love you perfectly."

"You've got all the answers, don't you, missy?"

Rachel smiled. It wasn't the first time Wanda had said that to her. "I try. Bad habit from years of teaching. Wanda, you've been a good mom. Look at your sons. All gainfully employed and happily married. They look after you."

"More or less."

"More or less. That's life. I remind myself every day that God loves me. Bubbie taught me that when I was nine years old. What else matters if He loves me? It'll all work out."

"Is that what makes you nice?"

"You think I'm nice?"

She gave her a smug smile as if she too had all the answers. "Vic wouldn't have married you otherwise."

Imagine *that!* "Well, my faith gives me deep contentment."

"Hmm."

Letting her ponder things, Rachel went back to praying and sitting on her hands in order not to bite her nails. Wanda offered to get coffee for her from the pot across the room. They flipped through magazines.

At long last, "Mrs. Koski?"

They both looked toward the door.

A nurse grinned. "Grandma and Great-Grandma? You can come in now. She's here!"

Rachel and Wanda shrieked. Rachel grabbed her mother-in-law in an embrace. Not only did the woman not resist, her wiry arms returned the hug forcefully.

They followed the nurse down the hall. Stan stood in the distance.

Wanda elbowed Rachel. "Look at him. Grinning like he had something to do with it. Which I guess he did." She giggled.

"He was there for Vic's conception! So, nurse, what does the baby weigh?"

"Seven and a half pounds. She is definitely not the preemie like we thought she'd be."

Wanda clapped her hands. "Ha! What did I say? Just like Vic! It must be hereditary."

Rachel smiled. *Thank You, Lord.*

Hands diligently scrubbed and wearing blue paper gowns, the three Koskis filed into Fiona's room. She was sitting up in bed, clearly exhausted and clearly beaming. Danny grinned more broadly from the chair where he sat cuddling a bundle wrapped in a pink blanket.

Rachel thought her heart would melt.

There were congratulations all around, and Rachel hugged Fiona. "Congratulations, Mommy."

"Thank you. Oh, she's perfect. Absolutely perfect. Is God good or what?"

"He is good."

Danny stood, nodding toward the chair. "Great-Grandma."

"Oh, no." Wanda shook her head. "Rachel should hold her first."

"Wanda," she said, "that's your honor. Go on."

A visible softness settled over the woman. The constant frown on her face relaxed. The shrink-wrap grew less distinct. Was that God's love breaking upon her?

She sat and Danny gently laid the baby in her arms. Stan cooed over her shoulder and said softly, "Merry Christmas, little girl."

Wanda said, "She's a Koski, that's for sure. Have you named her?"

Danny and Fiona exchanged a smile and he said, "Victoria Koski Gallagher."

Stan laughed. "That's a mouthful."

"It's a natural. Fiona's middle name is Victoria. And we want to honor her grandfather."

Wanda began to cry. "It's beautiful. Just like her. Look." She lifted a side of the little white cap on the baby's head. "Vic's ears."

Fiona groaned. "I noticed!"

"Rachel, honey." Wanda stood abruptly. "You hold her before she needs her mama."

Honey? "It's Stan's turn." She looked at her father-in-law.

"No. I don't hold 'em until they're two years old. Go for it, Grandma." He winked.

Wanda gently transferred the child into Rachel's arms.

The room faded from view as she settled into the chair and gazed at the sleeping Victoria. Such perfect, delicate features. Such a miracle in that tiny heartbeat.

Such a dream come true.

She thought she heard the echo of her husband's laughter. Smiling, she kissed the downy cheek and whispered, "Vic, look what I got for Christmas!"

$\mathcal{E}$pilogue

A light southerly breeze drifted across the patio, delivering the sweet scent of clover from some distant field. Under a cloudless July sky, Rachel and Terri sat in white wicker chairs padded with yellow-and-green floral print cushions. Large orange tumblers of iced tea sat on a round, glass-topped table between them.

Arms draped around a warm chubby bundle and nose pressed against a mass of fine, espresso brown hair, Rachel inhaled deeply. Baby shampoo. Sweeter than a thousand fields of clover blossoms. Six-month-old Victoria curled against her breast, fast asleep. More brilliant than the sun in the azure sky was the light radiating from the child into the dark corners of Rachel's life.

Terri picked up a glass of iced tea. "Like I said three months ago, you live in the absolute middle of nowhere!"

Rachel smiled and let her gaze sweep the area. The view struck her as it had every time since she first saw it in February: fresh and simple. If she squinted her eyes just so, she could make out filmy silken threads enfolding it all.

Her two-story condominium occupied a nice corner spot. The patio was divided from the neighbor's by a tall privacy fence. Potted red geraniums sat atop a low stone wall that squared off the concrete slab on its other two sides. Beyond that were fifty feet of grass, a row of maple saplings, and, lastly, undulating waves of cornfields rolling to the horizon.

"But," Terri said, "the absolute middle of nowhere must agree with you. I've never seen you looking healthier or more contented."

"That might have something to do with my granddaughter napping in my arms. Or the fact that she lives a six-minute walk from here, across my yard, down the gravel road a piece, and through two blocks of subdivision." She chuckled. "Did I mention she says 'Buh' when she sees me?"

"In an email, on the phone, and three times since I got here last night."

They laughed and the baby stirred.

"Say hello to Aunt Terri, sweetheart. She was out running when you came over to visit this morning."

As if she understood, Victoria twisted to her side, navy blue eyes still heavy with sleep, one cheek pink with creases. She smiled shyly at Terri.

"Well, greetings, Miss Victoria." She removed her sunglasses and whistled. "Get a load of those ears."

"Terri! You'll give her a complex, not to mention devastate her grandma's feelings. Tell her she's adorable."

"She looks like Vic, and I never considered him adorable."

"You need some aunt-ing lessons. Here." She stood and held the baby out over the table.

"Uh, how about I play ball with her when she's seven? I'm not too good with kids."

"Unless they're bleeding or choking. Take her. She's easygoing."

Terri slid her sunglasses back into place and accepted Victoria. A moment later the child sat happily, her chubby hand fingering a sports logo printed on Terri's T-shirt. "Cootchy coo."

"You can talk to her like she's a regular person, Auntie. Oh, I can't wait to show her off at the station next week."

"The guys will get a hoot out of seeing her. Especially her ears." She grinned.

"Hush."

"Hear that, Victoria? That's your Bubbie's mean teacher voice. Speaking of which." She glanced over at Rachel. "Have you heard anything more about that opening at the school here?"

"I didn't apply."

"Really." Her tone expressed no surprise. She had once said Rachel's actions had ceased to amaze her.

"Really." Rachel shrugged. "I'll sub fall semester and take a class in Iowa City. And keep babysitting *often*."

"There's no timetable. If you're not ready for your own class again, you're not ready."

"I know." She sighed. Eight days from now, on July eleventh, she would stand at Vic's grave and remember last July eleventh. "But still, you'd think after a year I'd miss what I've devoted half my life to."

"So much has happened though. Maybe a year isn't long enough to process all the changes. I mean, look at you. You're a grandma living in Eldridge, Iowa. And that's just for starters!"

They exchanged bittersweet smiles. She was a widow with a great hole within her where Vic used to live. She'd sold their house and moved away from all that was familiar. Her good friend Jessie had been hired to replace her as fourth grade teacher. And that too was just for starters in describing all the changes in her life. She switched topics.

"How are plans coming for the memorial service?" Next week she would travel with Fiona, Danny, and the baby to

Chicago. Vic's friends were commemorating him on the anniversary of his death.

"Everything is all set. Payton and Bryan will facilitate the program. Quite a few of us from the department are going to say a few words. We'll do that slide show again that was done at the funeral. And there will be music. I voted for his favorite hard rock stuff. Bryan probably would have agreed but the service is in Payton's church, and he said we have to keep things dignified."

She grinned. "Vic had his proper streak too. I'm so grateful you all came up with this idea. It'll be good for Fiona and Danny. They'll gain a better understanding of Vic, of what kind of a man he was."

"We couldn't let the date pass without paying tribute to him in some special way. Too many lives have been affected in major ways. We aren't what we were on July tenth last year. Especially me."

From the set of her friend's mouth, Rachel knew that behind the reflective lenses tears gathered. She blinked away her own. Still crying at the drop of a hat, though fewer hats dropped as the months wore on.

Terri said, "I read the Bible and have no boyfriend. Who would have imagined?"

"Vic."

"Yeah, Vic. So tell me, Bubbie, after three months, what do you think?"

"I think...I think home is here. Of course I knew that in December. If this condo had been built sooner, I would have moved long before April."

"Stan might have blocked your way if you hadn't waited for the DNA results."

They now had a formal proclamation, which stated that according to genetic testing, Vic was Fiona's father.

Rachel leaned across the table and touched her grand-daughter's arm. "Victoria, your great-grandpa is such a stickler for tying up loose ends!"

The baby squealed in delight. Then she grew quite somber and said, "Buh."

Rachel laughed loudly and clapped her hands.

Terri wiped a palm across her damp cheeks.

"Terri, what is it?"

"It's just— You're okay! You really are okay, aren't you?"

Rachel looked over her friend's shoulder toward the unhindered expanse of fields. She thought of Fiona and Danny almost within shouting distance...of her new friends at her new church...of her spare bedroom already occupied twice by Stan and Wanda...of the portable crib set up in the living room...of the fire station a mile down the highway...

Vic would approve of her new home. Yes, he would like it immensely.

She smiled. "Oh, Terri, I'm much more than okay. So much, much more."

Dear Reader,

Thank you for joining me on Rachel's journey. I hope that you laughed and cried with her, that you felt, as she did, a healing touch of the Lord Jesus Christ.

My constant prayer as I write is that the story will carry you for a time to an imaginary place that is at once very different from and yet very much like your own world. In the difference may you find respite, and in the sameness may you find yourself less alone. May God's faithfulness to these fictional characters enhance your relationship with Him.

I believe in joyful endings, even when the path is strewn with heartache. They are like a microcosm of God's plan: He promises that through Christ's work on the cross we will have a joyful ending when we finally, literally meet Him face-to-face. Though Rachel's epilogue isn't the typical happy-go-lucky conclusion, it is full of deep joy and a peace that will withstand any broken dream.

Many of you have written to me, and I am so grateful for your kindness. I treasure our long-distance fellowship and look forward to hearing from more of you.

I can be reached via email: sallyjohnbook@aol.com.

Or by mail in care of: Harvest House Publishers
990 Owen Loop North
Eugene, OR 97402-9173

Blessings on your day.
Sally John

Discussion Questions

Rachel's story is about trusting God, the Dream Maker, against all odds. Life can indeed change in the time it takes a heart to beat. Hopes and dreams are irrevocably affected, perhaps never to be fulfilled. We may even question God's love or His very existence.

1. When was your life changed in a heartbeat? (Examples: death, birth, salvation, (un)answered prayer, medical diagnosis, betrayal by a loved one.)

2. How did it affect your view of God?

3. What happened to your dreams?

4. What conclusions did you reach about God?

5. Ultimately Rachel did not need her new family in Fiona, Danny, and the baby in order for her healing to continue. What do you think her life might have looked like without them in it?

6. What were you able to imagine about God's character while reading *In a Heartbeat*?

7. Were any of your preconceived ideas of who God is affected by Rachel's story?

8. Brennan Manning writes, "There is an extraordinary power in storytelling that stirs the imagination and makes

an indelible impression on the mind." (*A Glimpse of Jesus* [San Francisco: HarperSanFrancisco, 2003], p. 67.)

  a. Did Rachel's story do this for you? If so, what images remain most vivid?

  b. What lasting impressions remain in your mind?

Books by Sally John

THE OTHER WAY HOME SERIES

A Journey by Chance
After All These Years
Just to See You Smile
The Winding Road Home

IN A HEARTBEAT SERIES

In a Heartbeat
Flash Point
Moment of Truth

Sally John is a former teacher and the author of several books, including the popular books of The Other Way Home series (*A Journey by Chance, After All These Years, Just to See You Smile,* and *The Winding Road Home*). *In a Heartbeat* is the first book in Sally's brand-new In a Heartbeat series. Sally and her husband, Tim, live in the country surrounded by woods and cornfields. The Johns have two grown children, a daughter-in-law, and a granddaughter.